LIFE'S HANDICAP

RUDYARD KIPLING

The Centenary Edition

LIFE'S HANDICAP

BEING STORIES
OF MINE OWN PEOPLE

BY

RUDYARD KIPLING

I met a hundred men on the road to
Delhi and they were all my brothers.
Native Proverb

ISBN (cased) 0 333 32801 9
ISBN (paper) 0 333 32802 7

MACMILLAN LONDON LIMITED
London and Basingstoke

Associated companies in Auckland, Dallas,
Delhi, Dublin, Hong Kong, Johannesburg,
Lagos, Manzini, Melbourne, Nairobi,
New York, Singapore, Tokyo, Washington
and Zaria

First edition 1891
Edition de Luxe 1898
Uniform edition 1899
Pocket edition 1907
Bombay edition 1913
Service edition 1915
Sussex edition 1937
Library edition 1950, 1964
Centenary edition (n.s.) 1982
Paperback edition 1982

Printed in Great Britain by
St. Edmundsbury Press
Bury St. Edmunds, Suffolk

PREFACE

In Northern India stood a monastery called The Chubára of Dhunni Bhagat. No one remembered who or what Dhunni Bhagat had been. He had lived his life, made a little money, and spent it all, as every good Hindu should do, on a work of piety—the Chubára. That was full of brick cells, gaily painted with the figures of Gods and kings and elephants, where worn-out priests could sit and meditate on the latter end of things : the paths were brick paved, and the naked feet of thousands had worn them into gutters. Clumps of mangoes sprouted from between the bricks ; great pipal trees overhung the well-windlass that whined all day ; and hosts of parrots tore through the trees. Crows and squirrels were tame in that place, for they knew that never a priest would touch them.

The wandering mendicants, charm-sellers, and holy vagabonds for a hundred miles round used to make the Chubára their place of call and rest. Mahomedan, Sikh, and Hindu mixed equally under the trees. They were old men, and when man has come to the turnstiles of Night all the creeds in the world seem to him wonderfully alike and colourless.

Gobind the one-eyed told me this. He was a holy man who lived on an island in the middle of a river and fed the fishes with little bread pellets twice a day. In flood-time, when swollen corpses stranded themselves at the foot of the island, Gobind would cause them to be piously burned, for the sake of the honour of mankind, and having regard to his own account with God hereafter. But when two-thirds of the island was torn away in a spate, Gobind came across the river to Dhunni Bhagat's Chubára, he and his brass drinking vessel with the well-cord round the neck, his short arm-rest crutch studded with brass nails, his roll of bedding, his big pipe, his umbrella, and his tall sugar-loaf hat with the nodding peacock feathers in it. He wrapped himself up in his patched quilt made of every colour and material in the world, sat down in a sunny corner of the very quiet Chubára, and, resting his arm on his short-handled crutch, waited for death. The people brought him food and little clumps of marigold flowers, and he gave his blessing in return. He was nearly blind, and his face was seamed and lined and wrinkled beyond belief, for he had lived in his time which was before the English came within five hundred miles of Dhunni Bhagat's Chubára.

When we grew to know each other well, Gobind would tell me tales in a voice most like the rumbling of heavy guns over a wooden bridge. His tales were true, but not one in twenty could be printed in an English book, because the English do not think as natives do. They brood over matters that a native would dismiss till a fitting occasion; and what they would not think twice about a native will brood over till a fitting occasion: then native and English stare at each other hopelessly across great gulfs of mis-comprehension.

'And what,' said Gobind one Sunday evening, 'is your honoured craft, and by what manner of means earn you your daily bread?'

'I am,' said I, 'a *kerani*—one who writes with a pen upon paper, not being in the service of the Government.'

'Then what do you write?' said Gobind. 'Come nearer, for I cannot see your countenance, and the light fails.'

'I write of all matters that lie within my under-standing, and of many that do not. But chiefly I write of Life and Death, and men and women, and Love and Fate according to the measure of my ability, telling the tale through the mouths of one, two, or more people. Then by the favour of God the tales are sold and money accrues to me that I may keep alive.'

'Even so,' said Gobind. 'That is the work of the bazar story-teller; but he speaks straight to men and women and does not write anything at all. Only when the tale has aroused expectation, and calamities are about to befall the virtuous, he stops suddenly and demands payment ere he continues the narration. Is it so in your craft, my son?'

'I have heard of such things when a tale is of great length, and is sold as a cucumber, in small pieces.'

'Ay, I was once a famed teller of stories when I was begging on the road between Koshin and Etra; before the last pilgrimage that ever I took to Orissa. I told many tales and heard many more at the rest-houses in the evening when we were merry at the end of the march. It is in my heart that grown men are but as little children in the matter of tales, and the oldest tale is the most beloved.'

'With your people that is truth,' said I. 'But in regard to our people they desire new tales, and when all is written they rise up and declare that the tale were better told in such and such a manner, and doubt either the truth or the invention thereof.'

'But what folly is theirs!' said Gobind, throwing out his knotted hand. 'A tale that is told is a true tale as long as the telling lasts. And of their talk upon it—you know how Bilas Khan, that was the prince of tale-tellers, said to one who mocked him in the great rest-house on the Jhelum road : "Go on, my brother, and finish that I have begun," and he who mocked took up the tale, but having neither voice nor manner for the task came to a standstill, and the pilgrims at supper made him eat abuse and stick half that night.'

'Nay, but with our people, money having passed, it is their right ; as we should turn against a shoeseller in regard to shoes if those wore out. If ever I make a book you shall see and judge.'

'And the parrot said to the falling tree, Wait, brother, till I fetch a prop !' said Gobind with a grim chuckle. 'God has given me eighty years, and it may be some over. I cannot look for more than day granted by day and as a favour at this tide. Be swift.'

'In what manner is it best to set about the task,' said I, 'oh chiefest of those who string pearls with their tongue ?'

'How do I know? Yet'—he thought for a little—'how should I not know? God has made very many heads, but there is only one heart in all the world among your people or my people. They are children in the matter of tales.'

'But none are so terrible as the little ones, if a man misplace a word, or in a second telling vary events by so much as one small devil.'

'Ay, I also have told tales to the little ones, but do thou this——' His old eyes fell on the gaudy paintings of the wall, the blue and red dome, and the flames of the poinsettias beyond. 'Tell them first of those things that thou hast seen and they have seen together. Thus their knowledge will piece out thy imperfections. Tell them of what thou alone hast seen, then what thou hast heard, and since they be children tell them of battles and kings, horses, devils, elephants, and angels, but omit not to tell them of love and such-like. All the earth is full of tales to him who listens and does not drive away the poor from his door. The poor are the best of tale-tellers; for they must lay their ear to the ground every night.'

After this conversation the idea grew in my head, and Gobind was pressing in his inquiries as to the health of the book.

Later, when we had been parted for months, it happened that I was to go away and far off, and I came to bid Gobind good-bye.

'It is farewell between us now, for I go a very long journey,' I said.

'And I also. A longer one than thou. But what of the book?' said he.

'It will be born in due season if it is so ordained.'

'I would I could see it,' said the old man, huddling beneath his quilt. 'But that will not be.

I die three days hence, in the night, a little before the dawn. The term of my years is accomplished.'

In nine cases out of ten a native makes no miscalculation as to the day of his death. He has the foreknowledge of the beasts in this respect.

'Then thou wilt depart in peace, and it is good talk, for thou hast said that life is no delight to thee.'

'But it is a pity that our book is not born. How shall I know that there is any record of my name?'

'Because I promise, in the forepart of the book, preceding everything else, that it shall be written, Gobind, sadhu, of the island in the river and awaiting God in Dhunni Bhagat's Chubára, first spoke of the book,' said I.

'And gave counsel—an old man's counsel. Gobind, son of Gobind of the Chumi village in the Karaon tehsil, in the district of Mooltan. Will that be written also?'

'That will be written also.'

'And the book will go across the Black Water to the houses of your people, and all the *Sahibs* will know of me who am eighty years old?'

'All who read the book shall know. I cannot promise for the rest.'

'That is good talk. Call aloud to all who are in the monastery, and I will tell them this thing.'

They trooped up, *faquirs, sadhus, sunnyasis,*

byragis, *nihangs*, and *mullahs*, priests of all faiths and every degree of raggedness, and Gobind, leaning upon his crutch, spoke so that they were visibly filled with envy, and a white-haired senior bade Gobind think of his latter end instead of transitory repute in the mouths of strangers. Then Gobind gave me his blessing and I came away.

These tales have been collected from all places, and all sorts of people, from priests in the Chubára, from Ala Yar the carver, Jiwun Singh the carpenter, nameless men on steamers and trains round the world, women spinning outside their cottages in the twilight, officers and gentlemen now dead and buried, and a few, but these are the very best, my father gave me. The greater part of them have been published in magazines and newspapers, to whose editors I am indebted ; but some are new on this side of the water, and some have not seen the light before.

The most remarkable stories are, of course, those which do not appear—for obvious reasons.

CONTENTS

xvi CONTENTS

The Incarnation of Krishna Mulvaney

Wohl auf, my bully cavaliers
We ride to church to-day,
The man that hasn't got a horse
Must steal one straight away.

. . . . .

Be reverent, men, remember
This is a Gottes haus.
Du, Conrad, cut along der aisle
And schenck der whiskey aus.
Hans Breitmann's Ride to Church.

ONCE upon a time, very far from England, there lived three men who loved each other so greatly that neither man nor woman could come between them. They were in no sense refined, nor to be admitted to the outer-door mats of decent folk, because they happened to be private soldiers in Her Majesty's Army; and private soldiers of our service have small time for self-culture. Their duty is to keep themselves and their accoutrements specklessly clean, to refrain from getting drunk more often than is necessary, to obey their superiors, and to pray for a war. All these things my friends accomplished; and of their own

motion threw in some fighting-work for which the
Army Regulations did not call. Their fate sent
them to serve in India, which is not a golden
country, though poets have sung otherwise. There
men die with great swiftness, and those who live
suffer many and curious things. I do not think
that my friends concerned themselves much with
the social or political aspects of the East. They
attended a not unimportant war on the northern
frontier, another one on our western boundary, and
a third in Upper Burma. Then their regiment
sat still to recruit, and the boundless monotony of
cantonment life was their portion. They were
drilled morning and evening on the same dusty
parade-ground. They wandered up and down the
same stretch of dusty white road, attended the
same church and the same grog-shop, and slept
in the same lime-washed barn of a barrack for two
long years. There was Mulvaney, the father in
the craft, who had served with various regiments
from Bermuda to Halifax, old in war, scarred,
reckless, resourceful, and in his pious hours an
unequalled soldier. To him turned for help and
comfort six and a half feet of slow-moving, heavy-
footed Yorkshireman, born on the wolds, bred in
the dales, and educated chiefly among the carriers'
carts at the back of York railway-station. His
name was Learoyd, and his chief virtue an unmitigated patience which helped him to win fights.
How Ortheris, a fox-terrier of a Cockney, ever
came to be one of the trio, is a mystery which
even to-day I cannot explain. 'There was always
three av us,' Mulvaney used to say. 'An' by the

grace av God, so long as our service lasts, three av us they'll always be. 'Tis betther so.'

They desired no companionship beyond their own, and it was evil for any man of the regiment who attempted dispute with them. Physical argument was out of the question as regarded Mulvaney and the Yorkshireman; and assault on Ortheris meant a combined attack from these twain—a business which no five men were anxious to have on their hands. Therefore they flourished, sharing their drinks, their tobacco, and their money; good luck and evil; battle and the chances of death; life and the chances of happiness from Calicut in southern, to Peshawur in northern India.

Through no merit of my own it was my good fortune to be in a measure admitted to their friendship—frankly by Mulvaney from the beginning, sullenly and with reluctance by Learoyd, and suspiciously by Ortheris, who held to it that no man not in the Army could fraternise with a redcoat. 'Like to like,' said he. 'I'm a bloomin' sodger—he's a bloomin' civilian. 'Tain't natural —that's all.'

But that was not all. They thawed progressively, and in the thawing told me more of their lives and adventures than I am ever likely to write.

Omitting all else, this tale begins with the Lamentable Thirst that was at the beginning of First Causes. Never was such a thirst—Mulvaney told me so. They kicked against their compulsory virtue, but the attempt was only successful in the case of Ortheris. He, whose talents were many, went forth into the highways and stole a dog from a ' civilian '—*videlicet*, some one, he knew not who, not in the Army. Now that civilian was but newly connected by marriage with the colonel of the regiment, and outcry was made from quarters least anticipated by Ortheris, and, in the end, he was forced, lest a worse thing should happen, to dispose at ridiculously unremunerative rates of as promising a small terrier as ever graced one end of a leading string. The purchase-money was barely sufficient for one small outbreak which led him to the guard-room. He escaped, however, with nothing worse than a severe reprimand, and a few hours of punishment drill. Not for nothing had he acquired the reputation of being ' the best soldier of his inches ' in the regiment. Mulvaney had taught personal cleanliness and efficiency as the first articles of his companions' creed. ' A dhirty man,' he was used to say, in the speech of his kind, ' goes to Clink for a weakness in the knees, an' is coort-martialled for a pair av socks missin'; but a clane man, such as is an ornament to his service—a man whose buttons are gold, whose coat is wax upon him, an' whose 'coutrements are widout a speck—*that* man may, spakin' in reason, do fwhat he likes an' dhrink from day to divil. That's the pride av bein' dacint.'

We sat together, upon a day, in the shade of a ravine far from the barracks, where a watercourse used to run in rainy weather. Behind us was the scrub jungle, in which jackals, peacocks, the gray wolves of the North-Western Provinces, and occasionally a tiger estrayed from Central India,

were supposed to dwell. In front lay the cantonment, glaring white under a glaring sun; and on
either side ran the broad road that led to Delhi.

It was the scrub that suggested to my mind the
wisdom of Mulvaney taking a day's leave and
going upon a shooting-tour. The peacock is a
holy bird throughout India, and he who slays
one is in danger of being mobbed by the nearest
villagers; but on the last occasion that Mulvaney
had gone forth, he had contrived, without in the
least offending local religious susceptibilities, to
return with six beautiful peacock skins which he
sold to profit. It seemed just possible then——

'But fwhat manner av use is ut to me goin'
out widout a dhrink? The ground's powdher-
dhry underfoot, an' ut gets unto the throat fit to
kill,' wailed Mulvaney, looking at me reproachfully.
'An' a peacock is not a bird you can catch the tail
av onless ye run. Can a man run on wather—an'
jungle-wather too?

Ortheris had considered the question in all its
bearings. He spoke, chewing his pipe-stem meditatively the while:

> 'Go forth, return in glory,
>   To Clusium's royal 'ome:
>   An' round these bloomin' temples 'ang
>   The bloomin' shields o' Rome.

You better go. You ain't like to shoot yourself
—not while there's a chanst of liquor. Me an'
Learoyd'll stay at 'ome an' keep shop—'case o'
anythin' turnin' up. But you go out with a gas-
pipe gun an' ketch the little peacockses or somethin'.
You kin get one day's leave easy as winkin'.

Go along an' get it, an' get peacockses or some-thin'.'

'Jock,' said Mulvaney, turning to Learoyd, who was half asleep under the shadow of the bank. He roused slowly.

'Sitha, Mulvaaney, go,' said he.

And Mulvaney went; cursing his allies with Irish fluency and barrack-room point.

'Take note,' said he, when he had won his holiday, and appeared dressed in his roughest clothes with the only other regimental fowling-piece in his hand. 'Take note, Jock, an' you Orth'ris, I am goin' in the face av my own will—all for to please you. I misdoubt anythin' will come av permiscuous huntin' afther peacockses in a desolit lan'; an' I know that I will lie down an' die wid thirrrst. Me catch peacockses for you, ye lazy scutts—an' be sacrificed by the peasanthry—Ugh!'

He waved a huge paw and went away.

At twilight, long before the appointed hour, he returned empty-handed, much begrimed with dirt.

'Peacockses?' queried Ortheris from the safe rest of a barrack-room table whereon he was smoking cross-legged, Learoyd fast asleep on a bench.

'Jock,' said Mulvaney without answering, as he stirred up the sleeper. 'Jock, can ye fight? Will ye fight?'

Very slowly the meaning of the words communicated itself to the half-roused man. He understood—and again—what might these things mean ? Mulvaney was shaking him savagely. Meantime the men in the room howled with delight. There was war in the confederacy at last—war and the breaking of bonds.

Barrack-room etiquette is stringent. On the direct challenge must follow the direct reply. This is more binding than the ties of tried friendship. Once again Mulvaney repeated the question. Learoyd answered by the only means in his power, and so swiftly that the Irishman had barely time to avoid the blow. The laughter around increased. Learoyd looked bewilderedly at his friend—himself as greatly bewildered. Ortheris dropped from the table because his world was falling.

'Come outside,' said Mulvaney, and as the occupants of the barrack-room prepared joyously to follow, he turned and said furiously, 'There will be no fight this night—onless any wan av you is wishful to assist. The man that does, follows on.'

No man moved. The three passed out into the moonlight, Learoyd fumbling with the buttons of his coat. The parade-ground was deserted except for the scurrying jackals. Mulvaney's impetuous rush carried his companions far into the open ere Learoyd attempted to turn round and continue the discussion.

'Be still now. 'Twas my fault for beginnin' things in the middle av an end, Jock. I should ha' comminst wid an explanation ; but Jock, dear, on your sowl are ye fit, think you, for the finest fight that iver was—betther than fightin' me? Considher before ye answer.'

More than ever puzzled, Learoyd turned round two or three times, felt an arm, kicked tentatively, and answered, ' Ah'm fit.' He was accustomed to fight blindly at the bidding of the superior mind.

They sat them down, the men looking on from afar, and Mulvaney untangled himself in mighty words.

' Followin' your fools' scheme I wint out into the thrackless desert beyond the barricks. An' there I met a pious Hindu dhriving a bullock-kyart. I tuk ut for granted he wud be delighted for to convoy me a piece, an' I jumped in——'

' You long, lazy, black-haired swine,' drawled Ortheris, who would have done the same thing under similar circumstances.

' 'Twas the height av policy. That naygur-man dhruv miles an' miles—as far as the new railway line they're buildin' now back av the Tavi river. " 'Tis a kyart for dhirt only," says he now an' again timoreously, to get me out av ut. " Dhirt I am," sez I, " an' the dhryest that you iver kyarted. Dhrive on, me son, an' glory be wid you." At that I wint to slape, an' took no heed till he pulled up on the embankmint av the line where the coolies were pilin' mud. There was a matther av two thousand coolies on that line —you remimber that. Prisintly a bell rang, an' they throops off to a big pay-shed. " Where's the white man in charge ? " sez I to my kyart-dhriver. " In the shed," sez he, " engaged on a riffle."—" A fwhat ? " sez I. " Riffle," sez he. " You take ticket. He take money. You get nothin'."—"Oho!" sez I, "that's fwhat the shuperior an' cultivated man calls a raffle, me misbeguided child av darkness an' sin. Lead on to that raffle, though fwhat the mischief 'tis doin' so far away from uts home—which is the charity-bazaar at Christmas, an' the colonel's wife grinnin' behind the tea-table—is more than I know." Wid that I wint to the shed an' found 'twas pay-day among the coolies. Their wages was on a table forninst a big, fine, red buck av a man—sivun fut high, four fut wide, an' three fut thick, wid a fist on him like a corn-sack. He was payin' the coolies fair an' easy, but he wud ask each man if he wud raffle that month, an each man sez, "Yes," av course. Thin he wud deduct from their wages accordin'. Whin all was paid, he filled an ould cigar-box full av gun-wads an' scatthered ut among the coolies. They did not take much joy av that performince, an' small wondher. A man close to me picks up a black gun-wad an' sings out, "I have ut."—"Good may ut do you," sez I. The coolie wint forward to this big, fine, red man, who threw a cloth off av the most sumpshus, jooled, enamelled an' variously bedivilled sedan-chair I iver saw.'

'Sedan-chair! Put your 'ead in a bag. That was a palanquin. Don't yer know a palanquin when you see it?' said Ortheris with great scorn.

'I chuse to call ut sedan-chair, an' chair ut shall be, little man,' continued the Irishman. ''Twas a most amazin' chair—all lined wid pink silk an' fitted wid red silk curtains. "Here ut is," sez the red man. "Here ut is," sez the coolie, an' he grinned weakly-ways. "Is ut any use to you?" sez the red man. "No," sez the coolie ; "I'd like to make a presint av ut to you."—"I am graciously pleased to accept that same," sez the red man ; an' at that all the coolies cried aloud in fwhat was mint for cheerful notes, an' wint back to their diggin', lavin' me alone in the shed. The red man saw me, an' his face grew blue on his big, fat neck. "Fwhat d'you want here?" sez he. "Standin'-room an' no more," sez I, "onless it may be fwhat ye niver had, an' that's manners, ye rafflin' ruffian," for I was not goin' to have the Service throd upon. "Out of this," sez he. "I'm in charge av this section av construction."—"I'm in charge av mesilf," sez I, "an' it's like I will stay a while. D'ye raffle much in these parts?"— "Fwhat's that to you?" sez he. "Nothin'," sez I, "but a great dale to you, for begad I'm thinkin' you get the full half av your revenue from that sedan-chair. Is ut always raffled so?" I sez, an' wid that I wint to a coolie to ask questions. Bhoys, that man's name is Dearsley, an' he's been rafflin' that ould sedan-chair monthly this matther av nine months. Ivry coolie on the section takes a ticket —or he gives 'em the go—wanst a month on pay-day. Ivry coolie that wins ut gives ut back to him, for 'tis too big to carry away, an' he'd sack the man that thried to sell ut. That Dearsley has been makin' the rowlin' wealth av Roshus by nefarious rafflin'. Think av the burnin' shame to the sufferin' coolie-man that the Army in Injia are bound to protect an' nourish in their bosoms! Two thousand coolies defrauded wanst a month ! '

'Dom t' coolies. Has't gotten t' cheer, man?'
said Learoyd.

'Hould on. Havin' onearthed this amazin' an'
stupenjus fraud committed by the man Dearsley, I
hild a council av war; he thryin' all the time to
sejuce me into a fight wid opprobrious language.
That sedan-chair niver belonged by right to any
foreman av coolies. 'Tis a king's chair or a quane's.
There's gold on ut an' silk an' all manner av
trapesemints. Bhoys, 'tis not for me to countenance any sort av wrong-doin'—me bein' the ould
man—but——anyway he has had ut nine months,
an' he dare not make throuble av ut was taken from
him. Five miles away, or ut may be six——'

There was a long pause, and the jackals howled
merrily. Learoyd bared one arm, and contemplated
it in the moonlight. Then he nodded partly to
himself and partly to his friends. Ortheris wriggled
with suppressed emotion.

'I thought ye wud see the reasonableness av ut,'
said Mulvaney. 'I made bould to say as much to
the man before. He was for a direct front attack
—fut, horse, an' guns——an' all for nothin', seein'
that I had no thransport to convey the machine
away. "I will not argue wid you," sez I, "this
day, but subsequintly, Mister Dearsley, me rafflin'
jool, we talk ut out lengthways. 'Tis no good
policy to swindle the naygur av his hard-earned
emolumints, an' by presint informashin'"—'twas
the kyart man that tould me—"ye've been per-
pethrating that same for nine months. But I'm a
just man," sez I, "an' overlookin' the presumpshin
that yondher settee wid the gilt top was not come

by honust"—at that he turned sky-green, so I
knew things was more thrue than tellable—"not
come by honust, I'm willin' to compound the felony
for this month's winnin's."'

'Ah! Ho!' from Learoyd and Ortheris.

'That man Dearsley's rushin' on his fate,'
continued Mulvaney, solemnly wagging his head.
'All Hell had no name bad enough for me that
tide. Faith, he called me a robber! Me! that
was savin' him from continuin' in his evil ways
widout a remonstrince—an' to a man av conscience
a remonstrince may change the chune av his life.
"'Tis not for me to argue," sez I, "fwhatever ye
are, Mister Dearsley, but, by my hand, I'll take
away the temptation for you that lies in that sedan-
chair."—"You will have to fight me for ut," sez he,
"for well I know you will never dare make report
to any one."—"Fight I will," sez I, "but not this
day, for I'm rejuced for want av nourishmint."—
"Ye're an ould bould hand," sez he, sizin' me up
an' down; "an' a jool av a fight we will have.
Eat now an' dhrink, an' go your way." Wid that
he gave me some hump an' whisky—good whisky
—an' we talked av this an' that the while. "It goes
hard on me now," sez I, wipin' my mouth, "to con-
fiscate that piece av furniture, but justice is justice."
—"Ye've not got ut yet," sez he; "there's the fight
between."—"There is," sez I, "an' a good fight.
Ye shall have the pick av the best quality in my
rigimint for the dinner you have given this day."
Thin I came hot-foot to you two. Hould your
tongue, the both. 'Tis this way. To-morrow we
three will go there an' he shall have his pick betune

me an' Jock. Jock's a deceivin' fighter, for he is all fat to the eye, an' he moves slow. Now I'm all beef to the look, an' I move quick. By my reckonin' the Dearsley man won't take me; so me an' Orth'ris 'll see fair play. Jock, I tell you, 'twill be big fightin'—whipped, wid the cream above the jam. Afther the business 'twill take a good three av us—Jock'll be very hurt—to haul away that sedan-chair.'

'Palanquin.' This from Ortheris.

'Fwhatever ut is, we must have ut. 'Tis the only sellin' piece av property widin reach that we can get so cheap. An' fwhat's a fight afther all? He has robbed the naygur-man, dishonust. We rob him honust for the sake av the whisky he gave me.'

'But wot'll we do with the bloomin' article when we've got it? Them palanquins are as big as 'ouses, an' uncommon 'ard to sell, as McCleary said when ye stole the sentry-box from the Curragh.'

'Who's goin' to do t' fightin'?' said Learoyd, and Ortheris subsided. The three returned to barracks without a word. Mulvaney's last argument clinched the matter. This palanquin was property, vendible and to be attained in the simplest and least embarrassing fashion. It would eventually become beer. Great was Mulvaney.

Next afternoon a procession of three formed itself and disappeared into the scrub in the direction of the new railway line. Learoyd alone was without care, for Mulvaney dived darkly into the future, and little Ortheris feared the unknown.

What befell at that interview in the lonely pay-shed by the side of the half-built embankment only a few hundred coolies know, and their tale is a confusing one, running thus—

'We were at work. Three men in red coats came. They saw the Sahib — Dearsley Sahib. They made oration ; and noticeably the small man among the red-coats. Dearsley Sahib also made oration, and used many very strong words. Upon this talk they departed together to an open space, and there the fat man in the red coat fought with Dearsley Sahib after the custom of white men— with his hands, making no noise, and never at all pulling Dearsley Sahib's hair. Such of us as were not afraid beheld these things for just so long a time as a man needs to cook the mid-day meal. The small man in the red coat had possessed himself of Dearsley Sahib's watch. No, he did not steal that watch. He held it in his hand, and at certain seasons made outcry, and the twain ceased their combat, which was like the combat of young bulls in spring. Both men were soon all red, but Dearsley Sahib was much more red than the other. Seeing this, and fearing for his life—because we greatly loved him—some fifty of us made shift to rush upon the red-coats. But a certain man—very black as to the hair, and in no way to be confused with the small man, or the fat man who fought— that man, we affirm, ran upon us, and of us he embraced some ten or fifty in both arms, and beat our heads together, so that our livers turned to water, and we ran away. It is not good to interfere in the fightings of white men. After that Dearsley

Sahib fell and did not rise, these men jumped upon his stomach and despoiled him of all his money, and attempted to fire the pay-shed, and departed. Is it true that Dearsley Sahib makes no complaint of these latter things having been done? We were senseless with fear, and do not at all remember. There was no palanquin near the pay-shed. What do we know about palanquins? Is it true that Dearsley Sahib does not return to this place, on account of his sickness, for ten days? This is the fault of those bad men in the red coats, who should be severely punished; for Dearsley Sahib is both our father and mother, and we love him much. Yet, if Dearsley Sahib does not return to this place at all, we will speak the truth. There was a palanquin, for the up-keep of which we were forced to pay nine-tenths of our monthly wage. On such mulctings Dearsley Sahib allowed us to make obeisance to him before the palanquin. What could we do? We were poor men. He took a full half of our wages. Will the Government repay us those moneys? Those three men in red coats bore the palanquin upon their shoulders and departed. All the money that Dearsley Sahib had taken from us was in the cushions of that palanquin. Therefore they stole it. Thousands of rupees were there—all our money. It was our bank-box, to fill which we cheerfully contributed to Dearsley Sahib three-sevenths of our monthly wage. Why does the white man look upon us with the eye of disfavour? Before God, there was a palanquin, and now there is no palanquin; and if they send the police here to make inquisition, we can only say that there never has been any palanquin. Why should a palanquin be near these works? We are poor men, and we know nothing.'

Such is the simplest version of the simplest story connected with the descent upon Dearsley. From the lips of the coolies I received it. Dearsley himself was in no condition to say anything, and Mulvaney preserved a massive silence, broken only by the occasional licking of the lips. He had seen a fight so gorgeous that even his power of speech was taken from him. I respected that reserve until, three days after the affair, I discovered in a disused stable in my quarters a palanquin of unchastened splendour—evidently in past days the litter of a queen. The pole whereby it swung between the shoulders of the bearers was rich with the painted *papier - maché* of Cashmere. The shoulder-pads were of yellow silk. The panels of the litter itself were ablaze with the loves of all the gods and goddesses of the Hindu Pantheon— lacquer on cedar. The cedar sliding doors were fitted with hasps of translucent Jaipur enamel and ran in grooves shod with silver. The cushions were of brocaded Delhi silk, and the curtains which once hid any glimpse of the beauty of the king's palace were stiff with gold. Closer investigation showed that the entire fabric was everywhere rubbed and discoloured by time and wear ; but even thus it was sufficiently gorgeous to deserve housing on the threshold of a royal zenana. I found no fault with it, except that it was in my stable. Then, trying to lift it by the silver-shod shoulder-pole, I laughed. The road from Dearsley's pay-shed to the cantonment was a narrow and uneven one, and, traversed by three very inexperienced palanquin-bearers, one of whom was sorely battered about the head, must have been a path of torment. Still I did not quite recognise the right of the three musketeers to turn me into a 'fence' for stolen property.

'I'm askin' you to warehouse ut,' said Mulvaney, when he was brought to consider the question. 'There's no steal in ut. Dearsley tould us we cud have ut if we fought. Jock fought—an', oh, sorr, when the throuble was at uts finest an' Jock was bleedin' like a stuck pig, an' little Orth'ris was shquealin' on one leg chewin' big bites out av Dearsley's watch, I wud ha' given my place at the fight to have had you see wan round. He tuk Jock, as I suspicioned he would, an' Jock was deceptive. Nine roun's they were even matched, an' at the tenth—— About that palanquin now. There's not the least throuble in the world, or we wud not ha' brought ut here. You will ondher-stand that the Queen—God bless her!—does not reckon for a privit soldier to kape elephints an' palanquins an' sich in barricks. Afther we had dhragged ut down from Dearsley's through that cruel scrub that near broke Orth'ris's heart, we set ut in the ravine for a night; an' a thief av a porcupine an' a civet-cat av a jackal roosted in ut, as well we knew in the mornin'. I put ut to you, sorr, is an elegint palanquin, fit for the princess, the natural abidin' place av all the vermin in canton-mints? We brought ut to you, afther dhark, and put ut in your shtable. Do not let your conscience

prick.   Think av the rejoicin' men in the pay-shed
yonder—lookin' at Dearsley wid his head tied up
in a towel—an' well knowin' that they can dhraw
their pay ivry month widout stoppages for riffles.
Indirectly, sorr, you have rescued from an on-
principled son av a night-hawk the peasanthry av a
numerous village.   An' besides, will I let that
sedan-chair rot on our hands ?   Not I.   'Tis not
every day a piece av pure joolry comes into the
market.   There's not a king widin these forty
miles'—he waved his hand round the dusty horizon
—'not a king wud not be glad to buy ut.   Some
day meself, whin I have leisure, I'll take ut up
along the road an' dishpose av ut.'

'How ?' said I, for I knew the man was
capable of anything.

'Get into ut, av coorse, and keep wan eye open
through the curtains.   Whin I see a likely man
av the native persuasion, I will descind blushin'
from my canopy and say, "Buy a palanquin, ye
black scutt ?"   I will have to hire four men to
carry me first, though ; and that's impossible till
next pay-day.'

Curiously enough, Learoyd, who had fought
for the prize, and in the winning secured the
highest pleasure life had to offer him, was altogether disposed to undervalue it, while Ortheris
openly said it would be better to break the thing
up.   Dearsley, he argued, might be a many-sided
man, capable, despite his magnificent fighting
qualities, of setting in motion the machinery of
the civil law—a thing much abhorred by the
soldier.   Under any circumstances their fun had

come and passed; the next pay-day was close at
hand, when there would be beer for all. Wherefore longer conserve the painted palanquin?

'A first-class rifle-shot an' a good little man
av your inches you are,' said Mulvaney. 'But
you niver had a head worth a soft-boiled egg.
'Tis me has to lie awake av nights schamin' an'
plottin' for the three av us. Orth'ris, me son, 'tis
no matther av a few gallons av beer—no, nor
twenty gallons—but tubs an' vats an' firkins in
that sedan-chair. Whose ut was, an' what ut was,
an' how ut got there, we do not know; but I
know in my bones that you an' me an' Jock wid
his sprained thumb will get a fortune thereby.
Lave me alone, an' let me think.'

Meantime the palanquin stayed in my stall, the
key of which was in Mulvaney's hands.

Pay-day came, and with it beer. It was not in
experience to hope that Mulvaney, dried by four
weeks' drought, would avoid excess. Next morning he and the palanquin had disappeared. He
had taken the precaution of getting three days'
leave 'to see a friend on the railway,' and the
colonel, well knowing that the seasonal outburst
was near, and hoping it would spend its force
beyond the limits of his jurisdiction, cheerfully
gave him all he demanded. At this point Mulvaney's history, as recorded in the mess-room,
stopped.

Ortheris carried it not much further. 'No, 'e
wasn't drunk,' said the little man loyally, 'the
liquor was no more than feelin' its way round
inside of 'im; but 'e went an' filled that 'ole

bloomin' palanquin with bottles 'fore 'e went off. E's gone an' 'ired six men to carry 'im, an' I 'ad to 'elp 'im into 'is nupshal couch, 'cause 'e wouldn't 'ear reason. 'E's gone off in 'is shirt an' trousies, swearin' tremenjus—gone down the road in the palanquin, wavin' 'is legs out o' windy.'

'Yes,' said I, 'but where?'

'Now you arx me a question. 'E said 'e was goin' to sell that palanquin, but from observations what happened when I was stuffin' 'im through the door, I fancy 'e's gone to the new embankment to mock at Dearsley. 'Soon as Jock's off duty I'm goin' there to see if 'e's safe—not Mulvaney, but t'other man. My saints, but I pity 'im as 'elps Terence out o' the palanquin when 'e's once fair drunk!'

'He'll come back without harm,' I said.

''Corse 'e will. On'y question is, what'll 'e be doin' on the road? Killing Dearsley, like as not. 'E shouldn't 'a gone without Jock or me.'

Reinforced by Learoyd, Ortheris sought the foreman of the coolie-gang. Dearsley's head was still embellished with towels. Mulvaney, drunk or sober, would have struck no man in that condition, and Dearsley indignantly denied that he would have taken advantage of the intoxicated brave.

'I had my pick o' you two,' he explained to Learoyd, 'and you got my palanquin—not before I'd made my profit on it. Why'd I do harm when everything's settled? Your man *did* come here—drunk as Davy's sow on a frosty night— came a-purpose to mock me—stuck his head out

of the door an' called me a crucified hodman. I
made him drunker, an' sent him along. But I
never touched him.'

To these things Learoyd, slow to perceive the
evidences of sincerity, answered only, 'If owt
comes to Mulvaaney 'long o' you, I'll gripple you,
clouts or no clouts on your ugly head, an' I'll
draw t' throat twistyways, man. See there now.'

The embassy removed itself, and Dearsley, the
battered, laughed alone over his supper that
evening.

Three days passed—a fourth and a fifth. The
week drew to a close and Mulvaney did not
return. He, his royal palanquin, and his six
attendants, had vanished into air. A very large
and very tipsy soldier, his feet sticking out of the
litter of a reigning princess, is not a thing to
travel along the ways without comment. Yet no
man of all the country round had seen any such
wonder. He was, and he was not ; and Learoyd
suggested the immediate smashment of Dearsley
as a sacrifice to his ghost. Ortheris insisted that
all was well, and in the light of past experience his
hopes seemed reasonable.

'When Mulvaney goes up the road,' said he,
''e's like to go a very long ways up, specially
when 'e's so blue drunk as 'e is now. But what
gits me is 'is not bein' 'eard of pullin' wool off
the niggers somewheres about. That don't look
good. The drink must ha' died out in 'im by
this, unless 'e's broke a bank, an' then—Why
don't 'e come back ? 'E didn't ought to ha' gone
off without us.'

Even Ortheris's heart sank at the end of the seventh day, for half the regiment were out scouring the countryside, and Learoyd had been forced to fight two men who hinted openly that Mulvaney had deserted. To do him justice, the colonel laughed at the notion, even when it was put forward by his much-trusted adjutant.

'Mulvaney would as soon think of deserting as you would,' said he. 'No; he's either fallen into a mischief among the villagers—and yet that isn't likely, for he'd blarney himself out of the Pit; or else he is engaged on urgent private affairs—some stupendous devilment that we shall hear of at mess after it has been the round of the barrack-rooms. The worst of it is that I shall have to give him twenty-eight days' confinement at least for being absent without leave, just when I most want him to lick the new batch of recruits into shape. I never knew a man who could put a polish on young soldiers as quickly as Mulvaney can. How does he do it?'

'With blarney and the buckle-end of a belt, sir,' said the adjutant. 'He is worth a couple of non-commissioned officers when we are dealing with an Irish draft, and the London lads seem to adore him. The worst of it is that if he goes to the cells the other two are neither to hold nor to bind till he comes out again. I believe Ortheris preaches mutiny on those occasions, and I know that the mere presence of Learoyd mourning for Mulvaney kills all the cheerfulness of his room. The sergeants tell me that he allows no man to laugh when he feels unhappy. They are a queer gang.'

'For all that, I wish we had a few more of them. I like a well-conducted regiment, but these pasty - faced, shifty-eyed, mealy-mouthed young slouchers from the depot worry me sometimes with their offensive virtue. They don't seem to have backbone enough to do anything but play cards and prowl round the married quarters. I believe I'd forgive that old villain on the spot if he turned up with any sort of explanation that I could in decency accept.'

'Not likely to be much difficulty about that, sir,' said the adjutant. 'Mulvaney's explanations are only one degree less wonderful than his performances. They say that when he was in the Black Tyrone, before he came to us, he was discovered on the banks of the Liffey trying to sell his colonel's charger to a Donegal dealer as a perfect lady's hack. Shackbolt commanded the Tyrone then.'

'Shackbolt must have had apoplexy at the thought of his ramping war-horses answering to that description. He used to buy unbacked devils, and tame them on some pet theory of starvation. What did Mulvaney say?'

'That he was a member of the Society for the Prevention of Cruelty to Animals, anxious to " sell the poor baste where he would get something to fill out his dimples." Shackbolt laughed, but I fancy that was why Mulvaney exchanged to ours.'

'I wish he were back,' said the colonel; 'for I like him and believe he likes me.'

That evening, to cheer our souls, Learoyd, Ortheris, and I went into the waste to smoke out a porcupine. All the dogs attended, but even their clamour—and they began to discuss the shortcomings of porcupines before they left cantonments—could not take us out of ourselves. A large, low moon turned the tops of the plume-grass to silver, and the stunted camelthorn bushes and sour tamarisks into the likenesses of trooping devils. The smell of the sun had not left the earth, and little aimless winds blowing across the rose-gardens to the southward brought the scent of dried roses and water. Our fire once started, and the dogs craftily disposed to wait the dash of the porcupine, we climbed to the top of a rain-scarred hillock of earth, and looked across the scrub seamed with cattle paths, white with the long grass, and dotted with spots of level pond-bottom, where the snipe would gather in winter.

'This,' said Ortheris, with a sigh, as he took in the unkempt desolation of it all, 'this is sanguinary. This is unusually sanguinary. Sort o' mad country. Like a grate when the fire's put out by the sun.' He shaded his eyes against the moonlight. 'An' there's a loony dancin' in the middle of it all. Quite right. I'd dance too if I wasn't so downheart.'

There pranced a Portent in the face of the moon—a huge and ragged spirit of the waste, that flapped its wings from afar. It had risen out of the earth; it was coming towards us, and its outline was never twice the same. The toga, tablecloth, or dressing-gown, whatever the creature wore, took a hundred shapes. Once it stopped on a neighbouring mound and flung all its legs and arms to the winds.

'My, but that scarecrow 'as got 'em bad!' said Ortheris. 'Seems like if 'e comes any furder we'll 'ave to argify with 'im.'

Learoyd raised himself from the dirt as a bull clears his flanks of the wallow. And as a bull bellows, so he, after a short minute at gaze, gave tongue to the stars.

'Mulvaaney! Mulvaaney! A-hoo!'

Oh then it was that we yelled, and the figure dipped into the hollow, till, with a crash of rending grass, the lost one strode up to the light of the fire, and disappeared to the waist in a wave of joyous dogs! Then Learoyd and Ortheris gave greeting, bass and falsetto together, both swallowing a lump in the throat.

'You damned fool!' said they, and severally pounded him with their fists.

'Go easy!' he answered; wrapping a huge arm round each. 'I would have you to know that I am a god, to be treated as such—tho', by my faith, I fancy I've got to go to the guard-room just like a privit soldier.'

The latter part of the sentence destroyed the suspicions raised by the former. Any one would have been justified in regarding Mulvaney as mad. He was hatless and shoeless, and his shirt and trousers were dropping off him. But he wore one wondrous garment—a gigantic cloak that fell from collar-bone to heel—of pale pink silk, wrought all over in cunningest needlework of hands long since dead, with the loves of the Hindu gods. The monstrous figures leaped in and out of the light of the fire as he settled the folds round him.

Ortheris handled the stuff respectfully for a moment while I was trying to remember where I had seen it before. Then he screamed, 'What 'ave you done with the palanquin ? You're wearin' the linin'.'

'I am,' said the Irishman, 'an' by the same token the 'broidery is scrapin' my hide off. I've lived in this sumpshus counterpane for four days. Me son, I begin to ondherstand why the naygur is no use. Widout me boots, an' me trousies like an openwork stocking on a gyurl's leg at a dance, I begin to feel like a naygur-man—all fearful an' timoreous. Give me a pipe an' I'll tell on.'

He lit a pipe, resumed his grip of his two friends, and rocked to and fro in a gale of laughter.

'Mulvaney,' said Ortheris sternly, ''taint no time for laughin'. You've given Jock an' me more trouble than you're worth. You 'ave been absent without leave an' you'll go into cells for that ; an' you 'ave come back disgustin'ly dressed an' most improper in the linin' o' that bloomin' palanquin. Instid of which you laugh. An' *we* thought you was dead all the time.'

'Bhoys,' said the culprit, still shaking gently, 'whin I've done my tale you may cry if you like, an' little Orth'ris here can thrample my inside out. Ha' done an' listen. My performinces have been stupenjus : my luck has been the blessed luck av the British Army—an' there's no bchter than that. I went out dhrunk an' dhrinkin' in the palanquin, and I have come back a pink god. Did any of you go to Dearsley afther my time was up? He was at the bottom of ut all.'

'Ah said so,' murmured Learoyd. 'To-morrow ah'll smash t' face in upon his heead.'

'Ye will not. Dearsley's a jool av a man. Afther Ortheris had put me into the palanquin an' the six bearer-men were gruntin' down the road, I tuk thought to mock Dearsley for that fight. So I tould thim, "Go to the embankmint," and there, bein' most amazin' full, I shtuck my head out av the concern an' passed compliments wid Dearsley. I must ha' miscalled him outrageous, for whin I am that way the power av the tongue comes on me. I can bare remimber tellin' him that his mouth opened endways like the mouth av a skate, which was thrue afther Learoyd had handled ut; an' I clear remimber his takin' no manner nor matter av offence, but givin' me a big dhrink of beer. 'Twas the beer did the thrick, for I crawled back into the palanquin, steppin' on me right ear wid me left foot, an' thin I slept like the dead. Wanst I half-roused, an' begad the noise in my head was tremenjus—roarin' an' rattlin' an' poundin', such as was quite new to me. "Mother av Mercy," thinks I, "phwat a concertina I will have on my shoulders whin I wake!" An' wid that I curls mysilf up to sleep before ut should get hould on me. Bhoys, that noise was not dhrink, 'twas the rattle av a thrain!'

There followed an impressive pause.

'Yes, he had put me on a thrain—put me, palanquin an' all, an' six black assassins av his own coolies that was in his nefarious confidence, on the flat av a ballast-thruck, and we were rowlin' an' bowlin' along to Benares. Glory be that I did not wake up thin an' introjuce mysilf to the coolies. As I was sayin', I slept for the betther part av a day an' a night. But remimber you, that that man Dearsley had packed me off on wan av his material-thrains to Benares, all for to make me overstay my leave an' get me into the cells.'

The explanation was an eminently rational one. Benares lay at least ten hours by rail from the cantonments, and nothing in the world could have saved Mulvaney from arrest as a deserter had he appeared there in the apparel of his orgies. Dearsley had not forgotten to take revenge. Learoyd, drawing back a little, began to place soft blows over selected portions of Mulvaney's body. His thoughts were away on the embankment, and they meditated evil for Dearsley. Mulvaney continued—

'Whin I was full awake the palanquin was set down in a street, I suspicioned, for I cud hear people passin' an' talkin'. But I knew well I was far from home. There is a queer smell upon our cantonments—a smell av dried earth and brick-kilns wid whiffs av cavalry stable-litter. This place smelt marigold flowers an' bad water, an' wanst somethin' alive came an' blew heavy with his muzzle at the chink av the shutter. "It's in a village I am," thinks I to mysilf, "an' the parochial buffalo is investigatin' the palanquin." But anyways I had no desire to move. Only lie still whin you're in foreign parts an' the standin' luck av the

British Army will carry ye through. That is an epigram. I made ut.

'Thin a lot av whishperin' divils surrounded the palanquin. "Take ut up," sez wan man. "But who'll pay us?" sez another. "The Maharanee's minister, av coorse," sez the man. "Oho!" sez I to mysilf, "I'm a quane in me own right, wid a minister to pay me expenses. I'll be an emperor if I lie still long enough; but this is no village I've found." I lay quiet, but I gummed me right eye to a crack av the shutters, an I saw that the whole street was crammed wid palanquins an' horses, an' a sprinklin' av naked priests all yellow powder an' tigers' tails. But I may tell you, Orth'ris, an' you, Learoyd, that av all the palanquins ours was the most imperial an' magnificent. Now a palanquin means a native lady all the world over, except whin a soldier av the Quane happens to be takin' a ride. "Women an' priests!" sez I. "Your father's son is in the right pew this time, Terence. There will be proceedin's." Six black divils in pink muslin tuk up the palanquin, an' oh! but the rowlin' an' the rockin' made me sick. Thin we got fair jammed among the palanquins— not more than fifty av them—an' we grated an' bumped like Queenstown potato-smacks in a runnin' tide. I cud hear the women gigglin' and squirkin' in their palanquins, but mine was the royal equipage. They made way for ut, an', begad, the pink muslin men o' mine were howlin', "Room for the Maharanee av Gokral-Seetarun." Do you know aught av the lady, sorr?'

'Yes,' said I. 'She is a very estimable old

queen of the Central Indian States, and they say
she is fat. How on earth could she go to Benares
without all the city knowing her palanquin? '

' 'Twas the eternal foolishness av the naygur-
man. They saw the palanquin lying loneful an'
forlornsome, an' the beauty av ut, after Dearsley's
men had dhropped ut and gone away, an' they
gave ut the best name that occurred to thim.
Quite right too. For aught we know the ould
lady was thravellin' *incog*—like me. I'm glad to
hear she's fat. I was no light weight mysilf, an'
my men were mortial anxious to dhrop me under
a great big archway promiscuously ornamented
wid the most improper carvin's an' cuttin's I iver
saw. Begad! they made me blush—like a—like
a Maharanee.'

' The temple of Prithi-Devi,' I murmured,
remembering the monstrous horrors of that sculp-
tured archway at Benares.

' Pretty Devilskins, savin' your presence, sorr!
There was nothin' pretty about ut, except me.
'Twas all half dhark, an' whin the coolies left they
shut a big black gate behind av us, an' half a
company av fat yellow priests began pully-haulin'
the palanquins into a dharker place yet—a big
stone hall full av pillars, an' gods, an' incense, an'
all manner av similar thruck. The gate discon-
certed me, for I perceived I wud have to go
forward to get out, my retreat bein' cut off. By
the same token a good priest makes a bad palan-
quin-coolie. Begad! they nearly turned me inside
out draggin' the palanquin to the temple. Now
the disposishin av the forces inside was this way.

The Maharanee av Gokral-Seetarun — that was me
— lay by the favour av Providence on the far left
flank behind the dhark av a pillar carved with
elephints' heads. The remainder av the palanquins
was in a big half circle facing in to the biggest,
fattest, an' most amazin' she-god that iver I
dreamed av. Her head ran up into the black
above us, an' her feet stuck out in the light av a
little fire av melted butter that a priest was feedin'
out av a butter-dish. Thin a man began to sing
an' play on somethin' back in the dhark, an' 'twas
a queer song. Ut made my hair lift on the back
av my neck. Thin the doors av all the palanquins
slid back, an' the women bundled out. I saw
what I'll niver see again. 'Twas more glorious
than thransformations at a pantomime, for they
was in pink an' blue an' silver an' red an' grass
green, wid dimonds an' imralds an' great red
rubies all over thim. But that was the least part
av the glory. O bhoys, they were more lovely
than the like av any loveliness in hiven ; ay, their
little bare feet were better than the white hands av
a lord's lady, an' their mouths were like puckered
roses, an' their eyes were bigger an' dharker than
the eyes av any livin' women I've seen Ye may
laugh, but I'm speakin' truth. I niver saw the
like, an' niver I will again.'

'Seeing that in all probability you were watching
the wives and daughters of most of the kings of
India, the chances are that you won't,' I said, for
it was dawning on me that Mulvaney had stumbled
upon a big Queens' Praying at Benares.

' I niver will,' he said mournfully. ' That

sight doesn't come twist to any man. It made me ashamed to watch. A fat priest knocked at my door. I didn't think he'd have the insolince to disturb the Maharanee av Gokral-Seetarun, so I lay still. "The old cow's asleep," sez he to another. "Let her be," sez that. "'Twill be long before she has a calf!" I might ha' known before he spoke that all a woman prays for in Injia—an' for matter o' that in England to—is childher. That made me more sorry I'd come, me bein', as you well know, a childless man.'

He was silent for a moment, thinking of his little son, dead many years ago.

'They prayed, an' the butter-fires blazed up, an' the incense turned everything blue, an' between that an' the fires the women looked as tho' they were all ablaze an' twinklin'. They took hold av the she-god's knees, they cried out an' they threw themselves about, an' that world-without-end-amen music was dhrivin' thim mad. Mother av Hiven! how they cried, an' the ould she-god grinni' above thim all so scornful! The dhrink was dyin' out in me fast, an' I was thinkin' harder than the thoughts wud go through my head—thinkin' how to get out, an' all manner of nonsense as well. The women were rockin' in rows, their di'mond belts clickin', an' the tears runnin' out betune their hands, an' the lights were goin' lower an' dharker. Thin there was a blaze like lightnin' from the roof, an' that showed me the inside av the palanquin, an' at the end where my foot was, stood the livin' spit an' image o' mysilf worked on the linin'. This man here, ut was.'

He hunted in the folds of his pink cloak, ran a hand under one, and thrust into the firelight a foot-long embroidered presentment of the great god Krishna, playing on a flute. The heavy jowl, the staring eye, and the blue-black moustache of the god made up a far-off resemblance to Mulvaney.

'The blaze was gone in a wink, but the whole schame came to me thin. I believe I was mad too. I slid the off-shutter open an' rowled out into the dhark behind the elephint-head pillar, tucked up my trousies to my knees, slipped off my boots an' tuk a general hould av all the pink linin' av the palanquin. Glory be, ut ripped out like a woman's dhriss when you tread on ut at a sergeants' ball, an' a bottle came with ut. I tuk the bottle an' the next minut I was out av the dhark av the pillar, the pink linin' wrapped round me most graceful, the music thunderin' like kettledrums, an' a could draft blowin' round my bare legs. By this hand that did ut, I was Krishna tootlin' on the flute—the god that the rig'mental chaplain talks about. A sweet sight I must ha' looked. I knew my eyes were big, and my face was wax-white, an' at the worst I must ha' looked like a ghost. But they took me for the livin' god. The music stopped, and the women were dead dumb, an' I crooked my legs like a shepherd on a china basin, an' I did the ghost-waggle with my feet as I had done ut at the rig'mental theatre many times, an' I slid acrost the width av that temple in front av the she-god tootlin' on the beer bottle.'

'Wot did you toot?' demanded Ortheris the practical.

'Me? Oh!' Mulvaney sprang up, suiting the action to the word, and sliding gravely in front of us, a dilapidated but imposing deity in the half light. 'I sang—

> 'Only say
> You'll be Mrs. Brallaghan.
> Don't say nay,
> Charmin' Judy Callaghan.

I didn't know me own voice when I sang. An' oh! 'twas pitiful to see the women The darlin's were down on their faces. Whin I passed the last wan I cud see her poor little fingers workin' one in another as if she wanted to touch my feet. So I dhrew the tail av this pink overcoat over her head for the greater honour, an' I slid into the dhark on the other side av the temple, and fetched up in the arms av a big fat priest. All I wanted was to get away clear. So I tuk him by his greasy throat an' shut the speech out av him. "Out!" sez I. "Which way, ye fat heathen?"—"Oh!" sez he. "Man," sez I. "White man, soldier man, common soldier man. Where in the name av confusion is the back door?" The women in the temple were still on their faces, an' a young priest was holdin' out his arms above their heads.

'"This way," sez my fat friend, duckin' behind a big bull-god an' divin' into a passage. Thin I remimbered that I must ha' made the miraculous reputation av that temple for the next fifty years. "Not so fast," I sez, an' I held out both my hands wid a wink. That ould thief smiled like a

father. I tuk him by the back av the neck in
case he should be wishful to put a knife into me
unbeknowst, an' I ran him up an' down the passage
twice to collect his sensibilities! "Be quiet," sez
he, in English. "Now you talk sense," I sez.
"Fwhat'll you give me for the use av that most
iligant palanquin I have no time to take away?"—
"Don't tell," sez he. "Is ut like?" sez I.
"But ye might give me my railway fare. I'm far
from my home an' I've done you a service."
Bhoys, 'tis a good thing to be a priest. The ould
man niver throubled himself to dhraw from a bank.
As I will prove to you subsequint, he philandered
all round the slack av his clothes an' began
dribblin' ten-rupee notes, old gold mohurs, and
rupees into my hand till I could hould no more.'

'You lie!' said Ortheris. 'You're mad or
sunstrook. A native don't give coin unless you
cut it out o' 'im. Tain't nature.'

'Then my lie an' my sunstroke is concealed
under that lump av sod yonder,' retorted Mulvaney
unruffled, nodding across the scrub. 'An' there's
a dale more in nature than your squidgy little legs
have iver taken you to, Orth'ris, me son. Four
hundred an' thirty-four rupees by my reckonin',
an' a big fat gold necklace that I took from him
as a remimbrancer, was our share in that business.'

'An' 'e give it you for love?' said Ortheris.

'We were alone in that passage. Maybe I was
a trifle too pressin', but considher fwhat I had done
for the good av the temple and the iverlastin' joy
av those women. 'Twas cheap at the price. I
wud ha' taken more if I cud ha' found ut. I

turned the ould man upside down at the last, but he was milked dhry. Thin he opened a door in another passage an' I found mysilf up to my knees in Benares river-water, an' bad smellin' ut is. More by token I had come out on the river-line close to the burnin' ghat and contagious to a cracklin' corpse. This was in the heart av the night, for I had been four hours in the temple. There was a crowd av boats tied up, so I tuk wan an' wint across the river. Thin I came home acrost country, lyin' up by day.'

'How on earth did you manage?' I said.

'How did Sir Frederick Roberts get from Cabul to Candahar? He marched an' he niver tould how near he was to breakin' down. That's why he is fwhat he is. An' now—' Mulvaney yawned portentously. 'Now I will go an' give myself up for absince widout leave. It's eight an' twenty days an' the rough end of the colonel's tongue in orderly room, any way you look at ut. But 'tis cheap at the price.'

'Mulvaney,' said I softly. 'If there happens to be any sort of excuse that the colonel can in any way accept, I have a notion that you'll get nothing more than the dressing-down. The new recruits are in, and——'

'Not a word more, sorr. Is ut excuses the old man wants? 'Tis not my way, but he shall have thim. I'll tell him I was engaged in financial operations connected wid a church,' and he flapped his way to cantonments and the cells, singing lustily—

'So they sent a corp'ril's file,
  And they put me in the gyard-room
  For conduck unbecomin' of a soldier.'

And when he was lost in the mist of the moonlight
we could hear the refrain—

'Bang upon the big drum, bash upon the cymbals,
  As we go marchin' along, boys, oh !
  For although in this campaign
  There's no whisky nor champagne,
  We'll keep our spirits goin' with a song, boys !'

Therewith he surrendered himself to the joyful
and almost weeping guard, and was made much of
by his fellows. But to the colonel he said that he
had been smitten with sunstroke and had lain in-
sensible on a villager's cot for untold hours ; and
between laughter and goodwill the affair was
smoothed over, so that he could, next day, teach
the new recruits how to 'Fear God, Honour the
Queen, Shoot Straight, and Keep Clean.'

The Courting of Dinah Shadd

> What did the colonel's lady think?
>   Nobody never knew.
> Somebody asked the sergeant's wife
>   An' she told 'em true.
> When you git to a man in the case
>   They're like a row o' pins,
> For the colonel's lady an' Judy O'Grady
>   Are sisters under their skins. .
>
> *Barrack-Room Ballad.*

ALL day I had followed at the heels of a pursuing army engaged on one of the finest battles that ever camp of exercise beheld. Thirty thousand troops had, by the wisdom of the Government of India, been turned loose over a few thousand square miles of country to practise in peace what they would never attempt in war. Consequently cavalry charged unshaken infantry at the trot. Infantry captured artillery by frontal attacks delivered in line of quarter columns, and mounted infantry skirmished up to the wheels of an armoured train which carried nothing more deadly than a twenty-five-pounder Armstrong, two Nordenfeldts, and a few score volunteers all cased in three-eighths-inch boiler-plate. Yet it was a very lifelike camp.

Operations did not cease at sundown ; nobody knew the country and nobody spared man or horse. There was unending cavalry scouting and almost unending forced work over broken ground. The Army of the South had finally pierced the centre of the Army of the North, and was pouring through the gap hot-foot to capture a city of strategic importance. Its front extended fanwise, the sticks being represented by regiments strung out along the line of route backwards to the divisional transport columns and all the lumber that trails behind an army on the move. On its right the broken left of the Army of the North was flying in mass, chased by the Southern horse and hammered by the Southern guns till these had been pushed far beyond the limits of their last support. Then the flying sat down to rest, while the elated commandant of the pursuing force telegraphed that he held all in check and observation.

Unluckily he did not observe that three miles to his right flank a flying column of Northern horse with a detachment of Ghoorkhas and British troops had been pushed round as fast as the failing light allowed, to cut across the entire rear of the Southern Army,—to break, as it were, all the ribs of the fan where they converged by striking at the transport, reserve ammunition, and artillery supplies. Their instructions were to go in, avoiding the few scouts who might not have been drawn off by the pursuit, and create sufficient excitement to impress the Southern Army with the wisdom of guarding their own flank and rear before they captured cities. It was a pretty manœuvre, neatly carried out.

Speaking for the second division of the Southern Army, our first intimation of the attack was at twilight, when the artillery were labouring in deep sand, most of the escort were trying to help them out, and the main body of the infantry had gone on. A Noah's Ark of elephants, camels, and the mixed menagerie of an Indian transport-train bubbled and squealed behind the guns, when there appeared from nowhere in particular British infantry to the extent of three companies, who sprang to the heads of the gun-horses and brought all to a standstill amid oaths and cheers.

'How's that, umpire?' said the major commanding the attack, and with one voice the drivers and limber gunners answered 'Hout!' while the colonel of artillery sputtered.

'All your scouts are charging our main body,' said the major. 'Your flanks are unprotected for two miles. I think we've broken the back of this division. And listen,—there go the Ghoorkhas!'

A weak fire broke from the rear-guard more than a mile away, and was answered by cheerful howlings. The Ghoorkhas, who should have swung clear of the second division, had stepped on its tail in the dark, but drawing off hastened to reach the next line of attack, which lay almost parallel to us five or six miles away.

Our column swayed and surged irresolutely,— three batteries, the divisional ammunition reserve, the baggage, and a section of the hospital and bearer corps. The commandant ruefully promised

to report himself 'cut up' to the nearest umpire,
and commending his cavalry and all other cavalry
to the special care of Eblis, toiled on to resume
touch with the rest of the division.

'We'll bivouac here to-night,' said the major,
'I have a notion that the Ghoorkhas will get caught.
They may want us to re-form on. Stand easy till
the transport gets away.'

A hand caught my beast's bridle and led him
out of the choking dust; a larger hand deftly
canted me out of the saddle; and two of the hugest
hands in the world received me sliding. Pleasant
is the lot of the special correspondent who falls
into such hands as those of Privates Mulvaney,
Ortheris, and Learoyd.

'An' that's all right,' said the Irishman calmly.
'We thought we'd find you somewheres here by.
Is there anything av yours in the transport?
Orth'ris'll fetch ut out.'

Ortheris did 'fetch ut out,' from under the
trunk of an elephant, in the shape of a servant and
an animal both laden with medical comforts. The
little man's eyes sparkled.

'If the brutil an' licentious soldiery av these
parts gets sight av the thruck,' said Mulvaney,
making practised investigation, 'they'll loot ev'ry-
thing. They're bein' fed on iron-filin's an' dog-
biscuit these days, but glory's no compensation
for a belly-ache. Praise be, we're here to protect
you, sorr. Beer, sausage, bread (soft an' that's a
cur'osity), soup in a tin, whisky by the smell av
ut, an' fowls! Mother av Moses, but ye take the
field like a confectioner! 'Tis scand'lus.'

'Ere's a orficer,' said Ortheris significantly.
'When the sergent's done lushin' the privit may
clean the pot.'

I bundled several things into Mulvaney's haver-
sack before the major's hand fell on my shoulder
and he said tenderly, ' Requisitioned for the Queen's
service. Wolseley was quite wrong about special
correspondents : they are the soldier's best friends.
Come and take pot-luck with us to-night.'

And so it happened amid laughter and shoutings
that my well-considered commissariat melted away
to reappear later at the mess-table, which was a
waterproof sheet spread on the ground. The
flying column had taken three days' rations with it,
and there be few things nastier than Government
rations—especially when Government is experi-
menting with German toys. Erbswurst, tinned
beef of surpassing tinniness, compressed vegetables,
and meat-biscuits may be nourishing, but what
Thomas Atkins needs is bulk in his inside. The
major, assisted by his brother officers, purchased
goats for the camp, and so made the experiment of
no effect. Long before the fatigue-party sent to
collect brushwood had returned, the men were
settled down by their valises, kettles and pots had
appeared from the surrounding country, and were
dangling over fires as the kid and the compressed
vegetable bubbled together ; there rose a cheerful
clinking of mess-tins ; outrageous demands for ' a
little more stuffin' with that there liver-wing ; '
and gust on gust of chaff as pointed as a bayonet
and as delicate as a gun-butt.

'The boys are in a good temper,' said the

major. 'They'll be singing presently. Well, a night like this is enough to keep them happy.'

Over our heads burned the wonderful Indian stars, which are not all pricked in on one plane, but, preserving an orderly perspective, draw the eye through the velvet darkness of the void up to the barred doors of heaven itself. The earth was a gray shadow more unreal than the sky. We could hear her breathing lightly in the pauses between the howling of the jackals, the movement of the wind in the tamarisks, and the fitful mutter of musketry-fire leagues away to the left. A native woman from some unseen hut began to sing, the mail-train thundered past on its way to Delhi, and a roosting crow cawed drowsily. Then there was a belt-loosening silence about the fires, and the even breathing of the crowded earth took up the story.

The men, full fed, turned to tobacco and song, —their officers with them. The subaltern is happy who can win the approval of the musical critics in his regiment, and is honoured among the more intricate step-dancers. By him, as by him who plays cricket cleverly, Thomas Atkins will stand in time of need, when he will let a better officer go on alone. The ruined tombs of forgotten Mussulman saints heard the ballad of *Agra Town*, *The Buffalo Battery*, *Marching to Kabul*, *The long, long Indian Day*, *The Place where the Punkah-coolie died*, and that crashing chorus which announces,

> Youth's daring spirit, manhood's fire,
> Firm hand and eagle eye,
> Must he acquire, who would aspire
> To see the gray boar die.

To-day, of all those jovial thieves who appropriated my commissariat and lay and laughed round that waterproof sheet, not one remains. They went to camps that were not of exercise and battles without umpires. Burma, the Soudan, and the frontier,—fever and fight,—took them in their time.

I drifted across to the men's fires in search of Mulvaney, whom I found strategically greasing his feet by the blaze. There is nothing particularly lovely in the sight of a private thus engaged after a long day's march, but when you reflect on the exact proportion of the 'might, majesty, dominion, and power' of the British Empire which stands on those feet you take an interest in the proceedings.

'There's a blister, bad luck to ut, on the heel,' said Mulvaney. 'I can't touch ut. Prick ut out, little man.'

Ortheris took out his house-wife, eased the trouble with a needle, stabbed Mulvaney in the calf with the same weapon, and was swiftly kicked into the fire.

'I've bruk the best av my toes over you, ye grinnin' child av disruption,' said Mulvaney, sitting cross-legged and nursing his feet ; then seeing me, 'Oh, ut's you, sorr ! Be welkim, an' take that maraudin' scutt's place. Jock, hold him down on the cindhers for a bit.'

But Ortheris escaped and went elsewhere, as I took possession of the hollow he had scraped for himself and lined with his greatcoat. Learoyd on the other side of the fire grinned affably and in a minute fell fast asleep.

'There's the height av politeness for you,' said Mulvaney, lighting his pipe with a flaming branch. 'But Jock's eaten half a box av your sardines at wan gulp, an' I think the tin too. What's the best wid you, sorr, an' how did you happen to be on the losin' side this day whin we captured you ?'

'The Army of the South is winning all along the line,' I said.

'Then that line's the hangman's rope, savin' your presence. You'll learn to-morrow how we rethreated to dhraw thim on before we made thim trouble, an' that's what a woman does. By the same tokin, we'll be attacked before the dawnin' an' ut would be betther not to slip your boots. How do I know that ? By the light av pure reason. Here are three companies av us ever so far inside av the enemy's flank an' a crowd av roarin', tarin', squealin' cavalry gone on just to turn out the whole hornet's nest av them. Av course the enemy will pursue, by brigades like as not, an' thin we'll have to run for ut. Mark my words. I am av the opinion av Polonius whin he said, "Don't fight wid ivry scutt for the pure joy av fightin', but if you do, knock the nose av him first an' frequint." We ought to ha' gone on an' helped the Ghoorkhas.'

'But what do you know about Polonius ?' I demanded. This was a new side of Mulvaney's character.

'All that Shakespeare iver wrote an' a dale more that the gallery shouted,' said the man of war, carefully lacing his boots. 'Did I not tell you av Silver's theatre in Dublin whin I was younger than I am now an' a patron av the drama? Ould Silver wud never pay actor-man or woman their just dues, an' by consequince his comp'nies was collapsible at the last minut. Thin the bhoys wud clamour to take a part, an' oft as not ould Silver made them pay for the fun. Faith, I've seen Hamlut played wid a new black eye an' the queen as full as a cornucopia. I remimber wanst Hogin that 'listed in the Black Tyrone an' was shot in South Africa, he sejuced ould Silver into givin' him Hamlut's part instid av me that had a fine fancy for rhetoric in those days. Av course I wint into the gallery an' began to fill the pit wid other people's hats, an' I passed the time av day to Hogin walkin' through Denmark like a hamstrung mule wid a pall on his back. "Hamlut," sez I, "there's a hole in your heel. Pull up your shtockin's, Hamlut," sez I. "Hamlut, Hamlut, for the love av decincy dhrop that skull an' pull up your shtockin's." The whole house begun to tell him that. He stopped his soliloquishms mid-between. "My shtockin's may be comin' down or they may not," sez he, screwin' his eye into the gallery, for well he knew who I was. "But afther this performince is over me an' the Ghost'll trample the tripes out av you, Terence, wid your ass's bray!" An' that's how I come to know about Hamlut. Eyah! Those days, those days! Did you iver have onendin' devilmint an' nothin' to pay for it in your life, sorr?'

'Never, without having to pay,' I said.

'That's thrue! 'Tis mane whin you considher on ut; but ut's the same wid horse or fut. A headache if you dhrink, an' a belly-ache if you eat too much, an' a heart-ache to kape all down. Faith, the beast only gets the colic, an' he's the lucky man.'

He dropped his head and stared into the fire, fingering his moustache the while. From the far side of the bivouac the voice of Corbet-Nolan, senior subaltern of B company, uplifted itself in an ancient and much appreciated song of sentiment, the men moaning melodiously behind him.

> The north wind blew coldly, she drooped from that hour,
> My own little Kathleen, my sweet little Kathleen,
> Kathleen, my Kathleen, Kathleen O'Moore !

With forty-five O's in the last word : even at that distance you might have cut the soft South Irish accent with a shovel.

'For all we take we must pay, but the price is cruel high,' murmured Mulvaney when the chorus had ceased.

'What's the trouble?' I said gently, for I knew that he was a man of an inextinguishable sorrow.

'Hear now,' said he. 'Ye know what I am now. *I* know what I mint to be at the beginnin' av my service. I've tould you time an' again, an' what I have not Dinah Shadd has. An' what am I ? Oh, Mary Mother av Hiven, an ould dhrunken, untrustable baste av a privit that has seen the reg'ment change out from colonel to drummer-boy, not wanst or twice, but scores av times ! Ay, scores ! An' me not so near gettin' promotion as in the first ! An' me livin' on an' kapin' clear av clink, not by my own good conduck, but the kindness av some orf'cer-bhoy young enough to be son to me ! Do I not know ut ? Can I not tell whin I'm passed over at p'rade, tho' I'm rockin' full av liquor an' ready to fall all in wan piece, such as even a suckin' child might see, bekaze, "Oh, 'tis only ould Mulvaney!" An' whin I'm let off in ord'ly-room through some thrick of the tongue an' a ready answer an' the ould man's mercy, is ut smilin' I feel whin I fall away an' go back to Dinah Shadd, thryin' to carry ut all off as a joke ? Not I ! 'Tis hell to me, dumb hell through ut all ; an' next time whin the fit comes I will be as bad again. Good cause the reg'ment has to know me for the best soldier in ut. Better cause have I to know mesilf for the worst man. I'm only fit to tache the new drafts what I'll niver learn myself ; an' I am sure, as tho' I heard ut, that the minut wan av these pink-eyed recruities gets away from my "Mind ye now," an' "Listen to this, Jim, bhoy,"—sure I am that the sergint houlds me up to him for a warnin'. So I tache, as they say at musketry-instruction, by direct and ricochet fire. Lord be good to me, for I have stud some throuble ! '

'Lie down and go to sleep,' said I, not being able to comfort or advise. 'You're the best man in the regiment, and, next to Ortheris, the biggest fool. Lie down and wait till we're attacked. What force will they turn out ? Guns, think you ? '

'Try that wid your lorrds an' ladies, twistin' an turnin' the talk, tho' you mint ut well. Ye cud say nothin' to help me, an' yet ye niver knew what cause I had to be what I am.'

'Begin at the beginning and go on to the end,' I said royally. 'But rake up the fire a bit first.'

I passed Ortheris's bayonet for a poker.

'That shows how little we know what we do,' said Mulvaney, putting it aside. 'Fire takes all the heart out av the steel, an' the next time, may be, that our little man is fighting for his life his bradawl'll break, an' so you'll ha' killed him, manin' no more than to kape yourself warm. 'Tis a recruity's thrick that. Pass the clanin'-rod, sorr.'

I snuggled down abashed; and after an interval the voice of Mulvaney began.

'Did I iver tell you how Dinah Shadd came to be wife av mine?'

I dissembled a burning anxiety that I had felt for some months—ever since Dinah Shadd, the strong, the patient, and the infinitely tender, had of her own good love and free will washed a shirt for me, moving in a barren land where washing was not.

'I can't remember,' I said casually. 'Was it before or after you made love to Annie Bragin, and got no satisfaction?'

The story of Annie Bragin is written in another place. It is one of the many less respectable episodes in Mulvaney's chequered career.

'Before—before—long before, was that business av Annie Bragin an' the corp'ril's ghost. Niver woman was the worse for me whin I had married Dinah. There's a time for all things, an' I know how to kape all things in place—barrin' the dhrink, that kapes me in my place wid no hope av comin' to be aught else.'

'Begin at the beginning,' I insisted. 'Mrs. Mulvaney told me that you married her when you were quartered in Krab Bokhar barracks.'

'An' the same is a cess-pit,' said Mulvaney piously. 'She spoke thrue, did Dinah. 'Twas this way. Talkin' av that, have ye iver fallen in love, sorr?'

I preserved the silence of the damned. Mulvaney continued—

'Thin I will assume that ye have not. *I* did. In the days av my youth, as I have more than wanst tould you, I was a man that filled the eye an' delighted the sowl av women. Niver man was hated as I have bin. Niver man was loved as I—no, not within half a day's march av ut! For the first five years av my service, whin I was what I wud give my sowl to be now, I tuk whatever was within my reach an' digested ut—an' that's more than most men can say. Dhrink I tuk, an' ut did me no harm. By the Hollow av Hiven, I cud play wid four women at wanst, an' kape them from findin' out anythin' about the other three, an' smile like a full-blown marigold through ut all. Dick Coulhan, av the battery we'll have down on us to-night, could drive his team no better than I mine, an' I hild the worser cattle! An' so I lived, an' so I was happy till afther that business wid Annie Bragin—she that turned me off as cool as a meat-safe, an' taught me where I stud in the mind av an honest woman. 'Twas no sweet dose to swallow.

'Afther that I sickened awhile an' tuk thought to my reg'mental work ; conceiting mesilf I wud study an' be a sargint, an' a major-gineral twinty minutes afther that. But on top av my ambitiousness there was an empty place in my sowl, an' me own opinion av mesilf cud not fill ut. Sez I to mesilf, "Terence, you're a great man an' the best set-up in the reg'mint. Go on an' get promotion." Sez mesilf to me, " What for ? " Sez I to mesilf, " For the glory av ut ! " Sez mesilf to me, " Will that fill these two strong arrums av yours, Terence ? "—" Go to the devil," sez I to mesilf. " Go to the married lines," sez mesilf to me. " 'Tis the same thing," sez I to mesilf. " Av you're the same man, ut is," said mesilf to me ; an' wid that I considhered on ut a long while. Did you iver feel that way, sorr ? '

I snored gently, knowing that if Mulvaney were uninterrupted he would go on. The clamour from the bivouac fires beat up to the stars, as the rival singers of the companies were pitted against each other.

'So I felt that way an' a bad time ut was. Wanst, bein' a fool, I wint into the married lines more for the sake av spakin' to our ould coloursergint Shadd than for any thruck wid women-folk. I was a corp'ril then—rejuced aftherwards, but a corp'ril then. I've got a photograft av mesilf to prove ut. "You'll take a cup av tay wid us?" sez Shadd. " I will that," I sez, " tho' tay is not my divarsion."

'"'Twud be better for you if ut were," sez ould Mother Shadd, an' she had ought to know, for Shadd, in the ind av his service, dhrank bung-full each night.

'Wid that I tuk off my gloves—there was pipeclay in thim, so that they stud alone—an' pulled up my chair, lookin' round at the china ornaments an' bits av things in the Shadds' quarters. They were things that belonged to a man, an' no camp-kit, here to-day an' dishipated next. "You're comfortable in this place, sergint," sez I. "'Tis the wife that did ut, boy," sez he, pointin' the stem av his pipe to ould Mother Shadd, an' she smacked the top av his bald head apon the compliment. "That manes you want money," sez she.

'An' thin—an' thin whin the kettle was to be filled, Dinah came in—my Dinah—her sleeves rowled up to the elbow an' her hair in a winkin' glory over her forehead, the big blue eyes beneath twinklin' like stars on a frosty night, an' the tread av her two feet lighter than waste-paper from the colonel's basket in ord'ly-room whin ut's emptied. Bein' but a shlip av a girl she went pink at seein' me, an' I twisted me moustache an' looked at a picture forninst the wall. Niver show a woman that ye care the snap av a finger for her, an' begad she'll come bleatin' to your boot-heels!'

'I suppose that's why you followed Annie Bragin till everybody in the married quarters laughed at you,' said I, remembering that un-hallowed wooing and casting off the disguise of drowsiness.

'I'm layin' down the gin'ral theory av the attack,' said Mulvaney, driving his boot into the dying fire. 'If you read the *Soldier's Pocket Book*, which niver any soldier reads, you'll see that there are exceptions. Whin Dinah was out av the door (an' 'twas as tho' the sunlight had shut too) —"Mother av Hiven, sergint," sez I, "but is that your daughter?"—"I've believed that way these eighteen years," sez ould Shadd, his eyes twinklin'; "but Mrs. Shadd has her own opinion, like iv'ry woman."—"'Tis wid yours this time, for a mericle," sez Mother Shadd. "Thin why in the name av fortune did I niver see her before?" sez I. "Bekaze you've been thrapesin' round wid the married women these three years past. She was a bit av a child till last year, an' she shot up wid the spring," sez ould Mother Shadd. "I'll thrapese no more," sez I. "D'you mane that?" sez ould Mother Shadd, lookin' at me side-ways like a hen looks at a hawk whin the chickens are runnin' free. "Try me, an' tell," sez I. Wid that I pulled on my gloves, dhrank off the tay, an' went out av the house as stiff as at gin'ral p'rade, for well I knew that Dinah Shadd's eyes were in the small av my back out av the scullery window. Faith! that was the only time I mourned I was not a cav'l'ry man for the pride av the spurs to jingle.

'I wint out to think, an' I did a powerful lot av thinkin', but ut all came round to that shlip av a girl in the dotted blue dhress, wid the blue eyes an' the sparkil in them. Thin I kept off canteen, an' I kept to the married quarthers, or near by, on the chanst av meetin' Dinah. Did I meet her? Oh, my time past, did I not; wid a lump in my throat as big as my valise an' my heart goin'

like a farrier's forge on a Saturday morning?
'Twas "Good day to ye, Miss Dinah," an "Good
day t'you, corp'ril," for a week or two, and divil
a bit further could I get bekaze av the respect I
had to that girl that I cud ha' broken betune finger
an' thumb.'

Here I giggled as I recalled the gigantic figure
of Dinah Shadd when she handed me my shirt.

'Ye may laugh,' grunted Mulvaney. 'But I'm
speakin' the trut', an' 'tis you that are in fault.
Dinah was a girl that wud ha' taken the imperious-
ness out av the Duchess av Clonmel in those days.
Flower hand, foot av shod air, an' the eyes av the
livin' mornin' she had that is my wife to-day—ould
Dinah, and niver aught else than Dinah Shadd to me.

' 'Twas after three weeks standin' off an' on, an'
niver makin' headway excipt through the eyes, that
a little drummer-boy grinned in me face whin I had
admonished him wid the buckle av my belt for
riotin' all over the place. "An' I'm not the only
wan that doesn't kape to barricks," sez he. I tuk
him by the scruff av his neck,—my heart was hung
on a hair-thrigger those days, you will onderstand
—an' "Out wid ut," sez I, "or I'll lave no bone
av you unbreakable."—"Speak to Dempsey," sez
he howlin'. "Dempsey which?" sez I, " ye un-
washed limb av Satan."—"Av the Bob-tailed
Dhragoons," sez he. "He's seen her home from
her aunt's house in the civil lines four times this
fortnight."—"Child!" sez I, dhroppin' him, "your
tongue's stronger than your body. Go to your
quarters. I'm sorry I dhressed you down."

'At that I went four ways to wanst huntin'

Dempsey. I was mad to think that wid all my airs among women I shud ha' been chated by a basin-faced fool av a cav'lryman not fit to trust on a trunk. Presently I found him in our lines—the Bobtails was quartered next us—an' a tallowy, topheavy son av a she-mule he was wid his big brass spurs an' his plastrons on his epigastrons an' all. But he niver flinched a hair.

' "A word wid you, Dempsey," sez I. "You've walked wid Dinah Shadd four times this fortnight gone."

' "What's that to you?" sez he. "I'll walk forty times more, an' forty on top av that, ye shovel-futted clod-breakin' infantry lance-corp'ril."

' Before I cud gyard he had his gloved fist home on my cheek an' down I went full-sprawl. "Will that content you?" sez he, blowin' on his knuckles for all the world like a Scots Greys orf'cer. "Content!" sez I. "For your own sake, man, take off your spurs, peel your jackut, an' onglove. 'Tis the beginnin' av the overture; stand up!"

' He stud all he knew, but he niver peeled his jacket, an' his shoulders had no fair play. I was fightin' for Dinah Shadd an' that cut on my cheek. What hope had he forninst me? "Stand up," sez I, time an' again whin he was beginnin' to quarter the ground an' gyard high an' go large. "This isn't ridin'-school," I sez. "O man, stand up an' let me get in at ye." But whin I saw he wud be runnin' about, I grup his shtock in my left an' his waist-belt in my right an' swung him clear to my right front, head undher, he hammerin' my nose till the wind was knocked out av him on the bare ground. "Stand up," sez I, "or I'll kick your head into your chest!" and I wud ha' done ut too, so ragin' mad I was.

'"My collar bone's bruk," sez he. "Help me back to lines. I'll walk wid her no more." So I helped him back.'

'And was his collar-bone broken?' I asked, for I fancied that only Learoyd could neatly accomplish that terrible throw.

'He pitched on his left shoulder-point. Ut was. Next day the news was in both barricks, an' whin I met Dinah Shadd wid a cheek on me like all the reg'mintal tailor's samples there was no "Good mornin', corp'ril," or aught else. "An' what have I done, Miss Shadd," sez I, very bould, plantin' mesilf forninst her, "that ye should not pass the time of day?"

'"Ye've half-killed rough-rider Dempsey," sez she, her dear blue eyes fillin' up.

'"Maybe," sez I. "Was he a friend av yours that saw ye home four times in the fortnight?"

'"Yes," sez she, but her mouth was down at the corners. "An'—an' what's that to you?" she sez.

'"Ask Dempsey," sez I, purtendin' to go away.

'"Did you fight for me then, ye silly man?" she sez, tho' she knew ut all along.

'"Who else?" sez I, an' I tuk wan pace to the front.

'"I wasn't worth ut," sez she, fingerin' in her apron.

'"That's for me to say," sez I. "Shall I say ut?"

' " Yes," sez she in a saint's whisper, an' at that I explained mesilf; and she tould me what ivry man that is a man, an' many that is a woman, hears wanst in his life.

' " But what made ye cry at startin', Dinah, darlin' ? " sez I.

' " Your—your bloody cheek," sez she, duckin' her little head down on my sash (I was on duty for the day) an' whimperin' like a sorrowful angil.

' Now a man cud take that two ways. I tuk ut as pleased me best an' my first kiss wid ut. Mother av Innocence! but I kissed her on the tip av the nose an' undher the eye ; an' a girl that lets a kiss come tumbleways like that has never been kissed before. Take note av that, sorr. Thin we wint hand in hand to ould Mother Shadd like two little childher, an' she said 'twas no bad thing, an' ould Shadd nodded behind his pipe, an' Dinah ran away to her own room. That day I throd on rollin' clouds. All earth was too small to hould me. Begad, I cud ha' hiked the sun out av the sky for a live coal to my pipe, so magnificent I was. But I tuk recruities at squad-drill instid, an' began wid general battalion advance whin I shud ha' been balance-steppin' them. Eyah ! that day ! that day ! '

A very long pause. ' Well ? ' said I.

' 'Twas all wrong,' said Mulvaney, with an enormous sigh. ' An' I know that ev'ry bit av ut was my own foolishness. That night I tuk maybe the half av three pints—not enough to turn the hair of a man in his natural senses. But I was more than half drunk wid pure joy, an' that canteen beer was so much whisky to me. I can't tell how it came about, but *bekaze* I had no thought for anywan except Dinah, *bekaze* I hadn't slipped her little white arms from my neck five minuts, *bekaze* the breath of her kiss was not gone from my mouth, I must go through the married lines on my way to quarters, an' I must stay talkin' to a red-headed Mullingar heifer av a girl, Judy Sheehy, that was daughter to Mother Sheehy, the wife of Nick Sheehy, the canteen-sergint—the Black Curse av Shielygh be on the whole brood that are above groun' this day !

' " An' what are ye houldin' your head that high for, corp'ril ? " sez Judy. " Come in an' thry a cup av tay," she sez, standin' in the doorway. Bein' an ontrustable fool, an' thinkin' av anything but tay, I wint.

' " Mother's at canteen," sez Judy, smoothin' the hair av hers that was like red snakes, an' lookin' at me corner-ways out av her green cats' eyes. " Ye will not mind, corp'ril ? "

' " I can endure," sez I ; ould Mother Sheehy bein' no divarsion av mine, nor her daughter too. Judy fetched the tea things an' put thim on the table, leanin' over me very close to get thim square. I dhrew back, thinkin' av Dinah.

' " Is ut afraid you are av a girl alone ? " sez Judy.

' " No," sez I. " Why should I be ? "

' " That rests wid the girl," sez Judy, dhrawin' her chair next to mine.

' " Thin there let ut rest," sez I ; an' thinkin' I'd been a trifle onpolite, I sez, " The tay's not quite sweet enough for my taste. Put your little finger in the cup, Judy. 'Twill make ut necthar."

' " What's necthar ? " sez she.

' " Somethin' very sweet," sez I ; an' for the sinful life av me I cud not help lookin' at her out av the corner av my eye, as I was used to look at a woman.

' " Go on wid ye, corp'ril," sez she. " You're a flirrt."

' " On me sowl I'm not," sez I.

' " Then you're a cruel handsome man, an' that's worse," sez she, heaving big sighs an' lookin' crossways.

' " You know your own mind," sez I.

' " 'Twud be better for me if I did not," she sez.

' " There's a dale to be said on both sides av that," sez I, unthinkin'.

' " Say your own part av ut, then, Terence, darlin'," sez she ; " for begad I'm thinkin' I've said too much or too little for an honest girl," an' wid that she put her arms round my neck an' kissed me.

' " There's no more to be said afther that," sez I, kissin' her back again—Oh, the mane scutt that I was, my head ringin' wid Dinah Shadd ! How does ut come about, sorr, that when a man has put the comether on wan woman, he's sure bound to put it on another ? 'Tis the same thing at musketry. Wan day ivry shot goes wide or into the bank, an' the next, lay high lay low, sight or snap, ye can't get off the bull's-eye for ten shots runnin'.'

'That only happens to a man who has had a good deal of experience. He does it without thinking,' I replied.

'Thankin' you for the complimint, sorr, ut may be so. But I'm doubtful whether you mint ut for a complimint. Hear now; I sat there wid Judy on my knee tellin' me all manner av nonsinse an' only sayin' "yes" an' "no," when I'd much better ha' kept tongue betune teeth. An' that was not an hour afther I had left Dinah! What I was thinkin' av I cannot say. Presintly, quiet as a cat, ould Mother Sheehy came in velvet-dhrunk. She had her daughter's red hair, but 'twas bald in patches, an' I cud see in her wicked ould face, clear as lightnin', what Judy wud be twenty years to come. I was for jumpin' up, but Judy niver moved.

'"Terence has promust, mother," sez she, an' the could sweat bruk out all over me. Ould Mother Sheehy sat down of a heap an' began playin' wid the cups. "Thin you're a well-matched pair," she sez very thick. "For he's the biggest rogue that iver spoiled the Queen's shoe-leather," an'——

'"I'm off, Judy," sez I. "Ye should not talk nonsinse to your mother. Get her to bed, girl."

'"Nonsinse!" sez the ould woman, prickin' up her ears like a cat an' grippin' the table-edge. "'Twill be the most nonsinsical nonsinse for you, ye grinnin' badger, if nonsinse 'tis. Git clear, you. I'm goin' to bed."

'I ran out into the dhark, my head in a stew

an' my heart sick, but I had sinse enough to see
that I'd brought ut all on mysilf. "It's this to
pass the time av day to a panjandhrum av hell-
cats," sez I. "What I've said, an' what I've not
said do not matther. Judy an' her dam will
hould me for a promust man, an' Dinah will give
me the go, an' I desarve ut. I will go an' get
dhrunk," sez I, "an' forget about ut, for 'tis plain
I'm not a marrin' man."

'On my way to canteen I ran against Lascelles,
colour-sergeant that was av E Comp'ny, a hard,
hard man, wid a torment av a wife. "You've the
head av a drowned man on your shoulders," sez
he; "an' you're goin' where you'll get a worse
wan. Come back," sez he. "Let me go," sez I.
"I've thrown my luck over the wall wid my own
hand!"—"Then that's not the way to get ut back
again," sez he. "Have out wid your throuble,
ye fool-bhoy." An' I tould him how the matther
was.

'He sucked in his lower lip. "You've been
thrapped," sez he. "Ju Sheehy wud be the
betther for a man's name to hers as soon as can.
An' ye thought ye'd put the comether on her,—
that's the natural vanity of the baste. Terence,
you're a big born fool, but you're not bad enough
to marry into that comp'ny. If you said anythin',
an' for all your protestations I'm sure ye did—or
did not, which is worse,—eat ut all—lie like the
father of all lies, but come out av ut free av Judy.
Do I not know what ut is to marry a woman that
was the very spit an' image av Judy whin she was
young? I'm gettin' old an' I've larnt patience,

but you, Terence, you'd raise hand on Judy an'
kill her in a year. Never mind if Dinah gives you
the go, you've desarved ut ; never mind if the
whole reg'mint laughs you all day. Get shut av
Judy an' her mother. They can't dhrag you to
church, but if they do, they'll dhrag you to hell.
Go back to your quarters and lie down," sez he.
Thin over his shoulder, " You *must* ha' done with
thim."

'Next day I wint to see Dinah, but there was
no tucker in me as I walked. I knew the throuble
wud come soon enough widout any handlin' av
mine, an' I dreaded ut sore.

'I heard Judy callin' me, but I hild straight
on to the Shadds' quarthers, an' Dinah wud ha'
kissed me but I put her back.

'"Whin all's said, darlin'," sez I, "you can
give ut me if ye will, tho' I misdoubt 'twill be so
easy to come by then."

'I had scarce begun to put the explanation into
shape before Judy an' her mother came to the door.
I think there was a verandah, but I'm forgettin'.'

'"Will ye not step in ?" sez Dinah, pretty and
polite, though the Shadds had no dealin's with the
Sheehys. Old Mother Shadd looked up quick, an'
she was the fust to see the throuble ; for Dinah
was her daughter.

'"I'm pressed for time to-day," sez Judy as
bould as brass ; "an' I've only come for Terence,—
my promust man. 'Tis strange to find him here
the day afther the day."

'Dinah looked at me as though I had hit her,
an' I answered straight.

' " There was some nonsinse last night at the Sheehys' quarthers, an' Judy's carryin' on the joke, darlin'," sez I.

' " At the Sheehys' quarthers ? " sez Dinah very slow, an' Judy cut in wid : " He was there from nine till ten, Dinah Shadd, an' the betther half av that time I was sittin' on his knee, Dinah Shadd. Ye may look and ye may look an' ye may look me up an' down, but ye won't look away that Terence is my promust man. Terence, darlin', 'tis time for us to be comin' home."

' Dinah Shadd niver said word to Judy. " Ye left me at half-past eight," she sez to me, " an' I niver thought that ye'd leave me for Judy,— promises or no promises. Go back wid her, you that have to be fetched by a girl ! I'm done with you," sez she, and she ran into her own room, her mother followin'. So I was alone wid those two women and at liberty to spake my sentiments."

' " Judy Sheehy," sez I, " if you made a fool av me betune the lights you shall not do ut in the day. I niver promised you words or lines."

' " You lie," sez ould Mother Sheehy, " an' may ut choke you where you stand ! " She was far gone in dhrink.

' " An' tho' ut choked me where I stud I'd not change," sez I. " Go home, Judy. I take shame for a decent girl like you dhraggin' your mother out bare - headed on this errand. Hear now, and have ut for an answer. I gave my word to Dinah Shadd yesterday, an', more blame to me, I was wid you last night talkin' nonsinse but nothin' more. You've chosen to thry to hould me on ut. I will not be held thereby for anythin' in the world. Is that enough?"

'Judy wint pink all over. "An' I wish you joy av the perjury," sez she, duckin' a curtsey. "You've lost a woman that would ha' wore her hand to the bone for your pleasure; an' 'deed, Terence, ye were not thrapped. . . ." Lascelles must ha' spoken plain to her. "I am such as Dinah is—'deed I am! Ye've lost a fool av a girl that'll niver look at you again, an' ye've lost what ye niver had,—your common honesty. If you manage your men as you manage your love-makin', small wondher they call you the worst corp'ril in the comp'ny. Come away, mother," sez she.

'But divil a fut would the ould woman budge! "D'you hould by that?" sez she, peerin' up under her thick gray eyebrows.

'"Ay, an' wud," sez I, "tho' Dinah gave me the go twinty times. I'll have no thruck with you or yours," sez I. "Take your child away, ye shameless woman."

'"An' am I shameless?" sez she, bringin' her hands up above her head. "Thin what are you, ye lyin', schamin', weak-kneed, dhirty-souled son av a sutler? Am I shameless? Who put the open shame on me an' my child that we shud go beggin' through the lines in the broad daylight for the broken word of a man? Double portion of my shame be on you, Terence Mulvaney, that think yourself so strong! By Mary and the saints, by blood and water an' by ivry sorrow that came into the world since the beginnin', the black blight fall on you and yours, so that you may niver be free from pain for another when ut's not your own! May your heart bleed in your breast drop by drop wid all your friends laughin' at the bleedin'! Strong you think yourself? May your strength be a curse to you to dhrive you into the divil's hands against your own will! Clear-eyed you are? May your eyes see clear evry step av the dark path you take till the hot cindhers av hell put thim out! May the ragin' dry thirst in my own ould bones go to you that you shall niver pass bottle full nor glass empty. God preserve the light av your onderstandin' to you, my jewel av a bhoy, that ye may niver forget what you mint to be an' do, whin you're wallowin' in the muck! May ye see the betther and follow the worse as long as there's breath in your body; an' may ye die quick in a strange land, watchin' your death before ut takes you, an' onable to stir hand or foot!"

'I heard a scufflin' in the room behind, and thin Dinah Shadd's hand dhropped into mine like a rose-leaf into a muddy road.

'"The half av that I'll take," sez she, "an' more too if I can. Go home, ye silly talkin' woman,—go home an' confess."

'"Come away! Come away!" sez Judy, pullin' her mother by the shawl. "'Twas none av Terence's fault. For the love av Mary stop the talkin'!"

'"An' you!" said ould Mother Sheehy, spinnin' round forninst Dinah. "Will ye take the half av that man's load? Stand off from him,

Dinah Shadd, before he takes you down too—you that look to be a quarther-master-sergeant's wife in five years. You look too high, child. You shall *wash* for the quarther-master-sergeant, whin he plases to give you the job out av charity; but a privit's wife you shall be to the end, an' evry sorrow of a privit's wife you shall know and niver a joy but wan, that shall go from you like the running tide from a rock. The pain av bearin' you shall know but niver the pleasure av giving the breast; an' you shall put away a man-child into the common ground wid niver a priest to say a prayer over him, an' on that man-child ye shall think ivry day av your life. Think long, Dinah Shadd, for you'll niver have another tho' you pray till your knees are bleedin'. The mothers av childer shall mock you behind your back when you're wringing over the wash-tub. You shall know what ut is to help a dhrunken husband home an' see him go to the gyard-room. Will that plase you, Dinah Shadd, that won't be seen talkin' to my daughter? You shall talk to worse than Judy before all's over. The sergints' wives shall look down on you contemptuous, daughter av a sergint, an' you shall cover ut all up wid a smiling face whin your heart's burstin'. Stand off av him, Dinah Shadd, for I've put the Black Curse of Shielygh upon him an' his own mouth shall make ut good."

'She pitched forward on her head an' began foamin' at the mouth. Dinah Shadd ran out wid water, an' Judy dhragged the ould woman into the verandah till she sat up.

' " I'm old an' forlore," she sez, thremblin' an' cryin', " and 'tis like I say a dale more than I mane."

' " When you're able to walk,—go," says ould Mother Shadd. " This house has no place for the likes av you that have cursed my daughter."

' " Eyah! " said the ould woman. " Hard words break no bones, an' Dinah Shadd 'll kape the love av her husband till my bones are green corn. Judy darlin', I misremember what I came here for. Can you lend us the bottom av a taycup av tay, Mrs. Shadd ? "

' But Judy dhragged her off cryin' as tho' her heart wud break. An' Dinah Shadd an' I, in ten minutes we had forgot ut all.'

' Then why do you remember it now ? ' said I.

' Is ut like I'd forget ? Ivry word that wicked ould woman spoke fell thrue in my life aftherwards, an' I cud ha' stud ut all—stud ut all,—excipt when my little Shadd was born. That was on the line av march three months afther the regiment was taken with cholera. We were betune Umballa an' Kalka thin, an' I was on picket. Whin I came off duty the women showed me the child, an' ut turned on uts side an' died as I looked. We buried him by the road, an' Father Victor was a day's march behind wid the heavy baggage, so the comp'ny captain read a prayer. An' since then I've been a childless man, an' all else that ould Mother Sheehy put upon me an' Dinah Shadd. What do you think, sorr ? '

I thought a good deal, but it seemed better

then to reach out for Mulvaney's hand. The demonstration nearly cost me the use of three fingers. Whatever he knows of his weaknesses, Mulvaney is entirely ignorant of his strength.

'But what do you think?' he repeated, as I was straightening out the crushed fingers.

My reply was drowned in yells and outcries from the next fire, where ten men were shouting for 'Orth'ris,' 'Privit Orth'ris,' 'Mistah Or—ther —ris!' 'Deah boy,' 'Cap'n Orth'ris,' 'Field-Marshal Orth'ris,' 'Stanley, you pen'north o' pop, come 'ere to your own comp'ny!' And the cockney, who had been delighting another audience with recondite and Rabelaisian yarns, was shot down among his admirers by the major force.

'You've crumpled my dress-shirt 'orrid,' said he, 'an' I shan't sing no more to this 'ere bloomin' drawin'-room.'

Learoyd, roused by the confusion, uncoiled himself, crept behind Ortheris, and slung him aloft on his shoulders.

'Sing, ye bloomin' hummin' bird!' said he, and Ortheris, beating time on Learoyd's skull, delivered himself, in the raucous voice of the Ratcliffe Highway, of this song :—

> My girl she give me the go onst,
>   When I was a London lad,
> An' I went on the drink for a fortnight,
>   An' then I went to the bad.
> The Queen she give me a shillin'
>   To fight for 'er over the seas ;
> But Guv'ment built me a fever-trap,
>   An' Injia give me disease.

Chorus.

> Ho ! don't you 'eed what a girl says,
>   An' don't you go for the beer ;
> But I was an ass when I was at grass,
>   An' that is why I'm here.

I fired a shot at a Afghan,
    The beggar e' fired again,
An' I lay on my bed with a 'ole in my 'ead,
    An' missed the next campaign !
I up with my gun at a Burman
    Who carried a bloomin' *dah*,
But the cartridge stuck and the bay'nit bruk,
    An' all I got was the scar.

Chorus.

> Ho ! don't you aim at a Afghan,
>   When you stand on the sky-line clear ;
> An' don't you go for a Burman
>   If none o' your friends is near.

I served my time for a corp'ral,
    An' wetted my stripes with pop,
For I went on the bend with a intimate friend,
    An' finished the night in the 'shop.'
I served my time for a sergeant ;
    The colonel 'e sez ' No !
The most you'll see is a full C.B.'[1]
    An' . . . very next night 'twas so.

Chorus.

> Ho ! don't you go for a corp'ral
>   Unless your 'ead is clear ;
> But I was an ass when I was at grass,
>   An' that is why I'm 'ere.

I've tasted the luck o' the army
    In barrack an' camp an' clink,
An' I lost my tip through the bloomin' trip
    Along o' the women an' drink.

---

[1] Confined to barracks.

I'm down at the heel o' my service,
    An' when I am laid on the shelf,
My very wust friend from beginning to end
    By the blood of a mouse was myself!

Chorus.

Ho ! don't you 'eed what a girl says,
    An' don't you go for the beer ;
But I was an ass when I was at grass
    An' that is why I'm 'ere.

'Ay, listen to our little man now, singin' an' shoutin' as tho' trouble had niver touched him. D' you remember when he went mad with the home-sickness ?' said Mulvaney, recalling a never-to-be-forgotten season when Ortheris waded through the deep waters of affliction and behaved abominably. 'But he's talkin' bitter truth, though.   Eyah !

'My very worst frind from beginnin' to ind
    By the blood av a mouse was mesilf !'

.   .   .   .   .

When I woke I saw Mulvaney, the night-dew gemming his moustache, leaning on his rifle at picket, lonely as Prometheus on his rock, with I know not what vultures tearing his liver.

On Greenhow Hill

To Love's low voice she lent a careless ear ;
Her hand within his rosy fingers lay,
A chilling weight.   She would not turn or hear ;
But with averted face went on her way.
But when pale Death, all featureless and grim,
Lifted his bony hand, and beckoning
Held out his cypress-wreath, she followed him,
And Love was left forlorn and wondering,
That she who for his bidding would not stay,
At Death's first whisper rose and went away.

Rivals.

'*Ohé, Ahmed Din! Shafiz Ullah ahoo!* Bahadur
Khan, where are you ? Come out of the tents, as
I have done, and fight against the English.   Don't
kill your own kin ! Come out to me !'

The deserter from a native corps was crawling
round the outskirts of the camp, firing at intervals,
and shouting invitations to his old comrades.   Mis-
led by the rain and the darkness, he came to the
English wing of the camp, and with his yelping
and rifle-practice disturbed the men.   They had
been making roads all day, and were tired.

Ortheris was sleeping at Learoyd's feet.   'Wot's
all that ?' he said thickly.   Learoyd snored, and a
Snider bullet ripped its way through the tent wall.

The men swore. 'It's that bloomin' deserter from the Aurangabadis,' said Ortheris. 'Git up, some one, an' tell 'im 'e's come to the wrong shop.'

'Go to sleep, little man,' said Mulvaney, who was steaming nearest the door. 'I can't arise an' expaytiate with him. 'Tis rainin' entrenchin' tools outside.'

' 'Tain't because you bloomin' can't. It's 'cause you bloomin' won't, ye long, limp, lousy, lazy beggar, you. 'Ark to 'im 'owlin'!'

'Wot's the good of argifying? Put a bullet into the swine! 'E's keepin' us awake!' said another voice.

A subaltern shouted angrily, and a dripping sentry whined from the darkness—

' 'Tain't no good, sir. I can't see 'im. 'E's 'idin' somewhere down 'ill.'

Ortheris tumbled out of his blanket. 'Shall I try to get 'im, sir?' said he.

'No,' was the answer. 'Lie down. I won't have the whole camp shooting all round the clock. Tell him to go and pot his friends.'

Ortheris considered for a moment. Then, putting his head under the tent wall, he called, as a 'bus conductor calls in a block, ' 'Igher up, there! 'Igher up!'

The men laughed, and the laughter was carried down wind to the deserter, who, hearing that he had made a mistake, went off to worry his own regiment half a mile away. He was received with shots; the Aurangabadis were very angry with him for disgracing their colours.

'An' that's all right,' said Ortheris, withdrawing

his head as he heard the hiccough of the Sniders in the distance. 'S'elp me Gawd, tho', that man's not fit to live — messin' with my beauty-sleep this way.'

'Go out and shoot him in the morning, then,' said the subaltern incautiously. 'Silence in the tents now. Get your rest, men.'

Ortheris lay down with a happy little sigh, and in two minutes there was no sound except the rain on the canvas and the all-embracing and elemental snoring of Learoyd.

The camp lay on a bare ridge of the Himalayas, and for a week had been waiting for a flying column to make connection. The nightly rounds of the deserter and his friends had become a nuisance.

In the morning the men dried themselves in hot sunshine and cleaned their grimy accoutrements. The native regiment was to take its turn of road-making that day while the Old Regiment loafed.

'I'm goin' to lay for a shot at that man,' said Ortheris, when he had finished washing out his rifle. ' 'E comes up the watercourse every evenin' about five o'clock. If we go and lie out on the north 'ill a bit this afternoon we'll get 'im.'

'You're a bloodthirsty little mosquito,' said Mulvaney, blowing blue clouds into the air. 'But I suppose I will have to come wid you. Fwhere's Jock ?'

'Gone out with the Mixed Pickles, 'cause 'e thinks 'isself a bloomin' marksman,' said Ortheris with scorn.

The 'Mixed Pickles' were a detachment of

picked shots, generally employed in clearing spurs
of hills when the enemy were too impertinent.
This taught the young officers how to handle men,
and did not do the enemy much harm. Mulvaney
and Ortheris strolled out of camp, and passed the
Aurangabadis going to their road-making.

'You've got to sweat to-day,' said Ortheris
genially. 'We're going to get your man. You
didn't knock 'im out last night by any chance,
any of you?'

'No. The pig went away mocking us. I had
one shot at him,' said a private. 'He's my cousin,
and _I_ ought to have cleared our dishonour. But
good luck to you.'

They went cautiously to the north hill, Ortheris
leading, because, as he explained, 'this is a long-
range show, an' I've got to do it.' His was an almost
passionate devotion to his rifle, which, by barrack-
room report, he was supposed to kiss every night
before turning in. Charges and scuffles he held in
contempt, and, when they were inevitable, slipped
between Mulvaney and Learoyd, bidding them to
fight for his skin as well as their own. They
never failed him. He trotted along, questing like
a hound on a broken trail, through the wood of
the north hill. At last he was satisfied, and threw
himself down on the soft pine-needled slope that
commanded a clear view of the watercourse and a
brown, bare hillside beyond it. The trees made a
scented darkness in which an army corps could
have hidden from the sun-glare without.

''Ere's the tail o' the wood,' said Ortheris.
''E's got to come up the watercourse, 'cause it

gives 'im cover. We'll lay 'ere. 'Tain't not arf so bloomin' dusty neither.'

He buried his nose in a clump of scentless white violets. No one had come to tell the flowers that the season of their strength was long past, and they had bloomed merrily in the twilight of the pines.

'This is something like,' he said luxuriously. 'Wot a 'evinly clear drop for a bullet acrost. How much d'you make it, Mulvaney?'

'Seven hunder. Maybe a trifle less, bekaze the air's so thin.'

Wop! wop! wop! went a volley of musketry on the rear face of the north hill.

'Curse them Mixed Pickles firin' at nothin'! They'll scare arf the country.'

'Thry a sightin' shot in the middle of the row,' said Mulvaney, the man of many wiles. 'There's a red rock yonder he'll be sure to pass. Quick!'

Ortheris ran his sight up to six hundred yards and fired. The bullet threw up a feather of dust by a clump of gentians at the base of the rock.

'Good enough!' said Ortheris, snapping the scale down. 'You snick your sights to mine or a little lower. You're always firin' high. But remember, first shot to me. O Lordy! but it's a lovely afternoon.'

The noise of the firing grew louder, and there was a tramping of men in the wood. The two lay very quiet, for they knew that the British soldier is desperately prone to fire at anything that moves or calls. Then Learoyd appeared, his tunic ripped across the breast by a bullet, looking ashamed of himself. He flung down on the pine-needles, breathing in snorts.

'One o' them damned gardeners o' th' Pickles,' said he, fingering the rent. 'Firin' to th' right flank, when he knowed I was there. If I knew who he was I'd 'a' rippen the hide offan him. Look at ma tunic!'

'That's the spishil trustability av a marksman. Train him to hit a fly wid a stiddy rest at seven hunder, an' he'll loose on anythin' he sees or hears up to th' mile. You're well out av that fancy-firin' gang, Jock. Stay here.'

'Bin firin' at the bloomin' wind in the bloomin' treetops,' said Ortheris with a chuckle. 'I'll show you some firin' later on.'

They wallowed in the pine-needles, and the sun warmed them where they lay. The Mixed Pickles ceased firing, and returned to camp, and left the wood to a few scared apes. The watercourse lifted up its voice in the silence, and talked foolishly to the rocks. Now and again the dull thump of a blasting charge three miles away told that the Aurangabadis were in difficulties with their road-making. The men smiled as they listened and lay still, soaking in the warm leisure. Presently Learoyd, between the whiffs of his pipe—

'Seems queer—about 'im yonder—desertin' at all.'

''E'll be a bloomin' side queerer when I've done with 'im,' said Ortheris. They were talking in whispers, for the stillness of the wood and the desire of slaughter lay heavy upon them.

'I make no doubt he had his reasons for

desertin'; but, my faith! I make less doubt ivry man has good reason for killin' him,' said Mulvaney.

'Happen there was a lass tewed up wi' it. Men do more than more for th' sake of a lass.'

'They make most av us 'list. They've no manner av right to make us desert.'

'Ah; they make us 'list, or their fathers do,' said Learoyd softly, his helmet over his eyes.

Ortheris's brows contracted savagely. He was watching the valley. 'If it's a girl I'll shoot the beggar twice over, an' second time for bein' a fool. You're blasted sentimental all of a sudden. Thinkin' o' your last near shave?'

'Nay, lad; ah was but thinkin' o' what has happened.'

'An' fwhat has happened, ye lumberin' child av calamity, that you're lowing like a cow-calf at the back av the pasture, an' suggestin' invidious excuses for the man Stanley's goin' to kill. Ye'll have to wait another hour yet, little man. Spit it out, Jock, an' bellow melojus to the moon. It takes an earthquake or a bullet graze to fetch aught out av you. Discourse, Don Juan! The a-moors av Lotharius Learoyd! Stanley, kape a rowlin' rig'mental eye on the valley.'

'It's along o' yon hill there,' said Learoyd, watching the bare sub-Himalayan spur that reminded him of his Yorkshire moors. He was speaking more to himself than his fellows. 'Ay,' said he, 'Rumbolds Moor stands up ower Skipton town, an' Greenhow Hill stands up ower Pately Brig. I reckon you've never heeard tell o' Greenhow Hill, but yon bit o' bare stuff if there was

nobbut a white road windin' is like ut; strangely
like. Moors an' moors an' moors, wi' never a
tree for shelter, an' gray houses wi' flagstone
rooves, and pewits cryin', an' a windhover goin' to
and fro just like these kites. And cold! A wind
that cuts you like a knife. You could tell Greenhow Hill folk by the red-apple colour o' their
cheeks an' nose tips, and their blue eyes, driven
into pin-points by the wind. Miners mostly,
burrowin' for lead i' th' hillsides, followin' the
trail of th' ore vein same as a field-rat. It was the
roughest minin' I ever seen. Yo'd come on a bit
o' creakin' wood windlass like a well-head, an' you
was let down i' th' bight of a rope, fendin' yoursen
off the side wi' one hand, carryin' a candle stuck in
a lump o' clay with t'other, an' clickin' hold of a
rope with t'other hand.'

'An' that's three of them,' said Mulvaney.
'Must be a good climate in those parts.'

Learoyd took no heed.

'An' then yo' came to a level, where you crept
on your hands and knees through a mile o' windin'
drift, an' you come out into a cave-place as big as
Leeds Townhall, with a engine pumpin' water from
workin's 'at went deeper still. It's a queer country,
let alone minin', for the hill is full of those natural
caves, an' the rivers an' the becks drops into what
they call pot-holes, an' come out again miles away.'

'Wot was you doin' there?' said Ortheris.

'I was a young chap then, an' mostly went wi'
'osses, leadin' coal and lead ore; but at th' time
I'm tellin' on I was drivin' the waggon-team i' th'
big sumph. I didn't belong to that country-side

by rights. I went there because of a little difference
at home, an' at fust I took up wi' a rough lot.
One night we'd been drinkin', an' I must ha' hed
more than I could stand, or happen th' ale was
none so good. Though i' them days, By for God,
I never seed bad ale.' He flung his arms over
his head, and gripped a vast handful of white
violets. 'Nah,' said he, 'I never seed the ale I
could not drink, the bacca I could not smoke, nor
the lass I could not kiss. Well, we mun have a
race home, the lot on us. I lost all th' others, an'
when I was climbin' ower one of them walls built
o' loose stones, I comes down into the ditch, stones
and all, an' broke my arm. Not as I knawed much
about it, for I fell on th' back of my head, an' was
knocked stupid like. An' when I come to mysen
it were mornin', an' I were lyin' on the settle i'
Jesse Roantree's house-place, an' 'Liza Roantree
was settin' sewin'. I ached all ovver, and my
mouth were like a lime-kiln. She gave me a
drink out of a china mug wi' gold letters—" A
Present from Leeds "—as I looked at many and
many a time at after. " Yo're to lie still while
Dr. Warbottom comes, because your arm's broken,
and father has sent a lad to fetch him. He found
yo' when he was goin' to work, an' carried you
here on his back," sez she. "Oa!" sez I; an'
I shet my eyes, for I felt ashamed o' mysen.
"Father's gone to his work these three hours, an'
he said he'd tell 'em to get somebody to drive the
tram." The clock ticked, an' a bee comed in the
house, an' they rung i' my head like mill-wheels.
An' she give me another drink an' settled the

pillow. "Eh, but yo're young to be getten drunk an' such like, but yo' won't do it again, will yo'?"—"Noa," sez I, "I wouldn't if she'd nobbut stop they mill-wheels clatterin'." '

'Faith, it's a good thing to be nursed by a woman when you're sick!' said Mulvaney. 'Dir' cheap at the price av twenty broken heads.'

Ortheris turned to frown across the valley. He had not been nursed by many women in his life.

'An' then Dr. Warbottom comes ridin' up, an' Jesse Roantree along with 'im. He was a high-larned doctor, but he talked wi' poor folk same as theirsens. "What's ta bin agaate on naa?" he sings out. "Brekkin' tha thick head?" An' he felt me all ovver. "That's none broken. Tha's nobbut knocked a bit sillier than ordinary, an' that's daaft eneaf." An' soa he went on, callin' me all the names he could think on, but settin' my arm, wi' Jesse's help, as careful as could be. "Yo' mun let the big oaf bide here a bit, Jesse," he says, when he hed strapped me up an' given me a dose o' physic; "an' you an' 'Liza will tend him, though he's scarcelins worth the trouble. An' tha'll lose tha work," sez he, "an' tha'll be upon th' Sick Club for a couple o' months an' more. Doesn't tha think tha's a fool?" '

'But whin was a young man, high or low, the other av a fool, I'd like to know?' said Mulvaney. 'Sure, folly's the only safe way to wisdom, for I've thried it.'

'Wisdom!' grinned Ortheris, scanning his comrades with uplifted chin. 'You're bloomin' Solomons, you two, ain't you?'

Learoyd went calmly on, with a steady eye like an ox chewing the cud.

'And that was how I comed to know 'Liza Roantree. There's some tunes as she used to sing —aw, she were always singin'—that fetches Greenhow Hill before my eyes as fair as yon brow across there. And she would learn me to sing bass, an' I was to go to th' chapel wi' 'em, where Jesse and she led the singin', th' old man playin' the fiddle. He was a strange chap, old Jesse, fair mad wi' music, an' he made me promise to learn the big fiddle when my arm was better. It belonged to him, and it stood up in a big case alongside o' th' eight-day clock, but Willie Satterthwaite, as played it in the chapel, had getten deaf as a door-post, and it vexed Jesse, as he had to rap him ower his head wi' th' fiddle-stick to make him give ower sawin' at th' right time.

'But there was a black drop in it all, an' it was a man in a black coat that brought it. When th' Primitive Methodist preacher came to Greenhow, he would always stop wi' Jesse Roantree, an' he laid hold of me from th' beginning. It seemed I wor a soul to be saved, and he meaned to do it. At th' same time I jealoused 'at he were keen o' savin' 'Liza Roantree's soul as well, and I could ha' killed him many a time. An' this went on till one day I broke out, an' borrowed th' brass for a drink from 'Liza. After fower days I come back, wi' my tail between my legs, just to see 'Liza again. But Jesse were at home an' th' preacher—th' Reverend Amos Barraclough. 'Liza said naught, but a bit o' red come into her face as were white of a regular thing. Says Jesse, tryin' his best to be civil, "Nay, lad, it's like this. You've getten to choose which way it's goin' to be. I'll ha' nobody across ma doorstep as goes a-drinkin', an' borrows my lass's money to spend i' their drink. Ho'd tha tongue, 'Liza," sez he, when she wanted to put in a word 'at I were welcome to th' brass, and she were none afraid that I wouldn't pay it back. Then the Reverend cuts in, seein' as Jesse were losin' his temper, an' they fair beat me among them. But it were 'Liza, as looked an' said naught, as did more than either o' their tongues, an' soa I concluded to get converted.'

'Fwhat!' shouted Mulvaney. Then, checking himself, he said softly, 'Let be! Let be! Sure the Blessed Virgin is the mother of all religion an' most women ; an' there's a dale av piety in a girl if the men would only let ut stay there. I'd ha' been converted myself under the circumstances.'

'Nay, but,' pursued Learoyd with a blush, 'I meaned it.'

Ortheris laughed as loudly as he dared, having regard to his business at the time.

'Ay, Ortheris, you may laugh, but you didn't know yon preacher Barraclough—a little white-faced chap, wi' a voice as 'ud wile a bird offan a bush, and a way o' layin' hold of folks as made them think they'd never had a live man for a friend before. You never saw him, an'—an'— you never seed 'Liza Roantree—never seed 'Liza Roantree. . . . Happen it was as much 'Liza as th' preacher and her father, but anyways they all meaned it, an' I was fair shamed o' mysen, an' so I become what they called a changed cháracter. And when I think on, it's hard to believe as yon chap going to prayer-meetin's, chapel, and class-meetin's were me. But I never had naught to say for mysen, though there was a deal o' shoutin', and old Sammy Strother, as were almost clemmed to death and doubled up with the rheumatics, would sing out, " Joyful! Joyful!" and 'at it were better to go up to heaven in a coal-basket than down to hell i' a coach an' six. And he would put his poor old claw on my shoulder, sayin', "Doesn't tha feel it, tha great lump? Doesn't tha feel it?" An' sometimes I thought I did, and then again I thought I didn't, an' how was that?'

'The iverlastin' nature av mankind,' said Mulvaney. 'An', furthermore, I misdoubt you were built for the Primitive Methodians. They're a new corps anyways. I hold by the Ould Church, for she's the mother of them all—ay, an' the father, too. I like her bekaze she's most remarkable regimental in her fittings. I may die in Honolulu, Nova Zambra, or Cape Cayenne, but wherever I die, me bein' fwhat I am, an' a priest handy, I go under the same orders an' the same words an' the same unction as tho' the Pope himself come down from the roof av St. Peter's to see me off. There's neither high nor low, nor broad nor deep, nor betwixt nor between wid her, an' that's what I like. But mark you, she's no manner av Church for a wake man, bekaze she takes the body and the soul av him, onless he has his proper work to do. I remember when my father died that was three months comin' to his grave ; begad he'd ha' sold the shebeen above our heads for ten minutes' quittance of purgathory. An' he did all he could. That's why I say ut takes a strong man to deal with the Ould Church, an' for that reason you'll find so many women go there. An' that sames a conundrum.'

'Wot's the use o' worrittin' 'bout these things ?' said Ortheris. 'You're bound to find all out quicker nor you want to, any'ow.' He jerked the cartridge out of the breech-block into the palm of his hand. ' 'Ere's my chaplain,' he said, and made the venomous black-headed bullet bow like a marionette. ' 'E's goin' to teach a man all about which is which, an' wot's true, after all, before sundown. But wot 'appened after that, Jock ? '

' There was one thing they boggled at, and almost shut th' gate i' my face for, and that were my dog Blast, th' only one saved out o' a litter o' pups as was blowed up when a keg o' minin' powder loosed off in th' store-keeper's hut. They liked his name no better than his business, which were fightin' every dog he comed across ; a rare good dog, wi' spots o' black and pink on his face, one ear gone, and lame o' one side wi' being driven in a basket through an iron roof, a matter of half a mile.

' They said I mun give him up 'cause he were worldly and low ; and would I let mysen be shut out of heaven for the sake on a dog ? "Nay," says I, "if th' door isn't wide enough for th' pair on us, we'll stop outside, for we'll none be parted."

And th' preacher spoke up for Blast, as had a likin' for him from th' first—I reckon that was why I come to like th' preacher—and wouldn't hear o' changin' his name to Bless, as some o' them wanted. So th' pair on us became reg'lar chapel-members. But it's hard for a young chap o' my build to cut traces from the world, th' flesh, an' the devil all uv a heap. Yet I stuck to it for a long time, while th' lads as used to stand about th' town-end an' lean ower th' bridge, spittin' into th' beck o' a Sunday, would call after me, "Sitha, Learoyd, when's ta bean to preach, 'cause we're comin' to hear tha."—"Ho'd tha jaw. He hasn't getten th' white choaker on ta morn," another lad would say, and I had to double my fists hard i' th' bottom of my Sunday coat, and say to mysen, "If 'twere Monday and I warn't a member o' the Primitive Methodists, I'd leather all th' lot of yond'." That was th' hardest of all—to know that I could fight and I mustn't fight.'

Sympathetic grunts from Mulvaney.

'So what wi' singin', practisin', and class-meetin's, and th' big fiddle, as he made me take between my knees, I spent a deal o' time i' Jesse Roantree's house-place. But often as I was there, th' preacher fared to me to go oftener, and both th' old man an' th' young woman were pleased to have him. He lived i' Pately Brig, as were a goodish step off, but he come. He come all the same. I liked him as well or better as any man I'd ever seen i' one way, and yet I hated him wi' all my heart i' t'other, and we watched each other like cat and mouse, but civil as you please, for I

was on my best behaviour, and he was that fair
and open that I was bound to be fair with him.
Rare good company he was, if I hadn't wanted to
wring his cliver little neck half of the time.   Often
and often when he was goin' from Jesse's I'd set
him a bit on the road.'

'See 'im 'ome, you mean ?' said Ortheris.

'Ay.   It's a way we have i' Yorkshire o' seein'
friends off.   Yon was a friend as I didn't want to
come back, and he didn't want me to come back
neither, and so we'd walk together towards Pately,
and then he'd set me back again, and there we'd
be wal two o'clock i' the mornin' settin' each other
to an' fro like a blasted pair o' pendulums twixt
hill and valley, long after th' light had gone out i'
'Liza's window, as both on us had been looking at,
pretending to watch the moon.'

'Ah !' broke in Mulvaney, 'ye'd no chanst
against the maraudin' psalm-singer.   They'll take
the airs an' the graces instid av the man nine times
out av ten, an' they only find the blunder later—
the wimmen.'

'That's just where yo're wrong,' said Learoyd,
reddening under the freckled tan of his cheeks.
'I was th' first wi 'Liza, an' yo'd think that were
enough.   But th' parson were a steady-gaited sort
o' chap, and Jesse were strong o' his side, and all
th' women i' the congregation dinned it to 'Liza
'at she were fair fond to take up wi' a wastrel
ne'er-do-weel like me, as was scarcelins respectable
an' a fighting dog at his heels.   It was all very
well for her to be doing me good and saving my
soul, but she must mind as she didn't do herself

harm.   They talk o' rich folk bein' stuck up an' genteel, but for cast-iron pride o' respectability there's naught like poor chapel folk.   It's as cold as th' wind o' Greenhow Hill—ay, and colder, for 'twill never change.   And now I come to think on it, one at strangest things I know is 'at they couldn't abide th' thought o' soldiering.   There's a vast o' fightin' i' th' Bible, and there's a deal of Methodists i' th' army ; but to hear chapel folk talk yo'd think that soldierin' were next door, an' t'other side, to hangin'.   I' their meetin's all their talk is o' fightin'.   When Sammy Strother were stuck for summat to say in his prayers, he'd sing out, "Th' sword o' th' Lord and o' Gideon." They were allus at it about puttin' on th' whole armour o' righteousness, an' fightin' the good fight o' faith.   And then, atop o' 't all, they held a prayer-meetin' ower a young chap as wanted to 'list, and nearly deafened him, till he picked up his hat and fair ran away.   And they'd tell tales in th' Sunday-school o' bad lads as had been thumped and brayed for bird-nesting o' Sundays and playin' truant o' week-days, and how they took to wrestlin', dog-fightin', rabbit-runnin', and drinkin', till at last, as if 'twere a hepitaph on a gravestone, they damned him across th' moors wi', "an' then he went and 'listed for a soldier," an' they'd all fetch a deep breath, and throw up their eyes like a hen drinkin'.'

'Fwhy is ut ?' said Mulvaney, bringing down his hand on his thigh with a crack.   'In the name av God, fwhy is ut ?   I've seen ut, tu.   They cheat an' they swindle an' they lie an' they slander,

an' fifty things fifty times worse ; but the last an'
the worst by their reckonin' is to serve the Widdy
honest. It's like the talk av childer—seein' things
all round.'

'Plucky lot of fightin' good fights of whatser-
name they'd do if we didn't see they had a quiet
place to fight in. And such fightin' as theirs is!
Cats on the tiles. T'other callin' to which to
come on. I'd give a month's pay to get some o'
them broad-backed beggars in London sweatin'
through a day's road-makin' an' a night's rain.
They'd carry on a deal afterwards—same as we're
supposed to carry on. I've bin turned out of a
measly arf-licence pub down Lambeth way, full o'
greasy kebmen, 'fore now,' said Ortheris with an
oath.

'Maybe you were dhrunk,' said Mulvaney
soothingly.

'Worse nor that. The Forders were drunk.
I was wearin' the Queen's uniform.'

'I'd no particular thought to be a soldier i'
them days,' said Learoyd, still keeping his eye on
the bare hill opposite, 'but this sort o' talk put it
i' my head. They was so good, th' chapel folk,
that they tumbled ower t'other side. But I stuck
to it for 'Liza's sake, specially as she was learning
me to sing the bass part in a horotorio as Jesse were
gettin' up. She sung like a throstle hersen, and
we had practisin's night after night for a matter
of three months.'

'I know what a horotorio is,' said Ortheris
pertly. 'It's a sort of chaplain's sing-song—words
all out of the Bible, and hullabaloojah choruses.'

'Most Greenhow Hill folks played some instrument or t'other, an' they all sung so you might have heard them miles away, and they were so pleased wi' the noise they made they didn't fare to want anybody to listen. The preacher sung high seconds when he wasn't playin' the flute, an' they set me, as hadn't got far with big fiddle, again Willie Satterthwaite, to jog his elbow when he had to get agate playin'. Old Jesse was happy if ever a man was, for he were th' conductor an' th' first fiddle an' th' leadin' singer, beatin' time wi' his fiddle-stick, till at times he'd rap with it on the table, and cry out, "Now, you mun all stop; it's my turn." And he'd face round to his front, fair sweating wi' pride, to sing th' tenor solos. But he were grandest i' th' choruses, waggin' his head, flinging his arms round like a windmill, and singin' hisself black in the face. A rare singer were Jesse.

'Yo' see, I was not o' much account wi' 'em all exceptin' to 'Liza Roantree, and I had a deal o' time settin' quiet at meetings and horotorio practices to hearken their talk, and if it were strange to me at beginnin', it got stranger still at after, when I was shut on it, and could study what it meaned.

'Just after th' horotorios came off, 'Liza, as had allus been weakly like, was took very bad. I walked Dr. Warbottom's horse up and down a deal of times while he were inside, where they wouldn't let me go, though I fair ached to see her.

'"She'll be better i' noo, lad—better i' noo," he used to say. "Tha mun ha' patience." Then

they said if I was quiet I might go in, and th'
Reverend Amos Barraclough used to read to her
lyin' propped up among th' pillows. Then she
began to mend a bit, and they let me carry her
on to th' settle, and when it got warm again she
went about same as afore. Th' preacher and me
and Blast was a deal together i' them days, and i'
one way we was rare good comrades. But I
could ha' stretched him time and again with a
good will. I mind one day he said he would like
to go down into th' bowels o' th' earth, and see
how th' Lord had builded th' framework o' th'
everlastin' hills. He were one of them chaps as
had a gift o' sayin' things. They rolled off the
tip of his clever tongue, same as Mulvaney here,
as would ha' made a rare good preacher if he had
nobbut given his mind to it. I lent him a suit o'
miner's kit as almost buried th' little man, and his
white face down i' th' coat-collar and hat-flap
looked like the face of a boggart, and he cowered
down i' th' bottom o' the waggon. I was drivin'
a tram as led up a bit of an incline up to th' cave
where the engine was pumpin', and where th' ore
was brought up and put into th' waggons as went
down o' themselves, me puttin' th' brake on and th'
horses a-trottin' after. Long as it was daylight
we were good friends, but when we got fair into
th' dark, and could nobbut see th' day shinin' at
the hole like a lamp at a street-end, I feeled down-
right wicked. Ma religion dropped all away from
me when I looked back at him as were always
comin' between me and 'Liza. The talk was 'at
they were to be wed when she got better, an' I

couldn't get her to say yes or nay to it. He began to sing a hymn in his thin voice, and I came out wi' a chorus that was all cussin' an' swearin' at my horses, an' I began to know how I hated him. He were such a little chap, too. I could drop him wi' one hand down Garstang's Copper-hole—a place where th' beck slithered ower th' edge on a rock, and fell wi' a bit of a whisper into a pit as no rope i' Greenhow could plump.'

Again Learoyd rooted up the innocent violets. 'Ay, he should see th' bowels o' th' earth an' never naught else. I could take him a mile or two along th' drift, and leave him wi' his candle doused to cry hallelujah, wi' none to hear him and say amen. I was to lead him down th' ladder-way to th' drift where Jesse Roantree was workin', and why shouldn't he slip on th' ladder, wi' my feet on his fingers till they loosed grip, and I put him down wi' my heel? If I went fust down th' ladder I could click hold on him and chuck him over my head, so as he should go squshin' down the shaft, breakin' his bones at ev'ry timberin' as Bill Appleton did when he was fresh, and hadn't a bone left when he wrought to th' bottom. Niver a blasted leg to walk from Pately. Niver an arm to put round 'Liza Roantree's waist. Niver no more—niver no more.'

The thick lips curled back over the yellow teeth, and that flushed face was not pretty to look upon. Mulvaney nodded sympathy, and Ortheris, moved by his comrade's passion, brought up the rifle to his shoulder, and searched the hillside for his quarry, muttering ribaldry about a sparrow, a spout, and a thunder-storm. The voice of the watercourse supplied the necessary small talk till Learoyd picked up his story.

'But it's none so easy to kill a man like yon. When I'd given up my horses to th' lad as took my place and I was showin' th' preacher th' workin's, shoutin' into his ear across th' clang o' th' pumpin' engines, I saw he were afraid o' naught ; and when the lamplight showed his black eyes, I could feel as he was masterin' me again. I were no better nor Blast chained up short and growlin' i' the depths of him while a strange dog went safe past.

'"Th'art a coward and a fool," I said to mysen ; an' I wrestled i' my mind again' him till, when we come to Garstang's Copper-hole, I laid hold o' the preacher and lifted him up over my head and held him into the darkest on it. "Now, lad," I says, "it's to be one or t'other on us—thee or me—for 'Liza Roantree. Why, isn't thee afraid for thysen ?" I says, for he were still i' my arms as a sack. "Nay ; I'm but afraid for thee, my poor lad, as knows naught," says he. I set him down on th' edge, an' th' beck run stiller, an' there was no more buzzin' in my head like when th' bee come through th' window o' Jesse's house. "What dost tha mean ?" says I.

'"I've often thought as thou ought to know," says he, "but 'twas hard to tell thee. 'Liza Roantree's for neither on us, nor for nobody o' this earth. Dr. Warbottom says—and he knows her, and her mother before her—that she is in a decline, and she cannot live six months longer.

He's known it for many a day. Steady, John!
Steady!" says he. And that weak little man
pulled me further back and set me again' him, and
talked it all over quiet and still, me turnin' a bunch
o' candles in my hand, and counting them ower
and ower again as I listened. A deal on it were
th' regular preachin' talk, but there were a vast lot
as made me begin to think as he were more of a
man than I'd ever given him credit for, till I were
cut as deep for him as I were for mysen.

'Six candles we had, and we crawled and
climbed all that day while they lasted, and I said
to mysen, "'Liza Roantree hasn't six months to
live." And when we came into th' daylight
again we were like dead men to look at, an' Blast
come behind us without so much as waggin' his
tail. When I saw 'Liza again she looked at me a
minute and says, "Who's telled tha? For I see
tha knows." And she tried to smile as she kissed
me, and I fair broke down.

'Yo'see, I was a young chap i' them days, and
had seen naught o' life, let alone death, as is allus
a-waitin'. She telled me as Dr. Warbottom said
as Greenhow air was too keen, and they were goin'
to Bradford, to Jesse's brother David, as worked
i' a mill, and I mun hold up like a man and a
Christian, and she'd pray for me. Well, and they
went away, and the preacher that same back end o'
th' year were appointed to another circuit, as they
call it, and I were left alone on Greenhow Hill.

'I tried, and I tried hard, to stick to th' chapel,
but 'tweren't th' same thing at after. I hadn't
'Liza's voice to follow i' th' singin', nor her eyes

a'shinin' acrost their heads. And i' th' class-meetings they said as I mun have some experiences to tell, and I hadn't a word to say for mysen.

'Blast and me moped a good deal, and happen we didn't behave ourselves over well, for they dropped us and wondered however they'd come to take us up. I can't tell how we got through th' time, while i' th' winter I gave up my job and went to Bradford. Old Jesse were at th' door o' th' house, in a long street o' little houses. He'd been sendin' th' children 'way as were clatterin' their clogs in th' causeway, for she were asleep.

'"Is it thee?" he says; "but you're not to see her. I'll none have her wakened for a nowt like thee. She's goin' fast, and she mun go in peace. Thou'lt never be good for naught i' th' world, and as long as thou lives thou'll never play the big fiddle. Get away, lad, get away!" So he shut the door softly i' my face.

'Nobody never made Jesse my master, but it seemed to me he was about right, and I went away into the town and knocked up against a recruiting sergeant. The old tales o' th' chapel folk came buzzin' into my head. I was to get away, and this were th' regular road for the likes o' me. I 'listed there and then, took th' Widow's shillin', and had a bunch o' ribbons pinned i' my hat.

'But next day I found my way to David Roantree's door, and Jesse came to open it. Says he, "Thou's come back again wi' th' devil's colours flyin'—thy true colours, as I always telled thee."

'But I begged and prayed of him to let me see her nobbut to say good-bye, till a woman calls down th' stair-way, "She says John Learoyd's to come up." Th' old man shifts aside in a flash, and lays his hand on my arm, quite gentle like. "But thou'lt be quiet, John," says he, "for she's rare and weak. Thou was allus a good lad."

'Her eyes were all alive wi' light, and her hair was thick on the pillow round her, but her cheeks were thin—thin to frighten a man that's strong. "Nay, father, yo' mayn't say th' devil's colours. Them ribbons is pretty." An' she held out her hands for th' hat, an' she put all straight as a woman will wi' ribbons. "Nay, but what they're pretty," she says. "Eh, but I'd ha' liked to see thee i' thy red coat, John, for thou was allus my own lad—my very own lad, and none else."

'She lifted up her arms, and they come round my neck i' a gentle grip, and they slacked away, and she seemed fainting. "Now yo' mun get away, lad," says Jesse, and I picked up my hat and I came downstairs.

'Th' recruiting sergeant were waitin' for me at th' corner public-house. "Yo've seen your sweetheart?" says he. "Yes, I've seen her," says I. "Well, we'll have a quart now, and you'll do your best to forget her," says he, bein' one o' them smart, bustlin' chaps. "Ay, sergeant," says I. "Forget her." And I've been forgettin' her ever since.'

He threw away the wilted clump of white violets as he spoke. Ortheris suddenly rose to his knees, his rifle at his shoulder, and peered across

the valley in the clear afternoon light. His chin
cuddled the stock, and there was a twitching of
the muscles of the right cheek as he sighted;
Private Stanley Ortheris was engaged on his business. A speck of white crawled up the watercourse.

'See that beggar? . . . Got 'im.'

Seven hundred yards away, and a full two
hundred down the hillside, the deserter of the
Aurangabadis pitched forward, rolled down a red
rock, and lay very still, with his face in a clump of
blue gentians, while a big raven flapped out of the
pine wood to make investigation.

'That's a clean shot, little man,' said Mulvaney.

Learoyd thoughtfully watched the smoke clear
away. 'Happen there was a lass tewed up wi'
him, too,' said he.

Ortheris did not reply. He was staring across
the valley, with the smile of the artist who looks
on the completed work.

The Man Who Was

The Earth gave up her dead that tide,
    Into our camp he came,
And said his say, and went his way,
    And left our hearts aflame.

Keep tally—on the gun-butt score
    The vengeance we must take,
When God shall bring full reckoning,
    For our dead comrade's sake.

Ballad.

Let it be clearly understood that the Russian is a delightful person till he tucks in his shirt. As an Oriental he is charming. It is only when he insists upon being treated as the most easterly of western peoples instead of the most westerly of easterns that he becomes a racial anomaly extremely difficult to handle. The host never knows which side of his nature is going to turn up next.

Dirkovitch was a Russian—a Russian of the Russians—who appeared to get his bread by serving the Czar as an officer in a Cossack regiment, and corresponding for a Russian newspaper with a name that was never twice alike. He was a handsome young Oriental, fond of wandering through unexplored portions of the earth, and he arrived in India from nowhere in particular. At least no living man could ascertain whether it was by way of Balkh, Badakshan, Chitral, Baluchistan, or Nepal, or anywhere else. The Indian Government, being in an unusually affable mood, gave orders that he was to be civilly treated and shown everything that was to be seen. So he drifted, talking bad English and worse French, from one city to another, till he foregathered with Her Majesty's White Hussars in the city of Peshawur, which stands at the mouth of that narrow swordcut in the hills that men call the Khyber Pass. He was undoubtedly an officer, and he was decorated after the manner of the Russians with little enamelled crosses, and he could talk, and (though this has nothing to do with his merits) he had been given up as a hopeless task, or cask, by the Black Tyrone, who individually and collectively, with hot whisky and honey, mulled brandy, and mixed spirits of every kind, had striven in all hospitality to make him drunk. And when the Black Tyrone, who are exclusively Irish, fail to disturb the peace of head of a foreigner—that foreigner is certain to be a superior man.

The White Hussars were as conscientious in choosing their wine as in charging the enemy. All that they possessed, including some wondrous brandy, was placed at the absolute disposition of Dirkovitch, and he enjoyed himself hugely—even more than among the Black Tyrones.

But he remained distressingly European through it all. The White Hussars were 'My dear true friends,' 'Fellow-soldiers glorious,' and 'Brothers inseparable.' He would unburden himself by the hour on the glorious future that awaited the combined arms of England and Russia when their hearts and their territories should run side by side, and the great mission of civilising Asia should begin. That was unsatisfactory, because Asia is not going to be civilised after the methods of the West. There is too much Asia and she is too old. You cannot reform a lady of many lovers, and Asia has been insatiable in her flirtations aforetime. She will never attend Sunday school or learn to vote save with swords for tickets.

Dirkovitch knew this as well as any one else, but it suited him to talk special-correspondently and to make himself as genial as he could. Now and then he volunteered a little, a very little, information about his own sotnia of Cossacks, left apparently to look after themselves somewhere at the back of beyond. He had done rough work in Central Asia, and had seen rather more help-yourself fighting than most men of his years. But he was careful never to betray his superiority, and more than careful to praise on all occasions the appearance, drill, uniform, and organisation of Her Majesty's White Hussars. And indeed they were a regiment to be admired. When Lady Durgan, widow of the late Sir John Durgan, arrived in their station, and after a short time had been proposed to by every single man at mess, she put the public sentiment very neatly when she explained that they were all so nice that unless she could marry them all, including the colonel and some majors already married, she was not going to content herself with one hussar. Wherefore she wedded a little man in a rifle regiment, being by nature contradictious ; and the White Hussars were going to wear crape on their arms, but compromised by attending the wedding in full force, and lining the aisle with unutterable reproach. She had jilted them all—from Basset-Holmer the senior captain to little Mildred the junior subaltern, who could have given her four thousand a year and a title.

The only persons who did not share the general regard for the White Hussars were a few thousand gentlemen of Jewish extraction who lived across the border, and answered to the name of Pathan. They had once met the regiment officially and for something less than twenty minutes, but the interview, which was complicated with many casualties, had filled them with prejudice. They even called the White Hussars children of the devil and sons of persons whom it would be perfectly impossible to meet in decent society. Yet they were not above making their aversion fill their money-belts. The regiment possessed carbines—beautiful Martini-Henry carbines that would lob a bullet into an enemy's camp at one thousand yards, and were even handier than the long rifle. Therefore they were coveted all along the border, and since demand inevitably breeds supply, they were supplied at the risk of life and limb for exactly their weight in coined silver—seven and one half pounds weight of rupees, or sixteen pounds sterling reckoning the rupee at par. They were stolen at night by snaky-haired thieves who crawled on their stomachs under the nose of the sentries ; they disappeared

mysteriously from locked arm-racks, and in the
hot weather, when all the barrack doors and
windows were open, they vanished like puffs of
their own smoke. The border people desired them
for family vendettas and contingencies. But in
the long cold nights of the northern Indian winter
they were stolen most extensively. The traffic of
murder was liveliest among the hills at that season,
and prices ruled high. The regimental guards
were first doubled and then trebled. A trooper
does not much care if he loses a weapon—Government must make it good—but he deeply resents
the loss of his sleep. The regiment grew very
angry, and one rifle-thief bears the visible marks of
their anger upon him to this hour. That incident
stopped the burglaries for a time, and the guards
were reduced accordingly, and the regiment devoted
itself to polo with unexpected results ; for it beat
by two goals to one that very terrible polo corps
the Lushkar Light Horse, though the latter had
four ponies apiece for a short hour's fight, as well
as a native officer who played like a lambent flame
across the ground.

They gave a dinner to celebrate the event.
The Lushkar team came, and Dirkovitch came, in
the fullest full uniform of a Cossack officer, which
is as full as a dressing-gown, and was introduced
to the Lushkars, and opened his eyes as he regarded.
They were lighter men than the Hussars, and they
carried themselves with the swing that is the
peculiar right of the Punjab Frontier Force and
all Irregular Horse. Like everything else in the
Service it has to be learnt, but, unlike many things,

it is never forgotten, and remains on the body till death.

The great beam-roofed mess-room of the White Hussars was a sight to be remembered. All the mess plate was out on the long table—the same table that had served up the bodies of five officers after a forgotten fight long and long ago—the dingy, battered standards faced the door of entrance, clumps of winter-roses lay between the silver candlesticks, and the portraits of eminent officers deceased looked down on their successors from between the heads of sambhur, nilghai, markhor, and, pride of all the mess, two grinning snow-leopards that had cost Basset-Holmer four months' leave that he might have spent in England, instead of on the road to Thibet and the daily risk of his life by ledge, snow-slide, and grassy slope.

The servants in spotless white muslin with the crest of their regiments on the brow of their turbans waited behind their masters, who were clad in the scarlet and gold of the White Hussars, and the cream and silver of the Lushkar Light Horse. Dirkovitch's dull green uniform was the only dark spot at the board, but his big onyx eyes made up for it. He was fraternising effusively with the captain of the Lushkar team, who was wondering how many of Dirkovitch's Cossacks his own dark wiry down-countrymen could account for in a fair charge. But one does not speak of these things openly.

The talk rose higher and higher, and the regimental band played between the courses, as is the

immemorial custom, till all tongues ceased for a
moment with the removal of the dinner-slips and
the first toast of obligation, when an officer rising
said, 'Mr. Vice, the Queen,' and little Mildred
from the bottom of the table answered, 'The
Queen, God bless her,' and the big spurs clanked
as the big men heaved themselves up and drank
the Queen upon whose pay they were falsely supposed to settle their mess-bills. That Sacrament
of the Mess never grows old, and never ceases to
bring a lump into the throat of the listener wherever he be by sea or by land. Dirkovitch rose
with his 'brothers glorious,' but he could not
understand. No one but an officer can tell what
the toast means ; and the bulk have more sentiment than comprehension. Immediately after the
little silence that follows on the ceremony there
entered the native officer who had played for the
Lushkar team. He could not, of course, eat with
the mess, but he came in at dessert, all six feet of
him, with the blue and silver turban atop, and the
big black boots below. The mess rose joyously
as he thrust forward the hilt of his sabre in token
of fealty for the colonel of the White Hussars to
touch, and dropped into a vacant chair amid shouts
of : '*Rung ho*, Hira Singh!' (which being translated means 'Go in and win'). 'Did I whack
you over the knee, old man?' 'Rissaldar Sahib,
what the devil made you play that kicking pig of
a pony in the last ten minutes?' '*Shabash*, Rissaldar Sahib!' Then the voice of the colonel,
'The health of Rissaldar Hira Singh!'

After the shouting had died away Hira Singh

rose to reply, for he was the cadet of a royal house, the son of a king's son, and knew what was due on these occasions.   Thus he spoke in the vernacular :—' Colonel Sahib and officers of this regiment.   Much honour have you done me. This will I remember.   We came down from afar to play you.   But we were beaten ' ('No fault of yours, Rissaldar Sahib.   Played on our own ground y' know.   Your ponies were cramped from the railway.   Don't apologise!')   'There-fore perhaps we will come again if it be so ordained.' ('Hear! Hear! Hear, indeed! Bravo! Hsh!') ' Then we will play you afresh ' ('Happy to meet you.')   'till there are left no feet upon our ponies. Thus far for sport.'   He dropped one hand on his sword-hilt and his eye wandered to Dirkovitch lolling back in his chair.   'But if by the will of God there arises any other game which is not the polo game, then be assured, Colonel Sahib and officers, that we will play it out side by side, though *they*,' again his eye sought Dirkovitch, ' though *they*, I say, have fifty ponies to our one horse.'   And with a deep-mouthed *Rung ho!* that sounded like a musket-butt on flagstones, he sat down amid leaping glasses.

Dirkovitch, who had devoted himself steadily to the brandy—the terrible brandy aforementioned —did not understand, nor did the expurgated translations offered to him at all convey the point. Decidedly Hira Singh's was the speech of the evening, and the clamour might have continued to the dawn had it not been broken by the noise of a shot without that sent every man feeling at his

defenceless left side.   Then there was a scuffle
and a yell of pain.

'Carbine-stealing again!' said the adjutant,
calmly sinking back in his chair.   'This comes of
reducing the guards.   I hope the sentries have
killed him.'

The feet of armed men pounded on the
verandah flags, and it was as though something
was being dragged.

'Why don't they put him in the cells till the
morning?' said the colonel testily.   'See if
they've damaged him, sergeant.'

The mess sergeant fled out into the darkness
and returned with two troopers and a corporal, all
very much perplexed.

'Caught a man stealin' carbines, sir,' said the
corporal.   'Leastways 'e was crawlin' towards the
barricks, sir, past the main road sentries, an' the
sentry 'e sez, sir——'

The limp heap of rags upheld by the three
men groaned.   Never was seen so destitute and
demoralised an Afghan.   He was turbanless, shoeless, caked with dirt, and all but dead with rough
handling.   Hira Singh started slightly at the
sound of the man's pain.   Dirkovitch took another
glass of brandy.

'*What* does the sentry say?' said the colonel.

'Sez 'e speaks English, sir,' said the corporal.

'So you brought him into mess instead of
handing him over to the sergeant!   If he spoke
all the Tongues of the Pentecost you've no business——'

Again the bundle groaned and muttered.   Little

Mildred had risen from his place to inspect. He jumped back as though he had been shot.

'Perhaps it would be better, sir, to send the men away,' said he to the colonel, for he was a much privileged subaltern. He put his arms round the rag-bound horror as he spoke, and dropped him into a chair. It may not have been explained that the littleness of Mildred lay in his being six feet four and big in proportion. The corporal seeing that an officer was disposed to look after the capture, and that the colonel's eye was beginning to blaze, promptly removed himself and his men. The mess was left alone with the carbine-thief, who laid his head on the table and wept bitterly, hopelessly, and inconsolably, as little children weep.

Hira Singh leapt to his feet. 'Colonel Sahib,' said he, 'that man is no Afghan, for they weep *Ai ! Ai !* Nor is he of Hindustan, for they weep *Oh ! Ho !* He weeps after the fashion of the white men, who say *Ow ! Ow !* '

'Now where the dickens did you get that knowledge, Hira Singh ?' said the captain of the Lushkar team.

'Hear him ! ' said Hira Singh simply, pointing at the crumpled figure that wept as though it would never cease.

'He said, "My God !"' said little Mildred. 'I heard him say it.'

The colonel and the mess-room looked at the man in silence. It is a horrible thing to hear a man cry. A woman can sob from the top of her palate, or her lips, or anywhere else, but a man must cry from his diaphragm, and it rends him to pieces.

'Poor devil!' said the colonel, coughing tremendously. 'We ought to send him to hospital. He's been man-handled.'

Now the adjutant loved his carbines. They were to him as his grandchildren, the men standing in the first place. He grunted rebelliously: 'I can understand an Afghan stealing, because he's built that way. But I can't understand his crying. That makes it worse.'

The brandy must have affected Dirkovitch, for he lay back in his chair and stared at the ceiling. There was nothing special in the ceiling beyond a shadow as of a huge black coffin. Owing to some peculiarity in the construction of the mess-room this shadow was always thrown when the candles were lighted. It never disturbed the digestion of the White Hussars. They were in fact rather proud of it.

'Is he going to cry all night?' said the colonel, 'or are we supposed to sit up with little Mildred's guest until he feels better?'

The man in the chair threw up his head and stared at the mess. 'Oh, my God!' he said, and every soul in the mess rose to his feet. Then the Lushkar captain did a deed for which he ought to have been given the Victoria Cross—distinguished gallantry in a fight against overwhelming curiosity. He picked up his team with his eyes as the hostess picks up the ladies at the opportune moment, and pausing only by the colonel's chair to say, 'This isn't *our* affair, you know, sir,' led them into the verandah and the gardens. Hira Singh was the last to go, and he looked at Dirkovitch. But Dirkovitch had departed into a brandy-paradise of his own. His lips moved without sound, and he was studying the coffin on the ceiling.

'White—white all over,' said Basset-Holmer, the adjutant. 'What a pernicious renegade he must be ! I wonder where he came from ?'

The colonel shook the man gently by the arm, and 'Who are you?' said he.

There was no answer. The man stared round the mess-room and smiled in the colonel's face. Little Mildred, who was always more of a woman than a man till 'Boot and saddle' was sounded, repeated the question in a voice that would have drawn confidences from a geyser. The man only smiled. Dirkovitch at the far end of the table slid gently from his chair to the floor. No son of Adam in this present imperfect world can mix the Hussars' champagne with the Hussars' brandy by five and eight glasses of each without remembering the pit whence he was digged and descending thither. The band began to play the tune with which the White Hussars from the date of their formation have concluded all their functions. They would sooner be disbanded than abandon that tune ; it is a part of their system. The man straightened himself in his chair and drummed on the table with his fingers.

'I don't see why we should entertain lunatics,' said the colonel. 'Call a guard and send him off to the cells. We'll look into the business in the morning. Give him a glass of wine first though.'

Little Mildred filled a sherry-glass with the brandy and thrust it over to the man. He drank, and the tune rose louder, and he straightened himself yet more. Then he put out his long-taloned hands to a piece of plate opposite and fingered it lovingly. There was a mystery connected with that piece of plate, in the shape of a spring which converted what was a seven-branched candlestick, three springs on each side and one in the middle, into a sort of wheel-spoke candelabrum. He found the spring, pressed it, and laughed weakly. He rose from his chair and inspected a picture on the wall, then moved on to another picture, the mess watching him without a word. When he came to the mantelpiece he shook his head and seemed distressed. A piece of plate representing a mounted hussar in full uniform caught his eye. He pointed to it, and then to the mantelpiece with inquiry in his eyes.

'What is it—Oh, what is it?' said little Mildred. Then as a mother might speak to a child, 'That is a horse. Yes, a horse.'

Very slowly came the answer in a thick, passionless guttural—'Yes, I—have seen. But— where is *the* horse?'

You could have heard the hearts of the mess beating as the men drew back to give the stranger full room in his wanderings. There was no question of calling the guard.

Again he spoke—very slowly, 'Where is *our* horse?'

There is but one horse in the White Hussars, and his portrait hangs outside the door of the mess-room. He is the piebald drum-horse, the king of the regimental band, that served the regiment for seven-and-thirty years, and in the end was shot for old age. Half the mess tore the thing down from its place and thrust it into the man's hands. He placed it above the mantelpiece, is clattered on the ledge as his poor hands dropped it, and he staggered towards the bottom of the table, falling into Mildred's chair. Then all the men spoke to one another something after this fashion, 'The drum-horse hasn't hung over the mantelpiece since '67.' 'How does he know?' 'Mildred, go and speak to him again.' 'Colonel, what are you going to do?' 'Oh, dry up, and give the poor devil a chance to pull himself together.' 'It isn't possible anyhow. The man's a lunatic.'

Little Mildred stood at the colonel's side talking in his ear. 'Will you be good enough to take your seats please, gentlemen!' he said, and the mess dropped into the chairs. Only Dirkovitch's seat, next to little Mildred's, was blank, and little Mildred himself had found Hira Singh's place. The wide-eyed mess-sergeant filled the glasses in dead silence. Once more the colonel rose, but his hand shook, and the port spilled on the table as he looked straight at the man in little Mildred's chair and said hoarsely, 'Mr. Vice, the Queen.' There was a little pause, but the man sprung to his feet and answered without hesitation, 'The Queen, God bless her!' and as he emptied the thin glass he snapped the shank between his fingers.

Long and long ago, when the Empress of

India was a young woman and there were no unclean ideals in the land, it was the custom of a few messes to drink the Queen's toast in broken glass, to the vast delight of the mess-contractors. The custom is now dead, because there is nothing to break anything for, except now and again the word of a Government, and that has been broken already.

'That settles it,' said the colonel, with a gasp. 'He's not a sergeant. What in the world is he?'

The entire mess echoed the word, and the volley of questions would have scared any man. It was no wonder that the ragged, filthy invader could only smile and shake his head.

From under the table, calm and smiling, rose Dirkovitch, who had been roused from healthful slumber by feet upon his body. By the side of the man he rose, and the man shrieked and grovelled. It was a horrible sight coming so swiftly upon the pride and glory of the toast that had brought the strayed wits together.

Dirkovitch made no offer to raise him, but little Mildred heaved him up in an instant. It is not good that a gentleman who can answer to the Queen's toast should lie at the feet of a subaltern of Cossacks.

The hasty action tore the wretch's upper clothing nearly to the waist, and his body was seamed with dry black scars. There is only one weapon in the world that cuts in parallel lines, and it is neither the cane nor the cat. Dirkovitch saw the marks, and the pupils of his eyes dilated. Also his face changed. He said something that sounded like *Shto ve takete*, and the man fawning answered, *Chetyre*.

' What's that ? ' said everybody together.

' His number. That is number four, you know.' Dirkovitch spoke very thickly.

' What has a Queen's officer to do with a qualified number ? ' said the colonel, and an unpleasant growl ran round the table.

' How can I tell ? ' said the affable Oriental with a sweet smile. ' He is a—how you have it ?—escape—run-a-way, from over there.' He nodded towards the darkness of the night.

'Speak to him if he'll answer you, and speak to him gently,' said little Mildred, settling the man in a chair. It seemed most improper to all present that Dirkovitch should sip brandy as he talked in purring, spitting Russian to the creature who answered so feebly and with such evident dread. But since Dirkovitch appeared to understand no one said a word. All breathed heavily, leaning forward, in the long gaps of the conversation. The next time that they have no engagements on hand the White Hussars intend to go to St. Petersburg in a body to learn Russian.

' He does not know how many years ago,' said Dirkovitch facing the mess, ' but he says it was very long ago in a war. I think that there was an accident. He says he was of this glorious and distinguished regiment in the war.'

' The rolls ! The rolls ! Holmer, get the rolls ! ' said little Mildred, and the adjutant dashed off bare-headed to the orderly-room, where the muster-rolls of the regiment were kept. He returned just in time to hear Dirkovitch conclude, 'Therefore, my dear friends, I am most sorry to say there was an accident which would have been reparable if he had apologised to that our colonel, which he had insulted.'

Then followed another growl which the colonel tried to beat down. The mess was in no mood just then to weigh insults to Russian colonels.

' He does not remember, but I think that there was an accident, and so he was not exchanged among the prisoners, but he was sent to another place—how do you say?—the country. *So*, he says, he came here. He does not know how he came. Eh? He was at Chepany'—the man caught the word, nodded, and shivered—'at Zhigansk and Irkutsk. I cannot understand how he escaped. He says, too, that he was in the forests for many years, but how many years he has forgotten—that with many things. It was an accident; done because he did not apologise to that our colonel. Ah!'

Instead of echoing Dirkovitch's sigh of regret, it is sad to record that the White Hussars livelily exhibited un-Christian delight and other emotions, hardly restrained by their sense of hospitality. Holmer flung the frayed and yellow regimental rolls on the table, and the men flung themselves at these.

'Steady! Fifty-six—fifty-five—fifty-four,' said Holmer. 'Here we are. "Lieutenant Austin Limmason. *Missing*." That was before Sebastopol. What an infernal shame! Insulted one of their colonels, and was quietly shipped off. Thirty years of his life wiped out.'

'But he never apologised. Said he'd see him damned first,' chorused the mess.

'Poor chap! I suppose he never had the chance afterwards. How did he come here?' said the colonel.

The dingy heap in the chair could give no answer.

'Do you know who you are?'

It laughed weakly.

'Do you know that you are Limmason—Lieutenant Limmason of the White Hussars?'

Swiftly as a shot came the answer, in a slightly surprised tone, 'Yes, I'm Limmason, of course.' The light died out in his eyes, and the man collapsed, watching every motion of Dirkovitch with terror. A flight from Siberia may fix a few elementary facts in the mind, but it does not seem to lead to continuity of thought. The man could not explain how, like a homing pigeon, he had found his way to his own old mess again. Of what he had suffered or seen he knew nothing. He cringed before Dirkovitch as instinctively as he had pressed the spring of the candlestick, sought the picture of the drum-horse, and answered to the toast of the Queen. The rest was a blank that the dreaded Russian tongue could only in part remove. His head bowed on his breast, and he giggled and cowered alternately.

The devil that lived in the brandy prompted Dirkovitch at this extremely inopportune moment to make a speech. He rose, swaying slightly, gripped the table-edge, while his eyes glowed like opals, and began :

'Fellow-soldiers glorious—true friends and hospitables. It was an accident, and deplorable—most deplorable.' Here he smiled sweetly all round the mess. 'But you will think of this little, little thing. So little, is it not? The Czar! Posh! I slap my fingers—I snap my fingers at him. Do I believe in him? No! But in us Slav who has done nothing, *him* I believe. Seventy—how much —millions peoples that have done nothing—not one thing. Posh! Napoleon was an episode.' He banged a hand on the table. 'Hear you, old peoples, we have done nothing in the world—out here. All our work is to do; and it shall be done, old peoples. Get a-way!' He waved his hand imperiously, and pointed to the man. 'You see him. He is not good to see. He was just one little—oh, so little—accident, that no one remembered. Now he is *That!* So will you be, brother soldiers so brave—so will you be. But you will never come back. You will all go where he is gone, or'—he pointed to the great coffin-shadow on the ceiling, and muttering, 'Seventy millions — get a-way, you old peoples,' fell asleep.

'Sweet, and to the point,' said little Mildred. 'What's the use of getting wroth? Let's make this poor devil comfortable.'

But that was a matter suddenly and swiftly taken from the loving hands of the White Hussars. The lieutenant had returned only to go away again three days later, when the wail of the Dead March, and the tramp of the squadrons, told the wondering Station, who saw no gap in the mess-table, that an officer of the regiment had resigned his new-found commission.

And Dirkovitch, bland, supple, and always genial, went away too by a night train. Little Mildred and another man saw him off, for he was the guest of the mess, and even had he smitten the colonel with the open hand, the law of that mess allowed no relaxation of hospitality.

'Good-bye, Dirkovitch, and a pleasant journey,' said little Mildred.

'*Au revoir*,' said the Russian.

'Indeed! But we thought you were going home?'

'Yes, but I will come again. My dear friends, is that road shut?' He pointed to where the North Star burned over the Khyber Pass.

'By Jove! I forgot. Of course. Happy to meet you, old man, any time you like. Got everything you want? Cheroots, ice, bedding? That's all right. Well, *au revoir*, Dirkovitch.'

'Um,' said the other man, as the tail-lights of the train grew small. 'Of—all—the—unmitigated——!'

Little Mildred answered nothing, but watched the North Star and hummed a selection from a recent Simla burlesque that had much delighted the White Hussars. It ran—

> I'm sorry for Mister Bluebeard,
> I'm sorry to cause him pain;
> But a terrible spree there's sure to be
> When he comes back again.

The Head of the District

There's a convict more in the Central Jail,
    Behind the old mud wall ;
There's a lifter less on the Border trail,
    And the Queen's Peace over all,
               Dear boys,
    The Queen's Peace over all.

For we must bear our leader's blame,
    On us the shame will fall,
If we lift our hand from a fettered land
    And the Queen's Peace over all,
               Dear boys,
    The Queen's Peace over all !
              The Running of Shindand.

I

THE Indus had risen in flood without warning. Last night it was a fordable shallow ; to-night five miles of raving muddy water parted bank and caving bank, and the river was still rising under the moon. A litter borne by six bearded men, all unused to the work, stopped in the white sand that bordered the whiter plain.

'It's God's will,' they said. 'We dare not cross to-night, even in a boat. Let us light a fire and cook food. We be tired men.'

They looked at the litter inquiringly.   Within, the Deputy Commissioner of the Kot-Kumharsen district lay dying of fever.   They had brought him across country, six fighting-men of a frontier clan that he had won over to the paths of a moderate righteousness, when he had broken down at the foot of their inhospitable hills.   And Tallantire, his assistant, rode with them, heavy-hearted as heavy-eyed with sorrow and lack of sleep.   He had served under the sick man for three years, and had learned to love him as men associated in toil of the hardest learn to love—or hate.   Dropping from his horse he parted the curtains of the litter and peered inside.

'Orde—Orde, old man, can you hear? We have to wait till the river goes down, worse luck.'

'I hear,' returned a dry whisper. 'Wait till the river goes down.   I thought we should reach camp before the dawn.   Polly knows.   She'll meet me.'

One of the litter-men stared across the river and caught a faint twinkle of light on the far side. He whispered to Tallantire, 'There are his camp-fires, and his wife.   They will cross in the morning, for they have better boats.   Can he live so long?'

Tallantire shook his head.   Yardley-Orde was very near to death.   What need to vex his soul with hopes of a meeting that could not be?   The river gulped at the banks, brought down a cliff of sand, and snarled the more hungrily.   The litter-men sought for fuel in the waste—dried camel-thorn and refuse of the camps that had waited at the ford.   Their sword-belts clinked as they moved softly in the haze of the moonlight, and Tallantire's horse coughed to explain that he would like a blanket.

'I'm cold too,' said the voice from the litter. 'I fancy this is the end. Poor Polly!'

Tallantire rearranged the blankets; Khoda Dad Khan, seeing this, stripped off his own heavy-wadded sheepskin coat and added it to the pile. 'I shall be warm by the fire presently,' said he. Tallantire took the wasted body of his chief into his arms and held it against his breast. Perhaps if they kept him very warm Orde might live to see his wife once more. If only blind Providence would send a three-foot fall in the river!

'That's better,' said Orde faintly. 'Sorry to be a nuisance, but is—is there anything to drink?'

They gave him milk and whisky, and Tallantire felt a little warmth against his own breast. Orde began to mutter.

'It isn't that I mind dying,' he said. 'It's leaving Polly and the district. Thank God! we have no children. Dick, you know, I'm dipped—awfully dipped—debts in my first five years' service. It isn't much of a pension, but enough for her. She has her mother at home. Getting there is the difficulty. And — and — you see, not being a soldier's wife——'

'We'll arrange the passage home, of course,' said Tallantire quietly.

'It's not nice to think of sending round the hat; but, good Lord! how many men I lie here and remember that had to do it! Morten's dead —he was of my year. Shaughnessy is dead, and he had children; I remember he used to read us their school-letters; what a bore we thought him! Evans is dead — Kot-Kumharsen killed him! Ricketts of Myndonie is dead—and I'm going too. "Man that is born of a woman is small potatoes and few in the hill." That reminds me, Dick; the four Khusru Kheyl villages in our border want a one-third remittance this spring. That's fair; their crops are bad. See that they get it, and speak to Ferris about the canal. I should like to have lived till that was finished; it means so much for the North-Indus villages—but Ferris is an idle beggar—wake him up. You'll have charge of the district till my successor comes. I wish they would appoint you permanently; you know the folk. I suppose it will be Bullows, though. 'Good man, but too weak for frontier work; and he doesn't understand the priests. The blind priest at Jagai will bear watching. You'll find it in my papers,—in the uniform case, I think. Call the Khusru Kheyl men up; I'll hold my last public audience. Khoda Dad Khan!'

The leader of the men sprang to the side of the litter, his companions following.

'Men, I'm dying,' said Orde quickly, in the vernacular; 'and soon there will be no more Orde Sahib to twist your tails and prevent you from raiding cattle.'

'God forbid this thing!' broke out the deep bass chorus. 'The Sahib is not going to die.'

'Yes, he is; and then he will know whether Mahomed speaks truth, or Moses. But you must be good men when I am not here. Such of you

as live in our borders must pay your taxes quietly
as before. I have spoken of the villages to be
gently treated this year. Such of you as live in
the hills must refrain from cattle-lifting, and burn
no more thatch, and turn a deaf ear to the voice
of the priests, who, not knowing the strength of
the Government, would lead you into foolish wars,
wherein you will surely die and your crops be
eaten by strangers. And you must not sack any
caravans, and must leave your arms at the police-
post when you come in ; as has been your custom,
and my order. And Tallantire Sahib will be with
you, but I do not know who takes my place. I
speak now true talk, for I am as it were already
dead, my children,—for though ye be strong men,
ye are children.'

'And thou art our father and our mother,' broke
in Khoda Dad Khan with an oath. 'What shall
we do, now there is no one to speak for us, or to
teach us to go wisely ! '

'There remains Tallantire Sahib. Go to him ;
he knows your talk and your heart. Keep the
young men quiet, listen to the old men, and obey.
Khoda Dad Khan, take my ring. The watch and
chain go to thy brother. Keep those things for
my sake, and I will speak to whatever God I may
encounter and tell him that the Khusru Kheyl are
good men. Ye have my leave to go.'

Khoda Dad Khan, the ring upon his finger,
choked audibly as he caught the well-known
formula that closed an interview. His brother
turned to look across the river. The dawn was
breaking, and a speck of white showed on the dull

silver of the stream. 'She comes,' said the man
under his breath. 'Can he live for another two
hours?' And he pulled the newly-acquired watch
out of his belt and looked uncomprehendingly at
the dial, as he had seen Englishmen do.

For two hours the bellying sail tacked and
blundered up and down the river, Tallantire still
clasping Orde in his arms, and Khoda Dad Khan
chafing his feet. He spoke now and again of the
district and his wife, but, as the end neared, more
frequently of the latter. They hoped he did not
know that she was even then risking her life in a
crazy native boat to regain him. But the awful
foreknowledge of the dying deceived them.
Wrenching himself forward, Orde looked through
the curtains and saw how near was the sail.
'That's Polly,' he said simply, though his mouth
was wried with agony. 'Polly and—the grimmest
practical joke ever played on a man. Dick—you'll
—have—to—explain.'

And an hour later Tallantire met on the bank
a woman in a gingham riding-habit and a sun-hat
who cried out to him for her husband—her boy
and her darling—while Khoda Dad Khan threw
himself face-down on the sand and covered his
eyes.

II

The very simplicity of the notion was its charm.
What more easy to win a reputation for far-seeing
statesmanship, originality, and, above all, deference
to the desires of the people, than by appointing a
child of the country to the rule of that country?

Two hundred millions of the most loving and grateful folk under Her Majesty's dominion would laud the fact, and their praise would endure for ever. Yet he was indifferent to praise or blame, as befitted the Very Greatest of All the Viceroys. His administration was based upon principle, and the principle must be enforced in season and out of season. His pen and tongue had created the New India, teeming with possibilities—loud-voiced, insistent, a nation among nations—all his very own. Wherefore the Very Greatest of All the Viceroys took another step in advance, and with it counsel of those who should have advised him on the appointment of a successor to Yardley-Orde. There was a gentleman and a member of the Bengal Civil Service who had won his place and a university degree to boot in fair and open competition with the sons of the English. He was cultured, of the world, and, if report spoke truly, had wisely and, above all, sympathetically ruled a crowded district in South-Eastern Bengal. He had been to England and charmed many drawing-rooms there. His name, if the Viceroy recollected aright, was Mr. Grish Chunder Dé, M.A. In short, did anybody see any objection to the appointment, always on principle, of a man of the people to rule the people? The district in South-Eastern Bengal might with advantage, he apprehended, pass over to a younger civilian of Mr. G. C. Dé's nationality (who had written a remarkably clever pamphlet on the political value of sympathy in administration); and Mr. G. C. Dé could be transferred northward to Kot-Kumharsen. The Viceroy was averse, on

principle, to interfering with appointments under
control of the Provincial Governments. He wished
it to be understood that he merely recommended
and advised in this instance.   As regarded the mere
question of race, Mr. Grish Chunder Dé was more
English than the English, and yet possessed of
that peculiar sympathy and insight which the best
among the best Service in the world could only
win to at the end of their service.

The stern, black-bearded kings who sit about
the Council-board of India divided on the step,
with the inevitable result of driving the Very
Greatest of All the Viceroys into the borders of
hysteria, and a bewildered obstinacy pathetic as
that of a child.

'The principle is sound enough,' said the weary-
eyed Head of the Red Provinces in which Kot-
Kumharsen lay, for he too held theories.   'The
only difficulty is——'

'Put the screw on the district officials ; brigade
Dé with a very strong Deputy Commissioner on
each side of him ; give him the best assistant in
the Province ; rub the fear of God into the people
beforehand ; and if anything goes wrong, say that
his colleagues didn't back him up.   All these lovely
little experiments recoil on the District-Officer in
the end,' said the Knight of the Drawn Sword with
a truthful brutality that made the Head of the Red
Provinces shudder.   And on a tacit understanding
of this kind the transfer was accomplished, as quietly
as might be for many reasons.

It is sad to think that what goes for public
opinion in India did not generally see the wisdom

of the Viceroy's appointment. There were not lacking indeed hireling organs, notoriously in the pay of a tyrannous bureaucracy, who more than hinted that His Excellency was a fool, a dreamer of dreams, a doctrinaire, and, worst of all, a trifler with the lives of men. 'The Viceroy's Excellence Gazette,' published in Calcutta, was at pains to thank 'Our beloved Viceroy for once more and again thus gloriously vindicating the potentialities of the Bengali nations for extended executive and administrative duties in foreign parts beyond our ken. We do not at all doubt that our excellent fellow-townsman, Mr. Grish Chunder Dé, Esq., M.A., will uphold the prestige of the Bengali, notwithstanding what underhand intrigue and *pesh-bundi* may be set on foot to insidiously nip his fame and blast his prospects among the proud civilians, some of which will now have to serve under a despised native and take orders too. How will you like that, Misters? We entreat our beloved Viceroy still to substantiate himself superiorly to race-prejudice and colour-blindness, and to allow the flower of this now *our* Civil Service all the full pays and allowances granted to his more fortunate brethren.'

III

'When does this man take over charge? I'm alone just now, and I gather that I'm to stand fast under him.'

'Would you have cared for a transfer?' said Bullows keenly. Then, laying his hand on Tallantire's shoulder: 'We're all in the same boat; don't

desert us.　And yet, why the devil should you stay,
if you can get another charge?

'It was Orde's,' said Tallantire simply.

'Well, it's Dé's now.　He's a Bengali of the
Bengalis, crammed with code and case law ; a
beautiful man so far as routine and deskwork go,
and pleasant to talk to.　They naturally have always
kept him in his own home district, where all his
sisters and his cousins and his aunts lived, somewhere south of Dacca.　He did no more than
turn the place into a pleasant little family preserve,
allowed his subordinates to do what they liked,
and let everybody have a chance at the shekels.
Consequently he's immensely popular down there.'

'I've nothing to do with that.　How on earth
am I to explain to the district that they are going
to be governed by a Bengali ?　Do you—does the
Government, I mean—suppose that the Khusru
Kheyl will sit quiet when they once know ?　What
will the Mahomedan heads of villages say ?　How
will the police—Muzbi Sikhs and Pathans—how
will *they* work under him ?　We couldn't say anything if the Government appointed a sweeper ; but
my people will say a good deal, you know that.
It's a piece of cruel folly ! '

'My dear boy, I know all that, and more.　I've
represented it, and have been told that I am ex-
hibiting "culpable and puerile prejudice."　By Jove,
if the Khusru Kheyl don't exhibit something worse
than that I don't know the Border !　The chances
are that you will have the district alight on your
hands, and I shall have to leave my work and help
you pull through.　I needn't ask you to stand by

the Bengali man in every possible way. You'll do that for your own sake.'

For Orde's. I can't say that I care twopence personally.'

'Don't be an ass. It's grievous enough, God knows, and the Government will know later on ; but that's no reason for your sulking. *You* must try to run the district ; *you* must stand between him and as much insult as possible ; *you* must show him the ropes ; *you* must pacify the Khusru Kheyl, and just warn Curbar of the Police to look out for trouble by the way. I'm always at the end of a telegraph-wire, and willing to peril my reputation to hold the district together. You'll lose yours, of course. If you keep things straight, and he isn't actually beaten with a stick when he's on tour, he'll get all the credit. If anything goes wrong, you'll be told that you didn't support him loyally.'

'I know what I've got to do,' said Tallantire wearily, 'and I'm going to it. But it's hard.'

'The work is with us, the event is with Allah,— as Orde used to say when he was more than usually in hot water.' And Bullows rode away.

That two gentlemen in Her Majesty's Bengal Civil Service should thus discuss a third, also in that service, and a cultured and affable man withal, seems strange and saddening. Yet listen to the artless babble of the Blind Mullah of Jagai, the priest of the Khusru Kheyl, sitting upon a rock overlooking the Border. Five years before, a chance-hurled shell from a screw-gun battery had dashed earth in the face of the Mullah, then urging a rush of Ghazis against half a dozen

British bayonets. So he became blind, and hated the English none the less for the little accident. Yardley-Orde knew his failing, and had many times laughed at him therefor.

'Dogs you are,' said the Blind Mullah to the listening tribesmen round the fire. 'Whipped dogs! Because you listened to Orde Sahib and called him father and behaved as his children, the British Government have proven how they regard you. Orde Sahib ye know is dead.'

'Ai! ai! ai!' said half a dozen voices.

'He was a man. Comes now in his stead, whom think ye? A Bengali of Bengal—an eater of fish from the South.'

'A lie!' said Khoda Dad Khan. 'And but for the small matter of thy priesthood, I'd drive my gun butt-first down thy throat.'

'Oho, art thou there, lickspittle of the English? Go in to-morrow across the Border to pay service to Orde Sahib's successor, and thou shalt slip thy shoes at the tent-door of a Bengali, as thou shalt hand thy offering to a Bengali's black fist. This I know; and in my youth, when a young man spoke evil to a Mullah holding the doors of Heaven and Hell, the gun-butt was not rammed down the Mullah's gullet. No!'

The Blind Mullah hated Khoda Dad Khan with Afghan hatred, both being rivals for the headship of the tribe; but the latter was feared for bodily as the other for spiritual gifts. Khoda Dad Khan looked at Orde's ring and grunted, 'I go in to-morrow because I am not an old fool, preaching war against the English. If the

Government, smitten with madness, have done this, then . . .'

'Then,' croaked the Mullah, 'thou wilt take out the young men and strike at the four villages within the Border ?'

'Or wring thy neck, black raven of Jehannum, for a bearer of ill-tidings.'

Khoda Dad Khan oiled his long locks with great care, put on his best Bokhara belt, a new turban-cap, and fine green shoes, and accompanied by a few friends came down from the hills to pay a visit to the new Deputy Commissioner of Kot-Kumharsen. Also he bore tribute—four or five priceless gold mohurs of Akbar's time in a white handkerchief. These the Deputy Commissioner would touch and remit. The little ceremony used to be a sign that, so far as Khoda Dad Khan's personal influence went, the Khusru Kheyl would be good boys,—till the next time ; especially if Khoda Dad Khan happened to like the new Deputy Commissioner. In Yardley-Orde's consul-ship his visit concluded with a sumptuous dinner and perhaps forbidden liquors ; certainly with some wonderful tales and great good-fellowship. Then Khoda Dad Khan would swagger back to his hold, vowing that Orde Sahib was one prince and Tallantire Sahib another, and that whosoever went a-raiding into British territory would be flayed alive. On this occasion he found the Deputy Commissioner's tents looking much as usual. Regarding himself as privileged he strode through the open door to confront a suave, portly Bengali in English costume writing at a table. Unversed in the elevating influence of education, and not in the least caring for university degrees, Khoda Dad Khan promptly set the man down for a Babu—the native clerk of the Deputy Commissioner — a hated and despised animal.

'Ugh !' said he cheerfully. 'Where's your master, Babujee ?'

'I am the Deputy Commissioner,' said the gentleman in English.

Now he overvalued the effects of university degrees, and stared Khoda Dad Khan in the face. But if from your earliest infancy you have been accustomed to look on battle, murder, and sudden death, if spilt blood affects your nerves as much as red paint, and, above all, if you have faithfully believed that the Bengali was the servant of all Hindustan, and that all Hindustan was vastly inferior to your own large, lustful self, you can endure, even though uneducated, a very large amount of looking over. You can even stare down a graduate of an Oxford college if the latter has been born in a hothouse, of stock bred in a hothouse, and fearing physical pain as some men fear sin ; especially if your opponent's mother has frightened him to sleep in his youth with horrible stories of devils inhabiting Afghanistan, and dismal legends of the black North. The eyes behind the gold spectacles sought the floor. Khoda Dad Khan chuckled, and swung out to find Tallantire hard by. 'Here,' said he roughly, thrusting the coins before him, 'touch and remit. That answers for *my* good behaviour. But, O Sahib, has the Government gone mad to send a black Bengali

dog to us ?   And am I to pay service to such an
one ?   And are you to work under him ?   What
does it mean ?'

'It is an order,' said Tallantire.   He had
expected something of this kind.   'He is a very
clever S-sahib.'

'He a Sahib!   He's a *kala admi* — a black
man—unfit to run at the tail of a potter's donkey.
All the peoples of the earth have harried Bengal.
It is written.   Thou knowest when we of the
North wanted women or plunder whither went
we ? To Bengal—where else ?   What child's talk
is this of Sahibdom—after Orde Sahib too !   Of a
truth the Blind Mullah was right.'

'What of him ?' asked Tallantire uneasily.
He mistrusted that old man with his dead eyes
and his deadly tongue.

'Nay, now, because of the oath that I sware to
Orde Sahib when we watched him die by the river
yonder, I will tell.   In the first place, is it true
that the English have set the heel of the Bengali on
their own neck, and that there is no more English
rule in the land ?'

'I am here,' said Tallantire, 'and I serve the
Maharanee of England.'

'The Mullah said otherwise, and further that
because we loved Orde Sahib the Government sent
us a pig to show that we were dogs, who till now
have been held by the strong hand.   Also that
they were taking away the white soldiers, that
more Hindustanis might come, and that all was
changing.'

This is the worst of ill-considered handling of

a very large country. What looks so feasible in Calcutta, so right in Bombay, so unassailable in Madras, is misunderstood by the North, and entirely changes its complexion on the banks of the Indus. Khoda Dad Khan explained as clearly as he could that, though he himself intended to be good, he really could not answer for the more reckless members of his tribe under the leadership of the Blind Mullah. They might or they might not give trouble, but they certainly had no intention whatever of obeying the new Deputy Commissioner. Was Tallantire perfectly sure that in the event of any systematic border-raiding the force in the district could put it down promptly?

'Tell the Mullah if he talks any more fool's talk,' said Tallantire curtly, 'that he takes his men on to certain death, and his tribe to blockade, trespass-fine, and blood-money. But why do I talk to one who no longer carries weight in the counsels of the tribe?'

Khoda Dad Khan pocketed that insult. He had learned something that he much wanted to know, and returned to his hills to be sarcastically complimented by the Mullah, whose tongue raging round the camp-fires was deadlier flame than ever dung-cake fed.

IV

Be pleased to consider here for a moment the unknown district of Kot-Kumharsen. It lay cut lengthways by the Indus under the line of the Khusru hills—ramparts of useless earth and tumbled stone. It was seventy miles long by fifty broad, maintained a population of something less than two hundred thousand, and paid taxes to the extent of forty thousand pounds a year on an area that was by rather more than half sheer, hopeless waste. The cultivators were not gentle people, the miners for salt were less gentle still, and the cattle-breeders least gentle of all. A police-post in the top right-hand corner and a tiny mud fort in the top left-hand corner prevented as much salt-smuggling and cattle-lifting as the influence of the civilians could not put down ; and in the bottom right-hand corner lay Jumala, the district headquarters—a pitiful knot of lime-washed barns facetiously rented as houses, reeking with frontier fever, leaking in the rain, and ovens in the summer.

It was to this place that Grish Chunder Dé was travelling, there formally to take over charge of the district. But the news of his coming had gone before. Bengalis were as scarce as poodles among the simple Borderers, who cut each other's heads open with their long spades and worshipped impartially at Hindu and Mahomedan shrines. They crowded to see him, pointing at him, and diversely comparing him to a gravid milch-buffalo, or a broken-down horse, as their limited range of metaphor prompted. They laughed at his police-guard, and wished to know how long the burly Sikhs were going to lead Bengali apes. They inquired whether he had brought his women with him, and advised him explicitly not to tamper with theirs. It remained for a wrinkled hag by

the roadside to slap her lean breasts as he passed,
crying, 'I have suckled six that could have eaten
six thousand of *him*. The Government shot them,
and made this That a king!' Whereat a blue-
turbaned huge - boned plough - mender shouted,
'Have hope, mother o' mine! He may yet go
the way of thy wastrels.' And the children, the
little brown puff-balls, regarded curiously. It was
generally a good thing for infancy to stray into
Orde Sahib's tent, where copper coins were to be
won for the mere wishing, and tales of the most
authentic, such as even their mothers knew but
the first half of. No! This fat black man could
never tell them how Pir Prith hauled the eye-teeth
out of ten devils ; how the big stones came to lie
all in a row on top of the Khusru hills, and
what happened if you shouted through the village-
gate to the gray wolf at even 'Badl Khas is dead.'
Meantime Grish Chunder Dé talked hastily and
much to Tallantire, after the manner of those who
are 'more English than the English,'—of Oxford
and 'home,' with much curious book-knowledge
of bump-suppers, cricket-matches, hunting-runs,
and other unholy sports of the alien. 'We must
get these fellows in hand,' he said once or twice
uneasily ; 'get them well in hand, and drive them
on a tight rein. No use, you know, being slack
with your district.'

And a moment later Tallantire heard Debendra
Nath Dé, who brotherliwise had followed his kins-
man's fortune and hoped for the shadow of his
protection as a pleader, whisper in Bengali, 'Better
are dried fish at Dacca than drawn swords at

Delhi. Brother of mine, these men are devils, as our mother said. And you will always have to ride upon a horse!'

That night there was a public audience in a broken-down little town thirty miles from Jumala, when the new Deputy Commissioner, in reply to the greetings of the subordinate native officials, delivered a speech. It was a carefully thought-out speech, which would have been very valuable had not his third sentence begun with three innocent words, '*Hamara hookum hai*—It is my order.' Then there was a laugh, clear and bell-like, from the back of the big tent, where a few border land-holders sat, and the laugh grew and scorn mingled with it, and the lean, keen face of Debendra Nath Dé paled, and Grish Chunder turning to Tallantire spake : '*You*—you put up this arrangement.' Upon that instant the noise of hoofs rang without, and there entered Curbar, the District Superintendent of Police, sweating and dusty. The State had tossed him into a corner of the province for seventeen weary years, there to check smuggling of salt, and to hope for promotion that never came. He had forgotten how to keep his white uniform clean, had screwed rusty spurs into patent-leather shoes, and clothed his head indifferently with a helmet or a turban. Soured, old, worn with heat and cold, he waited till he should be entitled to sufficient pension to keep him from starving.

'Tallantire,' said he, disregarding Grish Chunder Dé, 'come outside. I want to speak to you.' They withdrew. 'It's this,' continued Curbar,

'The Khusru Kheyl have rushed and cut up half a dozen of the coolies on Ferris's new canal-embankment; killed a couple of men and carried off a woman. I wouldn't trouble you about that —Ferris is after them and Hugonin, my assistant, with ten mounted police. But that's only the beginning, I fancy. Their fires are out on the Hassan Ardeb heights, and unless we're pretty quick there'll be a flare-up all along our Border. They are sure to raid the four Khusru villages on our side of the line : there's been bad blood between them for years ; and you know the Blind Mullah has been preaching a holy war since Orde went out. What's your notion ?'

'Damn!' said Tallantire thoughtfully. 'They've begun quick. Well, it seems to me I'd better ride off to Fort Ziar and get what men I can there to picket among the lowland villages, if it's not too late. Tommy Dodd commands at Fort Ziar, I think. Ferris and Hugonin ought to teach the canal-thieves a lesson, and—— No, we can't have the Head of the Police ostentatiously guarding the Treasury. You go back to the canal. I'll wire Bullows to come in to Jumala with a strong police-guard, and sit on the Treasury. They won't touch the place, but it looks well.'

'I—I—I insist upon knowing what this means,' said the voice of the Deputy Commissioner, who had followed the speakers.

'Oh !' said Curbar, who being in the Police could not understand that fifteen years of education must, on principle, change the Bengali into a Briton. 'There has been a fight on the Border, and heaps of men are killed. There's going to be another fight, and heaps more will be killed.'

' What for ? '

' Because the teeming millions of this district don't exactly approve of you, and think that under your benign rule they are going to have a good time. It strikes me that you had better make arrangements. I act, as you know, by your orders. What do you advise ? '

' I—I take you all to witness that I have not yet assumed charge of the district,' stammered the Deputy Commissioner, not in the tones of the ' more English.'

' Ah, I thought so. Well, as I was saying, Tallantire, your plan is sound. Carry it out. Do you want an escort ? '

' No ; only a decent horse. But how about wiring to headquarters ? '

' I fancy, from the colour of his cheeks, that your superior officer will send some wonderful telegrams before the night's over. Let him do that, and we shall have half the troops of the province coming up to see what's the trouble. Well, run along, and take care of yourself—the Khusru Kheyl jab upwards from below, remember. Ho! Mir Khan, give Tallantire Sahib the best of the horses, and tell five men to ride to Jumala with the Deputy Commissioner Sahib Bahadur. There is a hurry toward.'

There was ; and it was not in the least bettered by Debendra Nath Dé clinging to a policeman's bridle and demanding the shortest, the very shortest way to Jumala. Now originality is fatal to the

Bengali. Debendra Nath should have stayed with his brother, who rode steadfastly for Jumala on the railway-line, thanking gods entirely unknown to the most catholic of universities that he had not taken charge of the district, and could still—happy resource of a fertile race!—fall sick.

And I grieve to say that when he reached his goal two policemen, not devoid of rude wit, who had been conferring together as they bumped in their saddles, arranged an entertainment for his behoof. It consisted of first one and then the other entering his room with prodigious details of war, the massing of bloodthirsty and devilish tribes, and the burning of towns. It was almost as good, said these scamps, as riding with Curbar after evasive Afghans. Each invention kept the hearer at work for half an hour on telegrams which the sack of Delhi would hardly have justified. To every power that could move a bayonet or transfer a terrified man, Grish Chunder Dé appealed telegraphically. He was alone, his assistants had fled, and in truth he had not taken over charge of the district. Had the telegrams been despatched many things would have occurred ; but since the only signaller in Jumala had gone to bed, and the station-master, after one look at the tremendous pile of paper, discovered that railway regulations forbade the forwarding of imperial messages, policemen Ram Singh and Nihal Singh were fain to turn the stuff into a pillow and slept on it very comfortably.

Tallantire drove his spurs into a rampant skewbald stallion with china-blue eyes, and settled

himself for the forty-mile ride to Fort Ziar.
Knowing his district blindfold, he wasted no time
hunting for short cuts, but headed across the
richer grazing-ground to the ford where Orde had
died and been buried. The dusty ground deadened
the noise of his horse's hoofs, the moon threw his
shadow, a restless goblin, before him, and the
heavy dew drenched him to the skin. Hillock,
scrub that brushed against the horse's belly,
unmetalled road where the whip-like foliage of the
tamarisks lashed his forehead, illimitable levels of
lowland furred with bent and speckled with
drowsing cattle, waste, and hillock anew, dragged
themselves past, and the skewbald was labouring in
the deep sand of the Indus-ford. Tallantire was
conscious of no distinct thought till the nose of the
dawdling ferry-boat grounded on the farther side,
and his horse shied snorting at the white headstone
of Orde's grave. Then he uncovered, and shouted
that the dead might hear, 'They're out, old man!
Wish me luck.' In the chill of the dawn he was
hammering with a stirrup-iron at the gate of Fort
Ziar, where fifty sabres of that tattered regiment,
the Belooch Beshaklis, were supposed to guard Her
Majesty's interests along a few hundred miles of
Border. This particular fort was commanded by
a subaltern, who, born of the ancient family of the
Derouletts, naturally answered to the name of
Tommy Dodd. Him Tallantire found robed in a
sheepskin coat, shaking with fever like an aspen,
and trying to read the native apothecary's list of
invalids.

'So you've come, too,' said he. 'Well, we're

all sick here, and I don't think I can horse thirty men; but we're bub—bub—bub blessed willing. Stop, does this impress you as a trap or a lie?' He tossed a scrap of paper to Tallantire, on which was written painfully in crabbed Gurmukhi, 'We cannot hold young horses. They will feed after the moon goes down in the four border villages issuing from the Jagai pass on the next night.' Then in English round hand—'Your sincere friend.'

'Good man!' said Tallantire. 'That's Khoda Dad Khan's work, I know. It's the only piece of English he could ever keep in his head, and he is immensely proud of it. He is playing against the Blind Mullah for his own hand—the treacherous young ruffian!'

'Don't know the politics of the Khusru Kheyl, but if you're satisfied, I am. That was pitched in over the gatehead last night, and I thought we might pull ourselves together and see what was on. Oh, but we're sick with fever here and no mistake! Is this going to be a big business, think you?' said Tommy Dodd.

Tallantire gave him briefly the outlines of the case, and Tommy Dodd whistled and shook with fever alternately. That day he devoted to strategy, the art of war, and the enlivenment of the invalids, till at dusk there stood ready forty-two troopers, lean, worn, and dishevelled, whom Tommy Dodd surveyed with pride, and addressed thus, 'O men! If you die you will go to Hell. Therefore endeavour to keep alive. But if you go to Hell that place cannot be hotter than this place, and we are not told that we shall there suffer from fever. Consequently be not afraid of dying. File out there!' They grinned, and went.

V

It will be long ere the Khusru Kheyl forget their night attack on the lowland villages. The Mullah had promised an easy victory and unlimited plunder; but behold, armed troopers of the Queen had risen out of the very earth, cutting, slashing, and riding down under the stars, so that no man knew where to turn, and all feared that they had brought an army about their ears, and ran back to the hills. In the panic of that flight more men were seen to drop from wounds inflicted by an Afghan knife jabbed upwards, and yet more from long-range carbine-fire. Then there rose a cry of treachery, and when they reached their own guarded heights, they had left, with some forty dead and sixty wounded, all their confidence in the Blind Mullah on the plains below. They clamoured, swore, and argued round the fires; the women wailing for the lost, and the Mullah shrieking curses on the returned.

Then Khoda Dad Khan, eloquent and un-breathed, for he had taken no part in the fight, rose to improve the occasion. He pointed out that the tribe owed every item of its present misfortune to the Blind Mullah, who had lied in every possible particular and talked them into a trap. It was undoubtedly an insult that a Bengali, the son of a Bengali, should presume to administer the

Border, but that fact did not, as the Mullah pretended, herald a general time of licence and lifting ;
and the inexplicable madness of the English had
not in the least impaired their power of guarding
their marches. On the contrary, the baffled and
out-generalled tribe would now, just when their
food-stock was lowest, be blockaded from any
trade with Hindustan until they had sent hostages
for good behaviour, paid compensation for dis-
turbance, and blood-money at the rate of thirty-
six English pounds per head for every villager
that they might have slain. ' And ye know that
those lowland dogs will make oath that we have
slain scores. Will the Mullah pay the fines or
must we sell our guns ? ' A low growl ran round
the fires. ' Now, seeing that all this is the Mullah's
work, and that we have gained nothing but
promises of Paradise thereby, it is in my heart that
we of the Khusru Kheyl lack a shrine whereat to
pray. We are weakened, and henceforth how
shall we dare to cross into the Madar Kheyl border,
as has been our custom, to kneel to Pir Sajji's
tomb? The Madar men will fall upon us, and
rightly. But our Mullah is a holy man. He has
helped two score of us into Paradise this night.
Let him therefore accompany his flock, and we
will build over his body a dome of the blue tiles
of Mooltan, and burn lamps at his feet every
Friday night. He shall be a saint : we shall have
a shrine ; and there our women shall pray for fresh
seed to fill the gaps in our fighting-tale. How
think you ? '

A grim chuckle followed the suggestion, and

the soft *wheep*, *wheep* of unscabbarded knives followed the chuckle. It was an excellent notion, and met a long felt want of the tribe. The Mullah sprang to his feet, glaring with withered eyeballs at the drawn death he could not see, and calling down the curses of God and Mahomed on the tribe. Then began a game of blind man's buff round and between the fires, whereof Khuruk Shah, the tribal poet, has sung in verse that will not die.

They tickled him gently under the armpit with the knife-point. He leaped aside screaming, only to feel a cold blade drawn lightly over the back of his neck, or a rifle-muzzle rubbing his beard. He called on his adherents to aid him, but most of these lay dead on the plains, for Khoda Dad Khan had been at some pains to arrange their decease. Men described to him the glories of the shrine they would build, and the little children clapping their hands cried, 'Run, Mullah, run! There's a man behind you!' In the end, when the sport wearied, Khoda Dad Khan's brother sent a knife home between his ribs. 'Wherefore,' said Khoda Dad Khan with charming simplicity, 'I am now Chief of the Khusru Kheyl!' No man gainsaid him; and they all went to sleep very stiff and sore.

On the plain below Tommy Dodd was lecturing on the beauties of a cavalry charge by night, and Tallantire, bowed on his saddle, was gasping hysterically because there was a sword dangling from his wrist flecked with the blood of the Khusru Kheyl, the tribe that Orde had kept in leash so well. When a Rajpoot trooper pointed out that the skewbald's right ear had been taken off at the root by some blind slash of its unskilled rider, Tallantire broke down altogether, and laughed and sobbed till Tommy Dodd made him lie down and rest.

'We must wait about till the morning,' said he. 'I wired to the Colonel just before we left, to send a wing of the Beshaklis after us. He'll be furious with me for monopolising the fun, though. Those beggars in the hills won't give us any more trouble.'

'Then tell the Beshaklis to go on and see what has happened to Curbar on the canal. We must patrol the whole line of the Border. You're quite sure, Tommy, that—that stuff was—was only the skewbald's ear?'

'Oh, quite,' said Tommy. 'You just missed cutting off his head. *I* saw you when we went into the mess. Sleep, old man.'

Noon brought two squadrons of Beshaklis and a knot of furious brother officers demanding the court-martial of Tommy Dodd for 'spoiling the picnic,' and a gallop across country to the canal-works where Ferris, Curbar, and Hugonin were haranguing the terror-stricken coolies on the enormity of abandoning good work and high pay, merely because half a dozen of their fellows had been cut down. The sight of a troop of the Beshaklis restored wavering confidence, and the police-hunted section of the Khusru Kheyl had the joy of watching the canal-bank humming with life as usual, while such of their men as had taken refuge in the water-courses and ravines were being driven out by the troopers. By sundown began the remorseless patrol of the Border by police and trooper, most like the cow-boys' eternal ride round restless cattle.

'Now,' said Khoda Dad Khan to his fellows, pointing out a line of twinkling fires below, 'ye may see how far the old order changes. After their horse will come the little devil-guns that they can drag up to the tops of the hills, and, for aught I know, to the clouds when we crown the hills. If the tribe-council thinks good, I will go to Tallantire Sahib—who loves me—and see if I can stave off at least the blockade. Do I speak for the tribe?'

'Ay, speak for the tribe in God's name. How those accursed fires wink! Do the English send their troops on the wire—or is this the work of the Bengali?'

As Khoda Dad Khan went down the hill he was delayed by an interview with a hard-pressed tribesman, which caused him to return hastily for something he had forgotten. Then, handing himself over to the two troopers who had been chasing his friend, he claimed escort to Tallantire Sahib, then with Bullows at Jumala. The Border was safe, and the time for reasons in writing had begun.

'Thank Heaven,' said Bullows, 'that the trouble came at once. Of course we can never put down the reason in black and white, but all India will understand. And it is better to have a sharp short outbreak than five years of impotent administration inside the Border. It costs less.

Grish Chunder Dé has reported himself sick, and has been transferred to his own province without any sort of reprimand. He was strong on not having taken over the district.'

'Of course,' said Tallantire bitterly. 'Well, what am I supposed to have done that was wrong?'

'Oh, you will be told that you exceeded all your powers, and should have reported, and written, and advised for three weeks until the Khusru Kheyl could really come down in force. But I don't think the authorities will dare to make a fuss about it. They've had their lesson. Have you seen Curbar's version of the affair? He can't write a report, but he can speak the truth.'

'What's the use of the truth? He'd much better tear up the report. I'm sick and heartbroken over it all. It was so utterly unnecessary—except in that it rid us of that Babu.'

Entered unabashed Khoda Dad Khan, a stuffed forage-net in his hand, and the troopers behind him.

'May you never be tired!' said he cheerily. 'Well, Sahibs, that was a good fight, and Naim Shah's mother is in debt to you, Tallantire Sahib. A clean cut, they tell me, through jaw, wadded coat, and deep into the collarbone. Well done! But I speak for the tribe. There has been a fault —a great fault. Thou knowest that I and mine, Tallantire Sahib, kept the oath we sware to Orde Sahib on the banks of the Indus.'

'As an Afghan keeps his knife—sharp on one side, blunt on the other,' said Tallantire.

'The better swing in the blow, then. But I

speak God's truth. Only the Blind Mullah carried the young men on the tip of his tongue, and said that there was no more Border-law because a Bengali had been sent, and we need not fear the English at all. So they came down to avenge that insult and get plunder. Ye know what befell, and how far I helped. Now five score of us are dead or wounded, and we are all shamed and sorry, and desire no further war. Moreover, that ye may better listen to us, we have taken off the head of the Blind Mullah, whose evil counsels have led us to folly. I bring it for proof,'—and he heaved on the floor the head. ' He will give no more trouble, for *I* am chief now, and so I sit in a higher place at all audiences. Yet there is an offset to this head. That was another fault. One of the men found that black Bengali beast, through whom this trouble arose, wandering on horseback and weeping. Reflecting that he had caused loss of much good life, Alla Dad Khan, whom, if you choose, I will to-morrow shoot, whipped off this head, and I bring it to you to cover your shame, that ye may bury it. See, no man kept the spectacles, though they were of gold.'

Slowly rolled to Tallantire's feet the crop-haired head of a spectacled Bengali gentleman, open-eyed, open-mouthed—the head of Terror incarnate. Bullows bent down. 'Yet another blood-fine and a heavy one, Khoda Dad Khan, for this is the head of Debendra Nath, the man's brother. The Babu is safe long since. All but the fools of the Khusru Kheyl know that.'

'Well, I care not for carrion. Quick meat for

me. The thing was under our hills asking the road to Jumala, and Alla Dad Khan showed him the road to Jehannum, being, as thou sayest, but a fool. Remains now what the Government will do to us. As to the blockade——'

'Who art thou, seller of dog's flesh,' thundered Tallantire, 'to speak of terms and treaties? Get hence to the hills—go, and wait there starving, till it shall please the Government to call thy people out for punishment—children and fools that ye be! Count your dead, and be still. Rest assured that the Government will send you a *man!*'

'Ay,' returned Khoda Dad Khan, 'for we also be men.'

As he looked Tallantire between the eyes, he added, 'And by God, Sahib, mayest thou be that man!'

Without Benefit of Clergy

Before my Spring I garnered Autumn's gain,
Out of her time my field was white with grain,
    The year gave up her secrets to my woe.
Forced and deflowered each sick season lay,
In mystery of increase and decay ;
I saw the sunset ere men saw the day,
    Who am too wise in that I should not know.
                            Bitter Waters.

I

'But if it be a girl ? '

'Lord of my life, it cannot be. I have prayed
for so many nights, and sent gifts to Sheikh Badl's
shrine so often, that I know God will give us a
son—a man-child that shall grow into a man.
Think of this and be glad. My mother shall be
his mother till I can take him again, and the mullah
of the Pattan mosque shall cast his nativity—God
send he be born in an auspicious hour !—and then,
and then thou wilt never weary of me, thy slave.'

'Since when hast thou been a slave, my queen ? '

'Since the beginning—till this mercy came to
me. How could I be sure of thy love when I
knew that I had been bought with silver ? '

'Nay, that was the dowry. I paid it to thy
mother.'

'And she has buried it, and sits upon it all day long like a hen. What talk is yours of dower! I was bought as though I had been a Lucknow dancing-girl instead of a child.'

'Art thou sorry for the sale?'

'I have sorrowed; but to-day I am glad. Thou wilt never cease to love me now?—answer, my king.'

'Never—never. No.'

'Not even though the *mem-log*—the white women of thy own blood—love thee? And remember, I have watched them driving in the evening; they are very fair.'

'I have seen fire-balloons by the hundred. I have seen the moon, and—then I saw no more fire-balloons.'

Ameera clapped her hands and laughed. 'Very good talk,' she said. Then with an assumption of great stateliness, 'It is enough. Thou hast my permission to depart,—if thou wilt.'

The man did not move. He was sitting on a low red-lacquered couch in a room furnished only with a blue and white floor-cloth, some rugs, and a very complete collection of native cushions. At his feet sat a woman of sixteen, and she was all but all the world in his eyes. By every rule and law she should have been otherwise, for he was an Englishman, and she a Mussulman's daughter bought two years before from her mother, who, being left without money, would have sold Ameera shrieking to the Prince of Darkness if the price had been sufficient.

It was a contract entered into with a light

heart; but even before the girl had reached her bloom she came to fill the greater portion of John Holden's life. For her, and the withered hag her mother, he had taken a little house overlooking the great red-walled city, and found,—when the marigolds had sprung up by the well in the court-yard, and Ameera had established herself according to her own ideas of comfort, and her mother had ceased grumbling at the inadequacy of the cooking-places, the distance from the daily market, and at matters of house-keeping in general,—that the house was to him his home. Any one could enter his bachelor's bungalow by day or night, and the life that he led there was an unlovely one. In the house in the city his feet only could pass beyond the outer courtyard to the women's rooms; and when the big wooden gate was bolted behind him he was king in his own territory, with Ameera for queen. And there was going to be added to this kingdom a third person whose arrival Holden felt inclined to resent. It interfered with his perfect happiness. It disarranged the orderly peace of the house that was his own. But Ameera was wild with delight at the thought of it, and her mother not less so. The love of a man, and particularly a white man, was at the best an inconstant affair, but it might, both women argued, be held fast by a baby's hands. 'And then,' Ameera would always say, 'then he will never care for the white *mem-log*. I hate them all—I hate them all.'

'He will go back to his own people in time,' said the mother; 'but by the blessing of God that time is yet afar off.'

Holden sat silent on the couch thinking of the
future, and his thoughts were not pleasant. The
drawbacks of a double life are manifold. The
Government, with singular care, had ordered him
out of the station for a fortnight on special duty
in the place of a man who was watching by the
bedside of a sick wife. The verbal notification of
the transfer had been edged by a cheerful remark
that Holden ought to think himself lucky in being
a bachelor and a free man. He came to break the
news to Ameera.

'It is not good,' she said slowly, 'but it is not
all bad. There is my mother here, and no harm
will come to me—unless indeed I die of pure joy.
Go thou to thy work and think no troublesome
thoughts. When the days are done I believe . . .
nay, I am sure. And—and then I shall lay *him*
in thy arms, and thou wilt love me for ever. The
train goes to-night, at midnight, is it not ? Go
now, and do not let thy heart be heavy by cause
of me. But thou wilt not delay in returning ?
Thou wilt not stay on the road to talk to the bold
white *mem-log?* Come back to me swiftly, my life.'

As he left the courtyard to reach his horse that
was tethered to the gate-post, Holden spoke to
the white-haired old watchman who guarded the
house, and bade him under certain contingencies
despatch the filled-up telegraph-form that Holden
gave him. It was all that could be done, and
with the sensations of a man who has attended his
own funeral Holden went away by the night mail
to his exile. Every hour of the day he dreaded
the arrival of the telegram, and every hour of the

night he pictured to himself the death of Ameera. In consequence his work for the State was not of first-rate quality, nor was his temper towards his colleagues of the most amiable. The fortnight ended without a sign from his home, and, torn to pieces by his anxieties, Holden returned to be swallowed up for two precious hours by a dinner at the club, wherein he heard, as a man hears in a swoon, voices telling him how execrably he had performed the other man's duties, and how he had endeared himself to all his associates. Then he fled on horseback through the night with his heart in his mouth. There was no answer at first to his blows on the gate, and he had just wheeled his horse round to kick it in when Pir Khan appeared with a lantern and held his stirrup.

'Has aught occurred?' said Holden.

'The news does not come from my mouth, Protector of the Poor, but——' He held out his shaking hand as befitted the bearer of good news who is entitled to a reward.

Holden hurried through the courtyard. A light burned in the upper room. His horse neighed in the gateway, and he heard a shrill little wail that sent all the blood into the apple of his throat. It was a new voice, but it did not prove that Ameera was alive.

'Who is there?' he called up the narrow brick staircase.

There was a cry of delight from Ameera, and then the voice of the mother, tremulous with old age and pride—'We be two women and—the—man—thy—son.'

On the threshold of the room Holden stepped on a naked dagger, that was laid there to avert ill-luck, and it broke at the hilt under his impatient heel.

'God is great!' cooed Ameera in the half-light. 'Thou hast taken his misfortunes on thy head.'

'Ay, but how is it with thee, life of my life? Old woman, how is it with her?'

'She has forgotten her sufferings for joy that the child is born. There is no harm; but speak softly,' said the mother.

'It only needed thy presence to make me all well,' said Ameera. 'My king, thou hast been very long away. What gifts hast thou for me? Ah, ah! It is I that bring gifts this time. Look, my life, look. Was there ever such a babe? Nay, I am too weak even to clear my arm from him.'

'Rest then, and do not talk. I am here, *bachari* [little woman].'

'Well said, for there is a bond and a heel-rope [*peecharee*] between us now that nothing can break. Look—canst thou see in this light? He is without spot or blemish. Never was such a man-child. *Ya illah!* he shall be a pundit—no, a trooper of the Queen. And, my life, dost thou love me as well as ever, though I am faint and sick and worn? Answer truly.'

'Yea. I love as I have loved, with all my soul. Lie still, pearl, and rest.'

'Then do not go. Sit by my side here—so. Mother, the lord of this house needs a cushion. Bring it.' There was an almost imperceptible movement on the part of the new life that lay in the hollow of Ameera's arm. 'Aho!' she said, her voice breaking with love. 'The babe is a champion from his birth. He is kicking me in the side with mighty kicks. Was there ever such a babe! And he is ours to us—thine and mine. Put thy hand on his head, but carefully, for he is very young, and men are unskilled in such matters.'

Very cautiously Holden touched with the tips of his fingers the downy head.

'He is of the Faith,' said Ameera; 'for lying here in the night-watches I whispered the call to prayer and the profession of faith into his ears. And it is most marvellous that he was born upon a Friday, as I was born. Be careful of him, my life; but he can almost grip with his hands.'

Holden found one helpless little hand that closed feebly on his finger. And the clutch ran through his body till it settled about his heart. Till then his sole thought had been for Ameera. He began to realise that there was some one else in the world, but he could not feel that it was a veritable son with a soul. He sat down to think, and Ameera dozed lightly.

'Get hence, *sahib*,' said her mother under her breath. 'It is not good that she should find you here on waking. She must be still.'

'I go,' said Holden submissively. 'Here be rupees. See that my *baba* gets fat and finds all that he needs.'

The chink of the silver roused Ameera. 'I am his mother, and no hireling,' she said weakly.

'Shall I look to him more or less for the sake of money? Mother, give it back. I have borne my lord a son.'

The deep sleep of weakness came upon her almost before the sentence was completed. Holden went down to the courtyard very softly with his heart at ease. Pir Khan, the old watchman, was chuckling with delight. 'This house is now complete,' he said, and without further comment thrust into Holden's hands the hilt of a sabre worn many years ago when he, Pir Khan, served the Queen in the police. The bleat of a tethered goat came from the well-kerb.

'There be two,' said Pir Khan, 'two goats of the best. I bought them, and they cost much money; and since there is no birth-party assembled their flesh will be all mine. Strike craftily, *sahib!* 'Tis an ill-balanced sabre at the best. Wait till they raise their heads from cropping the marigolds.'

'And why?' said Holden, bewildered.

'For the birth-sacrifice. What else? Otherwise the child being unguarded from fate may die. The Protector of the Poor knows the fitting words to be said.'

Holden had learned them once with little thought that he would ever speak them in earnest. The touch of the cold sabre-hilt in his palm turned suddenly to the clinging grip of the child up-stairs —the child that was his own son—and a dread of loss filled him.

'Strike!' said Pir Khan. 'Never life came into the world but life was paid for it. See, the goats have raised their heads. Now! With a drawing cut!'

Hardly knowing what he did, Holden cut twice as he muttered the Mahomedan prayer that runs: 'Almighty! In place of this my son I offer life for life, blood for blood, head for head, bone for bone, hair for hair, skin for skin.' The waiting horse snorted and bounded in his pickets at the smell of the raw blood that spirted over Holden's riding-boots.

'Well smitten!' said Pir Khan wiping the sabre. 'A swordsman was lost in thee. Go with a light heart, Heaven-born. I am thy servant, and the servant of thy son. May the Presence live a thousand years and . . . the flesh of the goats is all mine?' Pir Khan drew back richer by a month's pay. Holden swung himself into the saddle and rode off through the low-hanging wood-smoke of the evening. He was full of riotous exultation, alternating with a vast vague tenderness directed towards no particular object, that made him choke as he bent over the neck of his uneasy horse. 'I never felt like this in my life,' he thought. 'I'll go to the club and pull myself together.'

A game of pool was beginning, and the room was full of men. Holden entered, eager to get to the light and the company of his fellows, singing at the top of his voice—

In Baltimore a-walking, a lady I did meet!

'Did you?' said the club-secretary from his corner. 'Did she happen to tell you that your boots were wringing wet ? Great goodness, man, it's blood ! '

' Bosh ! ' said Holden, picking his cue from the rack. ' May I cut in ? It's dew. I've been riding through high crops. My faith ! my boots are in a mess though !

> 'And if it be a girl she shall wear a wedding-ring,
> And if it be a boy he shall fight for his king,
> With his dirk, and his cap, and his little jacket blue,
> He shall walk the quarter-deck—'

' Yellow on blue—green next player,' said the marker monotonously.

' *He shall walk the quarter-deck*,—Am I green, marker ? *He shall walk the quarter-deck*,—eh ! that's a bad shot,—*As his daddy used to do !* '

' I don't see that you have anything to crow about,' said a zealous junior civilian acidly. ' The Government is not exactly pleased with your work when you relieved Sanders.'

' Does that mean a wigging from headquarters ? ' said Holden with an abstracted smile. ' I think I can stand it.'

The talk beat up round the ever-fresh subject of each man's work, and steadied Holden till it was time to go to his dark empty bungalow, where his butler received him as one who knew all his affairs. Holden remained awake for the greater part of the night, and his dreams were pleasant ones.

II

' How old is he now ? '

' *Ya illah !* What a man's question ! He is

all but six weeks old ; and on this night I go up
to the house-top with thee, my life, to count the
stars. For that is auspicious. And he was born
on a Friday under the sign of the Sun, and it has
been told to me that he will outlive us both and
get wealth. Can we wish for aught better, beloved ? '

'There is nothing better. Let us go up to the
roof, and thou shalt count the stars—but a few
only, for the sky is heavy with cloud.'

'The winter rains are late, and maybe they
come out of season. Come, before all the stars
are hid. I have put on my richest jewels.'

'Thou hast forgotten the best of all.'

' *Ai !* Ours. He comes also. He has never
yet seen the skies.'

Ameera climbed the narrow staircase that led
to the flat roof. The child, placid and unwinking,
lay in the hollow of her right arm, gorgeous in
silver-fringed muslin with a small skull-cap on
his head. Ameera wore all that she valued most.
The diamond nose-stud that takes the place of
the Western patch in drawing attention to the
curve of the nostril, the gold ornament in the
centre of the forehead studded with tallow-drop
emeralds and flawed rubies, the heavy circlet of
beaten gold that was fastened round her neck by
the softness of the pure metal, and the chinking
curb-patterned silver anklets hanging low over the
rosy ankle-bone. She was dressed in jade-green
muslin as befitted a daughter of the Faith, and
from shoulder to elbow and elbow to wrist ran
bracelets of silver tied with floss silk, frail glass

bangles slipped over the wrist in proof of the slenderness of the hand, and certain heavy gold bracelets that had no part in her country's ornaments, but, since they were Holden's gift and fastened with a cunning European snap, delighted her immensely.

They sat down by the low white parapet of the roof, overlooking the city and its lights.

'They are happy down there,' said Ameera. 'But I do not think that they are as happy as we. Nor do I think the white *mem-log* are as happy. And thou?'

'I know they are not.'

'How dost thou know?'

'They give their children over to the nurses.'

'I have never seen that,' said Ameera with a sigh, 'nor do I wish to see. *Ahi!*'—she dropped her head on Holden's shoulder,—'I have counted forty stars, and I am tired. Look at the child, love of my life, he is counting too.'

The baby was staring with round eyes at the dark of the heavens. Ameera placed him in Holden's arms, and he lay there without a cry.

'What shall we call him among ourselves?' she said. 'Look! Art thou ever tired of looking? He carries thy very eyes. But the mouth——'

'Is thine, most dear. Who should know better than I?'

''Tis such a feeble mouth. Oh, so small! And yet it holds my heart between its lips. Give him to me now. He has been too long away.'

'Nay, let him lie; he has not yet begun to cry.'

'When he cries thou wilt give him back—eh? What a man of mankind thou art! If he cried he were only the dearer to me. But, my life, what little name shall we give him?'

The small body lay close to Holden's heart. It was utterly helpless and very soft. He scarcely dared to breathe for fear of crushing it. The caged green parrot that is regarded as a sort of guardian-spirit in most native households moved on its perch and fluttered a drowsy wing.

'There is the answer,' said Holden. 'Mian Mittu has spoken. He shall be The Parrot. When he is ready he will talk mightily and run about. Mian Mittu is The Parrot in thy—in the Mussulman tongue, is it not?'

'Why put me so far off?' said Ameera fretfully. 'Let it be like unto some English name—but not wholly. For he is mine.'

'Then call him Tota, for that is likest English.'

'Ay, Tota, and that is still The Parrot. Forgive me, my lord, for a minute ago, but in truth he is too little to wear all the weight of Mian Mittu for name. He shall be Tota—our Tota to us. Hearest thou, oh, small one? Littlest, thou art Tota.' She touched the child's cheek, and he waking wailed, and it was necessary to return him to his mother, who soothed him with the wonderful rhyme of *Aré koko, Jaré koko!* which says—

'Oh, crow! Go, crow! Baby's sleeping sound,
And the wild plums grow in the jungle, only a penny a pound.
Only a penny a pound, *baba*, only a penny a pound.'

Reassured many times as to the price of those

plums, Tota cuddled himself down to sleep. The two sleek, white well-bullocks in the courtyard were steadily chewing the cud of their evening meal; old Pir Khan squatted at the head of Holden's horse, his police sabre across his knees, pulling drowsily at a big water-pipe that croaked like a bull-frog in a pond. Ameera's mother sat spinning in the lower verandah, and the wooden gate was shut and barred. The music of a marriage-procession came to the roof above the gentle hum of the city, and a string of flying-foxes crossed the face of the low moon.

'I have prayed,' said Ameera after a long pause, 'I have prayed for two things. First, that I may die in thy stead if thy death is demanded, and in the second, that I may die in the place of the child. I have prayed to the Prophet and to Beebee Miriam [the Virgin Mary]. Thinkest thou either will hear?'

'From thy lips who would not hear the lightest word?'

'I asked for straight talk, and thou hast given me sweet talk. Will my prayers be heard?'

'How can I say? God is very good.'

'Of that I am not sure. Listen now. When I die, or the child dies, what is thy fate? Living, thou wilt return to the bold white *mem-log*, for kind calls to kind.'

'Not always.'

'With a woman, no; with a man it is otherwise. Thou wilt in this life, later on, go back to thine own folk. That I could almost endure, for I should be dead. But in thy very death thou wilt be taken away to a strange place and a paradise that I do not know.'

'Will it be paradise?'

'Surely, for who would harm thee? But we two—I and the child—shall be elsewhere, and we cannot come to thee, nor canst thou come to us. In the old days, before the child was born, I did not think of these things; but now I think of them always. It is very hard talk.'

'It will fall as it will fall. To-morrow we do not know, but to-day and love we know well. Surely we are happy now.'

'So happy that it were well to make our happiness assured. And thy Beebee Miriam should listen to me ; for she is also a woman. But then she would envy me ! It is not seemly for men to worship a woman.'

Holden laughed aloud at Ameera's little spasm of jealousy.

'Is it not seemly ? Why didst thou not turn me from worship of thee, then ?'

'Thou a worshipper ! And of me? My king, for all thy sweet words, well I know that I am thy servant and thy slave, and the dust under thy feet. And I would not have it otherwise. See !'

Before Holden could prevent her she stooped forward and touched his feet ; recovering herself with a little laugh she hugged Tota closer to her bosom. Then, almost savagely—

'Is it true that the bold white *mem-log* live for three times the length of my life ? Is it true that they make their marriages not before they are old women ?'

'They marry as do others—when they are women.'

'That I know, but they wed when they are twenty-five. Is that true?'

'That is true.'

'*Ya illah!* At twenty-five! Who would of his own will take a wife even of eighteen? She is a woman—aging every hour. Twenty-five! I shall be an old woman at that age, and—— Those *mem-log* remain young for ever. How I hate them!'

'What have they to do with us?'

'I cannot tell. I know only that there may now be alive on this earth a woman ten years older than I who may come to thee and take thy love ten years after I am an old woman, gray-headed, and the nurse of Tota's son. That is unjust and evil. They should die too.'

'Now, for all thy years thou art a child, and shalt be picked up and carried down the staircase.'

'Tota! Have a care for Tota, my lord! Thou at least art as foolish as any babe!' Ameera tucked Tota out of harm's way in the hollow of her neck, and was carried downstairs laughing in Holden's arms, while Tota opened his eyes and smiled after the manner of the lesser angels.

He was a silent infant, and, almost before Holden could realise that he was in the world, developed into a small gold-coloured little god and unquestioned despot of the house overlooking the city. Those were months of absolute happiness to Holden and Ameera—happiness withdrawn from the world, shut in behind the wooden gate that Pir Khan guarded. By day Holden did his work with an immense pity for such as were not so fortunate as himself, and a sympathy for small children that amazed and amused many mothers at the little station-gatherings. At nightfall he returned to Ameera,—Ameera, full of the wondrous doings of Tota; how he had been seen to clap his hands together and move his fingers with intention and purpose—which was manifestly a miracle—how later, he had of his own initiative crawled out of his low bedstead on to the floor and swayed on both feet for the space of three breaths.

'And they were long breaths, for my heart stood still with delight,' said Ameera.

Then Tota took the beasts into his councils— the well-bullocks, the little gray squirrels, the mongoose that lived in a hole near the well, and especially Mian Mittu, the parrot, whose tail he grievously pulled, and Mian Mittu screamed till Ameera and Holden arrived.

'Oh, villain! Child of strength! This to thy brother on the house-top! *Tobah, tobah!* Fie! Fie! But I know a charm to make him wise as Suleiman and Aflatoun [Solomon and Plato]. Now look,' said Ameera. She drew from an embroidered bag a handful of almonds. 'See! we count seven. In the name of God!'

She placed Mian Mittu, very angry and rumpled, on the top of his cage, and seating herself between the babe and the bird she cracked and peeled an almond less white than her teeth. 'This is a true charm, my life, and do not laugh. See! I give the parrot one-half and Tota the other.' **Mian Mittu** with careful beak took his share from between Ameera's lips, and she kissed the other half into the mouth of the child, who ate it slowly with wondering eyes. ' This I will do each day of seven, and without doubt he who is ours will be a bold speaker and wise. Eh, Tota, what wilt thou be when thou art a man and I am gray-headed ? ' Tota tucked his fat legs into adorable creases. He could crawl, but he was not going to waste the spring of his youth in idle speech. He wanted Mian Mittu's tail to tweak.

When he was advanced to the dignity of a silver belt—which, with a magic square engraved on silver and hung round his neck, made up the greater part of his clothing—he staggered on a perilous journey down the garden to Pir Khan, and proffered him all his jewels in exchange for one little ride on Holden's horse, having seen his mother's mother chaffering with pedlars in the verandah. Pir Khan wept and set the untried feet on his own gray head in sign of fealty, and brought the bold adventurer to his mother's arms, vowing that Tota would be a leader of men ere his beard was grown.

One hot evening, while he sat on the roof between his father and mother watching the never-ending warfare of the kites that the city boys flew, he demanded a kite of his own with Pir Khan to fly it, because he had a fear of dealing with any-thing larger than himself, and when Holden called him a ' spark,' he rose to his feet and answered slowly in defence of his new-found individuality,

'*Hum 'park nahin hai.   Hum admi hai* [I am no spark, but a man.]'

The protest made Holden choke and devote himself very seriously to a consideration of Tota's future. He need hardly have taken the trouble. The delight of that life was too perfect to endure. Therefore it was taken away as many things are taken away in India—suddenly and without warning. The little lord of the house, as Pir Khan called him, grew sorrowful and complained of pains who had never known the meaning of pain. Ameera, wild with terror, watched him through the night, and in the dawning of the second day the life was shaken out of him by fever—the seasonal autumn fever. It seemed altogether impossible that he could die, and neither Ameera nor Holden at first believed the evidence of the little body on the bedstead. Then Ameera beat her head against the wall and would have flung herself down the well in the garden had Holden not restrained her by main force.

One mercy only was granted to Holden. He rode to his office in broad daylight and found waiting him an unusually heavy mail that demanded concentrated attention and hard work. He was not, however, alive to this kindness of the gods.

III

The first shock of a bullet is no more than a brisk pinch. The wrecked body does not send in its protest to the soul till ten or fifteen seconds later. Holden realised his pain slowly, exactly as

he had realised his happiness, and with the same
imperious necessity for hiding all trace of it.   In
the beginning he only felt that there had been a
loss, and that Ameera needed comforting, where
she sat with her head on her knees shivering as
Mian Mittu from the house-top called, *Tota!
Tota! Tota!*   Later all his world and the daily
life of it rose up to hurt him.   It was an outrage
that any one of the children at the band-stand in
the evening should be alive and clamorous, when
his own child lay dead.   It was more than mere
pain when one of them touched him, and stories
told by over-fond fathers of their children's latest
performances cut him to the quick.   He could
not declare his pain.   He had neither help, comfort,
nor sympathy ; and Ameera at the end of each
weary day would lead him through the hell of self-
questioning reproach which is reserved for those
who have lost a child, and believe that with a little
—just a little more care—it might have been saved.

   'Perhaps,' Ameera would say, 'I did not take
sufficient heed.   Did I, or did I not ?   The sun
on the roof that day when he played so long alone
and I was—*ahi!* braiding my hair—it may be that
the sun then bred the fever.   If I had warned him
from the sun he might have lived.   But, oh, my
life, say that I am guiltless!   Thou knowest that
I loved him as I love thee.   Say that there is no
blame on me, or I shall die—I shall die!'

   'There is no blame,—before God, none.   It
was written, and how could we do aught to save?
What has been, has been.   Let it go, beloved.'

   'He was all my heart to me.   How can I let

the thought go when my arm tells me every night that he is not here? *Ahi! Ahi!* Oh, Tota, come back to me—come back again, and let us be all together as it was before!'

'Peace, peace! For thine own sake, and for mine also, if thou lovest me—rest.'

'By this I know thou dost not care; and how shouldst thou? The white men have hearts of stone and souls of iron. Oh, that I had married a man of mine own people—though he beat me—and had never eaten the bread of an alien!'

'Am I an alien—mother of my son?'

'What else—*Sahib?* . . . Oh, forgive me—forgive! The death has driven me mad. Thou art the life of my heart, and the light of my eyes, and the breath of my life, and—and I have put thee from me, though it was but for a moment. If thou goest away, to whom shall I look for help? Do not be angry. Indeed, it was the pain that spoke and not thy slave.'

'I know, I know. We be two who were three. The greater need therefore that we should be one.'

They were sitting on the roof as of custom. The night was a warm one in early spring, and sheet-lightning was dancing on the horizon to a broken tune played by far-off thunder. Ameera settled herself in Holden's arms.

'The dry earth is lowing like a cow for the rain, and I—I am afraid. It was not like this when we counted the stars. But thou lovest me as much as before, though a bond is taken away? Answer!'

'I love more because a new bond has come out

of the sorrow that we have eaten together, and that thou knowest.'

'Yea, I knew,' said Ameera in a very small whisper. 'But it is good to hear thee say so, my life, who art so strong to help. I will be a child no more, but a woman and an aid to thee. Listen! Give me my *sitar* and I will sing bravely.'

She took the light silver-studded *sitar* and began a song of the great hero Rajah Rasalu. The hand failed on the strings, the tune halted, checked, and at a low note turned off to the poor little nursery-rhyme about the wicked crow—

'And the wild plums grow in the jungle, only a penny a pound.
　Only a penny a pound, *baba*—only . . .'

Then came the tears, and the piteous rebellion against fate till she slept, moaning a little in her sleep, with the right arm thrown clear of the body as though it protected something that was not there. It was after this night that life became a little easier for Holden. The ever-present pain of loss drove him into his work, and the work repaid him by filling up his mind for nine or ten hours a day. Ameera sat alone in the house and brooded, but grew happier when she understood that Holden was more at ease, according to the custom of women. They touched happiness again, but this time with caution.

'It was because we loved Tota that he died. The jealousy of God was upon us,' said Ameera. 'I have hung up a large black jar before our window to turn the evil eye from us, and we must make no protestations of delight, but go softly underneath the stars, lest God find us out. Is that not good talk, worthless one?'

She had shifted the accent on the word that means 'beloved,' in proof of the sincerity of her purpose. But the kiss that followed the new christening was a thing that any deity might have envied. They went about henceforward saying, 'It is naught, it is naught;' and hoping that all the Powers heard.

The Powers were busy on other things. They had allowed thirty million people four years of plenty, wherein men fed well and the crops were certain, and the birth-rate rose year by year; the districts reported a purely agricultural population varying from nine hundred to two thousand to the square mile of the overburdened earth; and the Member for Lower Tooting, wandering about India in top-hat and frock-coat, talked largely of the benefits of British rule, and suggested as the one thing needful the establishment of a duly qualified electoral system and a general bestowal of the franchise. His long-suffering hosts smiled and made him welcome, and when he paused to admire, with pretty picked words, the blossom of the blood-red *dhak*-tree that had flowered untimely for a sign of what was coming, they smiled more than ever.

It was the Deputy Commissioner of Kot-Kumharsen, staying at the club for a day, who lightly told a tale that made Holden's blood run cold as he overheard the end.

'He won't bother any one any more. Never saw a man so astonished in my life. By Jove, I thought he meant to ask a question in the House about it. Fellow-passenger in his ship—dined next him—bowled over by cholera and died in eighteen hours. You needn't laugh, you fellows. The Member for Lower Tooting is awfully angry about it; but he's more scared. I think he's going to take his enlightened self out of India.'

'I'd give a good deal if he were knocked over. It might keep a few vestrymen of his kidney to their own parish. But what's this about cholera? It's full early for anything of that kind,' said the warden of an unprofitable salt-lick.

'Don't know,' said the Deputy Commissioner reflectively. 'We've got locusts with us. There's sporadic cholera all along the north—at least we're calling it sporadic for decency's sake. The spring crops are short in five districts, and nobody seems to know where the rains are. It's nearly March now. I don't want to scare anybody, but it seems to me that Nature's going to audit her accounts with a big red pencil this summer.'

'Just when I wanted to take leave, too!' said a voice across the room.

'There won't be much leave this year, but there ought to be a great deal of promotion. I've come in to persuade the Government to put my pet canal on the list of famine-relief works. It's an ill-wind that blows no good. I shall get that canal finished at last.'

'Is it the old programme then,' said Holden; 'famine, fever, and cholera?'

'Oh no. Only local scarcity and an unusual prevalence of seasonal sickness. You'll find it all in the reports if you live till next year. You're a lucky chap. *You* haven't got a wife to send out of harm's way. The hill-stations ought to be full of women this year.'

' I think you're inclined to exaggerate the talk in the *bazars*,' said a young civilian in the Secretariat. ' Now I have observed——'

' I daresay you have,' said the Deputy Commissioner, ' but you've a great deal more to observe, my son. In the meantime, I wish to observe to you——' and he drew him aside to discuss the construction of the canal that was so dear to his heart. Holden went to his bungalow and began to understand that he was not alone in the world, and also that he was afraid for the sake of another, —which is the most soul-satisfying fear known to man.

Two months later, as the Deputy had foretold, Nature began to audit her accounts with a red pencil. On the heels of the spring-reapings came a cry for bread, and the Government, which had decreed that no man should die of want, sent wheat. Then came the cholera from all four quarters of the compass. It struck a pilgrim-gathering of half a million at a sacred shrine. Many died at the feet of their god ; the others broke and ran over the face of the land carrying the pestilence with them. It smote a walled city and killed two hundred a day. The people crowded the trains, hanging on to the footboards and squatting on the roofs of the carriages, and the cholera followed them, for

at each station they dragged out the dead and the
dying. They died by the roadside, and the horses
of the Englishmen shied at the corpses in the grass.
The rains did not come, and the earth turned to
iron lest man should escape death by hiding in her.
The English sent their wives away to the hills
and went about their work, coming forward as
they were bidden to fill the gaps in the fighting-
line. Holden, sick with fear of losing his chiefest
treasure on earth, had done his best to persuade
Ameera to go away with her mother to the
Himalayas.

'Why should I go?' said she, one evening on
the roof.

'There is sickness, and people are dying, and
all the white *mem-log* have gone.'

'All of them?'

'All—unless perhaps there remain some old
scald-head who vexes her husband's heart by
running risk of death.'

'Nay; who stays is my sister, and thou must
not abuse her, for I will be a scald-head too. I
am glad all the bold *mem-log* are gone.'

'Do I speak to a woman or a babe? Go to
the hills, and I will see to it that thou goest like
a queen's daughter. Think, child. In a red-
lacquered bullock cart, veiled and curtained, with
brass peacocks upon the pole and red cloth hang-
ings. I will send two orderlies for guard and——'

'Peace! Thou art the babe in speaking thus.
What use are those toys to me? *He* would have
patted the bullocks and played with the housings.
For his sake, perhaps,—thou hast made me very

English—I might have gone. Now, I will not. Let the *mem-log* run.'

'Their husbands are sending them, beloved.'

'Very good talk. Since when hast thou been my husband to tell me what to do? I have but borne thee a son. Thou art only all the desire of my soul to me. How shall I depart when I know that if evil befall thee by the breadth of so much as my littlest finger-nail—is that not small?—I should be aware of it though I were in paradise. And here, this summer thou mayest die—*ai, janee*, die! and in dying they might call to tend thee a white woman, and she would rob me in the last of thy love!'

'But love is not born in a moment or on a death-bed!'

'What dost thou know of love, stoneheart? She would take thy thanks at least and, by God and the Prophet and Beebee Miriam the mother of thy Prophet, that I will never endure. My lord and my love, let there be no more foolish talk of going away. Where thou art, I am. It is enough.' She put an arm round his neck and a hand on his mouth.

There are not many happinesses so complete as those that are snatched under the shadow of the sword. They sat together and laughed, calling each other openly by every pet name that could move the wrath of the gods. The city below them was locked up in its own torments. Sulphur fires blazed in the streets; the conches in the Hindu temples screamed and bellowed, for the gods were inattentive in those days. There was a service in the great Mahomedan shrine, and the call to prayer from the minarets was almost unceasing. They heard the wailing in the houses of the dead, and once the shriek of a mother who had lost a child and was calling for its return. In the gray dawn they saw the dead borne out through the city gates, each litter with its own little knot of mourners. Wherefore they kissed each other and shivered.

It was a red and heavy audit, for the land was very sick and needed a little breathing-space ere the torrent of cheap life should flood it anew. The children of immature fathers and undeveloped mothers made no resistance. They were cowed and sat still, waiting till the sword should be sheathed in November if it were so willed. There were gaps among the English, but the gaps were filled. The work of superintending famine-relief, cholera-sheds, medicine-distribution, and what little sanitation was possible, went forward because it was so ordered.

Holden had been told to keep himself in readiness to move to replace the next man who should fall. There were twelve hours in each day when he could not see Ameera, and she might die in three. He was considering what his pain would be if he could not see her for three months, or if she died out of his sight. He was absolutely certain that her death would be demanded—so certain, that when he looked up from the telegram and saw Pir Khan breathless in the doorway, he laughed aloud. 'And ?' said he,——

'When there is a cry in the night and the

spirit flutters into the throat, who has a charm that will restore? Come swiftly, Heaven-born! It is the black cholera.'

Holden galloped to his home. The sky was heavy with clouds, for the long-deferred rains were near and the heat was stifling. Ameera's mother met him in the courtyard, whimpering, 'She is dying. She is nursing herself into death. She is all but dead. What shall I do, *sahib*?'

Ameera was lying in the room in which Tota had been born. She made no sign when Holden entered, because the human soul is a very lonely thing and, when it is getting ready to go away, hides itself in a misty borderland where the living may not follow. The black cholera does its work quietly and without explanation. Ameera was being thrust out of life as though the Angel of Death had himself put his hand upon her. The quick breathing seemed to show that she was either afraid or in pain, but neither eyes nor mouth gave any answer to Holden's kisses. There was nothing to be said or done. Holden could only wait and suffer. The first drops of the rain began to fall on the roof and he could hear shouts of joy in the parched city.

The soul came back a little and the lips moved. Holden bent down to listen. 'Keep nothing of mine,' said Ameera. 'Take no hair from my head. *She* would make thee burn it later on. That flame I should feel. Lower! Stoop lower! Remember only that I was thine and bore thee a son. Though thou wed a white woman to-morrow, the pleasure of receiving in thy arms thy first son

is taken from thee for ever. Remember me when
thy son is born—the one that shall carry thy name
before all men. His misfortunes be on my head.
I bear witness—I bear witness'—the lips were
forming the words on his ear—'that there is no
God but—thee, beloved!'

Then she died. Holden sat still, and all
thought was taken from him,—till he heard
Ameera's mother lift the curtain.

'Is she dead, *sahib*?'

'She is dead.'

'Then I will mourn, and afterwards take an
inventory of the furniture in this house. For that
will be mine. The *sahib* does not mean to resume
it? It is so little, so very little, *sahib*, and I am
an old woman. I would like to lie softly.'

'For the mercy of God be silent a while. Go
out and mourn where I cannot hear.'

'*Sahib*, she will be buried in four hours.'

'I know the custom. I shall go ere she is
taken away. That matter is in thy hands. Look
to it that the bed on which—on which she
lies——'

'Aha! That beautiful red-lacquered bed. I
have long desired——'

'That the bed is left here untouched for my
disposal. All else in the house is thine. Hire a
cart, take everything, go hence, and before sun-
rise let there be nothing in this house but that
which I have ordered thee to respect.'

'I am an old woman. I would stay at least
for the days of mourning, and the rains have just
broken. Whither shall I go?'

'What is that to me? My order is that there is a going. The house-gear is worth a thousand rupees and my orderly shall bring thee a hundred rupees to-night.'

'That is very little. Think of the cart-hire.'

'It shall be nothing unless thou goest, and with speed. O woman, get hence and leave me with my dead!'

The mother shuffled down the staircase, and in her anxiety to take stock of the house-fittings forgot to mourn. Holden stayed by Ameera's side and the rain roared on the roof. He could not think connectedly by reason of the noise, though he made many attempts to do so. Then four sheeted ghosts glided dripping into the room and stared at him through their veils. They were the washers of the dead. Holden left the room and went out to his horse. He had come in a dead, stifling calm through ankle-deep dust. He found the courtyard a rain-lashed pond alive with frogs; a torrent of yellow water ran under the gate, and a roaring wind drove the bolts of the rain like buckshot against the mud-walls. Pir Khan was shivering in his little hut by the gate, and the horse was stamping uneasily in the water.

'I have been told the *sahib's* order,' said Pir Khan. 'It is well. This house is now desolate. I go also, for my monkey-face would be a re-minder of that which has been. Concerning the bed, I will bring that to thy house yonder in the morning; but remember, *sahib*, it will be to thee

a knife turning in a green wound. I go upon
a pilgrimage, and I will take no money. I have
grown fat in the protection of the Presence whose
sorrow is my sorrow. For the last time I hold
his stirrup.'

He touched Holden's foot with both hands and
the horse sprang out into the road, where the
creaking bamboos were whipping the sky and all
the frogs were chuckling. Holden could not see
for the rain in his face. He put his hands before
his eyes and muttered—

'Oh, you brute! You utter brute!'

The news of his trouble was already in his
bungalow. He read the knowledge in his butler's
eyes when Ahmed Khan brought in food, and for
the first and last time in his life laid a hand upon
his master's shoulder, saying, 'Eat, *sahib*, eat.
Meat is good against sorrow. I also have known.
Moreover the shadows come and go, *sahib*;
the shadows come and go. These be curried
eggs.'

Holden could neither eat nor sleep. The
heavens sent down eight inches of rain in that
night and washed the earth clean. The waters
tore down walls, broke roads, and scoured open
the shallow graves on the Mahomedan burying-
ground. All next day it rained, and Holden sat
still in his house considering his sorrow. On the
morning of the third day he received a telegram
which said only, 'Ricketts, Myndonie. Dying.
Holden relieve. Immediate.' Then he thought
that before he departed he would look at the
house wherein he had been master and lord.

There was a break in the weather, and the rank earth steamed with vapour.

He found that the rains had torn down the mud pillars of the gateway, and the heavy wooden gate that had guarded his life hung lazily from one hinge. There was grass three inches high in the courtyard; Pir Khan's lodge was empty, and the sodden thatch sagged between the beams. A gray squirrel was in possession of the verandah, as if the house had been untenanted for thirty years instead of three days. Ameera's mother had removed everything except some mildewed matting. The *tick-tick* of the little scorpions as they hurried across the floor was the only sound in the house. Ameera's room and the other one where Tota had lived were heavy with mildew; and the narrow staircase leading to the roof was streaked and stained with rain-borne mud. Holden saw all these things, and came out again to meet in the road Durga Dass, his landlord,—portly, affable, clothed in white muslin, and driving a Cee-spring buggy. He was overlooking his property to see how the roofs stood the stress of the first rains.

'I have heard,' said he, 'you will not take this place any more, *sahib* ?'

'What are you going to do with it ?'

'Perhaps I shall let it again.'

'Then I will keep it on while I am away.'

Durga Dass was silent for some time. 'You shall not take it on, *sahib*,' he said. 'When I was a young man I also——, but to-day I am a member of the Municipality. Ho! Ho! No. When the birds have gone what need to keep the nest ? I will have it pulled down—the timber will sell for something always. It shall be pulled down, and the Municipality shall make a road across, as they desire, from the burning-ghaut to the city wall, so that no man may say where this house stood.'

At the End of the Passage

The sky is lead and our faces are red,
    And the gates of Hell are opened and riven,
    And the winds of Hell are loosened and driven,
And the dust flies up in the face of Heaven,
    And the clouds come down in a fiery sheet,
Heavy to raise and hard to be borne.
    And the soul of man is turned from his meat,
Turned from the trifles for which he has striven
      Sick in his body, and heavy-hearted,
    And his soul flies up like the dust in the street,
      Breaks from his flesh and is gone and departed,
As the blasts they blow on the cholera-horn.

Himalayan.

FOUR men, each entitled to 'life, liberty, and the pursuit of happiness,' sat at a table playing whist. The thermometer marked—for them—one hundred and one degrees of heat. The room was darkened till it was only just possible to distinguish the pips of the cards and the very white faces of the players. A tattered, rotten punkah of whitewashed calico was puddling the hot air and whining dolefully at each stroke. Outside lay gloom of a November day in London. There was neither sky, sun, nor horizon,—nothing but a brown purple haze of heat. It was as though the earth were dying of apoplexy.

From time to time clouds of tawny dust rose from the ground without wind or warning, flung themselves tablecloth-wise among the tops of the parched trees, and came down again. Then a whirling dust-devil would scutter across the plain for a couple of miles, break, and fall outward, though there was nothing to check its flight save a long low line of piled railway-sleepers white with the dust, a cluster of huts made of mud, condemned rails, and canvas, and the one squat four-roomed bungalow that belonged to the assistant engineer in charge of a section of the Gaudhari State line then under construction.

The four, stripped to the thinnest of sleeping-suits, played whist crossly, with wranglings as to leads and returns. It was not the best kind of whist, but they had taken some trouble to arrive at it. Mottram of the Indian Survey had ridden thirty and railed one hundred miles from his lonely post in the desert since the night before ; Lowndes of the Civil Service, on special duty in the political department, had come as far to escape for an instant the miserable intrigues of an impoverished native State whose king alternately fawned and blustered for more money from the pitiful revenues contributed by hard-wrung peasants and despairing camel-breeders ; Spurstow, the doctor of the line, had left a cholera-stricken camp of coolies to look after itself for forty-eight hours while he associated with white men once more. Hummil, the assistant engineer, was the host. He stood fast and received his friends thus every Sunday if they could come in. When one of them failed to appear, he would send a telegram to his last address, in order that he might know whether the defaulter were dead or alive. There are very many places in the East where it is not good or kind to let your acquaintances drop out of sight even for one short week.

The players were not conscious of any special regard for each other. They squabbled whenever they met ; but they ardently desired to meet, as men without water desire to drink. They were lonely folk who understood the dread meaning of loneliness. They were all under thirty years of age,—which is too soon for any man to possess that knowledge.

' Pilsener ? ' said Spurstow, after the second rubber, mopping his forehead.

' Beer's out, I'm sorry to say, and there's hardly enough soda-water for to-night,' said Hummil.

' What filthy bad management ! ' Spurstow snarled.

' Can't help it. I've written and wired ; but the trains don't come through regularly yet. Last week the ice ran out,—as Lowndes knows.'

' Glad I didn't come. I could ha' sent you some if I had known, though. Phew ! it's too hot to go on playing bumblepuppy.' This with a savage scowl at Lowndes, who only laughed. He was a hardened offender.

Mottram rose from the table and looked out of a chink in the shutters.

' What a sweet day ! ' said he.

The company yawned all together and betook themselves to an aimless investigation of all Hummil's possessions,—guns, tattered novels, saddlery, spurs, and the like. They had fingered them a score of times before, but there was really nothing else to do.

' Got anything fresh ? ' said Lowndes.

' Last week's *Gazette of India*, and a cutting from a home paper. My father sent it out. It's rather amusing.'

' One of those vestrymen that call 'emselves M.P.'s again, is it ? ' said Spurstow, who read his newspapers when he could get them.

' Yes. Listen to this. It's to your address, Lowndes. The man was making a speech to his constituents, and he piled it on. Here's a sample, " And I assert unhesitatingly that the Civil Service in India is the preserve—the pet preserve—of the aristocracy of England. What does the democracy —what do the masses—get from that country, which we have step by step fraudulently annexed ? I answer, nothing whatever. It is farmed with a single eye to their own interests by the scions of the aristocracy. They take good care to maintain their lavish scale of incomes, to avoid or stifle any inquiries into the nature and conduct of their administration, while they themselves force the unhappy peasant to pay with the sweat of his brow for all the luxuries in which they are lapped." ' Hummil waved the cutting above his head. ' 'Ear! 'ear ! ' said his audience.

Then Lowndes, meditatively, ' I'd give—I'd give three months' pay to have that gentleman spend one month with me and see how the free and independent native prince works things. Old Timbersides '—this was his flippant title for an honoured and decorated feudatory prince—'has been wearing my life out this week past for money. By Jove, his latest performance was to send me one of his women as a bribe!'

'Good for you! Did you accept it?' said Mottram.

'No. I rather wish I had, now. She was a pretty little person, and she yarned away to me about the horrible destitution among the king's women-folk. The darlings haven't had any new clothes for nearly a month, and the old man wants to buy a new drag from Calcutta,—solid silver railings and silver lamps, and trifles of that kind. I've tried to make him understand that he has played the deuce with the revenues for the last twenty years and must go slow. He can't see it.'

'But he has the ancestral treasure-vaults to draw on. There must be three millions at least in jewels and coin under his palace,' said Hummil.

'Catch a native king disturbing the family treasure! The priests forbid it except as the last resort. Old Timbersides has added something like a quarter of a million to the deposit in his reign.'

'Where the mischief does it all come from?' said Mottram.

'The country. The state of the people is enough to make you sick. I've known the tax-men wait by a milch-camel till the foal was born and then hurry off the mother for arrears. And what can I do? I can't get the court clerks to give me any accounts; I can't raise anything more than a fat smile from the commander-in-chief when I find out the troops are three months in arrears; and old Timbersides begins to weep when I speak to him. He has taken to the King's Peg heavily,—liqueur brandy for whisky, and Heidsieck for soda-water.'

'That's what the Rao of Jubela took to. Even a native can't last long at that,' said Spurstow. 'He'll go out.'

'And a good thing, too. Then I suppose we'll have a council of regency, and a tutor for the young prince, and hand him back his kingdom with ten years' accumulations.'

'Whereupon that young prince, having been taught all the vices of the English, will play ducks and drakes with the money and undo ten years' work in eighteen months. I've seen that business before,' said Spurstow. 'I should tackle the king with a light hand if I were you, Lowndes. They'll hate you quite enough under any circumstances.'

'That's all very well. The man who looks on can talk about the light hand; but you can't clean a pig-stye with a pen dipped in rose-water. I know my risks; but nothing has happened yet. My servant's an old Pathan, and he cooks for me. They are hardly likely to bribe him, and I don't accept food from my true friends, as they call themselves. Oh, but it's weary work! I'd sooner be with you, Spurstow. There's shooting near your camp.'

'Would you? I don't think it. About fifteen deaths a day don't incite a man to shoot anything but himself. And the worst of it is that the poor devils look at you as though you ought to save them. Lord knows, I've tried everything. My

last attempt was empirical, but it pulled an old
man through. He was brought to me apparently
past hope, and I gave him gin and Worcester sauce
with cayenne. It cured him ; but I don't recommend it.'

'How do the cases run generally?' said Hummil.

'Very simply indeed. Chlorodyne, opium pill,
chlorodyne, collapse, nitre, bricks to the feet, and
then—the burning-ghaut. The last seems to be
the only thing that stops the trouble. It's black
cholera, you know. Poor devils ! But, I will
say, little Bunsee Lal, my apothecary, works like
a demon. I've recommended him for promotion
if he comes through it all alive.'

'And what are your chances, old man?' said
Mottram.

'Don't know ; don't care much ; but I've sent
the letter in. What are you doing with yourself
generally?'

'Sitting under a table in the tent and spitting
on the sextant to keep it cool,' said the man of the
Survey. 'Washing my eyes to avoid ophthalmia,
which I shall certainly get, and trying to make
a sub-surveyor understand that an error of five
degrees in an angle isn't quite so small as it looks.
I'm altogether alone, y' know, and shall be till the
end of the hot weather.'

'Hummil's the lucky man,' said Lowndes, flinging himself into a long chair. 'He has an actual
roof—torn as to the ceiling-cloth, but still a roof
—over his head. He sees one train daily. He
can get beer and soda-water and ice 'em when God
is good. He has books, pictures,'—they were

torn from the *Graphic*,—' and the society of the excellent sub-contractor Jevins, besides the pleasure of receiving us weekly.'

Hummil smiled grimly. 'Yes, I'm the lucky man, I suppose. Jevins is luckier.'

'How? Not——'

'Yes. Went out. Last Monday.'

'By his own hand?' said Spurstow quickly, hinting the suspicion that was in everybody's mind. There was no cholera near Hummil's section. Even fever gives a man at least a week's grace, and sudden death generally implied self-slaughter.

'I judge no man this weather,' said Hummil. 'He had a touch of the sun, I fancy; for last week, after you fellows had left, he came into the verandah and told me that he was going home to see his wife, in Market Street, Liverpool, that evening.

'I got the apothecary in to look at him, and we tried to make him lie down. After an hour or two he rubbed his eyes and said he believed he had had a fit,—hoped he hadn't said anything rude. Jevins had a great idea of bettering himself socially. He was very like Chucks in his language.'

'Well?'

'Then he went to his own bungalow and began cleaning a rifle. He told the servant that he was going to shoot buck in the morning. Naturally he fumbled with the trigger, and shot himself through the head—accidentally. The apothecary sent in a report to my chief, and Jevins is buried somewhere out there. I'd have wired to you, Spurstow, if you could have done anything.'

'You're a queer chap,' said Mottram. 'If you'd killed the man yourself you couldn't have been more quiet about the business.'

'Good Lord! what does it matter?' said Hummil calmly. 'I've got to do a lot of his overseeing work in addition to my own. I'm the only person that suffers. Jevins is out of it,—by pure accident, of course, but out of it. The apothecary was going to write a long screed on suicide. Trust a babu to drivel when he gets the chance.'

'Why didn't you let it go in as suicide?' said Lowndes.

'No direct proof. A man hasn't many privileges in this country, but he might at least be allowed to mishandle his own rifle. Besides, some day I may need a man to smother up an accident to myself. Live and let live. Die and let die.'

'You take a pill,' said Spurstow, who had been watching Hummil's white face narrowly. 'Take a pill, and don't be an ass. That sort of talk is skittles. Anyhow, suicide is shirking your work. If I were Job ten times over, I should be so interested in what was going to happen next that I'd stay on and watch.'

'Ah! I've lost that curiosity,' said Hummil.

'Liver out of order?' said Lowndes feelingly.

'No. Can't sleep. That's worse.'

'By Jove, it is!' said Mottram. 'I'm that way every now and then, and the fit has to wear itself out. What do you take for it?'

'Nothing. What's the use? I haven't had ten minutes' sleep since Friday morning.'

'Poor chap! Spurstow, you ought to attend tc

this,' said Mottram. 'Now you mention it, your eyes are rather gummy and swollen.'

Spurstow, still watching Hummil, laughed lightly. 'I'll patch him up, later on. Is it too hot, do you think, to go for a ride?'

'Where to?' said Lowndes wearily. 'We shall have to go away at eight, and there'll be riding enough for us then. I hate a horse when I have to use him as a necessity. Oh, heavens! what is there to do?'

'Begin whist again, at chick points ['a chick' is supposed to be eight shillings] and a gold mohur on the rub,' said Spurstow promptly.

'Poker. A month's pay all round for the pool,—no limit,—and fifty-rupee raises. Somebody would be broken before we got up,' said Lowndes.

'Can't say that it would give me any pleasure to break any man in this company,' said Mottram. 'There isn't enough excitement in it, and it's foolish.' He crossed over to the worn and battered little camp-piano,—wreckage of a married household that had once held the bungalow,—and opened the case.

'It's used up long ago,' said Hummil. 'The servants have picked it to pieces.'

The piano was indeed hopelessly out of order, but Mottram managed to bring the rebellious notes into a sort of agreement, and there rose from the ragged keyboard something that might once have been the ghost of a popular music-hall song. The men in the long chairs turned with evident interest as Mottram banged the more lustily.

'That's good!' said Lowndes. 'By Jove! the last time I heard that song was in '79, or thereabouts, just before I came out.'

'Ah!' said Spurstow with pride, 'I was home in '80.' And he mentioned a song of the streets popular at that date.

Mottram executed it roughly. Lowndes criticised and volunteered emendations. Mottram dashed into another ditty, not of the music-hall character, and made as if to rise.

'Sit down,' said Hummil. 'I didn't know that you had any music in your composition. Go on playing until you can't think of anything more. I'll have that piano tuned up before you come again. Play something festive.'

Very simple indeed were the tunes to which Mottram's art and the limitations of the piano could give effect, but the men listened with pleasure, and in the pauses talked all together of what they had seen or heard when they were last at home. A dense dust-storm sprung up outside, and swept roaring over the house, enveloping it in the choking darkness of midnight, but Mottram continued unheeding, and the crazy tinkle reached the ears of the listeners above the flapping of the tattered ceiling-cloth.

In the silence after the storm he glided from the more directly personal songs of Scotland, half humming them as he played, into the Evening Hymn.

'Sunday,' said he, nodding his head.

'Go on. Don't apologise for it,' said Spurstow.

Hummil laughed long and riotously. 'Play it,

by all means.   You're full of surprises to-day.   I
didn't know you had such a gift of finished sar-
casm.   How does that thing go?'

Mottram took up the tune.

'Too slow by half.   You miss the note of
gratitude,' said Hummil.   'It ought to go to the
"Grasshopper's Polka,"—this way.'   And he
chanted, *prestissimo*,—

> 'Glory to thee, my God, this night,
>   For all the blessings of the light.'

That shows we really feel our blessings.   How
does it go on?—

> If in the night I sleepless lie,
>   My soul with sacred thoughts supply;
>   May no ill dreams disturb my rest,'—

Quicker, Mottram!—

> 'Or powers of darkness me molest!'

'Bah! what an old hypocrite you are!'

'Don't be an ass,' said Lowndes.   'You are at
full liberty to make fun of anything else you like,
but leave that hymn alone.   It's associated in my
mind with the most sacred recollections——'

'Summer evenings in the country,—stained-
glass window,—light going out, and you and she
jamming your heads together over one hymn-
book,' said Mottram.

'Yes, and a fat old cockchafer hitting you in
the eye when you walked home.   Smell of hay,
and a moon as big as a bandbox sitting on the top
of a haycock; bats,—roses,—milk and midges,'
said Lowndes.

' Also mothers. I can just recollect my mother singing me to sleep with that when I was a little chap,' said Spurstow.

The darkness had fallen on the room. They could hear Hummil squirming in his chair.

' Consequently,' said he testily, ' you sing it when you are seven fathom deep in Hell! It's an insult to the intelligence of the Deity to pretend we're anything but tortured rebels.'

' Take *two* pills,' said Spurstow ; ' that's tortured liver.'

' The usually placid Hummil is in a vile bad temper. I'm sorry for his coolies to-morrow,' said Lowndes, as the servants brought in the lights and prepared the table for dinner.

As they were settling into their places about the miserable goat-chops, and the smoked tapioca pudding, Spurstow took occasion to whisper to Mottram, ' Well done, David !'

' Look after Saul, then,' was the reply.

' What are you two whispering about ?' said Hummil suspiciously.

' Only saying that you are a damned poor host. This fowl can't be cut,' returned Spurstow with a sweet smile. ' Call this a dinner ?'

' I can't help it. You don't expect a banquet, do you ?'

Throughout that meal Hummil contrived laboriously to insult directly and pointedly all his guests in succession, and at each insult Spurstow kicked the aggrieved persons under the table ; but he dared not exchange a glance of intelligence with either of them. Hummil's face was white and pinched, while his eyes were unnaturally large. No man dreamed for a moment of resenting his savage personalities, but as soon as the meal was over they made haste to get away.

'Don't go. You're just getting amusing, you fellows. I hope I haven't said anything that annoyed you. You're such touchy devils.' Then, changing the note into one of almost abject entreaty, Hummil added, 'I say, you surely aren't going?'

'In the language of the blessed Jorrocks, where I dines I sleeps,' said Spurstow. 'I want to have a look at your coolies to-morrow, if you don't mind. You can give me a place to lie down in, I suppose?'

The others pleaded the urgency of their several duties next day, and, saddling up, departed together, Hummil begging them to come next Sunday. As they jogged off, Lowndes unbosomed himself to Mottram—

'. . . And I never felt so like kicking a man at his own table in my life. He said I cheated at whist, and reminded me I was in debt! 'Told you you were as good as a liar to your face! You aren't half indignant enough over it.'

'Not I,' said Mottram. 'Poor devil! Did you ever know old Hummy behave like that before or within a hundred miles of it?'

'That's no excuse. Spurstow was hacking my shin all the time, so I kept a hand on myself. Else I should have——'

'No, you wouldn't. You'd have done as Hummy did about Jevins; judge no man this weather. By Jove! the buckle of my bridle is hot in my hand! Trot out a bit, and 'ware rat-holes.'

Ten minutes' trotting jerked out of Lowndes one very sage remark when he pulled up, sweating from every pore—

' 'Good thing Spurstow's with him to-night.'

'Ye-es. Good man, Spurstow. Our roads turn here. See you again next Sunday, if the sun doesn't bowl me over.'

'S'pose so, unless old Timbersides' finance minister manages to dress some of my food. Good-night, and—God bless you!'

'What's wrong now?'

'Oh, nothing.' Lowndes gathered up his whip, and, as he flicked Mottram's mare on the flank, added, 'You're not a bad little chap,—that's all.' And the mare bolted half a mile across the sand, on the word.

In the assistant engineer's bungalow Spurstow and Hummil smoked the pipe of silence together, each narrowly watching the other. The capacity of a bachelor's establishment is as elastic as its arrangements are simple. A servant cleared away the dining-room table, brought in a couple of rude native bedsteads made of tape strung on a light wood frame, flung a square of cool Calcutta matting over each, set them side by side, pinned two towels to the punkah so that their fringes should just sweep clear of the sleeper's nose and mouth, and announced that the couches were ready.

The men flung themselves down, ordering the punkah-coolies by all the powers of Hell to pull.

Every door and window was shut, for the outside air was that of an oven. The atmosphere within was only 104°, as the thermometer bore witness, and heavy with the foul smell of badly-trimmed kerosene lamps ; and this stench, combined with that of native tobacco, baked brick, and dried earth, sends the heart of many a strong man down to his boots, for it is the smell of the Great Indian Empire when she turns herself for six months into a house of torment. Spurstow packed his pillows craftily so that he reclined rather than lay, his head at a safe elevation above his feet. It is not good to sleep on a low pillow in the hot weather if you happen to be of thick-necked build, for you may pass with lively snores and gugglings from natural sleep into the deep slumber of heat-apoplexy.

'Pack your pillows,' said the doctor sharply, as he saw Hummil preparing to lie down at full length.

The night-light was trimmed ; the shadow of the punkah wavered across the room, and the 'flick' of the punkah-towel and the soft whine of the rope through the wall-hole followed it. Then the punkah flagged, almost ceased. The sweat poured from Spurstow's brow. Should he go out and harangue the coolie ? It started forward again with a savage jerk, and a pin came out of the towels. When this was replaced, a tomtom in the coolie-lines began to beat with the steady throb of a swollen artery inside some brain-fevered skull. Spurstow turned on his side and swore gently. There was no movement on Hummil's part. The man had composed himself as rigidly as a corpse, his hands clinched at his sides. The respiration was too hurried for any suspicion of sleep. Spurstow looked at the set face. The jaws were clinched, and there was a pucker round the quivering eyelids.

'He's holding himself as tightly as ever he can,' thought Spurstow. 'What in the world is the matter with him?—Hummil!'

'Yes,' in a thick constrained voice.

'Can't you get to sleep?'

'No.'

'Head hot? 'Throat feeling bulgy? or how?'

'Neither, thanks. I don't sleep much, you know.'

''Feel pretty bad?'

'Pretty bad, thanks. There is a tomtom outside, isn't there? I thought it was my head at first. . . . Oh, Spurstow, for pity's sake give me something that will put me asleep,—sound asleep, —if it's only for six hours!' He sprang up, trembling from head to foot. 'I haven't been able to sleep naturally for days, and I can't stand it!—I can't stand it!'

'Poor old chap!'

'That's no use. Give me something to make me sleep. I tell you I'm nearly mad. I don't know what I say half my time. For three weeks I've had to think and spell out every word that has come through my lips before I dared say it. Isn't that enough to drive a man mad? I can't see things correctly now, and I've lost my sense of touch. My skin aches—my skin aches! Make me sleep. Oh, Spurstow, for the love of God make me sleep sound. It isn't enough merely to let me dream. Let me sleep!'

'All right, old man, all right. Go slow; you aren't half as bad as you think.'

The flood-gates of reserve once broken, Hummil was clinging to him like a frightened child. 'You're pinching my arm to pieces.'

'I'll break your neck if you don't do something for me. No, I didn't mean that. Don't be angry, old fellow.' He wiped the sweat off himself as he fought to regain composure. 'I'm a bit restless and off my oats, and perhaps you could recommend some sort of sleeping mixture, — bromide of potassium.'

'Bromide of skittles! Why didn't you tell me this before? Let go of my arm, and I'll see if there's anything in my cigarette-case to suit your complaint.' Spurstow hunted among his day-clothes, turned up the lamp, opened a little silver cigarette-case, and advanced on the expectant Hummil with the daintiest of fairy squirts.

'The last appeal of civilisation,' said he, 'and a thing I hate to use. Hold out your arm. Well, your sleeplessness hasn't ruined your muscle; and what a thick hide it is! Might as well inject a buffalo subcutaneously. Now in a few minutes the morphia will begin working. Lie down and wait.'

A smile of unalloyed and idiotic delight began to creep over Hummil's face. 'I think,' he whispered,—'I think I'm going off now. Gad! it's positively heavenly! Spurstow, you must give me that case to keep; you——' The voice ceased as the head fell back.

'Not for a good deal,' said Spurstow to the unconscious form. 'And now, my friend, sleeplessness of your kind being very apt to relax the moral fibre in little matters of life and death, I'll just take the liberty of spiking your guns.'

He paddled into Hummil's saddle-room in his bare feet and uncased a twelve-bore rifle, an express, and a revolver. Of the first he unscrewed the nipples and hid them in the bottom of a saddlery-case; of the second he abstracted the lever, kicking it behind a big wardrobe. The third he merely opened, and knocked the doll-head bolt of the grip up with the heel of a riding-boot.

'That's settled,' he said, as he shook the sweat off his hands. 'These little precautions will at least give you time to turn. You have too much sympathy with gun-room accidents.'

And as he rose from his knees, the thick muffled voice of Hummil cried in the doorway, 'You fool!'

Such tones they use who speak in the lucid intervals of delirium to their friends a little before they die.

Spurstow started, dropping the pistol. Hummil stood in the doorway, rocking with helpless laughter.

'That was awf'ly good of you, I'm sure,' he said, very slowly, feeling for his words. 'I don't intend to go out by my own hand at present. I say, Spurstow, that stuff won't work. What shall I do? What shall I do?' And panic terror stood in his eyes.

'Lie down and give it a chance. Lie down at once.'

'I daren't. It will only take me half-way again, and I shan't be able to get away this time. Do you know it was all I could do to come out just now ? Generally I am as quick as lightning ; but you had clogged my feet. I was nearly caught.'

'Oh yes, I understand. Go and lie down.'

'No, it isn't delirium ; but it was an awfully mean trick to play on me. Do you know I might have died ?'

As a sponge rubs a slate clean, so some power unknown to Spurstow had wiped out of Hummil's face all that stamped it for the face of a man, and he stood at the doorway in the expression of his lost innocence. He had slept back into terrified childhood.

'Is he going to die on the spot?' thought Spurstow. Then, aloud, 'All right, my son. Come back to bed, and tell me all about it. You couldn't sleep ; but what was all the rest of the nonsense ?'

'A place,—a place down there,' said Hummil, with simple sincerity. The drug was acting on him by waves, and he was flung from the fear of a strong man to the fright of a child as his nerves gathered sense or were dulled.

'Good God ! I've been afraid of it for months past, Spurstow. It has made every night hell to me ; and yet I'm not conscious of having done anything wrong.'

'Be still, and I'll give you another dose. We'll stop your nightmares, you unutterable idiot !'

'Yes, but you must give me so much that I

can't get away. You must make me quite sleepy,
—not just a little sleepy. It's so hard to run
then.'

'I know it; I know it. I've felt it myself.
The symptoms are exactly as you describe.'

'Oh, don't laugh at me, confound you! Before
this awful sleeplessness came to me I've tried to rest
on my elbow and put a spur in the bed to sting
me when I fell back. Look!'

'By Jove! the man has been rowelled like
a horse! Ridden by the nightmare with a
vengeance! And we all thought him sensible
enough. Heaven send us understanding! You
like to talk, don't you?'

'Yes, sometimes. Not when I'm frightened.
Then I want to run. Don't you?'

'Always. Before I give you your second dose
try to tell me exactly what your trouble is.'

Hummil spoke in broken whispers for nearly
ten minutes, whilst Spurstow looked into the pupils
of his eyes and passed his hand before them once
or twice.

At the end of the narrative the silver cigarette-
case was produced, and the last words that Hummil
said as he fell back for the second time were, 'Put
me quite to sleep; for if I'm caught I die,—I
die!'

'Yes, yes; we all do that sooner or later,—
thank Heaven who has set a term to our miseries,'
said Spurstow, settling the cushions under the head.
'It occurs to me that unless I drink something I
shall go out before my time. I've stopped sweating, and—I wear a seventeen-inch collar.' He

brewed himself scalding hot tea, which is an excellent remedy against heat-apoplexy if you take three or four cups of it in time. Then he watched the sleeper.

'A blind face that cries and can't wipe its eyes, a blind face that chases him down corridors! H'm! Decidedly, Hummil ought to go on leave as soon as possible ; and, sane or otherwise, he undoubtedly did rowel himself most cruelly. Well, Heaven send us understanding !'

At mid-day Hummil rose, with an evil taste in his mouth, but an unclouded eye and a joyful heart.

'I was pretty bad last night, wasn't I ?' said he.

'I have seen healthier men. You must have had a touch of the sun. Look here : if I write you a swingeing medical certificate, will you apply for leave on the spot ?'

'No.'

'Why not ? You want it.'

'Yes, but I can hold on till the weather's a little cooler.'

'Why should you, if you can get relieved on the spot ?'

'Burkett is the only man who could be sent ; and he's a born fool.'

'Oh, never mind about the line. You aren't so important as all that. Wire for leave, if necessary.'

Hummil looked very uncomfortable.

'I can hold on till the Rains,' he said evasively.

'You can't. Wire to headquarters for Burkett.'

'I won't. If you want to know why, particularly, Burkett is married, and his wife's just had a kid, and she's up at Simla, in the cool, and Burkett has a very nice billet that takes him into Simla from Saturday to Monday. That little woman isn't at all well. If Burkett was transferred she'd try to follow him. If she left the baby behind she'd fret herself to death. If she came,—and Burkett's one of those selfish little beasts who are always talking about a wife's place being with her husband,—she'd die. It's murder to bring a woman here just now. Burkett hasn't the physique of a rat. If he came here he'd go out ; and I know she hasn't any money, and I'm pretty sure she'd go out too. I'm salted in a sort of way, and I'm not married. Wait till the Rains, and then Burkett can get thin down here. It'll do him heaps of good.'

'Do you mean to say that you intend to face —what you have faced, till the Rains break ?'

'Oh, it won't be so bad, now you've shown me a way out of it. I can always wire to you. Besides, now I've once got into the way of sleeping, it'll be all right. Anyhow, I shan't put in for leave. That's the long and the short of it.'

'My great Scott ! I thought all that sort of thing was dead and done with.'

'Bosh ! You'd do the same yourself. I feel a new man, thanks to that cigarette-case. You're going over to camp now, aren't you ?'

'Yes ; but I'll try to look you up every other day, if I can.'

'I'm not bad enough for that. I don't want you to bother. Give the coolies gin and ketchup.'

' Then you feel all right ? '

' Fit to fight for my life, but not to stand out in the sun talking to you. Go along, old man, and bless you !

Hummil turned on his heel to face the echoing desolation of his bungalow, and the first thing he saw standing in the verandah was the figure of himself. He had met a similar apparition once before, when he was suffering from overwork and the strain of the hot weather.

' This is bad,—already,' he said, rubbing his eyes. ' If the thing slides away from me all in one piece, like a ghost, I shall know it is only my eyes and stomach that are out of order. If it walks— my head is going.'

He approached the figure, which naturally kept at an unvarying distance from him, as is the use of all spectres that are born of overwork. It slid through the house and dissolved into swimming specks within the eyeball as soon as it reached the burning light of the garden. Hummil went about his business till even. When he came in to dinner he found himself sitting at the table. The vision rose and walked out hastily. Except that it cast no shadow it was in all respects real.

No living man knows what that week held for Hummil. An increase of the epidemic kept Spurstow in camp among the coolies, and all he could do was to telegraph to Mottram, bidding him go to the bungalow and sleep there. But Mottram was forty miles away from the nearest telegraph, and knew nothing of anything save the needs of the Survey till he met, early on Sunday morning, Lowndes and Spurstow heading towards Hummil's for the weekly gathering.

'Hope the poor chap's in a better temper,' said the former, swinging himself off his horse at the door. 'I suppose he isn't up yet.'

'I'll just have a look at him,' said the doctor. 'If he's asleep there's no need to wake him.'

And an instant later, by the tone of Spurstow's voice calling upon them to enter, the men knew what had happened. There was no need to wake him.

The punkah was still being pulled over the bed, but Hummil had departed this life at least three hours.

The body lay on its back, hands clinched by the side, as Spurstow had seen it lying seven nights previously. In the staring eyes was written terror beyond the expression of any pen.

Mottram, who had entered behind Lowndes, bent over the dead and touched the forehead lightly with his lips. 'Oh, you lucky, lucky devil!' he whispered.

But Lowndes had seen the eyes, and withdrew shuddering to the other side of the room.

'Poor chap! poor old chap! And the last time I met him I was angry. Spurstow, we should have watched him. Has he——?'

Deftly Spurstow continued his investigations, ending by a search round the room.

'No, he hasn't,' he snapped. 'There's no trace of anything. Call the servants.'

They came, eight or ten of them, whispering and peering over each other's shoulders.

'When did your Sahib go to bed?' said Spurstow.

'At eleven or ten, we think,' said Hummil's personal servant.

'He was well then? But how should you know?'

'He was not ill, as far as our comprehension extended. But he had slept very little for three nights. This I know, because I saw him walking much, and specially in the heart of the night.'

As Spurstow was arranging the sheet, a big straight-necked hunting-spur tumbled on the ground. The doctor groaned. The personal servant peeped at the body.

'What do you think, Chuma?' said Spurstow, catching the look on the dark face.

'Heaven-born, in my poor opinion, this that was my master has descended into the Dark Places, and there has been caught because he was not able to escape with sufficient speed. We have the spur for evidence that he fought with Fear. Thus have I seen men of my race do with thorns when a spell was laid upon them to overtake them in their sleeping hours and they dared not sleep.'

'Chuma, you're a mud-head. Go out and prepare seals to be set on the Sahib's property.'

'God has made the Heaven-born. God has made me. Who are we, to inquire into the dispensations of God? I will bid the other servants hold aloof while you are reckoning the tale of the Sahib's property. They are all thieves, and would steal.'

' As far as I can make out, he died from—oh, anything ; stoppage of the heart's action, heat-apoplexy, or some other visitation,' said Spurstow to his companions. ' We must make an inventory of his effects, and so on.'

' He was scared to death,' insisted Lowndes. ' Look at those eyes ! For pity's sake don't let him be buried with them open ! '

' Whatever it was, he's clear of all the trouble now,' said Mottram softly.

Spurstow was peering into the open eyes.

' Come here,' said he. ' Can you see anything there ? '

' I can't face it ! ' whimpered Lowndes. ' Cover up the face ! Is there any fear on earth that can turn a man into that likeness ? It's ghastly. Oh, Spurstow, cover it up ! '

' No fear—on earth,' said Spurstow. Mottram leaned over his shoulder and looked intently.

' I see nothing except some gray blurs in the pupil. There can be nothing there, you know.'

' Even so. Well, let's think. It'll take half a day to knock up any sort of coffin ; and he must have died at midnight. Lowndes, old man, go out and tell the coolies to break ground next to Jevins's grave. Mottram, go round the house with Chuma and see that the seals are put on things. Send a couple of men to me here, and I'll arrange.'

The strong-armed servants when they returned to their own kind told a strange story of the doctor Sahib vainly trying to call their master back to life by magic arts,—to wit, the holding of a little green box that clicked to each of the dead man's eyes, and of a bewildered muttering on the part of the doctor Sahib, who took the little green box away with him.

The resonant hammering of a coffin-lid is no pleasant thing to hear, but those who have experience maintain that much more terrible is the soft swish of the bed-linen, the reeving and unreeving of the bed-tapes, when he who has fallen by the roadside is apparelled for burial, sinking gradually as the tapes are tied over, till the swaddled shape touches the floor and there is no protest against the indignity of hasty disposal.

At the last moment Lowndes was seized with scruples of conscience. 'Ought you to read the service,—from beginning to end?' said he to Spurstow.

'I intend to. You're my senior as a civilian. You can take it if you like.'

'I didn't mean that for a moment. I only thought if we could get a chaplain from some-where,—I'm willing to ride anywhere,—and give poor Hummil a better chance. That's all.'

'Bosh!' said Spurstow, as he framed his lips to the tremendous words that stand at the head of the burial service.

After breakfast they smoked a pipe in silence to the memory of the dead. Then Spurstow said absently—

''Tisn't in medical science.'

'What?'

'Things in a dead man's eye.'

'For goodness' sake leave that horror alone!' said Lowndes. 'I've seen a native die of pure fright when a tiger chivied him. I know what killed Hummil.'

'The deuce you do! I'm going to try to see.' And the doctor retreated into the bath-room with a Kodak camera. After a few minutes there was the sound of something being hammered to pieces, and he emerged, very white indeed.

'Have you got a picture?' said Mottram. 'What does the thing look like?'

'It was impossible, of course. You needn't look, Mottram. I've torn up the films. There was nothing there. It was impossible.'

'That,' said Lowndes, very distinctly, watching the shaking hand striving to relight the pipe, 'is a damned lie.'

Mottram laughed uneasily. 'Spurstow's right,' he said. 'We're all in such a state now that we'd believe anything. For pity's sake let's try to be rational.'

There was no further speech for a long time. The hot wind whistled without, and the dry trees sobbed. Presently the daily train, winking brass, burnished steel, and spouting steam, pulled up panting in the intense glare. 'We'd better go on on that,' said Spurstow. 'Go back to work. I've written my certificate. We can't do any more good here, and work'll keep our wits together. Come on.'

No one moved. It is not pleasant to face railway journeys at mid-day in June. Spurstow gathered up his hat and whip, and, turning in the doorway, said—

> 'There may be Heaven,—there must be Hell.
> Meantime, there is our life here.   We-ell ?'

Neither Mottram nor Lowndes had any answer to the question.

The Mutiny of the Mavericks

Sec. 7. (1)	Causing Conspiring with other persons to cause	a mutiny sedition	in forces belonging to Her Majesty's	Regular forces, Reserve forces, Auxiliary forces, Navy.

WHEN three obscure gentlemen in San Francisco argued on insufficient premises they condemned a fellow-creature to a most unpleasant death in a far country, which had nothing whatever to do with the United States. They foregathered at the top of a tenement-house in Tehama Street, an unsavoury quarter of the city, and, there calling for certain drinks, they conspired because they were con-spirators by trade, officially known as the Third Three of the I.A.A.—an institution for the propagation of pure light, not to be confounded with any others, though it is affiliated to many. The Second Three live in Montreal, and work among the poor there; the First Three have their home in New York, not far from Castle Garden, and write regularly once a week to a small house near one of the big hotels at Boulogne. What happens after that, a particular section of Scotland Yard knows too well, and laughs at. A conspirator detests ridicule. More men have been stabbed with Lucrezia Borgia daggers and dropped into the Thames for laughing at Head Centres and Triangles than for betraying secrets; for this is human nature.

The Third Three conspired over whisky cocktails and a clean sheet of notepaper against the British Empire and all that lay therein. This work is very like what men without discernment call politics before a general election. You pick out and discuss, in the company of congenial friends, all the weak points in your opponents' organisation, and unconsciously dwell upon and exaggerate all their mishaps, till it seems to you a miracle that the hated party holds together for an hour.

'Our principle is not so much active demonstration—that we leave to others—as passive embarrassment, to weaken and unnerve,' said the first man. 'Wherever an organisation is crippled, wherever a confusion is thrown into any branch of any department, we gain a step for those who take on the work; we are but the forerunners.' He was a German enthusiast, and editor of a newspaper, from whose leading articles he quoted frequently.

'That cursed Empire makes so many blunders of her own that unless we doubled the year's average I guess it wouldn't strike her anything special had occurred,' said the second man. 'Are you prepared to say that all our resources are equal to blowing off the muzzle of a hundred-ton gun or spiking a ten-thousand-ton ship on a plain rock in clear daylight? They can beat us at our own game. 'Better join hands with the practical branches; we're in funds now. Try a direct scare in a crowded street. They value their greasy hides.' He was the drag upon the wheel, and an Americanised Irishman of the second generation, despising his own race and hating the other. He had learned caution.

The third man drank his cocktail and spoke no word. He was the strategist, but unfortunately his knowledge of life was limited. He picked a letter from his breast-pocket and threw it across the table. That epistle to the heathen contained some very concise directions from the First Three in New York. It said—

'*The boom in black iron has already affected the eastern markets, where our agents have been forcing down the English-held stock among the smaller buyers who watch the turn of shares. Any immediate operations, such as western bears, would increase their willingness to unload. This, however, cannot be expected till they see clearly that foreign iron-masters are willing to co-operate. Mulcahy should be dispatched to feel the pulse of the market, and act accordingly. Mavericks are at present the best for our purpose.—P.D.Q.*'

As a message referring to an iron crisis in Pennsylvania, it was interesting, if not lucid. As a new departure in organised attack on an out-lying English dependency, it was more than interesting.

The second man read it through and murmured—

'Already? Surely they are in too great a

hurry. All that Dhulip Singh could do in India he has done, down to the distribution of his photographs among the peasantry. Ho! Ho! The Paris firm arranged that, and he has no substantial money backing from the Other Power. Even our agents in India know he hasn't. What is the use of our organisation wasting men on work that is already done? Of course the Irish regiments in India are half mutinous as they stand.'

This shows how near a lie may come to the truth. An Irish regiment, for just so long as it stands still, is generally a hard handful to control, being reckless and rough. When, however, it is moved in the direction of musketry-firing, it becomes strangely and unpatriotically content with its lot. It has even been heard to cheer the Queen with enthusiasm on these occasions.

But the notion of tampering with the army was, from the point of view of Tehama Street, an altogether sound one. There is no shadow of stability in the policy of an English Government, and the most sacred oaths of England would, even if engrossed on vellum, find very few buyers among colonies and dependencies that have suffered from vain beliefs. But there remains to England always her army. That cannot change except in the matter of uniform and equipment. The officers may write to the papers demanding the heads of the Horse Guards in default of cleaner redress for grievances ; the men may break loose across a country town and seriously startle the publicans ; but neither officers nor men have it in their composition to mutiny after the continental manner. The English people, when they trouble to think about the army at all, are, and with justice, absolutely assured that it is absolutely trustworthy. Imagine for a moment their emotions on realising that such and such a regiment was in open revolt from causes directly due to England's management of Ireland. They would probably send the regiment to the polls forthwith and examine their own consciences as to their duty to Erin; but they would never be easy any more. And it was this vague, unhappy mistrust that the I.A.A. were labouring to produce.

'Sheer waste of breath,' said the second man after a pause in the council, 'I don't see the use of tampering with their fool-army, but it has been tried before and we must try it again. It looks well in the reports. If we send one man from here you may bet your life that other men are going too. Order up Mulcahy.'

They ordered him up—a slim, slight, dark-haired young man, devoured with that blind rancorous hatred of England that only reaches its full growth across the Atlantic. He had sucked it from his mother's breast in the little cabin at the back of the northern avenues of New York; he had been taught his rights and his wrongs, in German and Irish, on the canal fronts of Chicago; and San Francisco held men who told him strange and awful things of the great blind power over the seas. Once, when business took him across the Atlantic, he had served in an English regiment, and being insubordinate had suffered extremely. He drew all his ideas of England that were not bred by the cheaper patriotic prints from one iron-fisted colonel and an unbending adjutant. He would go to the mines if need be to teach his gospel. And he went as his instructions advised *p.d.q.*—which means 'with speed'—to introduce embarrassment into an Irish regiment, 'already half-mutinous, quartered among Sikh peasantry, all wearing miniatures of His Highness Dhulip Singh, Maharaja of the Punjab, next their hearts, and all eagerly expecting his arrival.' Other information equally valuable was given him by his masters. He was to be cautious, but never to grudge expense in winning the hearts of the men in the regiment. His mother in New York would supply funds, and he was to write to her once a month. Life is pleasant for a man who has a mother in New York to send him two hundred pounds a year over and above his regimental pay.

In process of time, thanks to his intimate knowledge of drill and musketry exercise, the excellent Mulcahy, wearing the corporal's stripe, went out in a troopship and joined Her Majesty's Royal Loyal Musketeers, commonly known as the 'Mavericks,' because they were masterless and unbranded cattle—sons of small farmers in County Clare, shoeless vagabonds of Kerry, herders of Ballyvegan, much wanted 'moonlighters' from the bare rainy headlands of the south coast, officered by O'Mores, Bradys, Hills, Kilreas, and the like. Never to outward seeming was there more promising material to work on. The First Three had chosen their regiment well. It feared nothing that moved or talked save the colonel and the regimental Roman Catholic chaplain, the fat Father Dennis, who held the keys of heaven and hell, and blared like an angry bull when he desired to be convincing. Him also it loved because on occasions of stress he was used to tuck up his cassock and charge with the rest into the merriest of the fray, where he always found, good man, that the saints sent him a revolver when there was a fallen private to be protected, or—but this came as an afterthought—his own gray head to be guarded.

Cautiously as he had been instructed, tenderly and with much beer, Mulcahy opened his projects to such as he deemed fittest to listen. And these were, one and all, of that quaint, crooked, sweet, profoundly irresponsible and profoundly lovable race that fight like fiends, argue like children, reason like women, obey like men, and jest like their own goblins of the rath through rebellion, loyalty, want, woe, or war. The underground work of a conspiracy is always dull and very much the same the world over. At the end of six months—the seed always falling on good ground —Mulcahy spoke almost explicitly, hinting darkly in the approved fashion at dread powers behind him, and advising nothing more nor less than mutiny. Were they not dogs, evilly treated ? had they not all their own and their national revenges to satisfy ? Who in these days would do aught to nine hundred men in rebellion ? Who, again, could stay them if they broke for the sea, licking up on their way other regiments only too anxious to join ? And afterwards . . . here followed windy promises of gold and preferment, office, and honour, ever dear to a certain type of Irishman.

As he finished his speech, in the dusk of a twilight, to his chosen associates, there was a sound of a rapidly unslung belt behind him. The arm of one Dan Grady flew out in the gloom and arrested something. Then said Dan—

'Mulcahy, you're a great man, an' you do credit to whoever sent you. Walk about a bit while we think of it.' Mulcahy departed elate. He knew his words would sink deep.

'Why the triple-dashed asterisks did ye not let me belt him?' grunted a voice.

'Because I'm not a fat-headed fool. Boys, 'tis what he's been driving at these six months— our superior corpril with his education and his copies of the Irish papers and his everlasting beer. He's been sent for the purpose and that's where the money comes from. Can ye not see? That man's a gold-mine, which Horse Egan here would have destroyed with a belt-buckle. It would be throwing away the gifts of Providence not to fall in with his little plans. Of coorse we'll mut'ny till all's dry. Shoot the colonel on the parade-ground, massacree the company officers, ransack the arsenal, and then—Boys, did he tell you what next? He told *me* the other night when he was beginning to talk wild. Then we're to join with the niggers, and look for help from Dhulip Singh and the Russians!'

'And spoil the best campaign that ever was this side of Hell! Danny, I'd have lost the beer to ha' given him the belting he requires.'

'Oh, let him go this awhile, man! He's got no—no constructiveness, but that's the egg-meat of his plan, and you must understand that I'm in with it, an' so are you. We'll want oceans of beer to convince us—firmaments full. We'll give him talk for his money, and one by one all the boys'll come in and he'll have a nest of nine hundred mutineers to squat in an' give drink to.'

'What makes me killing-mad is his wanting us to do what the niggers did thirty years gone. That an' his pig's cheek in saying that other regiments would come along,' said a Kerry man.

'That's not so bad as hintin' we should loose off on the colonel.'

'Colonel be sugared! I'd as soon as not put a shot through his helmet to see him jump and clutch his old horse's head. But Mulcahy talks o' shootin' our comp'ny orf'cers accidental.'

'He said that, did he?' said Horse Egan.

'Somethin' like that, anyways. Can't ye fancy ould Barber Brady wid a bullet in his lungs, coughin' like a sick monkey, an' sayin', "Bhoys, I do not mind your gettin' dhrunk, but you must hould your liquor like men. The man that shot me is dhrunk. I'll suspend investigations for six hours, while I get this bullet cut out, an' then——"'

'An' then,' continued Horse Egan, for the peppery Major's peculiarities of speech and manner were as well known as his tanned face; '"an' then, ye dissolute, half-baked, putty-faced scum o' Connemara, if I find a man so much as lookin' confused, begad, I'll coort-martial the whole company. A man that can't get over his liquor in six hours is not fit to belong to the Mavericks!"'

A shout of laughter bore witness to the truth of the sketch.

'It's pretty to think of,' said the Kerry man slowly. 'Mulcahy would have us do all the devilmint, and get clear himself, someways. He wudn't be takin' all this fool's throuble in shpoilin' the reputation of the regiment——'

'Reputation of your grandmother's pig!' said Dan.

'Well, an' *he* had a good reputation tu; so it's all right. Mulcahy must see his way to clear out behind him, or he'd not ha' come so far, talkin' powers of darkness.'

'Did you hear anything of a regimental court-martial among the Black Boneens, these days? Half a company of 'em took one of the new draft an' hanged him by his arms with a tent-rope from a third story verandah. They gave no reason for so doin', but he was half dead. I'm thinking that the Boneens are short-sighted. It was a friend of Mulcahy's, or a man in the same trade. They'd a deal better ha' taken his beer,' returned Dan reflectively.

'Better still ha' handed him up to the colonel,' said Horse Egan, 'onless—but sure the news wud be all over the counthry an' give the reg'ment a bad name.'

'An' there'd be no reward for that man—he but went about talkin',' said the Kerry man artlessly.

'You speak by your breed,' said Dan with a laugh. 'There was never a Kerry man yet that wudn't sell his brother for a pipe o' tobacco an' a pat on the back from a p'liceman.'

'Praise God I'm not a bloomin' Orangeman,' was the answer.

'No, nor never will be,' said Dan. 'They breed *men* in Ulster. Would you like to thry the taste of one?'

The Kerry man looked and longed, but forebore. The odds of battle were too great.

'Then you'll not even give Mulcahy a—a strike for his money,' said the voice of Horse Egan, who regarded what he called 'trouble' of any kind as the pinnacle of felicity.

Dan answered not at all, but crept on tip-toe, with large strides, to the mess-room, the men following. The room was empty. In a corner, cased like the King of Dahomey's state umbrella, stood the regimental colours. Dan lifted them tenderly and unrolled in the light of the candles the record of the Mavericks—tattered, worn, and hacked. The white satin was darkened everywhere with big brown stains, the gold threads on the crowned harp were frayed and discoloured, and the Red Bull, the totem of the Mavericks, was coffee-hued. The stiff, embroidered folds, whose price is human life, rustled down slowly. The Mavericks keep their colours long and guard them very sacredly.

'Vittoria, Salamanca, Toulouse, Waterloo, Moodkee, Ferozshah, an' Sobraon — that was fought close next door here, against the very

beggars he wants us to join. Inkerman, The
Alma, Sebastopol ! What are those little businesses
compared to the campaigns of General Mulcahy?
The Mut'ny, think o' that ; the Mut'ny an' some
dirty little matters in Afghanistan ; an' for that
an' these an' those '—Dan pointed to the names of
glorious battles — 'that Yankee man with the
partin' in his hair comes an' says as easy as " have
a drink." . . . Holy Moses, there's the captain ! '

But it was the mess-sergeant who came in just
as the men clattered out, and found the colours
uncased.

From that day dated the mutiny of the
Mavericks, to the joy of Mulcahy and the pride of
his mother in New York—the good lady who sent
the money for the beer. Never, so far as words
went, was such a mutiny. The conspirators, led
by Dan Grady and Horse Egan, poured in daily.
They were sound men, men to be trusted, and they
all wanted blood ; but first they must have beer.
They cursed the Queen, they mourned over
Ireland, they suggested hideous plunder of the
Indian country-side, and then, alas !—some of the
younger men would go forth and wallow on the
ground in spasms of wicked laughter. The genius
of the Irish for conspiracies is remarkable. None
the less they would swear no oaths but those of
their own making, which were rare and curious,
and they were always at pains to impress Mulcahy
with the risks they ran. Naturally the flood of
beer wrought demoralisation. But Mulcahy
confused the causes of things, and when a very
muzzy Maverick smote a sergeant on the nose or

called his commanding officer a bald-headed old lard-bladder, and even worse names, he fancied that rebellion and not liquor was at the bottom of the outbreak. Other gentlemen who have concerned themselves in larger conspiracies have made the same error.

The hot season, in which they protested no man could rebel, came to an end, and Mulcahy suggested a visible return for his teachings. As to the actual upshot of the mutiny he cared nothing. It would be enough if the English, infatuatedly trusting to the integrity of their army, should be startled with news of an Irish regiment revolting from political considerations. His persistent demands would have ended, at Dan's instigation, in a regimental belting which in all probability would have killed him and cut off the supply of beer, had not he been sent on special duty some fifty miles away from the cantonment to cool his heels in a mud fort and dismount obsolete artillery. Then the colonel of the Mavericks, reading his newspaper diligently, and scenting Frontier trouble from afar, posted to the army headquarters and pled with the Commander-in-chief for certain privileges, to be granted under certain contingencies; which contingencies came about only a week later, when the annual little war on the Border developed itself, and the colonel returned to carry the good news to the Mavericks. He held the promise of the Chief for active service, and the men must get ready.

On the evening of the same day, Mulcahy, an unconsidered corporal—yet great in conspiracy—

returned to cantonments, and heard sounds of strife and howlings from afar off. The mutiny had broken out and the barracks of the Mavericks were one white-washed pandemonium. A private tearing through the barrack-square gasped in his ear, 'Service! Active service. It's a burnin' shame.' Oh joy, the Mavericks had risen on the eve of battle! They would not—noble and loyal sons of Ireland—serve the Queen longer. The news would flash through the country-side and over to England, and he—Mulcahy—the trusted of the Third Three, had brought about the crash. The private stood in the middle of the square and cursed colonel, regiment, officers, and doctor, particularly the doctor, by his gods. An orderly of the native cavalry regiment clattered through the mob of soldiers. He was half lifted, half dragged from his horse, beaten on the back with mighty hand-claps till his eyes watered, and called all manner of endearing names. Yes, the Mavericks had fraternised with the native troops. Who then was the agent among the latter that had blindly wrought with Mulcahy so well?

An officer slunk, almost ran, from the mess to a barrack. He was mobbed by the infuriated soldiery, who closed round but did not kill him, for he fought his way to shelter, flying for the life. Mulcahy could have wept with pure joy and thankfulness. The very prisoners in the guard-room were shaking the bars of their cells and howling like wild beasts, and from every barrack poured the booming as of a big war-drum.

Mulcahy hastened to his own barrack. He

could hardly hear himself speak. Eighty men were pounding with fist and heel the tables and trestles—eighty men, flushed with mutiny, stripped to their shirt sleeves, their knapsacks half-packed for the march to the sea, made the two-inch boards thunder again as they chanted to a tune that Mulcahy knew well, the Sacred War Song of the Mavericks—

Listen in the north, my boys, there's trouble on the wind ;
Tramp o' Cossack hooves in front, gray great-coats behind,
Trouble on the Frontier of a most amazin' kind,
    Trouble on the waters o' the Oxus !

Then, as a table broke under the furious accompaniment—

Hurrah ! hurrah ! it's north by west we go ;
Hurrah ! hurrah ! the chance we wanted so ;
Let 'em hear the chorus from Umballa to Mos*cow*,
As we go marchin' to the Kremling.

'Mother of all the saints in bliss and all the devils in cinders, where's my fine new sock widout the heel?' howled Horse Egan, ransacking everybody's valise but his own. He was engaged in making up deficiencies of kit preparatory to a campaign, and in that work he steals best who steals last. 'Ah, Mulcahy, you're in good time,' he shouted. 'We've got the route, and we're off on Thursday for a pic-nic wid the Lancers next door.'

An ambulance orderly appeared with a huge basket full of lint rolls, provided by the forethought of the Queen for such as might need them later on. Horse Egan unrolled his bandage, and flicked it under Mulcahy's nose, chanting—

'Sheepskin an' bees' wax, thunder, pitch, and plaster,
The more you try to pull it off, the more it sticks the faster.
As I was goin' to New Orleans—

'You know the rest of it, my Irish-American-Jew-boy. By gad, ye have to fight for the Queen in the inside av a fortnight, my darlin'.'

A roar of laughter interrupted. Mulcahy looked vacantly down the room. Bid a boy defy his father when the pantomime-cab is at the door; or a girl develop a will of her own when her mother is putting the last touches to the first ball-dress; but do not ask an Irish regiment to embark upon mutiny on the eve of a campaign; when it has fraternised with the native regiment that accompanies it, and driven its officers into retirement with ten thousand clamorous questions, and the prisoners dance for joy, and the sick men stand in the open, calling down all known diseases on the head of the doctor, who has certified that they are "medically unfit for active service." At even the Mavericks might have been mistaken for mutineers by one so unversed in their natures as Mulcahy. At dawn a girls' school might have learned deportment from them. They knew that their colonel's hand had closed, and that he who broke that iron discipline would not go to the front: nothing in the world will persuade one of our soldiers when he is ordered to the north on the smallest of affairs, that he is not immediately going gloriously to slay Cossacks and cook his kettles in the palace of the Czar. A few of the younger men mourned for Mulcahy's beer, because the campaign was to be conducted on strict temperance principles, but as Dan and Horse Egan said sternly, ' We've got the beer-man with us. He shall drink now on his own hook.'

Mulcahy had not taken into account the possibility of being sent on active service. He had made up his mind that he would not go under any circumstances, but fortune was against him.

'Sick—you?' said the doctor, who had served an unholy apprenticeship to his trade in Tralee poorhouses. 'You're only home-sick, and what you call varicose veins come from over-eating. A little gentle exercise will cure that.' And later, ' Mulcahy, my man, everybody is allowed to apply for a sick-certificate *once*. If he tries it twice we call him by an ugly name. Go back to your duty, and let's hear no more of your diseases.'

I am ashamed to say that Horse Egan enjoyed the study of Mulcahy's soul in those days, and Dan took an equal interest. Together they would communicate to their corporal all the dark lore of death which is the portion of those who have seen men die. Egan had the larger experience, but Dan the finer imagination. Mulcahy shivered when the former spoke of the knife as an intimate acquaintance, or the latter dwelt with loving particularity on the fate of those who, wounded and helpless, had been overlooked by the ambulances, and had fallen into the hands of the Afghan women-folk.

Mulcahy knew that the mutiny, for the present at least, was dead, knew, too, that a change had come over Dan's usually respectful attitude to-wards him, and Horse Egan's laughter and frequent

allusions to abortive conspiracies emphasised all
that the conspirator had guessed. The horrible
fascination of the death-stories, however, made him
seek the men's society. He learnt much more
than he had bargained for ; and in this manner.
It was on the last night before the regiment en-
trained to the front. The barracks were stripped
of everything movable, and the men were too
excited to sleep. The bare walls gave out a heavy
hospital smell of chloride of lime.

'And what,' said Mulcahy in an awe-stricken
whisper, after some conversation on the eternal
subject, 'are you going to do to me, Dan?' This
might have been the language of an able conspirator
conciliating a weak spirit.

'You'll see,' said Dan grimly, turning over in
his cot, 'or I rather shud say you'll not see.'

This was hardly the language of a weak spirit.
Mulcahy shook under the bed-clothes.

'Be easy with him,' put in Egan from the next
cot. 'He has got his chanst o' goin' clean.
Listen, Mulcahy, all we want is for the good sake
of the regiment that you take your death standing
up, as a man shud. There's be heaps an' heaps of
enemy—plenshus heaps. Go there an' do all you
can and die decent. You'll die with a good name
there. 'Tis not a hard thing considerin'.'

Again Mulcahy shivered.

'An' how could a man wish to die better than
fightin',' added Dan consolingly.

'And if I won't?' said the corporal in a dry
whisper.

'There'll be a dale of smoke,' returned Dan,

sitting up and ticking off the situation on his fingers, 'sure to be, an' the noise of the firin' 'll be tremenjus, an' we'll be running about up and down, the regiment will. But *we*, Horse and I— we'll stay by you, Mulcahy, and never let you go. Maybe there'll be an accident.'

'It's playing it low on me. Let me go. For pity's sake let me go. I never did you harm, and —and I stood you as much beer as I could. Oh, don't be hard on me, Dan! You are—you were in it too. You won't kill me up there, will you ?'

'I'm not thinkin' of the treason ; though you shud be glad any honest boys drank with you. It's for the regiment. We can't have the shame o' you bringin' shame on us. You went to the doctor quiet as a sick cat to get and stay behind an' live with the women at the depôt—you that wanted us to run to the sea in wolf-packs like the rebels none of your black blood dared to be ! But *we* knew about your goin' to the doctor, for he told in mess, and it's all over the regiment. Bein', as we are, your best friends, we didn't allow any one to molest you *yet*. We will see to you ourselves. Fight which you will—us or the enemy—you'll never lie in that cot again, and there's more glory and maybe less kicks from fightin' the enemy. That's fair speakin'.'

'And he told us by word of mouth to go and join with the niggers—you've forgotten that, Dan,' said Horse Egan, to justify sentence.

'What's the use of plaguin' the man. One shot pays for all. Sleep ye sound, Mulcahy. But you onderstand, do ye not ?'

Mulcahy for some weeks understood very little of anything at all save that ever at his elbow, in camp, or at parade, stood two big men with soft voices adjuring him to commit *hara-kiri* lest a worse thing should happen—to die for the honour of the regiment in decency among the nearest knives. But Mulcahy dreaded death. He remembered certain things that priests had said in his infancy, and his mother—not the one at New York—starting from her sleep with shrieks to pray for a husband's soul in torment. It is well to be of a cultured intelligence, but in time of trouble the weak human mind returns to the creed it sucked in at the breast, and if that creed be not a pretty one trouble follows. Also, the death he would have to face would be physically painful. Most conspirators have large imaginations. Mulcahy could see himself, as he lay on the earth in the night, dying by various causes. They were all horrible ; the mother in New York was very far away, and the regiment, the engine that, once you fall in its grip, moves you forward whether you will or won't, was daily coming closer to the enemy !

.   .   .   .   .

They were brought to the field of Marzun-Katai, and with the Black Boneens to aid, they fought a fight that has never been set down in the newspapers. In response, many believe, to the fervent prayers of Father Dennis, the enemy not only elected to fight in the open, but made a beautiful fight, as many weeping Irish mothers knew later. They gathered behind walls or

flickered across the open in shouting masses, and
were pot-valiant in artillery. It was expedient to
hold a large reserve and wait for the psychological
moment that was being prepared by the shrieking
shrapnel. Therefore the Mavericks lay down in
open order on the brow of a hill to watch the play
till their call should come. Father Dennis, whose
duty was in the rear, to smooth the trouble of the
wounded, had naturally managed to make his way
to the foremost of his boys, and lay like a black
porpoise at length on the grass. To him crawled
Mulcahy, ashen-gray, demanding absolution.

'Wait till you're shot,' said Father Dennis
sweetly. 'There's a time for everything.'

Dan Grady chuckled as he blew for the fiftieth
time into the breech of his speckless rifle.
Mulcahy groaned and buried his head in his arms
till a stray shot spoke like a snipe immediately
above his head, and a general heave and tremour
rippled the line. Other shots followed and a few
took effect, as a shriek or a grunt attested. The
officers, who had been lying down with the men,
rose and began to walk steadily up and down the
front of their companies.

This manœuvre, executed, not for publication,
but as a guarantee of good faith, to soothe men,
demands nerve. You must not hurry, you must
not look nervous, though you know that you are
a mark for every rifle within extreme range, and
above all, if you are smitten you must make as
little noise as possible and roll inwards through
the files. It is at this hour, when the breeze
brings the first salt whiff of the powder to noses

rather cold at the tip, and the eye can quietly take in the appearance of each red casualty, that the strain on the nerves is strongest. Scotch regiments can endure for half a day and abate no whit of their zeal at the end ; English regiments sometimes sulk under punishment, while the Irish, like the French, are apt to run forward by ones and twos, which is just as bad as running back. The truly wise commandant of highly-strung troops allows them, in seasons of waiting, to hear the sound of their own voices uplifted in song. There is a legend of an English regiment that lay by its arms under fire chanting 'Sam Hall,' to the horror of its newly appointed and pious colonel. The Black Boneens, who were suffering more than the Mavericks, on a hill half a mile away, began presently to explain to all who cared to listen—

We'll sound the jubilee, from the centre to the sea,
And Ireland shall be free, says the Shan-van Vogh.

'Sing, boys,' said Father Dennis softly. 'It looks as if we cared for their Afghan peas.'

Dan Grady raised himself to his knees and opened his mouth in a song imparted to him, as to most of his comrades, in the strictest confidence by Mulcahy—that Mulcahy then lying limp and fainting on the grass, the chill fear of death upon him.

Company after company caught up the words which, the I.A.A. say, are to herald the general rising of Erin, and to breathe which, except to those duly appointed to hear, is death. Wherefore they are printed in this place.

The Saxon in Heaven's just balance is weighed,
His doom like Belshazzar's in death has been cast,
And the hand of the venger shall never be stayed
Till his race, faith, and speech are a dream of the past.

They were heart-filling lines and they ran with a swirl; the I.A.A. are better served by their pens than their petards. Dan clapped Mulcahy merrily on the back, asking him to sing up. The officers lay down again. There was no need to walk any more. Their men were soothing themselves thunderously, thus—

St. Mary in Heaven has written the vow
That the land shall not rest till the heretic blood,
From the babe at the breast to the hand at the plough,
Has rolled to the ocean like Shannon in flood!

'I'll speak to you after all's over,' said Father Dennis authoritatively in Dan's ear. 'What's the use of confessing to me when you do this foolishness? Dan, you've been playing with fire! I'll lay you more penance in a week than——'

'Come along to Purgatory with us, Father dear. The Boneens are on the move; they'll let us go now!'

The regiment rose to the blast of the bugle as one man; but one man there was who rose more swiftly than all the others, for half an inch of bayonet was in the fleshy part of his leg.

'You've got to do it,' said Dan grimly. 'Do it decent, anyhow;' and the roar of the rush drowned his words, for the rear companies thrust forward the first, still singing as they swung down the slope—

From the child at the breast to the hand at the plough,
   Shall roll to the ocean like Shannon in flood !

They should have sung it in the face of England, not of the Afghans, whom it impressed as much as did the wild Irish yell.

'They came down singing,' said the unofficial report of the enemy, borne from village to village the next day. 'They continued to sing, and it was written that our men could not abide when they came. It is believed that there was magic in the aforesaid song.'

Dan and Horse Egan kept themselves in the neighbourhood of Mulcahy. Twice the man would have bolted back in the confusion. Twice he was heaved, kicked, and shouldered back again into the unpaintable inferno of a hotly contested charge.

At the end, the panic excess of his fear drove him into madness beyond all human courage. His eyes staring at nothing, his mouth open and frothing, and breathing as one in a cold bath, he went forward demented, while Dan toiled after him. The charge checked at a high mud wall. It was Mulcahy who scrambled up tooth and nail and hurled down among the bayonets the amazed Afghan who barred his way. It was Mulcahy, keeping to the straight line of the rabid dog, who led a collection of ardent souls at a newly unmasked battery, and flung himself on the muzzle of a gun as his companions danced among the gunners. It was Mulcahy who ran wildly on from that battery into the open plain, where the enemy were retiring in sullen groups. His hands were empty, he had lost helmet and belt, and he was bleeding from a wound in the neck. Dan and Horse Egan, panting and distressed, had thrown themselves down on the ground by the captured guns, when they noticed Mulcahy's charge.

'Mad,' said Horse Egan critically. 'Mad with fear! He's going straight to his death, an' shouting's no use.'

'Let him go. Watch now! If we fire we'll hit him maybe.'

The last of a hurrying crowd of Afghans turned at the noise of shod feet behind him, and shifted his knife ready to hand. This, he saw, was no time to take prisoners. Mulcahy tore on, sobbing; the straight-held blade went home through the defenceless breast, and the body pitched forward almost before a shot from Dan's rifle brought down the slayer and still further hurried the Afghan retreat. The two Irishmen went out to bring in their dead.

'He was given the point and that was an easy death,' said Horse Egan, viewing the corpse. 'But would you ha' shot him, Danny, if he had lived?'

'He didn't live, so there's no sayin'. But I doubt I wud have bekase of the fun he gave us—let alone the beer. Hike up his legs, Horse, and we'll bring him in. Perhaps 'tis better this way.'

They bore the poor limp body to the mass of the regiment, lolling open-mouthed on their rifles; and there was a general snigger when one of the younger subalterns said, 'That was a good man!'

'Phew,' said Horse Egan, when a burial-party had taken over the burden. 'I'm powerful dhry, and this reminds me there'll be no more beer at all.'

'Fwhy not?' said Dan, with a twinkle in his eye as he stretched himself for rest. 'Are we not conspirin' all we can, an' while we conspire are we not entitled to free dhrinks? Sure his ould mother in New York would not let her son's comrades perish of drouth—if she can be reached at the end of a letter.'

'You're a janius,' said Horse Egan. 'O' coorse she will not. I wish this crool war was over, an' we'd get back to canteen. Faith, the Commander-in-Chief ought to be hanged in his own little sword-belt for makin' us work on wather.'

The Mavericks were generally of Horse Egan's opinion. So they made haste to get their work done as soon as possible, and their industry was rewarded by unexpected peace. 'We can fight the sons of Adam,' said the tribesmen, 'but we cannot fight the sons of Eblis, and this regiment never stays still in one place. Let us therefore come in.' They came in and 'this regiment' withdrew to conspire under the leadership of Dan Grady.

Excellent as a subordinate Dan failed altogether as a chief-in-command—possibly because he was too much swayed by the advice of the only man in the regiment who could manufacture more than one kind of handwriting. The same mail that bore to Mulcahy's mother in New York a letter from the colonel, telling her how valiantly her son had fought for the Queen, and how assuredly he would have been recommended for the Victoria Cross had he survived, carried a communication signed, I grieve to say, by that same colonel and all the officers of the regiment, explaining their willingness to do 'anything which is contrary to the regulations and all kinds of revolutions' if only a little money could be forwarded to cover incidental expenses. Daniel Grady, Esquire, would receive funds, *vice* Mulcahy, who 'was unwell at this present time of writing.'

Both letters were forwarded from New York to Tehama Street, San Francisco, with marginal comments as brief as they were bitter. The Third Three read and looked at each other. Then the Second Conspirator—he who believed in 'joining hands with the practical branches'—began to laugh, and on recovering his gravity said, 'Gentlemen, I consider this will be a lesson to us. We're left again. Those cursed Irish have let us down. I knew they would, but '—here he laughed afresh —'I'd give considerable to know what was at the back of it all.'

His curiosity would have been satisfied had he seen Dan Grady, discredited regimental conspirator, trying to explain to his thirsty comrades in India the non-arrival of funds from New York.

The Mark of the Beast

Your Gods and my Gods—do you or I know which are the stronger ?—*Native Proverb*.

EAST of Suez, some hold, the direct control of Providence ceases ; Man being there handed over to the power of the Gods and Devils of Asia, and the Church of England Providence only exercising an occasional and modified supervision in the case of Englishmen.

This theory accounts for some of the more unnecessary horrors of life in India: it may be stretched to explain my story.

My friend Strickland of the Police, who knows as much of natives of India as is good for any man, can bear witness to the facts of the case. Dumoise, our doctor, also saw what Strickland and I saw. The inference which he drew from the evidence was entirely incorrect. He is dead now ; he died in a rather curious manner, which has been elsewhere described.

When Fleete came to India he owned a little money and some land in the Himalayas, near a place called Dharmsala. Both properties had been left him by an uncle, and he came out to finance them. He was a big, heavy, genial, and inoffensive man. His knowledge of natives was, of course, limited, and he complained of the difficulties of the language.

He rode in from his place in the hills to spend New Year in the station, and he stayed with Strickland. On New Year's Eve there was a big dinner at the club, and the night was excusably wet. When men foregather from the uttermost ends of the Empire they have a right to be riotous. The Frontier had sent down a contingent o' Catch-'em-Alive-O's who had not seen twenty white faces for a year, and were used to ride fifteen miles to dinner at the next Fort at the risk of a Khyberee bullet where their drinks should lie. They profited by their new security, for they tried to play pool with a curled-up hedgehog found in the garden, and one of them carried the marker round the room in his teeth. Half a dozen planters had come in from the south and were talking 'horse' to the Biggest Liar in Asia, who was trying to cap all their stories at once. Everybody was there, and there was a general closing up of ranks and taking stock of our losses in dead or disabled that had fallen during the past year. It was a very wet night, and I remember that we sang 'Auld Lang Syne' with our feet in the Polo Championship Cup, and our heads among the stars, and swore that we were all dear friends. Then some of us went away and annexed Burma, and some tried to open up the Soudan and were opened up by Fuzzies in that cruel scrub outside Suakin, and some found stars and medals, and some were married, which was bad, and some did other things which were worse, and the others of us stayed in our chains and strove to make money on insufficient experiences.

Fleete began the night with sherry and bitters, drank champagne steadily up to dessert, then raw, rasping Capri with all the strength of whisky, took Benedictine with his coffee, four or five whiskies and sodas to improve his pool strokes, beer and bones at half-past two, winding up with old brandy. Consequently, when he came out, at half-past three in the morning, into fourteen degrees of frost, he was very angry with his horse for coughing, and tried to leapfrog into the saddle. The horse broke away and went to his stables; so Strickland and I formed a Guard of Dishonour to take Fleete home.

Our road lay through the bazaar, close to a little temple of Hanuman, the Monkey-god, who is a leading divinity worthy of respect. All gods have good points, just as have all priests. Personally, I attach much importance to Hanuman, and am kind to his people—the great gray apes of the hills. One never knows when one may want a friend.

There was a light in the temple, and as we passed we could hear voices of men chanting hymns. In a native temple the priests rise at all hours of the night to do honour to their god. Before we could stop him, Fleete dashed up the steps, patted two priests on the back, and was gravely grinding the ashes of his cigar-butt in to the forehead of the red stone image of Hanuman.

Strickland tried to drag him out, but he sat down and said solemnly :

'Shee that ? 'Mark of the B—beasht ! *I* made it. Ishn't it fine?'

In half a minute the temple was alive and noisy, and Strickland, who knew what came of polluting gods, said that things might occur. He, by virtue of his official position, long residence in the country, and weakness for going among the natives, was known to the priests and he felt unhappy. Fleete sat on the ground and refused to move. He said that 'good old Hanuman' made a very soft pillow.

Then, without any warning, a Silver Man came out of a recess behind the image of the god. He was perfectly naked in that bitter, bitter cold, and his body shone like frosted silver, for he was what the Bible calls 'a leper as white as snow.' Also he had no face, because he was a leper of some years' standing, and his disease was heavy upon him. We two stooped to haul Fleete up, and the temple was filling and filling with folk who seemed to spring from the earth, when the Silver Man ran in under our arms, making a noise exactly like the mewing of an otter, caught Fleete round the body and dropped his head on Fleete's breast before we could wrench him away. Then he retired to a corner and sat mewing while the crowd blocked all the doors.

The priests were very angry until the Silver Man touched Fleete. That nuzzling seemed to sober them.

At the end of a few minutes' silence one of the priests came to Strickland and said, in perfect

English, 'Take your friend away. He has done with Hanuman but Hanuman has not done with him.' The crowd gave room and we carried Fleete into the road.

Strickland was very angry. He said that we might all three have been knifed, and that Fleete should thank his stars that he had escaped without injury.

Fleete thanked no one. He said that he wanted to go to bed. He was gorgeously drunk.

We moved on, Strickland silent and wrathful, until Fleete was taken with violent shivering fits and sweating. He said that the smells of the bazaar were overpowering, and he wondered why slaughter-houses were permitted so near English residences. 'Can't you smell the blood?' said Fleete.

We put him to bed at last, just as the dawn was breaking, and Strickland invited me to have another whisky and soda. While we were drinking he talked of the trouble in the temple, and admitted that it baffled him completely. Strickland hates being mystified by natives, because his business in life is to overmatch them with their own weapons. He has not yet succeeded in doing this, but in fifteen or twenty years he will have made some small progress.

'They should have mauled us,' he said, 'instead of mewing at us. I wonder what they meant. I don't like it one little bit.'

I said that the Managing Committee of the temple would in all probability bring a criminal action against us for insulting their religion.

There was a section of the Indian Penal Code which exactly met Fleete's offence. Strickland said he only hoped and prayed that they would do this. Before I left I looked into Fleete's room, and saw him lying on his right side, scratching his left breast. Then I went to bed cold, depressed, and unhappy, at seven o'clock in the morning.

At one o'clock I rode over to Strickland's house to inquire after Fleete's head. I imagined that it would be a sore one. Fleete was breakfasting and seemed unwell. His temper was gone, for he was abusing the cook for not supplying him with an underdone chop. A man who can eat raw meat after a wet night is a curiosity. I told Fleete this and he laughed.

'You breed queer mosquitoes in these parts,' he said. 'I've been bitten to pieces, but only in one place.'

'Let's have a look at the bite,' said Strickland. 'It may have gone down since this morning.'

While the chops were being cooked, Fleete opened his shirt and showed us, just over his left breast, a mark, the perfect double of the black rosettes—the five or six irregular blotches arranged in a circle—on a leopard's hide. Strickland looked and said, 'It was only pink this morning. It's grown black now.'

Fleete ran to a glass.

'By Jove!' he said, 'this is nasty. What is it?'

We could not answer. Here the chops came in, all red and juicy, and Fleete bolted three in a most offensive manner. He ate on his right grinders only, and threw his head over his right shoulder as he snapped the meat. When he had finished, it struck him that he had been behaving strangely, for he said apologetically, 'I don't think I ever felt so hungry in my life. I've bolted like an ostrich.'

After breakfast Strickland said to me, 'Don't go. Stay here, and stay for the night.'

Seeing that my house was not three miles from Strickland's, this request was absurd. But Strickland insisted, and was going to say something, when Fleete interrupted by declaring in a shamefaced way that he felt hungry again. Strickland sent a man to my house to fetch over my bedding and a horse, and we three went down to Strickland's stables to pass the hours until it was time to go out for a ride. The man who has a weakness for horses never wearies of inspecting them; and when two men are killing time in this way they gather knowledge and lies the one from the other.

There were five horses in the stables, and I shall never forget the scene as we tried to look them over. They seemed to have gone mad. They reared and screamed and nearly tore up their pickets; they sweated and shivered and lathered and were distraught with fear. Strickland's horses used to know him as well as his dogs; which made the matter more curious. We left the stable for fear of the brutes throwing themselves in their panic. Then Strickland turned back and called me. The horses were still frightened, but they let us 'gentle' and make much of them, and put their heads in our bosoms.

'They aren't afraid of *us*,' said Strickland. 'D' you know, I'd give three months' pay if *Outrage* here could talk.'

But *Outrage* was dumb, and could only cuddle up to his master and blow out his nostrils, as is the custom of horses when they wish to explain things but can't. Fleete came up when we were in the stalls, and as soon as the horses saw him, their fright broke out afresh. It was all that we could do to escape from the place unkicked. Strickland said, 'They don't seem to love you, Fleete.'

'Nonsense, said Fleete ; 'my mare will follow me like a dog.' He went to her ; she was in a loose-box ; but as he slipped the bars she plunged, knocked him down, and broke away into the garden. I laughed, but Strickland was not amused. He took his moustache in both fists and pulled at it till it nearly came out. Fleete, instead of going off to chase his property, yawned, saying that he felt sleepy. He went to the house to lie down, which was a foolish way of spending New Year's Day.

Strickland sat with me in the stables and asked if I had noticed anything peculiar in Fleete's manner. I said that he ate his food like a beast ; but that this might have been the result of living alone in the hills out of the reach of society as refined and elevating as ours for instance. Strickland was not amused. I do not think that he listened to me, for his next sentence referred to the mark on Fleete's breast, and I said that it might have been caused by blister-flies, or that it was possibly a birth-mark newly born and now visible for the first time. We both agreed that it was unpleasant to look at, and Strickland found occasion to say that I was a fool.

'I can't tell you what I think now,' said he, 'because you would call me a madman; but you must stay with me for the next few days, if you can. I want you to watch Fleete, but don't tell me what you think till I have made up my mind.'

'But I am dining out to-night,' I said.

'So am I,' said Strickland, 'and so is Fleete. At least if he doesn't change his mind.'

We walked about the garden smoking, but saying nothing—because we were friends, and talking spoils good tobacco—till our pipes were out. Then we went to wake up Fleete. He was wide awake and fidgeting about his room.

'I say, I want some more chops,' he said. 'Can I get them?'

We laughed and said, 'Go and change. The ponies will be round in a minute.'

'All right,' said Fleete. 'I'll go when I get the chops—underdone ones, mind.'

He seemed to be quite in earnest. It was four o'clock, and we had had breakfast at one; still, for a long time, he demanded those underdone chops. Then he changed into riding clothes and went out into the verandah. His pony—the mare had not been caught—would not let him come near. All three horses were unmanageable—mad with fear—and finally Fleete said that he would stay at home and get something to eat. Strickland and I rode out wondering. As we passed the temple of Hanuman the Silver Man came out and mewed at us.

'He is not one of the regular priests of the temple,' said Strickland. 'I think I should peculiarly like to lay my hands on him.'

There was no spring in our gallop on the race-course that evening. The horses were stale, and moved as though they had been ridden out.

'The fright after breakfast has been too much for them,' said Strickland.

That was the only remark he made through the remainder of the ride. Once or twice, I think, he swore to himself; but that did not count.

We came back in the dark at seven o'clock, and saw that there were no lights in the bungalow. 'Careless ruffians my servants are!' said Strickland.

My horse reared at something on the carriage drive, and Fleete stood up under its nose.

'What are you doing, grovelling about the garden?' said Strickland.

But both horses bolted and nearly threw us. We dismounted by the stables and returned to Fleete, who was on his hands and knees under the orange-bushes.

'What the devil's wrong with you?' said Strickland.

'Nothing, nothing in the world,' said Fleete, speaking very quickly and thickly. 'I've been gardening—botanising, you know. The smell of the earth is delightful. I think I'm going for a walk—a long walk—all night.'

Then I saw that there was something excessively

out of order somewhere, and I said to Strickland, 'I am not dining out.'

'Bless you!' said Strickland. 'Here, Fleete, get up. You'll catch fever there. Come in to dinner and let's have the lamps lit. We'll all dine at home.'

Fleete stood up unwillingly, and said, 'No lamps—no lamps. It's much nicer here. Let's dine outside and have some more chops—lots of 'em and underdone—bloody ones with gristle.'

Now a December evening in Northern India is bitterly cold, and Fleete's suggestion was that of a maniac.

'Come in,' said Strickland sternly. 'Come in at once.'

Fleete came, and when the lamps were brought, we saw that he was literally plastered with dirt from head to foot. He must have been rolling in the garden. He shrank from the light and went to his room. His eyes were horrible to look at. There was a green light behind them, not in them, if you understand, and the man's lower lip hung down.

Strickland said, 'There is going to be trouble—big trouble—to-night. Don't you change your riding-things.'

We waited and waited for Fleete's reappearance, and ordered dinner in the meantime. We could hear him moving about his own room, but there was no light there. Presently from the room came the long-drawn howl of a wolf.

People write and talk lightly of blood running cold and hair standing up, and things of that kind. Both sensations are too horrible to be trifled with.

My heart stopped as though a knife had been driven through it, and Strickland turned as white as the tablecloth.

The howl was repeated, and was answered by another howl far across the fields.

That set the gilded roof on the horror. Strickland dashed into Fleete's room. I followed, and we saw Fleete getting out of the window. He made beast-noises in the back of his throat. He could not answer us when we shouted at him. He spat.

I don't quite remember what followed, but I think that Strickland must have stunned him with the long boot-jack, or else I should never have been able to sit on his chest. Fleete could not speak, he could only snarl, and his snarls were those of a wolf, not of a man. The human spirit must have been giving way all day and have died out with the twilight. We were dealing with a beast that had once been Fleete.

The affair was beyond any human and rational experience. I tried to say 'Hydrophobia,' but the word wouldn't come, because I knew that I was lying.

We bound this beast with leather thongs of the punkah-rope, and tied its thumbs and big toes together, and gagged it with a shoe-horn, which makes a very efficient gag if you know how to arrange it. Then we carried it into the dining-room, and sent a man to Dumoise, the doctor, telling him to come over at once. After we had despatched the messenger and were drawing breath, Strickland said, 'It's no good. This isn't any doctor's work.' I, also, knew that he spoke the truth.

The beast's head was free, and it threw it about from side to side. Any one entering the room would have believed that we were curing a wolf's pelt. That was the most loathsome accessory of all.

Strickland sat with his chin in the heel of his fist, watching the beast as it wriggled on the ground, but saying nothing. The shirt had been torn open in the scuffle and showed the black rosette mark on the left breast. It stood out like a blister.

In the silence of the watching we heard something without mewing like a she-otter. We both rose to our feet, and, I answer for myself, not Strickland, felt sick—actually and physically sick. We told each other, as did the men in *Pinafore*, that it was the cat.

Dumoise arrived, and I never saw a little man so unprofessionally shocked. He said that it was a heart-rending case of hydrophobia, and that nothing could be done. At least any palliative measures would only prolong the agony. The beast was foaming at the mouth. Fleete, as we told Dumoise, had been bitten by dogs once or twice. Any man who keeps half a dozen terriers must expect a nip now and again. Dumoise could offer no help. He could only certify that Fleete was dying of hydrophobia. The beast was then howling, for it had managed to spit out the shoe-horn. Dumoise said that he would be ready to certify to the cause of death, and that the end was

certain.   He was a good little man, and he offered
to remain with us ; but Strickland refused the
kindness.   He did not wish to poison Dumoise's
New Year.   He would only ask him not to give
the real cause of Fleete's death to the public.

So Dumoise left, deeply agitated ; and as soon
as the noise of the cart-wheels had died away,
Strickland told me, in a whisper, his suspicions.
They were so wildly improbable that he dared not
say them out aloud ; and I, who entertained all
Strickland's beliefs, was so ashamed of owning to
them that I pretended to disbelieve.

'Even if the Silver Man had bewitched Fleete
for polluting the image of Hanuman, the punishment could not have fallen so quickly.'

As I was whispering this the cry outside the
house rose again, and the beast fell into a fresh
paroxysm of struggling till we were afraid that the
thongs that held it would give way.

'Watch !' said Strickland.   'If this happens
six times I shall take the law into my own hands.
I order you to help me.'

He went into his room and came out in a few
minutes with the barrels of an old shot-gun, a
piece of fishing-line, some thick cord, and his
heavy wooden bedstead.   I reported that the con-
vulsions had followed the cry by two seconds in
each case, and the beast seemed perceptibly
weaker.

Strickland muttered, 'But he can't take away
the life !   He can't take away the life !'

I said, though I knew that I was arguing
against myself, 'It may be a cat.   It must be a

cat. If the Silver Man is responsible, why does he dare to come here?'

Strickland arranged the wood on the hearth, put the gun-barrels into the glow of the fire, spread the twine on the table, and broke a walking stick in two. There was one yard of fishing line, gut lapped with wire, such as is used for *mahseer*-fishing, and he tied the two ends together in a loop.

Then he said, 'How can we catch him? He must be taken alive and unhurt.'

I said that we must trust in Providence, and go out softly with polo-sticks into the shrubbery at the front of the house. The man or animal that made the cry was evidently moving round the house as regularly as a night-watchman. We could wait in the bushes till he came by and knock him over.

Strickland accepted this suggestion, and we slipped out from a bath-room window into the front verandah and then across the carriage drive into the bushes.

In the moonlight we could see the leper coming round the corner of the house. He was perfectly naked, and from time to time he mewed and stopped to dance with his shadow. It was an unattractive sight, and thinking of poor Fleete, brought to such degradation by so foul a creature, I put away all my doubts and resolved to help Strickland from the heated gun-barrels to the loop of twine—from the loins to the head and back again—with all tortures that might be needful.

The leper halted in the front porch for a

moment and we jumped out on him with the sticks. He was wonderfully strong, and we were afraid that he might escape or be fatally injured before we caught him. We had an idea that lepers were frail creatures, but this proved to be incorrect. Strickland knocked his legs from under him and I put my foot on his neck. He mewed hideously, and even through my riding-boots I could feel that his flesh was not the flesh of a clean man.

He struck at us with his hand and feet-stumps. We looped the lash of a dog-whip round him, under the arm-pits, and dragged him backwards into the hall and so into the dining-room where the beast lay. There we tied him with trunk-straps. He made no attempt to escape, but mewed.

When we confronted him with the beast the scene was beyond description. The beast doubled backwards into a bow as though he had been poisoned with strychnine, and moaned in the most pitiable fashion. Several other things happened also, but they cannot be put down here.

'I think I was right,' said Strickland. 'Now we will ask him to cure this case.'

But the leper only mewed. Strickland wrapped a towel round his hand and took the gun-barrels out of the fire. I put the half of the broken walking stick through the loop of fishing-line and buckled the leper comfortably to Strickland's bed-stead. I understood then how men and women and little children can endure to see a witch burnt alive ; for the beast was moaning on the floor, and though the Silver Man had no face, you could see horrible feelings passing through the slab that took its place, exactly as waves of heat play across red-hot iron—gun-barrels for instance.

Strickland shaded his eyes with his hands for a moment and we got to work. This part is not to be printed.

.   .   .   .   .

The dawn was beginning to break when the leper spoke. His mewings had not been satisfactory up to that point. The beast had fainted from exhaustion and the house was very still. We unstrapped the leper and told him to take away the evil spirit. He crawled to the beast and laid his hand upon the left breast. That was all. Then he fell face down and whined, drawing in his breath as he did so.

We watched the face of the beast, and saw the soul of Fleete coming back into the eyes. Then a sweat broke out on the forehead and the eyes— they were human eyes—closed. We waited for an hour, but Fleete still slept. We carried him to his room and bade the leper go, giving him the bedstead, and the sheet on the bedstead to cover his nakedness, the gloves and the towels with which we had touched him, and the whip that had been hooked round his body. He put the sheet about him and went out into the early morning without speaking or mewing.

Strickland wiped his face and sat down. A night-gong, far away in the city, made seven o'clock.

'Exactly four-and-twenty hours!' said Strickland. 'And I've done enough to ensure my dismissal from the service, besides permanent quarters in a lunatic asylum. Do you believe that we are awake?'

The red-hot gun-barrel had fallen on the floor and was singeing the carpet. The smell was entirely real.

That morning at eleven we two together went to wake up Fleete. We looked and saw that the black leopard-rosette on his chest had disappeared. He was very drowsy and tired, but as soon as he saw us, he said, 'Oh! Confound you fellows. Happy New Year to you. Never mix your liquors. I'm nearly dead.'

'Thanks for your kindness, but you're over time,' said Strickland. 'To-day is the morning of the second. You've slept the clock round with a vengeance.'

The door opened, and little Dumoise put his head in. He had come on foot, and fancied that we were laying out Fleete.

'I've brought a nurse,' said Dumoise. 'I suppose that she can come in for . . . what is necessary.'

'By all means,' said Fleete cheerily, sitting up in bed. 'Bring on your nurses.'

Dumoise was dumb. Strickland led him out and explained that there must have been a mistake in the diagnosis. Dumoise remained dumb and left the house hastily. He considered that his professional reputation had been injured, and was inclined to make a personal matter of the recovery. Strickland went out too. When he came back, he said that he had been to call on the Temple of Hanuman to offer redress for the pollution of the god, and had been solemnly assured that no white man had ever touched the idol, and that he was an incarnation of all the virtues labouring under a delusion. 'What do you think?' said Strickland.

I said, '"There are more things . . "'

But Strickland hates that quotation. He says that I have worn it threadbare.

One other curious thing happened which frightened me as much as anything in all the night's work. When Fleete was dressed he came into the dining-room and sniffed. He had a quaint trick of moving his nose when he sniffed. 'Horrid doggy smell, here,' said he. 'You should really keep those terriers of yours in better order. Try sulphur, Strick.'

But Strickland did not answer. He caught hold of the back of a chair, and, without warning, went into an amazing fit of hysterics. It is terrible to see a strong man overtaken with hysteria. Then it struck me that we had fought for Fleete's soul with the Silver Man in that room, and had disgraced ourselves as Englishmen for ever, and I laughed and gasped and gurgled just as shamefully as Strickland, while Fleete thought that we had both gone mad. We never told him what we had done.

Some years later, when Strickland had married and was a church-going member of society for his wife's sake, we reviewed the incident dispassionately, and Strickland suggested that I should put it before the public.

I cannot myself see that this step is likely to clear up the mystery ; because, in the first place, no one will believe a rather unpleasant story, and, in the second, it is well known to every right-minded man that the gods of the heathen are stone and brass, and any attempt to deal with them otherwise is justly condemned.

The Return of Imray

The doors were wide, the story saith,
Out of the night came the patient wraith,
He might not speak, and he could not stir
A hair of the Baron's miniver—
Speechless and strengthless, a shadow thin,
He roved the castle to seek his kin.
And oh, 'twas a piteous thing to see
The dumb ghost follow his enemy!

The Baron.

IMRAY achieved the impossible. Without warning, for no conceivable motive, in his youth, at the threshold of his career he chose to disappear from the world—which is to say, the little Indian station where he lived.

Upon a day he was alive, well, happy, and in great evidence among the billiard-tables at his Club. Upon a morning he was not, and no manner of search could make sure where he might be. He had stepped out of his place; he had not appeared at his office at the proper time, and his dogcart was not upon the public roads. For these reasons, and because he was hampering, in a microscopical degree, the administration of the Indian Empire, that Empire paused for one microscopical moment to make inquiry into the fate of Imray. Ponds were dragged, wells were plumbed, telegrams were despatched down the lines of railways and to the nearest seaport town— twelve hundred miles away ; but Imray was not at the end of the drag-ropes nor the telegraph wires. He was gone, and his place knew him no more. Then the work of the great Indian Empire swept forward, because it could not be delayed, and Imray from being a man became a mystery— such a thing as men talk over at their tables in the Club for a month, and then forget utterly. His guns, horses, and carts were sold to the highest bidder. His superior officer wrote an altogether absurd letter to his mother, saying that Imray had unaccountably disappeared, and his bungalow stood empty.

After three or four months of the scorching hot weather had gone by, my friend Strickland, of the Police, saw fit to rent the bungalow from the native landlord. This was before he was engaged to Miss Youghal—an affair which has been described in another place—and while he was pursuing his investigations into native life. His own life was sufficiently peculiar, and men complained of his manners and customs. There was always food in his house, but there were no regular times for meals. He ate, standing up and walking about, whatever he might find at the sideboard, and this is not good for human beings. His domestic equipment was limited to six rifles, three shot-guns, five saddles, and a collection of stiff-jointed mahseer-rods, bigger and stronger than the largest salmon-rods. These occupied one-half of his bungalow, and the other half was given up to Strickland and his dog Tietjens—an enormous Rampur slut who devoured daily the rations of two men. She spoke to Strickland in a language of her own ; and whenever, walking abroad, she saw things calculated to destroy the peace of Her Majesty the Queen-Empress, she returned to her master and laid information. Strickland would take steps at once, and the end of his labours was trouble and fine and imprisonment for other people. The natives believed that Tietjens was a familiar spirit, and treated her with the great reverence that is born of hate and fear. One room in the bungalow was set apart for her special use. She owned a bedstead, a blanket, and a drinking-trough, and if any one came into Strickland's room at night her custom was to knock down the invader and give tongue till some one came with a light. Strickland owed his life to her when he was on the Frontier, in search of a local murderer, who came in the gray dawn to send Strickland much farther than the Andaman Islands. Tietjens caught the man as he was crawling into Strickland's tent with a dagger between his teeth ; and after his record of iniquity was established in the eyes of the law he was hanged. From that date Tietjens wore a collar of rough silver, and employed a monogram on her night-blanket ; and the blanket was of double woven Kashmir cloth, for she was a delicate dog.

Under no circumstances would she be separated from Strickland ; and once, when he was ill with fever, made great trouble for the doctors, because she did not know how to help her master and would not allow another creature to attempt aid. Macarnaght, of the Indian Medical Service, beat her over her head with a gun-butt before she could understand that she must give room for those who could give quinine.

A short time after Strickland had taken Imray's bungalow, my business took me through that Station, and naturally, the Club quarters being full, I quartered myself upon Strickland. It was a desirable bungalow, eight-roomed and heavily thatched against any chance of leakage from rain. Under the pitch of the roof ran a ceiling-cloth which looked just as neat as a white-washed ceiling. The landlord had repainted it when Strickland took the bungalow. Unless you knew how Indian bungalows were built you would never have suspected that above the cloth lay the dark three-cornered cavern of the roof, where the beams and the underside of the thatch harboured all manner of rats, bats, ants, and foul things.

Tietjens met me in the verandah with a bay like the boom of the bell of St. Paul's, putting her paws on my shoulder to show she was glad to see me. Strickland had contrived to claw together a sort of meal which he called lunch, and immediately after it was finished went out about his business. I was left alone with Tietjens and my own affairs. The heat of the summer had broken up and turned to the warm damp of the rains. There was no motion in the heated air, but the rain fell like ramrods on the earth, and flung up a blue mist

when it splashed back.   The bamboos, and the
custard-apples, the poinsettias, and the mango-trees
in the garden stood still while the warm water
lashed through them, and the frogs began to sing
among the aloe hedges.   A little before the light
failed, and when the rain was at its worst, I sat in
the back verandah and heard the water roar from
the eaves, and scratched myself because I was
covered with the thing called prickly-heat.   Tietjens came out with me and put her head in my lap
and was very sorrowful ; so I gave her biscuits
when tea was ready, and I took tea in the back
verandah on account of the little coolness found
there.   The rooms of the house were dark behind
me.   I could smell Strickland's saddlery and the
oil on his guns, and I had no desire to sit among
these things.   My own servant came to me in
the twilight, the muslin of his clothes clinging
tightly to his drenched body, and told me that a
gentleman had called and wished to see some one.
Very much against my will, but only because of
the darkness of the rooms, I went into the naked
drawing-room, telling my man to bring the lights.
There might or might not have been a caller
waiting—it seemed to me that I saw a figure by
one of the windows—but when the lights came
there was nothing save the spikes of the rain without, and the smell of the drinking earth in my
nostrils.   I explained to my servant that he was
no wiser than he ought to be, and went back to
the verandah to talk to Tietjens.   She had gone
out into the wet, and I could hardly coax her back
to me, even with biscuits with sugar tops.   Strick-

land came home, dripping wet, just before dinner, and the first thing he said was,

'Has any one called?'

I explained, with apologies, that my servant had summoned me into the drawing-room on a false alarm; or that some loafer had tried to call on Strickland, and thinking better of it had fled after giving his name.   Strickland ordered dinner, without comment, and since it was a real dinner with a white tablecloth attached, we sat down.

At nine o'clock Strickland wanted to go to bed, and I was tired too.   Tietjens, who had been lying underneath the table, rose up, and swung into the least exposed verandah as soon as her master moved to his own room, which was next to the stately chamber set apart for Tietjens.   If a mere wife had wished to sleep out of doors in that pelting rain it would not have mattered; but Tietjens was a dog, and therefore the better animal.   I looked at Strickland, expecting to see him flay her with a whip.   He smiled queerly, as a man would smile after telling some unpleasant domestic tragedy. 'She has done this ever since I moved in here,' said he.   'Let her go.'

The dog was Strickland's dog, so I said nothing, but I felt all that Strickland felt in being thus made light of.   Tietjens encamped outside my bedroom window, and storm after storm came up, thundered on the thatch, and died away.   The lightning spattered the sky as a thrown egg spatters a barn-door, but the light was pale blue, not yellow; and, looking through my split-bamboo blinds, I could see the great dog standing, not sleeping, in the verandah, the hackles alift on her back, and her feet anchored as tensely as the drawn wire-rope of a suspension bridge. In the very short pauses of the thunder I tried to sleep, but it seemed that some one wanted me very urgently. He, who-ever he was, was trying to call me by name, but his voice was no more than a husky whisper. The thunder ceased, and Tietjens went into the garden and howled at the low moon. Somebody tried to open my door, walked about and about through the house, and stood breathing heavily in the verandahs, and just when I was falling asleep I fancied that I heard a wild hammering and clamour-ing above my head or on the door.

I ran into Strickland's room and asked him whether he was ill, and had been calling for me. He was lying on his bed half dressed, a pipe in his mouth. 'I thought you'd come,' he said. 'Have I been walking round the house recently?'

I explained that he had been tramping in the dining-room and the smoking-room and two or three other places; and he laughed and told me to go back to bed. I went back to bed and slept till the morning, but through all my mixed dreams I was sure I was doing some one an injustice in not attending to his wants. What those wants were I could not tell; but a fluttering, whispering, bolt-fumbling, lurking, loitering Someone was reproaching me for my slackness, and, half awake, I heard the howling of Tietjens in the garden and the threshing of the rain.

I lived in that house for two days. Strickland went to his office daily, leaving me alone for eight or ten hours with Tietjens for my only companion. As long as the full light lasted I was comfortable, and so was Tietjens; but in the twilight she and I moved into the back verandah and cuddled each other for company. We were alone in the house, but none the less it was much too fully occupied by a tenant with whom I did not wish to interfere. I never saw him, but I could see the curtains between the rooms quivering where he had just passed through; I could hear the chairs creaking as the bamboos sprung under a weight that had just quitted them; and I could feel when I went to get a book from the dining-room that somebody was waiting in the shadows of the front verandah till I should have gone away. Tietjens made the twilight more interesting by glaring into the darkened rooms with every hair erect, and following the motions of something that I could not see. She never entered the rooms, but her eyes moved interestedly : that was quite sufficient. Only when my servant came to trim the lamps and make all light and habitable she would come in with me and spend her time sitting on her haunches, watching an invisible extra man as he moved about behind my shoulder. Dogs are cheerful companions.

I explained to Strickland, gently as might be, that I would go over to the Club and find for myself quarters there. I admired his hospitality, was pleased with his guns and rods, but I did not much care for his house and its atmosphere. He heard me out to the end, and then smiled very wearily, but without contempt, for he is a man who understands things. 'Stay on,' he said, 'and see what this thing means. All you have talked about I have known since I took the bungalow. Stay on and wait. Tietjens has left me. Are you going too?'

I had seen him through one little affair, connected with a heathen idol, that had brought me to the doors of a lunatic asylum, and I had no desire to help him through further experiences. He was a man to whom unpleasantnesses arrived as do dinners to ordinary people.

Therefore I explained more clearly than ever that I liked him immensely, and would be happy to see him in the daytime; but that I did not care to sleep under his roof. This was after dinner, when Tietjens had gone out to lie in the verandah.

''Pon my soul, I don't wonder,' said Strickland, with his eyes on the ceiling-cloth. 'Look at that!'

The tails of two brown snakes were hanging between the cloth and the cornice of the wall. They threw long shadows in the lamplight.

'If you are afraid of snakes of course——' said Strickland.

I hate and fear snakes, because if you look into the eyes of any snake you will see that it knows all and more of the mystery of man's fall, and that it feels all the contempt that the Devil felt when Adam was evicted from Eden. Besides which its bite is generally fatal, and it twists up trouser legs.

'You ought to get your thatch overhauled,' I said. 'Give me a mahseer-rod, and we'll poke 'em down.'

'They'll hide among the roof-beams,' said Strickland. 'I can't stand snakes overhead. I'm going up into the roof.   If I shake 'em down, stand by with a cleaning-rod and break their backs.'

I was not anxious to assist Strickland in his work, but I took the cleaning-rod and waited in the dining-room, while Strickland brought a gardener's ladder from the verandah, and set it against the side of the room.   The snake-tails drew themselves up and disappeared.   We could hear the dry rushing scuttle of long bodies running over the baggy ceiling cloth.   Strickland took a lamp with him, while I tried to make clear to him the danger of hunting roof-snakes between a ceiling-cloth and a thatch, apart from the deterioration of property caused by ripping out ceiling-cloths.

'Nonsense!' said Strickland.   'They're sure to hide near the walls by the cloth.   The bricks are too cold for 'em, and the heat of the room is just what they like.'   He put his hand to the corner of the stuff and ripped it from the cornice. It gave with a great sound of tearing, and Strickland put his head through the opening into the dark of the angle of the roof-beams.   I set my teeth and lifted the rod, for I had not the least knowledge of what might descend.

'H'm!' said Strickland, and his voice rolled and rumbled in the roof.   'There's room for another set of rooms up here, and, by Jove, some one is occupying 'em!'

'Snakes?' I said from below.

'No.   It's a buffalo.   Hand me up the two last joints of a mahseer-rod, and I'll prod it.   It's lying on the main roof-beam.'

I handed up the rod.

'What a nest for owls and serpents! No wonder the snakes live here,' said Strickland, climbing farther into the roof. I could see his elbow thrusting with the rod. 'Come out of that, whoever you are! Heads below there! It's falling.'

I saw the ceiling cloth nearly in the centre of the room bag with a shape that was pressing it downwards and downwards towards the lighted lamp on the table. I snatched the lamp out of danger and stood back. Then the cloth ripped out from the walls, tore, split, swayed, and shot down upon the table something that I dared not look at, till Strickland had slid down the ladder and was standing by my side.

He did not say much, being a man of few words; but he picked up the loose end of the tablecloth and threw it over the remnants on the table.

'It strikes me,' said he, putting down the lamp, 'our friend Imray has come back. Oh! you would, would you?'

There was a movement under the cloth, and a little snake wriggled out, to be back-broken by the butt of the mahseer-rod. I was sufficiently sick to make no remarks worth recording.

Strickland meditated, and helped himself to drinks. The arrangement under the cloth made no more signs of life.

'Is it Imray?' I said.

Strickland turned back the cloth for a moment, and looked.

'It is Imray,' he said; 'and his throat is cut from ear to ear.'

Then we spoke, both together and to ourselves : 'That's why he whispered about the house.'

Tietjens, in the garden, began to bay furiously. A little later her great nose heaved open the dining-room door.

She snuffed and was still.   The tattered ceiling-cloth hung down almost to the level of the table, and there was hardly room to move away from the discovery.

Tietjens came in and sat down ; her teeth bared under her lip and her forepaws planted.   She looked at Strickland.

'It's a bad business, old lady,' said he.   'Men don't climb up into the roofs of their bungalows to die, and they don't fasten up the ceiling cloth behind 'em.   Let's think it out.'

'Let's think it out somewhere else,' I said.

'Excellent idea !   Turn the lamps out.   We'll get into my room.'

I did not turn the lamps out.   I went into Strickland's room first, and allowed him to make the darkness.   Then he followed me, and we lit tobacco and thought.   Strickland thought.   I smoked furiously, because I was afraid.

'Imray is back,' said Strickland.   'The question is—who killed Imray?   Don't talk, I've a notion of my own.   When I took this bungalow I took over most of Imray's servants.   Imray was guileless and inoffensive, wasn't he ? '

I agreed ; though the heap under the cloth had looked neither one thing nor the other.

'If I call in all the servants they will stand fast

in a crowd and lie like Aryans. What do you suggest?'

'Call 'em in one by one,' I said.

'They'll run away and give the news to all their fellows,' said Strickland. 'We must segregate 'em. Do you suppose your servant knows anything about it?'

'He may, for aught I know; but I don't think it's likely. He has only been here two or three days,' I answered. 'What's your notion?'

'I can't quite tell. How the dickens did the man get the wrong side of the ceiling-cloth?'

There was a heavy coughing outside Strickland's bedroom door. This showed that Bahadur Khan, his body-servant, had waked from sleep and wished to put Strickland to bed.

'Come in,' said Strickland. 'It's a very warm night, isn't it?'

Bahadur Khan, a great, green-turbaned, six-foot Mahomedan, said that it was a very warm night; but that there was more rain pending, which, by his Honour's favour, would bring relief to the country.

'It will be so, if God pleases,' said Strickland, tugging off his boots. 'It is in my mind, Bahadur Khan, that I have worked thee remorselessly for many days—ever since that time when thou first camest into my service. What time was that?'

'Has the Heaven-born forgotten? It was when Imray Sahib went secretly to Europe without warning given; and I—even I—came into the honoured service of the protector of the poor.'

'And Imray Sahib went to Europe?'

'It is so said among those who were his servants.'

'And thou wilt take service with him when he returns?'

'Assuredly, Sahib. He was a good master, and cherished his dependants.'

'That is true. I am very tired, but I go buck-shooting to-morrow. Give me the little sharp rifle that I use for black-buck; it is in the case yonder.'

The man stooped over the case; handed barrels, stock, and fore-end to Strickland, who fitted all together, yawning dolefully. Then he reached down to the gun-case, took a solid-drawn cartridge, and slipped it into the breech of the ·360 Express.

'And Imray Sahib has gone to Europe secretly! That is very strange, Bahadur Khan, is it not?'

'What do I know of the ways of the white man, Heaven-born?'

'Very little, truly. But thou shalt know more anon. It has reached me that Imray Sahib has returned from his so long journeyings, and that even now he lies in the next room, waiting his servant.'

'Sahib!'

The lamplight slid along the barrels of the rifle as they levelled themselves at Bahadur Khan's broad breast.

'Go and look!' said Strickland. 'Take a lamp. Thy master is tired, and he waits thee. Go!'

The man picked up a lamp, and went into the dining-room, Strickland following, and almost pushing him with the muzzle of the rifle. He looked for a moment at the black depths behind the ceiling-cloth; at the writhing snake under foot; and last, a gray glaze settling on his face, at the thing under the tablecloth.

'Hast thou seen?' said Strickland after a pause.

'I have seen. I am clay in the white man's hands. What does the Presence do?'

'Hang thee within the month. What else?'

'For killing him? Nay, Sahib, consider. Walking among us, his servants, he cast his eyes upon my child, who was four years old. Him he bewitched, and in ten days he died of the fever— my child!'

'What said Imray Sahib?'

'He said he was a handsome child, and patted him on the head; wherefore my child died. Wherefore I killed Imray Sahib in the twilight, when he had come back from office, and was sleeping. Wherefore I dragged him up into the roof-beams and made all fast behind him. The Heaven-born knows all things. I am the servant of the Heaven-born.'

Strickland looked at me above the rifle, and said, in the vernacular, 'Thou art witness to this saying? He has killed.'

Bahadur Khan stood ashen gray in the light of the one lamp. The need for justification came upon him very swiftly. 'I am trapped,' he said, 'but the offence was that man's. He cast an evil

eye upon my child, and I killed and hid him.
Only such as are served by devils,' he glared at
Tietjens, couched stolidly before him, 'only such
could know what I did.'

'It was clever.   But thou shouldst have lashed
him to the beam with a rope.   Now, thou thyself
wilt hang by a rope.   Orderly!'

A drowsy policeman answered Strickland's call.
He was followed by another, and Tietjens sat
wondrous still.

'Take him to the police-station,' said Strickland.
'There is a case toward.'

'Do I hang, then?' said Bahadur Khan, making
no attempt to escape, and keeping his eyes on the
ground.

'If the sun shines or the water runs—yes!'
said Strickland.

Bahadur Khan stepped back one long pace,
quivered, and stood still.   The two policemen
waited further orders.

'Go!' said Strickland.

'Nay; but I go very swiftly,' said Bahadur Khan.   'Look!   I am even now a dead
man.'

He lifted his foot, and to the little toe there
clung the head of the half-killed snake, firm fixed
in the agony of death.

'I come of land-holding stock,' said Bahadur
Khan, rocking where he stood.   'It were a
disgrace to me to go to the public scaffold:
therefore I take this way.   Be it remembered that
the Sahib's shirts are correctly enumerated, and
that there is an extra piece of soap in his wash-

basin. My child was bewitched, and I slew the wizard. Why should you seek to slay me with the rope? My honour is saved, and—and—I die.'

At the end of an hour he died, as they die who are bitten by the little brown *karait*, and the policemen bore him and the thing under the tablecloth to their appointed places. All were needed to make clear the disappearance of Imray.

'This,' said Strickland, very calmly, as he climbed into bed, 'is called the nineteenth century. Did you hear what that man said?'

'I heard,' I answered. 'Imray made a mistake.'

'Simply and solely through not knowing the nature of the Oriental, and the coincidence of a little seasonal fever. Bahadur Khan had been with him for four years.'

I shuddered. My own servant had been with me for exactly that length of time. When I went over to my own room I found my man waiting, impassive as the copper head on a penny, to pull off my boots.

'What has befallen Bahadur Khan?' said I.

'He was bitten by a snake and died. The rest the Sahib knows,' was the answer.

'And how much of this matter hast thou known?'

'As much as might be gathered from One coming in in the twilight to seek satisfaction. Gently, Sahib. Let me pull off those boots.'

I had just settled to the sleep of exhaustion when I heard Strickland shouting from his side of the house—

'Tietjens has come back to her place!'

And so she had. The great deerhound was couched statelily on her own bedstead on her own blanket, while, in the next room, the idle, empty, ceiling-cloth waggled as it trailed on the table.

Namgay Doola

There came to the beach a poor exile of Erin,
The dew on his wet robe hung heavy and chill ;
Ere the steamer that brought him had passed out of hearin',
He was Alderman Mike inthrojuicin' a bill !

American Song.

ONCE upon a time there was a King who lived
on the road to Thibet, very many miles in the
Himalayas. His Kingdom was eleven thousand
feet above the sea and exactly four miles square ;
but most of the miles stood on end owing to the
nature of the country. His revenues were rather
less than four hundred pounds yearly, and they
were expended in the maintenance of one elephant
and a standing army of five men. He was tributary
to the Indian Government, who allowed him certain
sums for keeping a section of the Himalaya-Thibet
road in repair. He further increased his revenues
by selling timber to the Railway companies ; for
he would cut the great deodar trees in his one
forest, and they fell thundering into the Sutlej river
and were swept down to the plains three hundred
miles away and became railway-ties. Now and
again this King, whose name does not matter,
would mount a ringstraked horse and ride scores

of miles to Simla-town to confer with the Lieutenant-Governor on matters of state, or to assure the Viceroy that his sword was at the service of the Queen-Empress. Then the Viceroy would cause a ruffle of drums to be sounded, and the ringstraked horse and the cavalry of the State—two men in tatters—and the herald who bore the silver stick before the King, would trot back to their own place, which lay between the tail of a heaven-climbing glacier and a dark birch-forest.

Now, from such a King, always remembering that he possessed one veritable elephant, and could count his descent for twelve hundred years, I expected, when it was my fate to wander through his dominions, no more than mere licence to live.

The night had closed in rain, and rolling clouds blotted out the lights of the villages in the valley. Forty miles away, untouched by cloud or storm, the white shoulder of Donga Pa—the Mountain of the Council of the Gods—upheld the Evening Star. The monkeys sang sorrowfully to each other as they hunted for dry roosts in the fern-wreathed trees, and the last puff of the day-wind brought from the unseen villages the scent of damp wood-smoke, hot cakes, dripping undergrowth, and rotting pine-cones. That is the true smell of the Himalayas, and if once it creeps into the blood of a man, that man will at the last, forgetting all else, return to the hills to die. The clouds closed and the smell went away, and there remained nothing in all the world except chilling white mist and the boom of the Sutlej river racing through the valley below. A fat-tailed sheep, who did not want to die, bleated piteously at my tent door. He was scuffling with the Prime Minister and the Director-General of Public Education, and he was a royal gift to me and my camp servants. I expressed my thanks suitably, and asked if I might have audience of the King. The Prime Minister readjusted his turban, which had fallen off in the struggle, and assured me that the King would be very pleased to see me. Therefore I despatched two bottles as a foretaste, and when the sheep had entered upon another incarnation went to the King's Palace through the wet. He had sent his army to escort me, but the army stayed to talk with my cook. Soldiers are very much alike all the world over.

The Palace was a four-roomed, and white-washed mud-and-timber house, the finest in all the hills for a day's journey. The King was dressed in a purple velvet jacket, white muslin trousers, and a saffron-yellow turban of price. He gave me audience in a little carpeted room opening off the palace courtyard which was occupied by the Elephant of State. The great beast was sheeted and anchored from trunk to tail, and the curve of his back stood out grandly against the mist.

The Prime Minister and the Director-General of Public Education were present to introduce me, but all the court had been dismissed, lest the two bottles aforesaid should corrupt their morals. The King cast a wreath of heavy-scented flowers round my neck as I bowed, and inquired how my honoured presence had the felicity to be. I said that through seeing his auspicious countenance the mists of the night had turned into sunshine, and

that by reason of his beneficent sheep his good
deeds would be remembered by the Gods. He
said that since I had set my magnificent foot in his
Kingdom the crops would probably yield seventy
per cent more than the average. I said that the
fame of the King had reached to the four corners
of the earth, and that the nations gnashed their
teeth when they heard daily of the glories of his
realm and the wisdom of his moon-like Prime
Minister and lotus-like Director-General of Public
Education.

Then we sat down on clean white cushions, and
I was at the King's right hand. Three minutes
later he was telling me that the state of the maize
crop was something disgraceful, and that the Railway companies would not pay him enough for his
timber. The talk shifted to and fro with the
bottles, and we discussed very many stately things,
and the King became confidential on the subject of
Government generally. Most of all he dwelt on
the shortcomings of one of his subjects, who, from
all I could gather, had been paralyzing the
executive.

' In the old days,' said the King, ' I could have
ordered the Elephant yonder to trample him to
death. Now I must e'en send him seventy miles
across the hills to be tried, and his keep would be
upon the State. The Elephant eats everything.'

' What be the man's crimes, Rajah Sahib ? '
said I.

' Firstly, he is an outlander and no man of
mine own people. Secondly, since of my favour
I gave him land upon his first coming, he refuses

to pay revenue. Am I not the lord of the earth, above and below, entitled by right and custom to one-eighth of the crop? Yet this devil, establishing himself, refuses to pay a single tax; and he brings a poisonous spawn of babes.'

'Cast him into jail,' I said.

'Sahib,' the King answered, shifting a little on the cushions, 'once and only once in these forty years sickness came upon me so that I was not able to go abroad. In that hour I made a vow to my God that I would never again cut man or woman from the light of the sun and the air of God; for I perceived the nature of the punishment. How can I break my vow? Were it only the lopping of a hand or a foot I should not delay. But even that is impossible now that the English have rule. One or another of my people' —he looked obliquely at the Director-General of Public Education—'would at once write a letter to the Viceroy, and perhaps I should be deprived of my ruffle of drums.'

He unscrewed the mouthpiece of his silver water-pipe, fitted a plain amber mouthpiece, and passed his pipe to me. 'Not content with refusing revenue,' he continued, 'this outlander refuses also the *begar*' (this was the corvée or forced labour on the roads) 'and stirs my people up to the like treason. Yet he is, when he wills, an expert log-snatcher. There is none better or bolder among my people to clear a block of the river when the logs stick fast.'

'But he worships strange Gods,' said the Prime Minister deferentially.

'For that I have no concern,' said the King, who was as tolerant as Akbar in matters of belief. 'To each man his own God and the fire or Mother Earth for us all at last. It is the rebellion that offends me.'

'The King has an army, I suggested. 'Has not the King burned the man's house and left him naked to the night dews?'

'Nay, a hut is a hut, and it holds the life of a man. But once, I sent my army against him when his excuses became wearisome : of their heads he brake three across the top with a stick. The other two men ran away. Also the guns would not shoot.'

I had seen the equipment of the infantry. One-third of it was an old muzzle-loading fowling-piece, with a ragged rust-hole where the nipples should have been, one-third a wire-bound match-lock with a worm-eaten stock, and one-third a four-bore flint duck-gun without a flint.

'But it is to be remembered,' said the King, reaching out for the bottle, 'that he is a very expert log-snatcher and a man of a merry face. What shall I do to him, Sahib?'

This was interesting. The timid hill-folk would as soon have refused taxes to their King as revenues to their Gods.

'If it be the King's permission,' I said, 'I will not strike my tents till the third day and I will see this man. The mercy of the King is God-like, and rebellion is like unto the sin of witchcraft. Moreover, both the bottles and another be empty.'

'You have my leave to go,' said the King.

Next morning a crier went through the State proclaiming that there was a log-jam on the river and that it behoved all loyal subjects to remove it. The people poured down from their villages to the moist, warm valley of poppy-fields ; and the King and I went with them. Hundreds of dressed deodar-logs had caught on a snag of rock, and the river was bringing down more logs every minute to complete the blockade. The water snarled and wrenched and worried at the timber, and the population of the State began prodding the nearest logs with a pole in the hope of starting a general movement. Then there went up a shout of 'Namgay Doola ! Namgay Doola !' and a large red-haired villager hurried up, stripping off his clothes as he ran.

'That is he. That is the rebel,' said the King. 'Now will the dam be cleared.'

'But why has he red hair ?' I asked, since red hair among hill-folks is as common as blue or green.

'He is an outlander,' said the King. 'Well done ! Oh, well done !'

Namgay Doola had scrambled out on the jam and was clawing out the butt of a log with a rude sort of boat-hook. It slid forward slowly as an alligator moves, three or four others followed it, and the green water spouted through the gaps they had made. Then the villagers howled and shouted and scrambled across the logs, pulling and pushing the obstinate timber, and the red head of Namgay Doola was chief among them all. The logs swayed and chafed and groaned as fresh consignments from upstream battered the now weakening dam. All gave way at last in a smother of foam, racing logs, bobbing black heads and confusion indescribable. The river tossed everything before it. I saw the red head go down with the last remnants of the jam and disappear between the great grinding tree-trunks. It rose close to the bank and blowing like a grampus. Namgay Doola wrung the water out of his eyes and made obeisance to the King. I had time to observe him closely. The virulent redness of his shock head and beard was most startling; and in the thicket of hair wrinkled above high cheek bones shone two very merry blue eyes. He was indeed an outlander, but yet a Thibetan in language, habit, and attire. He spoke the Lepcha dialect with an indescribable softening of the gutturals. It was not so much a lisp as an accent.

'Whence comest thou?' I asked.

'From Thibet.' He pointed across the hills and grinned. That grin went straight to my heart. Mechanically I held out my hand and Namgay Doola shook it. No pure Thibetan would have understood the meaning of the gesture. He went away to look for his clothes, and as he climbed back to his village, I heard a joyous yell that seemed unaccountably familiar. It was the whooping of Namgay Doola.

'You see now,' said the King, 'why I would not kill him. He is a bold man among my logs, but,' and he shook his head like a schoolmaster, 'I know that before long there will be complaints of him in the court. Let us return to the Palace and do justice.' It was that King's custom to judge his subjects every day between eleven and three o'clock. I saw him decide equitably in weighty matters of trespass, slander, and a little wife-stealing. Then his brow clouded and he summoned me.

'Again it is Namgay Doola,' he said despairingly. 'Not content with refusing revenue on his own part, he has bound half his village by an oath to the like treason. Never before has such a thing befallen me! Nor are my taxes heavy.'

A rabbit-faced villager, with a blush-rose stuck behind his ear, advanced trembling. He had been in the conspiracy, but had told everything and hoped for the King's favour.

'O King,' said I. 'If it be the King's will let this matter stand over till the morning. Only the Gods can do right swiftly, and it may be that yonder villager has lied.'

'Nay, for I know the nature of Namgay Doola; but since a guest asks let the matter remain. Wilt thou speak harshly to this red-headed outlander? He may listen to thee.'

I made an attempt that very evening, but for the life of me I could not keep my countenance. Namgay Doola grinned persuasively, and began to tell me about a big brown bear in a poppy-field by the river. Would I care to shoot it? I spoke austerely on the sin of conspiracy, and the certainty of punishment. Namgay Doola's face clouded for a moment. Shortly afterwards he withdrew from my tent, and I heard him singing to himself softly among the pines. The words were unintelligible to me, but the tune, like his liquid insinuating speech, seemed the ghost of something strangely familiar.

Dir hané mard-i-yemen dir
To weeree ala gee,

sang Namgay Doola again and again, and I racked my brain for that lost tune. It was not till after dinner that I discovered some one had cut a square foot of velvet from the centre of my best camera-cloth. This made me so angry that I wandered down the valley in the hope of meeting the big brown bear. I could hear him grunting like a discontented pig in the poppy-field, and I waited shoulder deep in the dew-dripping Indian corn to catch him after his meal. The moon was at full and drew out the rich scent of the tasselled crop. Then I heard the anguished bellow of a Himalayan cow, one of the little black crummies no bigger than Newfoundland dogs. Two shadows that looked like a bear and her cub hurried past me. I was in act to fire when I saw that they had each a brilliant red head. The lesser animal was trailing some rope behind it that left a dark track on the path. They passed within six feet of me, and the shadow of the moonlight lay velvet-black on their faces. Velvet-black was exactly the word, for by all the powers of moonlight they were masked in the velvet of my camera-cloth! I marvelled and went to bed.

Next morning the Kingdom was in uproar. Namgay Doola, men said, had gone forth in the night and with a sharp knife had cut off the tail of a cow belonging to the rabbit-faced villager who had betrayed him. It was sacrilege unspeakable against the Holy Cow. The State desired his blood, but he had retreated into his hut, barricaded the doors and windows with big stones, and defied the world.

The King and I and the Populace approached the hut cautiously. There was no hope of capturing the man without loss of life, for from a hole in the wall projected the muzzle of an extremely well-cared-for gun—the only gun in the State that could shoot. Namgay Doola had narrowly missed a villager just before we came up. The Standing Army stood. It could do no more, for when it advanced pieces of sharp shale flew from the windows. To these were added from time to time showers of scalding water. We saw red heads bobbing up and down in the hut. The family of Namgay Doola were aiding their sire, and blood-curdling yells of defiance were the only answers to our prayers.

'Never,' said the King, puffing, 'has such a thing befallen my State. Next year I will certainly buy a little cannon.' He looked at me imploringly.

'Is there any priest in the Kingdom to whom he will listen?' said I, for a light was beginning to break upon me.

'He worships his own God,' said the Prime Minister. 'We can starve him out.'

'Let the white man approach,' said Namgay Doola from within. 'All others I will kill. Send me the white man.'

The door was thrown open and I entered the

smoky interior of a Thibetan hut crammed with children. And every child had flaming red hair. A raw cow's-tail lay on the floor, and by its side two pieces of black velvet—my black velvet—rudely hacked into the semblance of masks.

'And what is this shame, Namgay Doola?' said I.

He grinned more winningly than ever. 'There is no shame,' said he. 'I did but cut off the tail of that man's cow. He betrayed me. I was minded to shoot him, Sahib. But not to death. Indeed not to death. Only in the legs.'

'And why at all, since it is the custom to pay revenue to the King? Why at all?'

'By the God of my father I cannot tell,' said Namgay Doola.

'And who was thy father?'

'The same that had this gun.' He showed me his weapon—a Tower musket bearing date 1832 and the stamp of the Honourable East India Company.

'And thy father's name?' said I.

'Timlay Doola,' said he. 'At the first, I being then a little child, it is in my mind that he wore a red coat.'

'Of that I have no doubt. But repeat the name of thy father thrice or four times.'

He obeyed, and I understood whence the puzzling accent in his speech came. 'Thimla Dhula,' said he excitedly. 'To this hour I worship his God.'

'May I see that God?'

'In a little while—at twilight time.'

'Rememberest thou aught of thy father's speech?'

'It is long ago. But there is one word which he said often. Thus "*Shun*." Then I and my brethren stood upon our feet, our hands to our sides. Thus.'

'Even so. And what was thy mother?

'A woman of the hills. We be Lepchas of Darjeeling, but me they call an outlander because my hair is as thou seest.'

The Thibetan woman, his wife, touched him on the arm gently. The long parley outside the fort had lasted far into the day. It was now close upon twilight—the hour of the Angelus. Very solemnly, the red-headed brats rose from the floor and formed a semicircle. Namgay Doola laid his gun against the wall, lighted a little oil lamp, and set it before a recess in the wall. Pulling aside a curtain of dirty cloth he revealed a worn brass crucifix leaning against the helmet-badge of a long forgotten East India regiment. 'Thus did my father,' he said, crossing himself clumsily. The wife and children followed suit. Then all together they struck up the wailing chant that I heard on the hillside—

> Dir hané mard-i-yemen dir
> To weeree ala gee.

I was puzzled no longer. Again and again they crooned as if their hearts would break, their version of the chorus of *The Wearing of the Green*—

> They're hanging men and women too,
> For wearing of the green.

A diabolical inspiration came to me. One of the brats, a boy about eight years old, was watching me as he sang. I pulled out a rupee, held the coin between finger and thumb, and looked—only looked—at the gun against the wall. A grin of brilliant and perfect comprehension overspread the face of the child. Never for an instant stopping the song he held out his hand for the money, and then slid the gun to my hand. I might have shot Namgay Doola as he chanted. But I was satisfied. The blood-instinct of the race held true. Namgay Doola drew the curtain across the recess. Angelus was over.

'Thus my father sang. There was much more, but I have forgotten, and I do not know the purport of these words, but it may be that the God will understand. I am not of this people, and I will not pay revenue.'

'And why?'

Again that soul-compelling grin. 'What occupation would be to me between crop and crop? It is better than scaring bears. But these people do not understand.' He picked the masks from the floor, and looked in my face as simply as a child.

'By what road didst thou attain knowledge to make these devilries?' I said, pointing.

'I cannot tell. I am but a Lepcha of Darjeeling, and yet the stuff——'

'Which thou hast stolen.'

'Nay, surely. Did I steal? I desired it so. The stuff—the stuff—what else should I have done with the stuff?' He twisted the velvet between his fingers.

'But the sin of maiming the cow — consider that?'

'That is true; but oh, Sahib, that man betrayed me and I had no thought—but the heifer's tail waved in the moonlight and I had my knife. What else should I have done? The tail came off ere I was aware. Sahib, thou knowest more than I.'

'That is true,' said I. 'Stay within the door. I go to speak to the King.'

The population of the State were ranged on the hillsides. I went forth and spoke to the King.

'O King,' said I. 'Touching this man there be two courses open to thy wisdom. Thou canst either hang him from a tree, he and his brood, till there remains no hair that is red within the land.'

'Nay,' said the King. 'Why should I hurt the little children?'

They had poured out of the hut door and were making plump obeisance to everybody. Namgay Doola waited with his gun across his arm.

'Or thou canst, discarding the impiety of the cow-maiming, raise him to honour in thy Army. He comes of a race that will not pay revenue. A red flame is in his blood which comes out at the top of his head in that glowing hair. Make him chief of the Army. Give him honour as may befall, and full allowance of work, but look to it, O King, that neither he nor his hold a foot of earth from thee henceforward. Feed him with words and favour, and also liquor from certain bottles that thou knowest of, and he will be a bulwark of defence. But deny him even a tuft of

grass for his own. This is the nature that God
has given him. Moreover he has brethren——'

The State groaned unanimously.

'But if his brethren come, they will surely fight
with each other till they die ; or else the one will
always give information concerning the other.
Shall he be of thy Army, O King ? Choose.'

The King bowed his head, and I said, 'Come
forth, Namgay Doola, and command the King's
Army. Thy name shall no more be Namgay in
the mouths of men, but Patsay Doola, for as thou
hast said, I know.'

Then Namgay Doola, new christened Patsay
Doola, son of Timlay Doola, which is Tim Doolan
gone very wrong indeed, clasped the King's feet,
cuffed the standing Army, and hurried in an agony
of contrition from temple to temple, making
offerings for the sin of cattle maiming.

And the King was so pleased with my perspi-
cacity that he offered to sell me a village for
twenty pounds sterling. But I buy no villages in
the Himalayas so long as one red head flares
between the tail of the heaven-climbing glacier
and the dark birch-forest.

I know that breed.

The Lang Men o' Larut

THE Chief Engineer's sleeping suit was of yellow
striped with blue, and his speech was the speech
of Aberdeen. They sluiced the deck under him,
and he hopped on to the ornamental capstan, a
black pipe between his teeth, though the hour was
not seven of the morn.

'Did you ever hear o' the Lang Men o'
Larut?' he asked when the Man from Orizava
had finished a story of an aboriginal giant discovered in the wilds of Brazil. There was never
story yet passed the lips of teller but the Man
from Orizava could cap it.

'No, we never did,' we responded with one
voice. The Man from Orizava watched the Chief
keenly, as a possible rival.

'I'm not telling the story for the sake of
talking merely,' said the Chief, 'but as a warning against betting, unless you bet on a perrfect
certainty. The Lang Men o' Larut were just
a certainty. I have had talk wi' them. Now
Larut, you will understand, is a dependency, or
it may be an outlying possession, o' the island o'
Penang, and there they will get you tin and

manganese, an' it may hap mica, and all manner o' meenerals. Larut is a great place.'

'But what about the population?' said the Man from Orizava.

'The population,' said the Chief slowly, 'were few but enorrmous. You must understand that, exceptin' the tin-mines, there is no special induce-ment to Europeans to reside in Larut. The climate is warm and remarkably like the climate o' Calcutta ; and in regard to Calcutta, it cannot have escaped your obsairvation that——'

'Calcutta isn't Larut ; and we've only just come from it,' protested the Man from Orizava. 'There's a meteorological department in Calcutta, too.'

'Ay, but there's no meteorological department in Larut. Each man is a law to himself. Some drink whisky, and some drink *brandipanee*, and some drink cocktails—vara bad for the coats o' the stomach is a cocktail—and some drink sangaree, so I have been credibly informed ; but one and all they sweat like the packing of a piston-head on a fourrteen-days' voyage with the screw racing half her time   But, as I was saying, the population o' Larut was five all told of English—that is to say, Scotch—an' I'm Scotch, ye know,' said the Chief.

The Man from Orizava lit another cigarette, and waited patiently. It was hopeless to hurry the Chief Engineer.

'I am not pretending to account for the population o' Larut being laid down according to such fabulous dimensions. O' the five white men engaged upon the extraction o' tin ore and mercantile pursuits, there were three o' the sons o' Anak. Wait while I remember. Lammitter was the first by two inches—a giant in the land, an' a terreefic man to cross in his ways. From heel to head he was six feet nine inches, and proportionately built across and through the thickness of his body. Six good feet nine inches—an overbearin' man. Next to him, and I have forgotten his precise business, was Sandy Vowle. And he was six feet seven, but lean and lathy, and it was more in the elasteecity of his neck that the height lay than in any honesty o' bone and sinew. Five feet and a few odd inches may have been his real height. The remainder came out when he held up his head, and six feet seven he was upon the door-sills. I took his measure in chalk standin' on a chair. And next to him, but a proportionately made man, ruddy and of a fair countenance, was Jock Coan— that they called the Fir Cone. He was but six feet five, and a child beside Lammitter and Vowle. When the three walked out together, they made a scunner run through the colony o' Larut. The Malays ran round them as though they had been the giant trees in the Yosemite Valley—these three Lang Men o' Larut. It was perfectly ridiculous— a *lusus naturæ*—that one little place should have contained maybe the three tallest ordinar' men upon the face o' the earth.

'Obsairve now the order o' things. For it led to the finest big drink in Larut, and six sore heads the morn that endured for a week. I am against immoderate liquor, but the event to follow was a justification. You must understand that many

coasting steamers call at Larut wi' strangers o' the
mercantile profession. In the spring time, when
the young cocoa-nuts were ripening, and the trees
o' the forests were putting forth their leaves, there
came an American man to Larut, and he was six
feet three, or it may have been four, in his stockings.
He came on business from Sacramento, but he
stayed for pleasure wi' the Lang Men o' Larut.
Less than a half o' the population were ordinar' in
their girth and stature, ye will understand—
Howson and Nailor, merchants, five feet nine or
thereabouts. He had business with those two,
and he stood above them from the six feet three-
dom o' his height till they went to drink. In the
course o' conversation he said, as tall men will,
things about his height, and the trouble of it to
him. That was his pride o' the flesh.

'"As the longest man in the island——"
he said, but there they took him up and asked if
he were sure.

'"I say I am the longest man in the island,"
he said, "and on that I'll bet my substance."

'They laid down the bed-plates of a big drink
then and there, and put it aside while they called
Jock Coan from his house, near by among the
fireflies' winking.

'"How's a' wi' you?" said Jock, and came in
by the side o' the Sacramento profligate, two inches,
or it may have been one, taller than he.

'"You're long," said the man opening his eyes.
"But I am longer." An' they sent a whistle
through the night an' howkit out Sandy Vowle
from his bit bungalow, and he came in an' stood

by the side o' Jock, an' the pair just fillit the room to the ceiling-cloth.

'The Sacramento man was a euchre-player and a most profane sweerer. "You hold both Bowers," he said, "but the Joker is with me."

'"Fair an' softly," says Nailor. "Jock, whaur's Lang Lammitter?"

'"Here," says that man, putting his leg through the window and coming in like an anaconda o' the desert furlong by furlong, one foot in Penang and one in Batavia, and a hand in North Borneo it may be.

'"Are you suited?" said Nailor, when the hinder end o' Lang Lammitter was slidden through the sill an' the head of Lammitter was lost in the smoke away above.

'The American man took out his card and put it on the table. "Esdras B. Longer is my name, America is my nation, 'Frisco is my resting-place, but this here beats Creation," said he. "Boys, giants—side-show giants—I minded to slide out of my bet if I had been overtopped, on the strength of the riddle on this paste-board. I would have done it if you had topped me even by three inches, but when it comes to feet—yards—miles, I am not the man to shirk the biggest drink that ever made the travellers'-joy palm blush with virginal indignation, or the orang-outang and the perambulating dyak howl with envy. Set them up and continue till the final conclusion."

'O mon, I tell you 'twas an awful sight to see those four giants threshing about the house and the island, and tearin' down the pillars thereof an' throwing palm-trees broadcast, and currling their long legs round the hills o' Larut. An awfu' sight! I was there. I did not mean to tell you, but it's out now. I was not overcome, for I e'en sat me down under the pieces o' the table at four the morn an' meditated upon the strangeness of things.

'Losh, yon's the breakfast-bell!'

Bertran and Bimi

THE orang-outang in the big iron cage lashed to the sheep-pen began the discussion. The night was stiflingly hot, and as I and Hans Breitmann, the big-beamed German, passed him, dragging our bedding to the fore-peak of the steamer, he roused himself and chattered obscenely. He had been caught somewhere in the Malayan Archipelago, and was going to England to be exhibited at a shilling a head. For four days he had struggled, yelled, and wrenched at the heavy bars of his prison without ceasing, and had nearly slain a Lascar, incautious enough to come within reach of the great hairy paw.

'It would be well for you, mine friend, if you was a liddle seasick,' said Hans Breitmann, pausing by the cage. 'You haf too much Ego in your Cosmos.'

The orang-outang's arm slid out negligently from between the bars. No one would have believed that it would make a sudden snakelike rush at the German's breast. The thin silk of the sleeping-suit tore out; Hans stepped back unconcernedly to pluck a banana from a bunch hanging close to one of the boats.

'Too much Ego,' said he, peeling the fruit and offering it to the caged devil, who was rending the silk to tatters.

Then we laid out our bedding in the bows among the sleeping Lascars, to catch any breeze that the pace of the ship might give us. The sea was like smoky oil, except where it turned to fire under our forefoot and whirled back into the dark in smears of dull flame. There was a thunderstorm some miles away; we could see the glimmer of the lightning. The ship's cow, distressed by the heat and the smell of the ape-beast in the cage, lowed unhappily from time to time in exactly the same key as that in which the look-out man answered the hourly call from the bridge. The trampling tune of the engines was very distinct, and the jarring of the ash-lift, as it was tipped into the sea, hurt the procession of hushed noise. Hans lay down by my side and lighted a good-night cigar. This was naturally the beginning of conversation. He owned a voice as soothing as the wash of the sea, and stores of experiences as vast as the sea itself; for his business in life was to wander up and down the world, collecting orchids and wild beasts and ethnological specimens for German and American dealers. I watched the glowing end of his cigar wax and wane in the gloom, as the sentences rose and fell, till I was nearly asleep. The orang-outang, troubled by some dream of the forests of his freedom, began to yell like a soul in purgatory, and to pluck madly at the bars of the cage.

'If he was out now dere would not be much of

us left hereabout,' said Hans lazily. 'He screams goot. See, now, how I shall tame him when he stops himself.'

There was a pause in the outcry, and from Hans' mouth came an imitation of a snake's hiss, so perfect that I almost sprang to my feet. The sustained murderous sound rang along the deck, and the wrenching at the bars ceased. The orang-outang was quaking in an ecstasy of pure terror.

'Dot stopped him,' said Hans. 'I learned dot trick in Mogoung Tanjong when I was collecting liddle monkeys for some peoples in Berlin. Efery one in der world is afraid of der monkeys—except der snake. So I blay snake against monkey, and he keep quite still. Dere was too much Ego in his Cosmos. Dot is der soul-custom of monkeys. Are you asleep, or will you listen, and I will tell a dale dot you shall not pelief?'

'There's no tale in the wide world that I can't believe,' I said.

'If you haf learned pelief you haf learned some-dings. Now I shall try your pelief. Goot! When I was collecting dose liddle monkeys—it was in '79 or '80, und I was in der islands of der Archipelago—over dere in der dark'—he pointed southward to New Guinea generally—'Mein Gott! I would sooner collect life red devils than liddle monkeys. When dey do not bite off your thumbs dey are always dying from nostalgia—home-sick—for dey haf der imperfect soul, which is midway arrested in defelopment—und too much Ego. I was dere for nearly a year, und dere I found a man dot was called Bertran. He was a Frenchman, und he

was goot man—naturalist to his bone. Dey said
he was an escaped convict, but he was naturalist,
und dot was enough for me. He would call all
der life beasts from der forest, und dey would
come. I said he was St. Francis of Assisi in a
new dransmigration produced, und he laughed
und said he haf never preach to der fishes. He
sold dem for tripang—*béche-de-mer*.

'Und dot man, who was king of beasts-tamer
men, he had in der house shust such anoder as
dot devil-animal in der cage—a great orang-outang
dot thought he was a man. He haf found him
when he was a child—der orang-outang—und he
was child und brother und opera comique all
round to Bertran. He had his room in dot house
—not a cage, but a room—mit a bed und sheets,
und he would go to bed und get up in der
morning und smoke his cigar und eat his dinner
mit Bertran, und walk mit him hand in hand,
which was most horrible. Herr Gott! I haf seen
dot beast throw himself back in his chair und
laugh when Bertran haf made fun of me. He was
not a beast; he was a man, und he talked to
Bertran, und Bertran comprehend, for I have seen
dem. Und he was always politeful to me except
when I talk too long to Bertran und say nodings
at all to him. Den he would pull me away—dis
great, dark devil, mit his enormous paws—shust
as if I was a child. He was not a beast; he was a
man. Dis I saw pefore I know him three months,
und Bertran he haf saw the same; and Bimi, der
orang-outang, haf understood us both, mit his
cigar between his big dog-teeth und der blue gum.

'I was dere a year, dere und at dere oder islands—somedimes for monkeys und somedimes for butterflies und orchits. One time Bertran says to me dot he will be married, because he haf found a girl dot was goot, und he enquire if this marrying idee was right. I would not say, pecause it was not me dot was going to be married. Den he go off courting der girl—she was a half-caste French girl—very pretty. Haf you got a new light for my cigar? Ouf! Very pretty. Only I say, "Haf you thought of Bimi? If he pull me away when I talk to you, what will he do to your wife? He will pull her in pieces. If I was you, Bertran, I would gif my wife for wedding-present der stuff figure of Bimi." By dot time I had learned some dings about der monkey peoples. "Shoot him?" says Bertran. "He is your beast," I said; "if he was mine he would be shot now!"

'Den I felt at der back of my neck der fingers of Bimi. Mein Gott! I tell you dot he talked through dose fingers. It was der deaf-and-dumb alphabet all gomplete. He slide his hairy arm round my neck, und he tilt up my chin und look into my face, shust to see if I understood his talk so well as he understood mine.

'"See now dere!" says Bertran, "und you would shoot him while he is cuddlin' you? Dot is der Teuton ingrate!"

'But I knew dot I had made Bimi a life's-enemy, pecause his fingers haf talk murder through the back of my neck. Next dime I see Bimi dere was a pistol in my belt, und he touch it once, und I open der breech to show him it was loaded. He

haf seen der liddle monkeys killed in der woods :
he understood.

'So Bertran he was married, and he forgot clean
about Bimi dot was skippin' alone on der beach
mit der half of a human soul in his belly. I was
see him skip, und he took a big bough und thrash
der sand till he haf made a great hole like a grave.
So I says to Bertran, "For any sakes, kill Bimi.
He is mad mit der jealousy."

'Bertran haf said "He is not mad at all. He
haf obey und lofe my wife, und if she speak he
will get her slippers," und he looked at his wife
agross der room. She was a very pretty girl.

'Den I said to him, "Dost dou pretend to know
monkeys und dis beast dot is lashing himself mad
upon der sands, pecause you do not talk to him ?
Shoot him when he comes to der house, for he haf
der light in his eye dot means killing—und killing."
Bimi come to der house, but dere was no light in
his eye. It was all put away, cunning—so cunning
—und he fetch der girl her slippers, und Bertran
turn to me und say, "Dost dou know him in nine
months more dan I haf known him in twelve years ?
Shall a child stab his fader ? I haf fed him, und
he was my child. Do not speak dis nonsense to
my wife or to me any more."

'Dot next day Bertran came to my house to
help me make some wood cases for der specimens,
und he tell me dot he haf left his wife a liddle
while mit Bimi in der garden. Den I finish my
cases quick, und I say, "Let us go to your houses
und get a trink." He laugh und say, "Come
along, dry mans."

'His wife was not in der garden, und Bimi did
not come when Bertran called. Und his wife did
not come when he called, und he knocked at her
bedroom door und dot was shut tight—locked.
Den he look at me, und his face was white. I
broke down der door mit my shoulder, und der
thatch of der roof was torn into a great hole, und
der sun came in upon der floor. Haf you ever
seen paper in der waste-basket, or cards at whist on
der table scattered? Dere was no wife dot could
be seen. I tell you dere was nodings in dot room
dot might be a woman. Dere was stuff on der
floor und dot was all. I looked at dese things und
I was very sick ; but Bertran looked a liddle
longer at what was upon the floor und der walls,
und der hole in der thatch. Den he pegan to
laugh, soft und low, und I knew und thank Gott
dot he was mad. He nefer cried, he nefer prayed.
He stood all still in der doorway und laugh to
himself. Den he said, " She haf locked herself in
dis room, und he haf torn up der thatch. *Fi donc !*
Dot is so. We will mend der thatch und wait for
Bimi. He will surely come."
'I tell you we waited ten days in dot house,
after der room was made into a room again, und
once or twice we saw Bimi comin' a liddle way from
der woods. He was afraid pecause he haf done
wrong. Bertran called him when he was come to
look on the tenth day, und Bimi come skipping
along der beach und making noises, mit a long
piece of black hair in his hands. Den Bertran
laugh und say, " *Fi donc !* " shust as if it was a
glass broken upon der table ; und Bimi come

nearer, und Bertran was honey-sweet in his voice und laughed to himself. For three days he made love to Bimi, pecause Bimi would not let himself be touched. Den Bimi come to dinner at der same table mit us, und the hair on his hands was all black und thick mit—mit what had dried on der hands. Bertran gave him sangaree till Bimi was drunk und stupid, und den——'

Hans paused to puff at his cigar.

' And then?' said I.

'Und den Bertran he kill him mit his hands, und I go for a walk upon der beach. It was Bertran's own piziness. When I come back der ape he was dead, und Bertran he was dying abofe him; but still he laughed liddle und low und he was quite content. Now you know der formula of der strength of der orang-outang—it is more as seven to one in relation to man. But Bertran, he haf killed Bimi mit sooch dings as Gott gif him. Dot was der miracle.'

The infernal clamour in the cage recommenced. ' Aha! Dot friend of ours haf still too much Ego in his Cosmos. Be quiet, dou!'

Hans hissed long and venomously. We could hear the great beast quaking in his cage.

' But why in the world didn't you help Bertran instead of letting him be killed?' I asked.

' My friend,' said Hans, composedly stretching himself to slumber, ' it was not nice even to mine-self dot I should live after I haf seen dot room mit der hole in der thatch. Und Bertran, he was her husband. Goot-night, und—sleep well.'

Reingelder and the German Flag

Hans Breitmann paddled across the deck in his pink pyjamas, a cup of tea in one hand and a cheroot in the other, when the steamer was sweltering down the coast on her way to Singapore. He drank beer all day and all night, and played a game called 'Scairt' with three compatriots.

'I haf washed,' said he in a voice of thunder, 'but, dere is no use washing on these hell-seas. Look at me—I am still all wet und schweatin'. It is der tea dot makes me so. Boy, bring me Bilsener on ice.'

'You will die if you drink beer before breakfast,' said one man. 'Beer is the worst thing in the world for——'

'Ya, I know—der liver. I haf no liver, und I shall not die. At least I will not die obon dese benny sdeamers dot haf no beer fit to trink. If I should haf died, I will haf don so a hoondert dimes before now—in Shermany, in New York, in Japan, in Assam, und all over der inside barts of South Amerique. Also in Shamaica should I haf died or in Siam, but I am here; und der are my orchits dot I have drafelled all the vorld round to find.'

He pointed towards the wheel, where, in two

rough wooden boxes, lay a mass of shrivelled vegetation, supposed by all the ship to represent Assam orchids of fabulous value.

Now, orchids do not grow in the main streets of towns, and Hans Breitmann had gone far to get his. There was nothing that he had not collected that year, from kingcrabs to white kangaroos.

'Lisden now,' said he, after he had been speaking for not much more than ten minutes without a pause; 'Lisden und I will dell you a sdory to show how bad und worse it is to go gollectin' und belief vot anoder fool haf said. Dis was in Uruguay which was in Amerique—North or Sout' you would not know—und I was hoontin' orchits und aferydings else dot I could back in my kanasters—dot is drafelling sbecimen-gaces. Dere vas den mit me anoder man—Reingelder, dot vas his name—und he vas hoontin' also, but only coralsnakes—joost Uruguay coral-snakes—aferykind you could imagine. I dell you a coral-snake is a peauty—all red und white like coral dot has been gestrung in bands upon der neck of a girl. Dere is one snake howefer dot we who gollect know ash der Sherman Flag, pecause id is red und plack und white, joost like a sausage mit druffles. Reingelder he was naturalist—goot man—goot trinker—better as me! "By Gott," said Reingelder, "I will get a Sherman Flag snake or I will die." Und we toorned all Uruguay upside-behint all pecause of dot Sherman Flag.

'Von day when we was in none knows where —shwingin' in our hummocks among der woods, oop comes a natif woman mit a Sherman Flag in

a bickle-bottle—my bickle-bottle—und we both
fell from our hummocks flat ubon our pot—what
you call stomach—mit shoy at dis thing. Now
I was gollectin' orchits also, und I knowed dot
der idee of life to Reingelder vas dis Sherman
Flag. Derefore I bicked myselfs oop und I said,
"Reingelder, dot is *your* find."—"Heart's true
friend, dou art a goot man," said Reingelder, und
mit dot he obens der bickle-bottle, und der natif
woman she shqueals, "Herr Gott! It will bite."
I said—pecause in Uruguay a man must be careful
of der insects—"Reingelder shpifligate her in der
alcohol und den she will be all right."—"Nein,"
said Reingelder, "I will der shnake alife examine.
Dere is no fear. Der coral-snakes are mitout
shting-apparatus brofided."   Boot I looked at her
het, und she vas der het of a boison-shnake—der
true viper cranium, narrow und contract.   "It is
not goot," said I, "she may bite und den—we
are tree hoondert mile from aferywheres. Broduce
der alcohol und bickle him alife."   Reingelder he
had him in his hand—grawlin' und grawlin' as
slow as a woorm und dwice as guiet.   "Nonsense,"
says Reingelder.   "Yates haf said dot not von of
der coral-snakes haf der sack of boison."   Yates
vas der crate authorité ubon der reptilia of Sout'
Amerique.   He haf written a book. You do not
know, of course, but he vas a crate authorité.

'I gum my eye upon der Sherman Flag, grawlin'
und grawlin' in Reingelder's fist, und der het vas
not der het of innocence.   "Mein Gott," I said.
"It is you dot will get der sack—der sack from
dis life here pelow!"

' " Den you may haf der snake," says Reingelder, pattin' it ubon her het. " See now, I will show you vat Yates haf written ! "

' Und mit dot he went indo his dent, unt brung out his big book of Yates ; der Sherman Flag grawlin' in his fist. " Yates haf said," said Reingelder, und he throwed oben der book in der fork of his fist und read der passage, proofin' conglusivement dot nefer coral-snake bite vas boison. Den he shut der book mit a bang, und dot shqueeze der Sherman Flag, und she nip once und dwice.

' " Der liddle fool he haf bit me," says Reingelder.

' Dese things was before we know apout der permanganat-potash injection. I was discomfordable.

' " Die oop der arm, Reingelder," said I, " und trink whisky ontil you can no more trink."

' " Trink ten tousand tevils ! I will go to dinner," said Reingelder, und he put her afay, und it vas very red mit emotion.

' We lifed upon soup, horse-flesh, und beans for dinner, but before we vas eaten der soup, Reingelder he haf hold of his arm und cry, " It is genumben to der clavicle. I am a dead man ; und Yates he haf lied in brint ! "

' I dell you it vas most sad, for der symbtoms dot came vas all dose of strychnine. He vas doubled into big knots, und den undoubled, und den redoubled mooch worse dan pefore, und he frothed. I vas mit him, saying " Reingelder, dost dou know me ? " but he himself, der inward gonciousness part, was peyond knowledge, und so I know he vas not in bain. Den he wrop himself oop in von dremendous knot und den he died— all alone mit me in Uruguay. I was sorry for I lofed Reingelder, und I puried him, und den I took der coral-snake—dot Sherman Flag—so bad und dreacherous, und I bickled him alife.

'So I got him : und so I lost Reingelder.'

The Wandering Jew

'IF you go once round the world in an easterly direction, you gain one day,' said the men of science to John Hay. In after years John Hay went east, west, north, and south, transacted business, made love, and begat a family, as have done many men, and the scientific information above recorded lay neglected in the deeps of his mind with a thousand other matters of equal importance.

When a rich relative died, he found himself wealthy beyond any reasonable expectation that he had entertained in his previous career, which had been a chequered and evil one. Indeed, long before the legacy came to him, there existed in the brain of John Hay a little cloud—a momentary obscuration of thought that came and went almost before he could realise that there was any solution of continuity. So do the bats flit round the eaves of a house to show that the darkness is falling. He entered upon great possessions, in money, land, and houses ; but behind his delight stood a ghost that cried out that his enjoyment of these things should not be of long duration. It was the ghost of the rich relative, who had been permitted to return to earth to torture his nephew into the grave. Wherefore, under the spur of this constant reminder, John Hay, always preserving the air of heavy business-like stolidity that hid the shadow on his mind, turned investments, houses, and lands into sovereigns—rich, round, red, English sovereigns, each one worth twenty shillings. Lands may become valueless, and houses fly heavenward on the wings of red flame, but till the Day of Judgment a sovereign will always be a sovereign—that is to say, a king of pleasures.

Possessed of his sovereigns, John Hay would fain have spent them one by one on such coarse amusements as his soul loved ; but he was haunted by the instant fear of Death ; for the ghost of his relative stood in the hall of his house close to the hat-rack, shouting up the stairway that life was short, that there was no hope of increase of days, and that the undertakers were already roughing out his nephew's coffin. John Hay was generally alone in the house, and even when he had company, his friends could not hear the clamorous uncle. The shadow inside his brain grew larger and blacker. His fear of death was driving John Hay mad.

Then, from the deeps of his mind, where he had stowed away all his discarded information, rose to light the scientific fact of the easterly journey. On the next occasion that his uncle shouted up the stairway urging him to make haste and live, a shriller voice cried, 'Who goes round the world once easterly, gains one day.'

His growing diffidence and distrust of mankind

made John Hay unwilling to give this precious message of hope to his friends. They might take it up and analyse it. He was sure it was true, but it would pain him acutely were rough hands to examine it too closely. To him alone of all the toiling generations of mankind had the secret of immortality been vouchsafed. It would be impious —against all the designs of the Creator—to set mankind hurrying eastward. Besides, this would crowd the steamers inconveniently, and John Hay wished of all things to be alone. If he could get round the world in two months—some one of whom he had read, he could not remember the name, had covered the passage in eighty days—he would gain a clear day ; and by steadily continuing to do it for thirty years, would gain one hundred and eighty days, or nearly the half of a year. It would not be much, but in course of time, as civilisation advanced, and the Euphrates Valley Railway was opened, he could improve the pace.

Armed with many sovereigns, John Hay, in the thirty-fifth year of his age, set forth on his travels, two voices bearing him company from Dover as he sailed to Calais. Fortune favoured him. The Euphrates Valley Railway was newly opened, and he was the first man who took ticket direct from Calais to Calcutta—thirteen days in the train. Thirteen days in the train are not good for the nerves ; but he covered the world and returned to Calais from America in twelve days over the two months, and started afresh with four and twenty hours of precious time to his credit.

Three years passed, and John Hay religiously went round this earth seeking for more time wherein to enjoy the remainder of his sovereigns. He became known on many lines as the man who wanted to go on ; when people asked him what he was and what he did, he answered—

'I'm the person who intends to live, and I am trying to do it now.'

His days were divided between watching the white wake spinning behind the stern of the swiftest steamers, or the brown earth flashing past the windows of the fastest trains ; and he noted in a pocket-book every minute that he had railed or screwed out of remorseless eternity.

'This is better than praying for long life,' quoth John Hay as he turned his face eastward for his twentieth trip. The years had done more for him than he dared to hope. By the extension of the Brahmaputra Valley line to meet the newly-developed China Midland, the Calais railway ticket held good *via* Karachi and Calcutta to Hongkong. The round trip could be managed in a fraction over forty-seven days, and, filled with fatal exultation, John Hay told the secret of his longevity to his only friend, the house-keeper of his rooms in London. He spoke and passed ; but the woman was one of resource, and immediately took counsel with the lawyers who had first informed John Hay of his golden legacy. Very many sovereigns still remained, and another Hay longed to spend them on things more sensible than railway tickets and steamer accommodation.

The chase was long, for when a man is journeying literally for the dear life, he does not tarry upon the road. Round the world Hay swept anew, and overtook the wearied Doctor, who had been sent out to look for him, in Madras. It was there that he found the reward of his toil and the assurance of a blessed immortality. In half an hour the Doctor, watching always the parched lips, the shaking hands, and the eye that turned eternally to the east, won John Hay to rest in a little house close to the Madras surf. All that Hay need do was to hang by ropes from the roof of the room and let the round earth swing free beneath him. This was better than steamer or train, for he gained a day in a day, and was thus the equal of the undying sun. The other Hay would pay his expenses throughout eternity.

.   .   .   .   .

It is true that we cannot yet take tickets from Calais to Hongkong, though that will come about in fifteen years ; but men say that if you wander along the southern coast of India you shall find in a neatly whitewashed little bungalow, sitting in a chair swung from the roof, over a sheet of thin steel which he knows so well destroys the attraction of the earth, an old and worn man who for ever faces the rising sun, a stop-watch in his hand, racing against eternity. He cannot drink, he does not smoke, and his living expenses amount to perhaps twenty-five rupees a month, but he is John Hay, the Immortal. Without, he hears the thunder of the wheeling world with which he is careful to explain he has no connection whatever ; but if you say that it is only the noise of the surf, he will cry bitterly, for the shadow on his brain is passing away as the brain ceases to work, and he doubts sometimes whether the Doctor spoke the truth.

'Why does not the sun always remain over my head?' asks John Hay.

Through the Fire

THE Policeman rode through the Himalayan forest, under the moss-draped oaks, and his orderly trotted after him.

'It's an ugly business, Bhere Singh,' said the Policeman. 'Where are they?'

'It is a very ugly business,' said Bhere Singh; 'and as for *them*, they are, doubtless, now frying in a hotter fire than was ever made of spruce-branches.'

'Let us hope not,' said the Policeman, 'for, allowing for the difference between race and race, it's the story of Francesca da Rimini, Bhere Singh.'

Bhere Singh knew nothing about Francesca da Rimini, so he held his peace until they came to the charcoal-burners' clearing where the dying flames said '*whit, whit, whit*' as they fluttered and whispered over the white ashes. It must have been a great fire when at full height. Men had seen it at Donga Pa across the valley winking and blazing through the night, and said that the charcoal-burners of Kodru were getting drunk. But it was only Suket Singh, Sepoy of the 102d Punjab Native Infantry, and Athira, a woman, burning—burning—burning.

This was how things befell ; and the Policeman's Diary will bear me out.

Athira was the wife of Madu, who was a charcoal-burner, one-eyed and of a malignant disposition. A week after their marriage, he beat Athira with a heavy stick. A month later, Suket Singh, Sepoy, came that way to the cool hills on leave from his regiment, and electrified the villagers of Kodru with tales of service and glory under the Government, and the honour in which he, Suket Singh, was held by the Colonel Sahib Bahadur. And Desdemona listened to Othello as Desdemonas have done all the world over, and, as she listened, she loved.

'I've a wife of my own,' said Suket Singh, 'though that is no matter when you come to think of it. I am also due to return to my regiment after a time, and I cannot be a deserter—I who intend to be Havildar.' There is no Himalayan version of 'I could not love thee, dear, so much, Loved I not Honour more ;' but Suket Singh came near to making one.

'Never mind,' said Athira, 'stay with me, and, if Madu tries to beat me, you beat him.'

'Very good,' said Suket Singh ; and he beat Madu severely, to the delight of all the charcoal-burners of Kodru.

'That is enough,' said Suket Singh, as he rolled Madu down the hillside. 'Now we shall have peace.' But Madu crawled up the grass slope again, and hovered round his hut with angry eyes.

'He'll kill me dead,' said Athira to Suket Singh. 'You must take me away.'

'There'll be a trouble in the Lines. My wife will pull out my beard ; but never mind,' said Suket Singh, 'I will take you.'

There was loud trouble in the Lines, and Suket Singh's beard was pulled, and Suket Singh's wife went to live with her mother and took away the children. 'That's all right,' said Athira ; and Suket Singh said, 'Yes, that's all right.'

So there was only Madu left in the hut that looks across the valley to Donga Pa ; and, since the beginning of time, no one has had any sympathy for husbands so unfortunate as Madu.

He went to Juseen Dazé, the wizard-man who keeps the Talking Monkey's Head.

'Get me back my wife,' said Madu.

'I can't,' said Juseen Dazé, 'until you have made the Sutlej in the valley run up the Donga Pa.'

'No riddles,' said Madu, and he shook his hatchet above Juseen Dazé's white head.

'Give all your money to the headmen of the village,' said Juseen Dazé ; 'and they will hold a communal Council, and the Council will send a message that your wife must come back.'

So Madu gave up all his worldly wealth, amounting to twenty-seven rupees, eight annas, three pice, and a silver chain, to the Council of Kodru. And it fell as Juseen Dazé foretold.

They sent Athira's brother down into Suket Singh's regiment to call Athira home. Suket Singh kicked him once round the Lines, and then handed him over to the Havildar, who beat him with a belt.

'Come back,' yelled Athira's brother.

'Where to?' said Athira.

'To Madu,' said he.

'Never,' said she.

'Then Juseen Dazé will send a curse, and you will wither away like a barked tree in the springtime,' said Athira's brother. Athira slept over these things.

Next morning she had rheumatism. 'I am beginning to wither away like a barked tree in the springtime,' she said. 'That is the curse of Juseen Dazé.'

And she really began to wither away because her heart was dried up with fear, and those who believe in curses die from curses. Suket Singh, too, was afraid because he loved Athira better than his very life. Two months passed, and Athira's brother stood outside the regimental Lines again and yelped, 'Aha! You are withering away. Come back.'

'I will come back,' said Athira.

'Say rather that *we* will come back,' said Suket Singh.

'Ai; but when?' said Athira's brother.

'Upon a day very early in the morning,' said Suket Singh; and he tramped off to apply to the Colonel Sahib Bahadur for one week's leave.

'I am withering away like a barked tree in the spring,' moaned Athira.

'You will be better soon,' said Suket Singh; and he told her what was in his heart, and the two laughed together softly, for they loved each other. But Athira grew better from that hour.

They went away together, travelling third-class by train as the regulations provided, and then in a cart to the low hills, and on foot to the high ones. Athira sniffed the scent of the pines of her own hills, the wet Himalayan hills. 'It is good to be alive,' said Athira.

'Hah!' said Suket Singh. 'Where is the Kodru road, and where is the Forest Ranger's house? . . .'

'It cost forty rupees twelve years ago,' said the Forest Ranger, handing the gun.

'Here are twenty,' said Suket Singh, 'and you must give me the best bullets.'

'It is *very* good to be alive,' said Athira wistfully, sniffing the scent of the pine-mould ; and they waited till the night had fallen upon Kodru and the Donga Pa. Madu had stacked the dry wood for the next day's charcoal-burning on the spur above his house. 'It is courteous in Madu to save us this trouble,' said Suket Singh, as he stumbled on the pile, which was twelve feet square and four high. 'We must wait till the moon rises.'

When the moon rose, Athira knelt upon the pile. 'If it were only a Government Snider,' said Suket Singh ruefully, squinting down the wire-bound barrel of the Forest Ranger's gun.

'Be quick,' said Athira ; and Suket Singh was quick ; but Athira was quick no longer. Then he lit the pile at the four corners and climbed on to it, re-loading the gun.

The little flames began to peer up between the big logs atop of the brushwood. 'The Government should teach us to pull the triggers with our toes,' said Suket Singh grimly to the moon. That was the last public observation of Sepoy Suket Singh.

.   .   .   .   .

Upon a day, early in the morning, Madu came to the pyre and shrieked very grievously, and ran away to catch the Policeman who was on tour in the district.

'The base-born has ruined four rupees' worth of charcoal wood,' Madu gasped. 'He has also killed my wife, and he has left a letter which I cannot read, tied to a pine bough.'

In the stiff, formal hand taught in the regimental school, Sepoy Suket Singh had written—

'Let us be burned together, if anything remain over, for we have made the necessary prayers. We have also cursed Madu, and Malak the brother of Athira—both evil men. Send my service to the Colonel Sahib Bahadur.'

The Policeman looked long and curiously at the marriage bed of red and white ashes on which lay, dull black, the barrel of the Ranger's gun. He drove his spurred heel absently into a half-charred log, and the chattering sparks flew upwards. 'Most extraordinary people,' said the Policeman.

'*Whe-w, whew, ouiou,*' said the little flames.

The Policeman entered the dry bones of the case, for the Punjab Government does not approve of romancing, in his Diary.

'But who will pay me those four rupees?' said Madu.

The Finances of the Gods

THE evening meal was ended in Dhunni Bhagat's Chubara, and the old priests were smoking or counting their beads. A little naked child pattered in, with its mouth wide open, a handful of marigold flowers in one hand, and a lump of conserved tobacco in the other. It tried to kneel and make obeisance to Gobind, but it was so fat that it fell forward on its shaven head, and rolled on its side, kicking and gasping, while the marigolds tumbled one way and the tobacco the other. Gobind laughed, set it up again, and blessed the marigold flowers as he received the tobacco.

'From my father,' said the child. 'He has the fever, and cannot come. Wilt thou pray for him, father?'

'Surely, littlest; but the smoke is on the ground, and the night-chill is in the air, and it is not good to go abroad naked in the autumn.'

'I have no clothes,' said the child, 'and all to-day I have been carrying cow-dung cakes to the bazar. It was very hot, and I am very tired.' It shivered a little, for the twilight was cool.

Gobind lifted an arm under his vast tattered

quilt of many colours, and made an inviting little nest by his side. The child crept in, and Gobind filled his brass-studded leather waterpipe with the new tobacco. When I came to the Chubara the shaven head with the tuft atop, and the beady black eyes looked out of the folds of the quilt as a squirrel looks out from his nest, and Gobind was smiling while the child played with his beard.

I would have said something friendly, but remembered in time that if the child fell ill afterwards I should be credited with the Evil Eye, and that is a horrible possession.

'Sit thou still, Thumbling,' I said, as it made to get up and run away. 'Where is thy slate, and why has the teacher let such an evil character loose on the streets when there are no police to protect us weaklings? In which ward dost thou try to break thy neck with flying kites from the house-tops?'

'Nay, Sahib, nay,' said the child, burrowing its face into Gobind's beard, and twisting uneasily. 'There was a holiday to-day among the schools, and I do not always fly kites. I play ker-li-kit like the rest.'

Cricket is the national game among the school-boys of the Punjab, from the naked hedge-school children, who use an old kerosene-tin for wicket, to the B.A.'s of the University, who compete for the Championship belt.

'Thou play kerlikit! Thou art half the height of the bat!' I said.

The child nodded resolutely. 'Yea, I *do* play. *Perlay-ball. Ow-at! Ran, ran, ran!* I know it all.'

'But thou must not forget with all this to pray to the Gods according to custom,' said Gobind, who did not altogether approve of cricket and Western innovations.

'I do not forget,' said the child in a hushed voice.

'Also to give reverence to thy teacher, and'— Gobind's voice softened—'to abstain from pulling holy men by the beard, little badling. Eh, eh, eh?'

The child's face was altogether hidden in the great white beard, and it began to whimper till Gobind soothed it as children are soothed all the world over, with the promise of a story.

'I did not think to frighten thee, senseless little one. Look up! Am I angry? Aré, aré, aré! Shall I weep too, and of our tears make a great pond and drown us both, and then thy father will never get well, lacking thee to pull his beard? Peace, peace, and I will tell thee of the Gods. Thou hast heard many tales?'

'Very many, father.'

'Now, this is a new one which thou hast not heard. Long and long ago when the Gods walked with men as they do to-day, but that we have not faith to see, Shiv, the greatest of Gods, and Parbati his wife, were walking in the garden of a temple.'

'Which temple? That in the Nandgaon ward?' said the child.

'Nay, very far away. Maybe at Trimbak or Hurdwar, whither thou must make pilgrimage when thou art a man. Now, there was sitting in the garden under the jujube trees, a mendicant that had worshipped Shiv for forty years, and he lived on the offerings of the pious, and meditated holiness night and day.'

'O father, was it thou?' said the child, looking up with large eyes.

'Nay, I have said it was long ago, and, moreover, this mendicant was married.'

'Did they put him on a horse with flowers on his head, and forbid him to go to sleep all night long? Thus they did to me when they made my wedding,' said the child, who had been married a few months before.

'And what didst thou do?' said I.

'I wept, and they called me evil names, and then I smote *her*, and we wept together.'

'Thus did not the mendicant,' said Gobind; 'for he was a holy man, and very poor. Parbati perceived him sitting naked by the temple steps where all went up and down, and she said to Shiv, "What shall men think of the Gods when the Gods thus scorn their worshippers? For forty years yonder man has prayed to us, and yet there be only a few grains of rice and some broken cowries before him after all. Men's hearts will be hardened by this thing." And Shiv said, "It shall be looked to," and so he called to the temple which was the temple of his son, Ganesh of the elephant head, saying, "Son, there is a mendicant without who is very poor. What wilt thou do for him?" Then that great elephant-headed One awoke in the dark and answered, "In three days, if it be thy will, he shall have one lakh of rupees." Then Shiv and Parbati went away.

'But there was a money-lender in the garden hidden among the marigolds'——the child looked at the ball of crumpled blossoms in its hands—'ay, among the yellow marigolds, and he heard the Gods talking. He was a covetous man, and of a black heart, and he desired that lakh of rupees for himself. So he went to the mendicant and said, "Oh brother, how much do the pious give thee daily?" The mendicant said, "I cannot tell. Sometimes a little rice, sometimes a little pulse, and a few cowries and, it has been, pickled mangoes, and dried fish."

'That is good,' said the child, smacking its lips.

'Then said the money-lender, "Because I have long watched thee, and learned to love thee and thy patience, I will give thee now five rupees for all thy earnings of the three days to come. There is only a bond to sign on the matter." But the mendicant said, "Thou art mad. In two months I do not receive the worth of five rupees," and he told the thing to his wife that evening. She, being a woman, said, "When did money-lender ever make a bad bargain? The wolf runs through the corn for the sake of the fat deer. Our fate is in the hands of the Gods. Pledge it not even for three days."

'So the mendicant returned to the money-lender, and would not sell. Then that wicked man sat all day before him offering more and more for those three days' earnings. First, ten, fifty, and a hundred rupees; and then, for he did not know when the Gods would pour down their gifts, rupees by the thousand, till he had offered half a lakh of rupees. Upon this sum the mendicant's wife shifted her counsel, and the mendicant signed the bond, and the money was paid in silver ; great white bullocks bringing it by the cartload. But saving only all that money, the mendicant received nothing from the Gods at all, and the heart of the money-lender was uneasy on account of expectation. Therefore at noon of the third day the money-lender went into the temple to spy upon the councils of the Gods, and to learn in what manner that gift might arrive. Even as he was making his prayers, a crack between the stones of the floor gaped, and, closing, caught him by the heel. Then he heard the Gods walking in the temple in the darkness of the columns, and Shiv called to his son Ganesh, saying "Son, what hast thou done in regard to the lakh of rupees for the mendicant ? " And Ganesh woke, for the money-lender heard the dry rustle of his trunk uncoiling, and he answered, "Father, one-half of the money has been paid, and the debtor for the other half I hold here fast by the heel." '

The child bubbled with laughter. ' And the money-lender paid the mendicant ? ' it said.

' Surely, for he whom the Gods hold by the heel must pay to the uttermost. The money was paid at evening, all silver, in great carts, and thus Ganesh did his work.'

' Nathu ! Ohē Nathu ! '

A woman was calling in the dusk by the door of the courtyard.

The child began to wriggle. ' That is my mother,' it said.

'Go then, littlest,' answered Gobind ; 'but stay a moment.'

He ripped a generous yard from his patchwork-quilt, put it over the child's shoulders, and the child ran away.

The Amir's Homily

His Royal Highness Abdur Rahman, Amir of Afghanistan, G.C.S.I., and trusted ally of Her Imperial Majesty the Queen of England and Empress of India, is a gentleman for whom all right-thinking people should have a profound regard. Like most other rulers, he governs not as he would, but as he can, and the mantle of his authority covers the most turbulent race under the stars. To the Afghan neither life, property, law, nor kingship are sacred when his own lusts prompt him to rebel. He is a thief by instinct, a murderer by heredity and training, and frankly and bestially immoral by all three. None the less he has his own crooked notions of honour, and his character is fascinating to study. On occasion he will fight without reason given till he is hacked in pieces ; on other occasions he will refuse to show fight till he is driven into a corner. Herein he is as unaccountable as the gray wolf, who is his blood-brother.

And these men His Highness rules by the only weapon that they understand—the fear of death, which among some Orientals is the beginning of wisdom. Some say that the Amir's authority reaches no farther than a rifle bullet can range ; but as none are quite certain when their king may be in their midst, and as he alone holds every one of the threads of Government, his respect is increased among men. Gholam Hyder, the Commander-in-Chief of the Afghan army, is feared reasonably, for he can impale ; all Kabul city fears the Governor of Kabul, who has power of life and death through all the wards ; but the Amir of Afghanistan, though outlying tribes pretend otherwise when his back is turned, is dreaded beyond chief and governor together. His word is red law ; by the gust of his passion falls the leaf of man's life, and his favour is terrible. He has suffered many things, and been a hunted fugitive before he came to the throne, and he understands all the classes of his people. By the custom of the East any man or woman having a complaint to make, or an enemy against whom to be avenged, has the right of speaking face to face with the king at the daily public audience. This is personal government, as it was in the days of Harun al Raschid of blessed memory, whose times exist still and will exist long after the English have passed away.

The privilege of open speech is of course exercised at certain personal risk. The king may be pleased, and raise the speaker to honour for that very bluntness of speech which three minutes later brings a too imitative petitioner to the edge of the ever ready blade. And the people love to have it so, for it is their right.

It happened upon a day in Kabul that the Amir chose to do his day's work in the Baber Gardens, which lie a short distance from the city of Kabul. A light table stood before him, and round the table in the open air were grouped generals and finance ministers according to their degree. The Court and the long tail of feudal chiefs—men of blood, fed and cowed by blood— stood in an irregular semicircle round the table, and the wind from the Kabul orchards blew among them. All day long sweating couriers dashed in with letters from the outlying districts with rumours of rebellion, intrigue, famine, failure of payments, or announcements of treasure on the road ; and all day long the Amir would read the dockets, and pass such of these as were less private to the officials whom they directly concerned, or call up a waiting chief for a word of explanation. It is well to speak clearly to the ruler of Afghanistan. Then the grim head, under the black astrakhan cap with the diamond star in front, would nod gravely, and that chief would return to his fellows. Once that afternoon a woman clamoured for divorce against her husband, who was bald, and the Amir, hearing both sides of the case, bade her pour curds over the bare scalp, and lick them off, that the hair might grow again, and she be contented. Here the Court laughed, and the woman withdrew, cursing her king under her breath.

But when twilight was falling, and the order of the Court was a little relaxed, there came before the king, in custody, a trembling haggard wretch,

sore with much buffeting, but of stout enough
build, who had stolen three rupees—of such small
matters does His Highness take cognisance.

'Why did you steal?' said he; and when the
king asks questions they do themselves service
who answer directly.

'I was poor, and no one gave. Hungry, and
there was no food.'

'Why did you not work?'

'I could find no work, Protector of the Poor,
and I was starving.'

'You lie. You stole for drink, for lust, for
idleness, for anything but hunger, since any man
who will may find work and daily bread.'

The prisoner dropped his eyes. He had
attended the Court before, and he knew the ring
of the death-tone.

'Any man may get work. Who knows this
so well as I do? for I too have been hungered—
not like you, bastard scum, but as any honest man
may be, by the turn of Fate and the will of God.'

Growing warm, the Amir turned to his nobles
all arow and thrust the hilt of his sabre aside with
his elbow.

'You have heard this Son of Lies? Hear me
tell a true tale. I also was once starved, and
tightened my belt on the sharp belly-pinch. Nor
was I alone, for with me was another, who did not
fail me in my evil days, when I was hunted, before
ever I came to this throne. And wandering like
a houseless dog by Kandahar, my money melted,
melted, melted till——' He flung out a bare
palm before the audience. 'And day upon day,

faint and sick, I went back to that one who waited, and God knows how we lived, till on a day I took our best *lihaf*—silk it was, fine work of Iran, such as no needle now works, warm, and a coverlet for two, and all that we had. I brought it to a money-lender in a by-lane, and I asked for three rupees upon it. He said to me, who am now the King, "You are a thief. This is worth three hundred."—"I am no thief," I answered, "but a prince of good blood, and I am hungry." —"Prince of wandering beggars," said that money-lender, "I have no money with me, but go to my house with my clerk and he will give you two rupees eight annas, for that is all I will lend." So I went with the clerk to the house, and we talked on the way, and he gave me the money. We lived on it till it was spent, and we fared hard. And then that clerk said, being a young man of a good heart, "Surely the money-lender will lend yet more on that *lihaf*," and he offered me two rupees. These I refused, saying, "Nay; but get me some work." And he got me work, and I, even I, Abdur Rahman, Amir of Afghanistan, wrought day by day as a coolie, bearing burdens, and labouring of my hands, receiving four annas wage a day for my sweat and backache. But he, this bastard son of naught, must steal! For a year and four months I worked, and none dare say that I lie, for I have a witness, even that clerk who is now my friend.'

Then there rose in his place among the Sirdars and the nobles one clad in silk, who folded his hands and said, 'This is the truth of God, for I, who by the favour of God and the Amir, am such as you know, was once clerk to that money-lender.'

There was a pause, and the Amir cried hoarsely to the prisoner, throwing scorn upon him, till he ended with the dread '*Dar arid*,' which clinches justice.

So they led the thief away, and the whole of him was seen no more together; and the Court rustled out of its silence, whispering, 'Before God and the Prophet, but this is a man!'

Jews in Shushan

My newly-purchased house furniture was, at the least, insecure ; the legs parted from the chairs, and the tops from the tables on the slightest provocation. But such as it was, it was to be paid for, and Ephraim, agent and collector for the local auctioneer, waited in the verandah with the receipt. He was announced by the Mahomedan servant as 'Ephraim, Yahudi'—Ephraim the Jew. He who believes in the Brotherhood of Man should hear my Elahi Bukhsh grinding the second word through his white teeth with all the scorn he dare show before his master. Ephraim was, personally, meek in manner—so meek, indeed, that one could not understand how he had fallen into the profession of bill-collecting. He resembled an over-fed sheep, and his voice suited his figure. There was a fixed, unvarying mask of childish wonder upon his face. If you paid him, he was as one marvelling at your wealth ; if you sent him away he seemed puzzled at your hard-heartedness. Never was Jew more unlike his dread breed.

Ephraim wore list slippers and coats of duster-cloth, so preposterously patterned that the most brazen of British Subalterns would have shied from them in fear. Very slow and deliberate was his speech, and carefully guarded to give offence to no one. After many weeks, Ephraim was induced to speak to me of his friends.

'There be eight of us in Shushan, and we are waiting till there are ten. Then we shall apply for a synagogue, and get leave from Calcutta. To-day we have no synagogue ; and I, only I, am Priest and Butcher to our people. I am of the tribe of Judah — I think, but I am not sure. My father was of the tribe of Judah, and we wish much to get our synagogue. I shall be a priest of that synagogue.'

Shushan is a big city in the North of India, counting its dwellers by the ten thousand ; and these eight of the Chosen People were shut up in its midst, waiting till time or chance sent them their full congregation.

Miriam the wife of Ephraim, two little children, an orphan boy of their people, Ephraim's uncle Jackrael Israel, a white-haired old man, his wife Hester, a Jew from Cutch, one Hyem Benjamin, and Ephraim, Priest and Butcher, made up the list of the Jews in Shushan. They lived in one house, on the outskirts of the great city, amid heaps of saltpetre, rotten bricks, herds of kine, and a fixed pillar of dust caused by the incessant passing of the beasts to the river to drink. In the evening the children of the City came to the waste place to fly their kites, and Ephraim's sons held aloof, watching the sport from the roof, but never descending to take part in it. At the back of the house stood a small brick enclosure, in which Ephraim prepared the daily meat for his people after the custom of the Jews. Once the rude door of the square was suddenly smashed open by a struggle from inside, and showed the meek bill-collector at his work, nostrils dilated, lips drawn back over his teeth, and his hands upon a half-maddened sheep. He was attired in strange raiment, having no relation whatever to duster coats or list slippers, and a knife was in his mouth. As he struggled with the animal between the walls, the breath came from him in thick sobs, and the nature of the man seemed changed. When the ordained slaughter was ended, he saw that the door was open and shut it hastily, his hand leaving a red mark on the timber, while his children from the neighbouring house-top looked down awe-stricken and open-eyed. A glimpse of Ephraim busied in one of his religious capacities was no thing to be desired twice.

Summer came upon Shushan, turning the trodden waste-ground to iron, and bringing sickness to the city.

'It will not touch us,' said Ephraim confidently. 'Before the winter we shall have our synagogue. My brother and his wife and children are coming up from Calcutta, and *then* I shall be the priest of the synagogue.'

Jackrael Israel, the old man, would crawl out in the stifling evenings to sit on the rubbish-heap and watch the corpses being borne down to the river.

'It will not come near us,' said Jackrael Israel feebly, 'for we are the People of God, and my nephew will be priest of our synagogue. Let them die.' He crept back to his house again and barred the door to shut himself off from the world of the Gentile.

But Miriam, the wife of Ephraim, looked out of the window at the dead as the biers passed and said that she was afraid. Ephraim comforted her with hopes of the synagogue to be, and collected bills as was his custom.

In one night the two children died and were buried early in the morning by Ephraim. The deaths never appeared in the City returns. 'The sorrow is my sorrow,' said Ephraim; and this to him seemed a sufficient reason for setting at naught the sanitary regulations of a large, flourishing, and remarkably well-governed Empire.

The orphan boy, dependent on the charity of Ephraim and his wife, could have felt no gratitude, and must have been a ruffian. He begged for whatever money his protectors would give him, and with that fled down-country for his life. A week after the death of her children Miriam left her bed at night and wandered over the country to find them. She heard them crying behind every bush, or drowning in every pool of water in the fields, and she begged the cartmen on the Grand Trunk Road not to steal her little ones from her. In the morning the sun rose and beat upon her bare head, and she turned into the cool wet crops to lie down and never came back; though Hyem Benjamin and Ephraim sought her for two nights.

The look of patient wonder on Ephraim's face

deepened, but he presently found an explanation. 'There are so few of us here, and these people are so many,' said he, 'that, it may be, our God has forgotten us.'

In the house on the outskirts of the city old Jackrael Israel and Hester grumbled that there was no one to wait on them, and that Miriam had been untrue to her race. Ephraim went out and collected bills, and in the evenings smoked with Hyem Benjamin till, one dawning, Hyem Benjamin died, having first paid all his debts to Ephraim. Jackrael Israel and Hester sat alone in the empty house all day, and, when Ephraim returned, wept the easy tears of age till they cried themselves asleep.

A week later Ephraim, staggering under a huge bundle of clothes and cooking-pots, led the old man and woman to the railway station, where the bustle and confusion made them whimper.

'We are going back to Calcutta,' said Ephraim, to whose sleeve Hester was clinging. 'There are more of us there, and here my house is empty.'

He helped Hester into the carriage and, turning back, said to me, 'I should have been priest of the synagogue if there had been ten of us. Surely we must have been forgotten by our God.'

The remnant of the broken colony passed out of the station on their journey south; while a Sub-altern, turning over the books on the bookstall, was whistling to himself 'The Ten Little Nigger Boys.'

But the tune sounded as solemn as the Dead March.

It was the dirge of the Jews in Shushan.

The Limitations of Pambé Serang

IF you consider the circumstances of the case, it was the only thing that he could do. But Pambé Serang has been hanged by the neck till he is dead, and Nurkeed is dead also.

Three years ago, when the Elsass-Lothringen steamer *Saarbruck* was coaling at Aden and the weather was very hot indeed, Nurkeed, the big fat Zanzibar stoker who fed the second right furnace thirty feet down in the hold, got leave to go ashore. He departed a 'Seedee boy,' as they call the stokers; he returned the full-blooded Sultan of Zanzibar—His Highness Sayyid Burgash, with a bottle in each hand. Then he sat on the fore-hatch grating, eating salt fish and onions, and singing the songs of a far country. The food belonged to Pambé, the Serang or head man of the lascar sailors. He had just cooked it for himself, turned to borrow some salt, and when he came back Nurkeed's dirty black fingers were spading into the rice.

A serang is a person of importance, far above a stoker, though the stoker draws better pay. He sets the chorus of 'Hya! Hulla! Hee-ah!

Heh ! ' when the captain's gig is pulled up to the davits ; he heaves the lead too ; and sometimes, when all the ship is lazy, he puts on his whitest muslin and a big red sash, and plays with the passengers' children on the quarter-deck. Then the passengers give him money, and he saves it all up for an orgie at Bombay or Calcutta, or Pulu Penang.

'Ho ! you fat black barrel, you're eating my food !' said Pambé, in the Other Lingua Franca that begins where the Levant tongue stops, and runs from Port Said eastward till east is west, and the sealing-brigs of the Kurile Islands gossip with the strayed Hakodate junks.

'Son of Eblis, monkey-face, dried shark's liver, pig-man, I am the Sultan Sayyid Burgash, and the commander of all this ship. Take away your garbage ;' and Nurkeed thrust the empty pewter rice-plate into Pambé's hand.

Pambé beat it into a basin over Nurkeed's woolly head. Nurkeed drew his sheath-knife and stabbed Pambé in the leg. Pambé drew *his* sheath-knife ; but Nurkeed dropped down into the darkness of the hold and spat through the grating at Pambé, who was staining the clean fore-deck with his blood.

Only the white moon saw these things ; for the officers were looking after the coaling, and the passengers were tossing in their close cabins. 'All right,' said Pambé—and went forward to tie up his leg—'we will settle the account later on.'

He was a Malay born in India : married once in Burma, where his wife had a cigar-shop on the

Shwe-Dagon road ; once in Singapore, to a Chinese
girl ; and once in Madras, to a Mahomedan
woman who sold fowls. The English sailor
cannot, owing to postal and telegraph facilities,
marry as profusely as he used to do ; but native
sailors can, being uninfluenced by the barbarous
inventions of the Western savage. Pambé was a
good husband when he happened to remember the
existence of a wife ; but he was also a very good
Malay ; and it is not wise to offend a Malay,
because he does not forget anything. Moreover,
in Pambé's case blood had been drawn and food
spoiled.

Next morning Nurkeed rose with a blank mind.
He was no longer Sultan of Zanzibar, but a very
hot stoker. So he went on deck and opened his
jacket to the morning breeze, till a sheath-knife
came like a flying-fish and stuck into the woodwork of the cook's galley half an inch from his
right armpit. He ran down below before his
time, trying to remember what he could have said
to the owner of the weapon. At noon, when all
the ship's lascars were feeding, Nurkeed advanced
into their midst, and, being a placid man with a
large regard for his own skin, he opened negotia-
tions, saying, ' Men of the ship, last night I was
drunk, and this morning I know that I behaved
unseemly to some one or another of you. Who
was that man, that I may meet him face to face
and say that I was drunk ? '

Pambé measured the distance to Nurkeed's
naked breast. If he sprang at him he might be
tripped up, and a blind blow at the chest some-

times only means a gash on the breast-bone. Ribs are difficult to thrust between unless the subject be asleep. So he said nothing; nor did the other lascars. Their faces immediately dropped all expression, as is the custom of the Oriental when there is killing on the carpet or any chance of trouble. Nurkeed looked long at the white eyeballs. He was only an African, and could not read characters. A big sigh—almost a groan—broke from him, and he went back to the furnaces. The lascars took up the conversation where he had interrupted it. They talked of the best methods of cooking rice.

Nurkeed suffered considerably from lack of fresh air during the run to Bombay. He only came on deck to breathe when all the world was about; and even then a heavy block once dropped from a derrick within a foot of his head, and an apparently firm-lashed grating on which he set his foot began to turn over with the intention of dropping him on the cased cargo fifteen feet below; and one insupportable night the sheath-knife dropped from the fo'c's'le, and this time it drew blood. So Nurkeed made complaint; and, when the *Saarbruck* reached Bombay, fled and buried himself among eight hundred thousand people, and did not sign articles till the ship had been a month gone from the port. Pambé waited too; but his Bombay wife grew clamorous, and he was forced to sign in the *Spicheren* to Hongkong, because he realised that all play and no work gives Jack a ragged shirt. In the foggy China seas he thought a great deal of Nurkeed, and, when Elsass-Loth-

ringen steamers lay in port with the *Spicheren*,
inquired after him and found he had gone to
England *via* the Cape, on the *Gravelotte*. Pambé
came to England on the *Worth*. The *Spicheren*
met her by the Nore Light. Nurkeed was going
out with the *Spicheren* to the Calicut coast.

' Want to find a friend, my trap-mouthed coal-
scuttle?' said a gentleman in the mercantile service.
'Nothing easier. Wait at the Nyanza Docks till
he comes. Every one comes to the Nyanza
Docks. Wait, you poor heathen.' The gentleman
spoke truth. There are three great doors in the
world where, if you stand long enough, you shall
meet any one you wish. The head of the Suez
Canal is one, but there Death comes also ; Charing
Cross Station is the second—for inland work ; and
the Nyanza Docks is the third. At each of these
places are men and women looking eternally for
those who will surely come. So Pambé waited at
the docks. Time was no object to him ; and the
wives could wait, as he did from day to day, week
to week, and month to month, by the Blue
Diamond funnels, the Red Dot smoke-stacks, the
Yellow Streaks, and the nameless dingy gypsies of
the sea that loaded and unloaded, jostled, whistled,
and roared in the everlasting fog. When money
failed, a kind gentleman told Pambé to become a
Christian ; and Pambé became one with great
speed, getting his religious teachings between ship
and ship's arrival, and six or seven shillings a week
for distributing tracts to mariners. What the
faith was Pambé did not in the least care ; but he
knew if he said 'Native Ki-lis-ti-an, Sar' to men

with long black coats he might get a few coppers; and the tracts were vendible at a little public-house that sold shag by the 'dottle,' which is even smaller weight than the 'half-screw,' which is less than the half-ounce, and a most profitable retail trade.

But after eight months Pambé fell sick with pneumonia, contracted from long standing still in slush; and much against his will he was forced to lie down in his two-and-sixpenny room raging against Fate.

The kind gentleman sat by his bedside, and grieved to find that Pambé talked in strange tongues, instead of listening to good books, and almost seemed to become a benighted heathen again—till one day he was roused from semi-stupor by a voice in the street by the dock-head. 'My friend—he,' whispered Pambé. 'Call now—call Nurkeed. Quick! God has sent him!'

'He wanted one of his own race,' said the kind gentleman; and, going out, he called 'Nurkeed!' at the top of his voice. An excessively coloured man in a rasping white shirt and brand-new slops, a shining hat, and a breast-pin, turned round. Many voyages had taught Nurkeed how to spend his money and made him a citizen of the world.

'Hi! Yes!' said he, when the situation was explained. 'Command him—black nigger—when I was in the *Saarbruck*. Ole Pambé, good ole Pambé. Dam lascar. Show him up, Sar;' and he followed into the room. One glance told the stoker what the kind gentleman had overlooked. Pambé was desperately poor. Nurkeed drove his hands deep into his pockets, then advanced with clenched fists on the sick, shouting, 'Hya, Pambé. Hya! Hee-ah! Hulla! Heh! Takilo! Takilo! Make fast aft, Pambé. You know, Pambé. You know me. Dekho, jee! Look! Dam big fat lazy lascar!'

Pambé beckoned with his left hand. His right was under his pillow. Nurkeed removed his gorgeous hat and stooped over Pambé till he could catch a faint whisper. 'How beautiful!' said the kind gentleman. 'How these Orientals love like children!'

'Spit him out,' said Nurkeed, leaning over Pambé yet more closely.

'Touching the matter of that fish and onions ——' said Pambé—and sent the knife home under the edge of the rib-bone upwards and forwards.

There was a thick sick cough, and the body of the African slid slowly from the bed, his clutching hands letting fall a shower of silver pieces that ran across the room.

'Now I can die!' said Pambé.

But he did not die. He was nursed back to life with all the skill that money could buy, for the Law wanted him; and in the end he grew sufficiently healthy to be hanged in due and proper form.

Pambé did not care particularly; but it was a sad blow to the kind gentleman.

Little Tobrah

'PRISONER's head did not reach to the top of the dock,' as the English newspapers say. This case, however, was not reported because nobody cared by so much as a hempen rope for the life or death of Little Tobrah. The assessors in the red court-house sat upon him all through the long hot afternoon, and whenever they asked him a question he salaamed and whined. Their verdict was that the evidence was inconclusive, and the Judge concurred. It was true that the dead body of Little Tobrah's sister had been found at the bottom of the well, and Little Tobrah was the only human being within a half mile radius at the time ; but the child might have fallen in by accident. Therefore Little Tobrah was acquitted, and told to go where he pleased. This permission was not so generous as it sounds, for he had nowhere to go to, nothing in particular to eat, and nothing whatever to wear.

He trotted into the court-compound, and sat upon the well-kerb, wondering whether an unsuccessful dive into the black water below would end in a forced voyage across the other Black

Water. A groom put down an emptied nose-bag on the bricks, and Little Tobrah, being hungry, set himself to scrape out what wet grain the horse had overlooked.

'O Thief—and but newly set free from the terror of the Law! Come along!' said the groom, and Little Tobrah was led by the ear to a large and fat Englishman, who heard the tale of the theft.

'Hah!' said the Englishman three times (only he said a stronger word). 'Put him into the net and take him home.' So Little Tobrah was thrown into the net of the cart, and, nothing doubting that he should be stuck like a pig, was driven to the Englishman's house. 'Hah!' said the Englishman as before. 'Wet grain, by Jove! Feed the little beggar, some of you, and we'll make a riding-boy of him! See? Wet grain, good Lord!'

'Give an account of yourself,' said the Head of the Grooms to Little Tobrah after the meal had been eaten, and the servants lay at ease in their quarters behind the house. 'You are not of the groom caste, unless it be for the stomach's sake. How came you into the court, and why? Answer, little devil's spawn!'

'There was not enough to eat,' said Little Tobrah calmly. 'This is a good place.'

'Talk straight talk,' said the Head Groom, 'or I will make you clean out the stable of that large red stallion who bites like a camel.'

'We be *Telis*, oil-pressers,' said Little Tobrah, scratching his toes in the dust. 'We were *Telis*—

my father, my mother, my brother, the elder by four years, myself, and the sister.'

'She who was found dead in the well?' said one who had heard something of the trial.

'Even so,' said Little Tobrah gravely. 'She who was found dead in the well. It befell upon a time, which is not in my memory, that the sickness came to the village where our oil-press stood, and first my sister was smitten as to her eyes, and went without sight, for it was *mata*—the small-pox. Thereafter, my father and my mother died of that same sickness, so we were alone—my brother who had twelve years, I who had eight, and the sister who could not see. Yet were there the bullock and the oil-press remaining, and we made shift to press the oil as before. But Surjun Dass, the grain-seller, cheated us in his dealings; and it was always a stubborn bullock to drive. We put marigold flowers for the Gods upon the neck of the bullock, and upon the great grinding-beam that rose through the roof; but we gained nothing thereby, and Surjun Dass was a hard man.'

'*Bapri-bap*,' muttered the grooms' wives, 'to cheat a child so! But *we* know what the *bunnia*-folk are, sisters.'

'The press was an old press, and we were not strong men—my brother and I; nor could we fix the neck of the beam firmly in the shackle.'

'Nay, indeed,' said the gorgeously-clad wife of the Head Groom, joining the circle. 'That is a strong man's work. When I was a maid in my father's house——'

'Peace, woman,' said the Head Groom. 'Go on, boy.'

'It is nothing,' said Little Tobrah. 'The big beam tore down the roof upon a day which is not in my memory, and with the roof fell much of the hinder wall, and both together upon our bullock, whose back was broken. Thus we had neither home, nor press, nor bullock—my brother, myself, and the sister who was blind. We went crying away from that place, hand-in-hand, across the fields; and our money was seven annas and six pies. There was a famine in the land. I do not know the name of the land. So, on a night when we were sleeping, my brother took the five annas that remained to us and ran away. I do not know whither he went. The curse of my father be upon him. But I and the sister begged food in the villages, and there was none to give. Only all men said—"Go to the Englishmen and they will give." I did not know what the Englishmen were; but they said that they were white, living in tents. I went forward; but I cannot say whither I went, and there was no more food for myself or the sister. And upon a hot night, she weeping and calling for food, we came to a well, and I bade her sit upon the kerb, and thrust her in, for, in truth, she could not see; and it is better to die than to starve.'

'Ai! Ahi!' wailed the grooms' wives in chorus; 'he thrust her in, for it is better to die than to starve!'

'I would have thrown myself in also, but that she was not dead and called to me from the bottom of the well, and I was afraid and ran. And one came out of the crops saying that I had killed her and defiled the well, and they took me before an Englishman, white and terrible, living in a tent, and me he sent here. But there were no witnesses, and it is better to die than to starve. She, furthermore, could not see with her eyes, and was but a little child.'

'Was but a little child,' echoed the Head Groom's wife. 'But who art thou, weak as a fowl and small as a day-old colt, what art *thou*?'

'I who was empty am now full,' said Little Tobrah, stretching himself upon the dust. 'And I would sleep.'

The groom's wife spread a cloth over him while Little Tobrah slept the sleep of the just.

Moti Guj—Mutineer

Once upon a time there was a coffee-planter in India who wished to clear some forest land for coffee-planting. When he had cut down all the trees and burned the under-wood the stumps still remained. Dynamite is expensive and slow-fire slow. The happy medium for stump-clearing is the lord of all beasts, who is the elephant. He will either push the stump out of the ground with his tusks, if he has any, or drag it out with ropes. The planter, therefore, hired elephants by ones and twos and threes, and fell to work. The very best of all the elephants belonged to the very worst of all the drivers or mahouts ; and the superior beast's name was Moti Guj. He was the absolute property of his mahout, which would never have been the case under native rule, for Moti Guj was a creature to be desired by kings ; and his name, being translated, meant the Pearl Elephant. Because the British Government was in the land, Deesa, the mahout, enjoyed his property undisturbed. He was dissipated. When he had made much money through the strength of his elephant, he would get extremely drunk and give Moti Guj a beating with a tent-peg over the tender nails of the forefeet. Moti Guj never trampled the life out of Deesa on these occasions, for he knew that after the beating was over Deesa would embrace his trunk, and weep and call him his love and his life and the liver of his soul, and give him some liquor. Moti Guj was very fond of liquor—arrack for choice, though he would drink palm-tree toddy if nothing better offered. Then Deesa would go to sleep between Moti Guj's forefeet, and as Deesa generally chose the middle of the public road, and as Moti Guj mounted guard over him and would not permit horse, foot, or cart to pass by, traffic was congested till Deesa saw fit to wake up.

There was no sleeping in the daytime on the planter's clearing: the wages were too high to risk. Deesa sat on Moti Guj's neck and gave him orders, while Moti Guj rooted up the stumps—for he owned a magnificent pair of tusks ; or pulled at the end of a rope—for he had a magnificent pair of shoulders, while Deesa kicked him behind the ears and said he was the king of elephants. At evening time Moti Guj would wash down his three hundred pounds' weight of green food with a quart of arrack, and Deesa would take a share and sing songs between Moti Guj's legs till it was time to go to bed. Once a week Deesa led Moti Guj down to the river, and Moti Guj lay on his side luxuriously in the shallows, while Deesa went over him with a coir-swab and a brick. Moti Guj never mistook the pounding blow of the latter for the smack of the former that warned him to get up and turn over on the other side. Then Deesa would look at his feet, and examine his eyes, and turn up the fringes of his mighty ears in case of sores or budding ophthalmia. After inspection, the two would 'come up with a song from the sea,' Moti Guj all black and shining, waving a torn tree branch twelve feet long in his trunk, and Deesa knotting up his own long wet hair.

It was a peaceful, well-paid life till Deesa felt the return of the desire to drink deep. He wished for an orgy. The little draughts that led nowhere were taking the manhood out of him.

He went to the planter, and 'My mother's dead,' said he, weeping.

'She died on the last plantation two months ago ; and she died once before that when you were working for me last year,' said the planter, who knew something of the ways of nativedom.

'Then it's my aunt, and she was just the same as a mother to me,' said Deesa, weeping more than ever. 'She has left eighteen small children entirely without bread, and it is I who must fill their little stomachs,' said Deesa, beating his head on the floor.

'Who brought you the news ?' said the planter.

'The post,' said Deesa.

'There hasn't been a post here for the past week. Get back to your lines ! '

'A devastating sickness has fallen on my village, and all my wives are dying,' yelled Deesa, really in tears this time.

'Call Chihun, who comes from Deesa's village,' said the planter. 'Chihun, has this man a wife ?'

'He!' said Chihun. 'No. Not a woman of our village would look at him. They'd sooner marry the elephant.' Chihun snorted. Deesa wept and bellowed.

'You will get into a difficulty in a minute,' said the planter. 'Go back to your work!'

'Now I will speak Heaven's truth,' gulped Deesa, with an inspiration. 'I haven't been drunk for two months. I desire to depart in order to get properly drunk afar off and distant from this heavenly plantation. Thus I shall cause no trouble.'

A flickering smile crossed the planter's face. 'Deesa,' said he, 'you've spoken the truth, and I'd give you leave on the spot if anything could be done with Moti Guj while you're away. You know that he will only obey your orders.'

'May the Light of the Heavens live forty thousand years. I shall be absent but ten little days. After that, upon my faith and honour and soul, I return. As to the inconsiderable interval, have I the gracious permission of the Heaven-born to call up Moti Guj?'

Permission was granted, and, in answer to Deesa's shrill yell, the lordly tusker swung out of the shade of a clump of trees where he had been squirting dust over himself till his master should return.

'Light of my heart, Protector of the Drunken, Mountain of Might, give ear,' said Deesa, standing in front of him.

Moti Guj gave ear, and saluted with his trunk. 'I am going away,' said Deesa.

Moti Guj's eyes twinkled. He liked jaunts as

well as his master. One could snatch all manner
of nice things from the roadside then.

'But you, you fubsy old pig, must stay behind
and work.'

The twinkle died out as Moti Guj tried to look
delighted. He hated stump-hauling on the plantation. It hurt his teeth.

'I shall be gone for ten days, oh Delectable One.
Hold up your near forefoot and I'll impress the
fact upon it, warty toad of a dried mud-puddle.'
Deesa took a tent-peg and banged Moti Guj ten
times on the nails. Moti Guj grunted and shuffled
from foot to foot.

'Ten days,' said Deesa, 'you must work and
haul and root trees as Chihun here shall order you.
Take up Chihun and set him on your neck!' Moti
Guj curled the tip of his trunk, Chihun put his foot
there and was swung on to the neck. Deesa handed
Chihun the heavy *ankus*, the iron elephant-goad.

Chihun thumped Moti Guj's bald head as a
paviour thumps a kerbstone.

Moti Guj trumpeted.

'Be still, hog of the backwoods. Chihun's
your mahout for ten days. And now bid me
good-bye, beast after mine own heart. Oh, my
lord, my king! Jewel of all created elephants,
lily of the herd, preserve your honoured health;
be virtuous. Adieu!'

Moti Guj lapped his trunk round Deesa and
swung him into the air twice. That was his way
of bidding the man good-bye.

'He'll work now,' said Deesa to the planter.
'Have I leave to go?'

The planter nodded, and Deesa dived into the woods. Moti Guj went back to haul stumps.

Chihun was very kind to him, but he felt unhappy and forlorn notwithstanding. Chihun gave him balls of spices, and tickled him under the chin, and Chihun's little baby cooed to him after work was over, and Chihun's wife called him a darling ; but Moti Guj was a bachelor by instinct, as Deesa was. He did not understand the domestic emotions. He wanted the light of his universe back again—the drink and the drunken slumber, the savage beatings and the savage caresses.

None the less he worked well, and the planter wondered. Deesa had vagabonded along the roads till he met a marriage procession of his own caste and, drinking, dancing, and tippling, had drifted past all knowledge of the lapse of time.

The morning of the eleventh day dawned, and there returned no Deesa. Moti Guj was loosed from his ropes for the daily stint. He swung clear, looked round, shrugged his shoulders, and began to walk away, as one having business elsewhere.

'Hi ! ho ! Come back you,' shouted Chihun. 'Come back, and put me on your neck, Misborn Mountain. Return, Splendour of the Hillsides. Adornment of all India, heave to, or I'll bang every toe off your fat forefoot !'

Moti Guj gurgled gently, but did not obey. Chihun ran after him with a rope and caught him up. Moti Guj put his ears forward, and Chihun knew what that meant, though he tried to carry it off with high words.

'None of your nonsense with me,' said he. 'To your pickets, Devil-son.'

'Hrrump!' said Moti Guj, and that was all— that and the forebent ears.

Moti Guj put his hands in his pockets, chewed a branch for a toothpick, and strolled about the clearing, making jest of the other elephants, who had just set to work.

Chihun reported the state of affairs to the planter, who came out with a dog-whip and cracked it furiously. Moti Guj paid the white man the compliment of charging him nearly a quarter of a mile across the clearing and 'Hrrumphing' him into the verandah. Then he stood outside the house chuckling to himself, and shaking all over with the fun of it, as an elephant will.

'We'll thrash him,' said the planter. 'He shall have the finest thrashing that ever elephant received. Give Kala Nag and Nazim twelve foot of chain apiece, and tell them to lay on twenty blows.'

Kala Nag — which means Black Snake — and Nazim were two of the biggest elephants in the lines, and one of their duties was to administer the graver punishments, since no man can beat an elephant properly.

They took the whipping-chains and rattled them in their trunks as they sidled up to Moti Guj, meaning to hustle him between them. Moti Guj had never, in all his life of thirty-nine years, been whipped, and he did not intend to open new experiences. So he waited, weaving his head from right to left, and measuring the precise spot in Kala Nag's fat side where a blunt tusk would sink deepest. Kala Nag had no tusks ; the chain was his badge of authority ; but he judged it good to swing wide of Moti Guj at the last minute, and seem to appear as if he had brought out the chain for amusement. Nazim turned round and went home early. He did not feel fighting-fit that morning, and so Moti Guj was left standing alone with his ears cocked.

That decided the planter to argue no more, and Moti Guj rolled back to his inspection of the clearing. An elephant who will not work, and is not tied up, is not quite so manageable as an eighty-one ton gun loose in a heavy sea-way. He slapped old friends on the back and asked them if the stumps were coming away easily; he talked nonsense concerning labour and the inalienable rights of elephants to a long 'nooning ' ; and, wandering to and fro, thoroughly demoralised the garden till sundown, when he returned to his pickets for food.

'If you won't work you shan't eat,' said Chihun angrily. 'You're a wild elephant, and no educated animal at all. Go back to your jungle.'

Chihun's little brown baby, rolling on the floor of the hut, stretched its fat arms to the huge shadow in the doorway. Moti Guj knew well that it was the dearest thing on earth to Chihun. He swung out his trunk with a fascinating crook at the end, and the brown baby threw itself shouting upon it. Moti Guj made fast and pulled up till the brown baby was crowing in the air twelve feet above his father's head.

'Great Chief !' said Chihun. 'Flour cakes of

the best, twelve in number, two feet across, and soaked in rum shall be yours on the instant, and two hundred pounds' weight of fresh-cut young sugar-cane therewith. Deign only to put down safely that insignificant brat who is my heart and my life to me.'

Moti Guj tucked the brown baby comfortably between his forefeet, that could have knocked into toothpicks all Chihun's hut, and waited for his food. He ate it, and the brown baby crawled away. Moti Guj dozed, and thought of Deesa. One of many mysteries connected with the elephant is that his huge body needs less sleep than anything else that lives. Four or five hours in the night suffice—two just before midnight, lying down on one side ; two just after one o'clock, lying down on the other. The rest of the silent hours are filled with eating and fidgeting and long grumbling soliloquies.

At midnight, therefore, Moti Guj strode out of his pickets, for a thought had come to him that Deesa might be lying drunk somewhere in the dark forest with none to look after him. So all that night he chased through the undergrowth, blowing and trumpeting and shaking his ears. He went down to the river and blared across the shallows where Deesa used to wash him, but there was no answer. He could not find Deesa, but he disturbed all the elephants in the lines, and nearly frightened to death some gipsies in the woods.

At dawn Deesa returned to the plantation. He had been very drunk indeed, and he expected to fall into trouble for outstaying his leave. He drew a long breath when he saw that the bungalow and the plantation were still uninjured; for he knew something of Moti Guj's temper; and reported himself with many lies and salaams. Moti Guj had gone to his pickets for breakfast. His night exercise had made him hungry.

'Call up your beast,' said the planter, and Deesa shouted in the mysterious elephant-language, that some mahouts believe came from China at the birth of the world, when elephants and not men were masters. Moti Guj heard and came. Elephants do not gallop. They move from spots at varying rates of speed. If an elephant wished to catch an express train he could not gallop, but he could catch the train. Thus Moti Guj was at the planter's door almost before Chihun noticed that he had left his pickets. He fell into Deesa's arms trumpeting with joy, and the man and beast wept and slobbered over each other, and handled each other from head to heel to see that no harm had befallen.

'Now we will get to work,' said Deesa. 'Lift me up, my son and my joy.'

Moti Guj swung him up and the two went to the coffee-clearing to look for irksome stumps.

The planter was too astonished to be very angry.

Bubbling Well Road

Look out on a large scale map the place where the Chenab river falls into the Indus fifteen miles or so above the hamlet of Chachuran. Five miles west of Chachuran lies Bubbling Well Road, and the house of the *gosain* or priest of Arti-goth. It was the priest who showed me the road, but it is no thanks to him that I am able to tell this story.

Five miles west of Chachuran is a patch of the plumed jungle-grass, that turns over in silver when the wind blows, from ten to twenty feet high and from three to four miles square. In the heart of the patch hides the *gosain* of Bubbling Well Road. The villagers stone him when he peers into the daylight, although he is a priest, and he runs back again as a strayed wolf turns into tall crops. He is a one-eyed man and carries, burnt between his brows, the impress of two copper coins. Some say that he was tortured by a native prince in the old days ; for he is so old that he must have been capable of mischief in the days of Runjit Singh. His most pressing need at present is a halter, and the care of the British Government.

These things happened when the jungle-grass

was tall ; and the villagers of Chachuran told me that a sounder of pig had gone into the Arti-goth patch. To enter jungle-grass is always an unwise proceeding, but I went, partly because I knew nothing of pig-hunting, and partly because the villagers said that the big boar of the sounder owned foot long tushes. Therefore I wished to shoot him, in order to produce the tushes in after years, and say that I had ridden him down in fair chase. I took a gun and went into the hot, close patch, believing that it would be an easy thing to unearth one pig in ten square miles of jungle. Mr. Wardle, the terrier, went with me because he believed that I was incapable of existing for an hour without his advice and countenance. He managed to slip in and out between the grass clumps, but I had to force my way, and in twenty minutes was as completely lost as though I had been in the heart of Central Africa. I did not notice this at first till I had grown wearied of stumbling and pushing through the grass, and Mr. Wardle was beginning to sit down very often and hang out his tongue very far. There was nothing but grass everywhere, and it was impossible to see two yards in any direction. The grass stems held the heat exactly as boiler-tubes do.

In half an hour, when I was devoutly wishing that I had left the big boar alone, I came to a narrow path which seemed to be a compromise between a native foot-path and a pig-run. It was barely six inches wide, but I could sidle along it in comfort. The grass was extremely thick here, and where the path was ill defined it was necessary to crush into the tussocks either with both hands before the face, or to back into it, leaving both hands free to manage the rifle. None the less it was a path, and valuable because it might lead to a place.

At the end of nearly fifty yards of fair way, just when I was preparing to back into an unusually stiff tussock, I missed Mr. Wardle, who for his girth is an unusually frivolous dog and never keeps to heel. I called him three times and said aloud, ' Where has the little beast gone ? ' Then I stepped backwards several paces, for almost under my feet a deep voice repeated, ' Where has the little beast gone ? ' To appreciate an unseen voice thoroughly you should hear it when you are lost in stifling jungle grass. I called Mr. Wardle again and the underground echo assisted me. At that I ceased calling and listened very attentively, because I thought I heard a man laughing in a peculiarly offensive manner. The heat made me sweat, but the laughter made me shake. There is no earthly need for laughter in high grass. It is indecent, as well as impolite. The chuckling stopped, and I took courage and continued to call till I thought that I had located the echo some-where behind and below the tussock into which I was preparing to back just before I lost Mr. Wardle. I drove my rifle up to the triggers between the grass-stems in a downward and for-ward direction. Then I waggled it to and fro, but it did not seem to touch ground on the far side of the tussock as it should have done. Every time that I grunted with the exertion of driving a heavy rifle through thick grass, the grunt was faithfully repeated from below, and when I stopped to wipe my face the sound of low laughter was distinct beyond doubting.

I went into the tussock, face first, an inch at a time, my mouth open and my eyes fine, full, and prominent. When I had overcome the resistance of the grass I found that I was looking straight across a black gap in the ground. That I was actually lying on my chest leaning over the mouth of a well so deep I could scarcely see the water in it.

There were things in the water,— black things, —and the water was as black as pitch with blue scum atop. The laughing sound came from the noise of a little spring, spouting half-way down one side of the well. Sometimes as the black things circled round, the trickle from the spring fell upon their tightly-stretched skins, and then the laughter changed into a sputter of mirth. One thing turned over on its back, as I watched, and drifted round and round the circle of the mossy brickwork with a hand and half an arm held clear of the water in a stiff and horrible flourish, as though it were a very wearied guide paid to exhibit the beauties of the place.

I did not spend more than half-an-hour in creeping round that well and finding the path on the other side. The remainder of the journey I accomplished by feeling every foot of ground in front of me, and crawling like a snail through every tussock. I carried Mr. Wardle in my arms and he licked my nose. He was not frightened in the least, nor was I, but we wished to reach open ground in order to enjoy the view. My knees were loose, and the apple in my throat refused to slide up and down. The path on the far side of the well was a very good one, though boxed in on all sides by grass, and it led me in time to a priest's hut in the centre of a little clearing. When that priest saw my very white face coming through the grass he howled with terror and embraced my boots ; but when I reached the bedstead set outside his door I sat down quickly and Mr. Wardle mounted guard over me. I was not in a condition to take care of myself.

When I awoke I told the priest to lead me into the open, out of the Arti-goth patch and to walk slowly in front of me. Mr. Wardle hates natives, and the priest was more afraid of Mr. Wardle than of me, though we were both angry. He walked very slowly down a narrow little path from his hut. That path crossed three paths, such as the one I had come by in the first instance, and every one of the three headed towards the Bubbling Well. Once when we stopped to draw breath, I heard the Well laughing to itself alone in the thick grass, and only my need for his services prevented my firing both barrels into the priest's back.

When we came to the open the priest crashed back into cover, and I went to the village of Arti-goth for a drink. It was pleasant to be able to see the horizon all round, as well as the ground underfoot.

The villagers told me that the patch of grass was full of devils and ghosts, all in the service of the priest, and that men and women and children had entered it and had never returned. They said the priest used their livers for purposes of witchcraft. When I asked why they had not told me of this at the outset, they said that they were afraid they would lose their reward for bringing news of the pig.

Before I left I did my best to set the patch alight, but the grass was too green. Some fine summer day, however, if the wind is favourable, a file of old newspapers and a box of matches will make clear the mystery of Bubbling Well Road.

'The City of Dreadful Night'

THE dense wet heat that hung over the face of land, like a blanket, prevented all hope of sleep in the first instance. The cicalas helped the heat, and the yelling jackals the cicalas. It was impossible to sit still in the dark, empty, echoing house and watch the punkah beat the dead air. So, at ten o'clock of the night, I set my walking-stick on end in the middle of the garden, and waited to see how it would fall. It pointed directly down the moon-lit road that leads to the City of Dreadful Night. The sound of its fall disturbed a hare. She limped from her form and ran across to a disused Mahomedan burial-ground, where the jawless skulls and rough-butted shank-bones, heartlessly exposed by the July rains, glimmered like mother o' pearl on the rain-channelled soil. The heated air and the heavy earth had driven the very dead upward for coolness' sake. The hare limped on ; snuffed curiously at a fragment of a smoke-stained lamp-shard, and died out, in the shadow of a clump of tamarisk trees.

The mat-weaver's hut under the lee of the Hindu temple was full of sleeping men who lay like sheeted corpses. Overhead blazed the un-winking eye of the Moon. Darkness gives at least a false impression of coolness. It was hard not to believe that the flood of light from above was warm. Not so hot as the Sun, but still sickly warm, and heating the heavy air beyond what was our due. Straight as a bar of polished steel ran the road to the City of Dreadful Night ; and on either side of the road lay corpses disposed on beds in fantastic attitudes—one hundred and seventy bodies of men. Some shrouded all in white with bound-up mouths ; some naked and black as ebony in the strong light; and one—that lay face upwards with dropped jaw, far away from the others—silvery white and ashen gray.

'A leper asleep; and the remainder wearied coolies, servants, small shopkeepers, and drivers from the hack-stand hard by. The scene—a main approach to Lahore city, and the night a warm one in August.' This was all that there was to be seen ; but by no means all that one could see. The witchery of the moonlight was everywhere ; and the world was horribly changed. The long line of the naked dead, flanked by the rigid silver statue, was not pleasant to look upon. It was made up of men alone. Were the women-kind, then, forced to sleep in the shelter of the stifling mud-huts as best they might ? The fretful wail of a child from a low mud-roof answered the question. Where the children are the mothers must be also to look after them. They need care on these sweltering nights. A black little bullet-head peeped over the coping, and a thin—a painfully thin—brown leg was slid over on to the gutter pipe. There was a sharp clink of glass bracelets ; a woman's arm showed for an instant above the parapet, twined itself round the lean little neck, and the child was dragged back, protesting, to the shelter of the bedstead. His thin, high-pitched shriek died out in the thick air almost as soon as it was raised ; for even the children of the soil found it too hot to weep.

More corpses ; more stretches of moonlit, white road ; a string of sleeping camels at rest by the wayside ; a vision of scudding jackals ; ekka-ponies asleep—the harness still on their backs, and the brass-studded country carts, winking in the moonlight—and again more corpses. Wherever a grain cart atilt, a tree trunk, a sawn log, a couple of bamboos and a few handfuls of thatch cast a shadow, the ground is covered with them. They lie—some face downwards, arms folded, in the dust ; some with clasped hands flung up above their heads; some curled up dog-wise ; some thrown like limp gunny-bags over the side of the grain carts ; and some bowed with their brows on their knees in the full glare of the Moon. It would be a comfort if they were only given to snoring ; but they are not, and the likeness to corpses is unbroken in all respects save one. The lean dogs snuff at them and turn away. Here and there a tiny child lies on his father's bedstead, and a protecting arm is thrown round it in every instance. But, for the most part, the children sleep with their mothers on the housetops. Yellow-skinned white-toothed pariahs are not to be trusted within reach of brown bodies.

A stifling hot blast from the mouth of the Delhi Gate nearly ends my resolution of entering the City of Dreadful Night at this hour. It is a compound of all evil savours, animal and vegetable, that a walled city can brew in a day and a night. The temperature within the motionless groves of plantain and orange-trees outside the city walls seems chilly by comparison. Heaven help all sick persons and young children within the city to-night! The high house-walls are still radiating heat savagely, and from obscure side gullies fetid breezes eddy that ought to poison a buffalo. But the buffaloes do not heed. A drove of them are parading the vacant main street; stopping now and then to lay their ponderous muzzles against the closed shutters of a grain-dealer's shop, and to blow thereon like grampuses.

Then silence follows—the silence that is full of the night noises of a great city. A stringed instrument of some kind is just, and only just audible. High over head some one throws open a window, and the rattle of the woodwork echoes down the empty street. On one of the roofs a hookah is in full blast; and the men are talking softly as the pipe gutters. A little farther on the noise of conversation is more distinct. A slit of light shows itself between the sliding shutters of a shop. Inside, a stubble-bearded, weary-eyed trader is balancing his account-books among the bales of cotton prints that surround him. Three sheeted figures bear him company, and throw in a remark from time to time. First he makes an entry, then a remark ; then passes the back of his hand across his streaming forehead. The heat in the built-in street is fearful. Inside the shops it must be almost unendurable. But the work goes on steadily ; entry, guttural growl, and uplifted hand-stroke succeeding each other with the precision of clock-work.

A policeman—turbanless and fast asleep—lies across the road on the way to the Mosque of Wazir Khan. A bar of moonlight falls across the forehead and eyes of the sleeper, but he never stirs. It is close upon midnight, and the heat seems to be increasing. The open square in front of the Mosque is crowded with corpses ; and a man must pick his way carefully for fear of treading on them. The moonlight stripes the Mosque's high front of coloured enamel work in broad diagonal bands ; and each separate dreaming pigeon in the niches and corners of the masonry throws a squab little shadow. Sheeted ghosts rise up wearily from their pallets, and flit into the dark depths of the building. Is it possible to climb to the top of the great Minars, and thence to look down on the city ? At all events the attempt is worth making, and the chances are that the door of the staircase will be unlocked. Unlocked it is ; but a deeply sleeping janitor lies across the threshold, face turned to the Moon. A rat dashes out of his turban at the sound of approaching footsteps. The man grunts, opens his eyes for a minute, turns round, and goes to sleep again. All the heat of a decade of fierce Indian summers is stored in the pitch-black, polished walls of the corkscrew stair-case. Half-way up there is something alive, warm, and feathery; and it snores. Driven from step to step as it catches the sound of my advance, it flutters to the top and reveals itself as a yellow-eyed, angry kite. Dozens of kites are asleep on this and the other Minars, and on the domes below. There is the shadow of a cool, or at least a less sultry breeze at this height; and, refreshed thereby, I turn to look on the City of Dreadful Night.

Doré might have drawn it! Zola could describe it—this spectacle of sleeping thousands in the moonlight and in the shadow of the Moon. The roof-tops are crammed with men, women, and children; and the air is full of undistinguishable noises. They are restless in the City of Dreadful Night; and small wonder. The marvel is that they can even breathe. If you gaze intently at the multitude you can see that they are almost as uneasy as a daylight crowd; but the tumult is subdued. Everywhere, in the strong light, you can watch the sleepers turning to and fro; shifting their beds and again resettling them. In the pit-like courtyards of the houses there is the same movement.

The pitiless Moon shows it all. Shows, too, the plains outside the city, and here and there a hand's-breadth of the Ravee without the walls. Shows lastly, a splash of glittering silver on a house-top almost directly below the mosque Minar. Some poor soul has risen to throw a jar of water over his fevered body; the tinkle of the falling

water strikes faintly on the ear. Two or three
other men, in far-off corners of the City of Dreadful Night, follow his example, and the water flashes
like heliographic signals. A small cloud passes
over the face of the Moon, and the city and its
inhabitants—clear drawn in black and white before
—fade into masses of black and deeper black.
Still the unrestful noise continues, the sigh of a
great city overwhelmed with the heat, and of a
people seeking in vain for rest. It is only the
lower-class women who sleep on the house-tops.
What must the torment be in the latticed zenanas,
where a few lamps are still twinkling ? There are
footfalls in the court below. It is the *Muezzin*—
faithful minister ; but he ought to have been here
an hour ago to tell the Faithful that prayer is
better than sleep—the sleep that will not come to
the city.

The *Muezzin* fumbles for a moment with the
door of one of the Minars, disappears awhile, and
a bull-like roar—a magnificent bass thunder—tells
that he has reached the top of the Minar. They
must hear the cry to the banks of the shrunken
Ravee itself! Even across the courtyard it is
almost overpowering. The cloud drifts by and
shows him outlined in black against the sky, hands
laid upon his ears, and broad chest heaving with
the play of his lungs—'Allah ho Akbar'; then a
pause while another *Muezzin* somewhere in the
direction of the Golden Temple takes up the call
—'Allah ho Akbar.' Again and again ; four
times in all ; and from the bedsteads a dozen men
have risen up already.—'I bear witness that there

is no God but God.' What a splendid cry it is, the proclamation of the creed that brings men out of their beds by scores at midnight! Once again he thunders through the same phrase, shaking with the vehemence of his own voice; and then, far and near, the night air rings with 'Mahomed is the Prophet of God.' It is as though he were flinging his defiance to the far-off horizon, where the summer lightning plays and leaps like a bared sword. Every *Muezzin* in the city is in full cry, and some men on the roof-tops are beginning to kneel. A long pause precedes the last cry, 'La ilaha Illallah,' and the silence closes up on it, as the ram on the head of a cotton-bale.

The *Muezzin* stumbles down the dark stairway grumbling in his beard. He passes the arch of the entrance and disappears. Then the stifling silence settles down over the City of Dreadful Night. The kites on the Minar sleep again, snoring more loudly, the hot breeze comes up in puffs and lazy eddies, and the Moon slides down towards the horizon. Seated with both elbows on the parapet of the tower, one can watch and wonder over that heat-tortured hive till the dawn. 'How do they live down there? What do they think of? When will they awake?' More tinkling of sluiced water-pots; faint jarring of wooden bedsteads moved into or out of the shadows; uncouth music of stringed instruments softened by distance into a plaintive wail, and one low grumble of far-off thunder. In the courtyard of the mosque the janitor, who lay across the threshold of the Minar when I came up, starts wildly in his sleep, throws his hands above his head, mutters something, and falls back again. Lulled by the snoring of the kites—they snore like over-gorged humans—I drop off into an uneasy doze, conscious that three o'clock has struck, and that there is a slight—a very slight—coolness in the atmosphere. The city is absolutely quiet now, but for some vagrant dog's love-song. Nothing save dead heavy sleep.

Several weeks of darkness pass after this. For the Moon has gone out. The very dogs are still, and I watch for the first light of the dawn before making my way homeward. Again the noise of shuffling feet. The morning call is about to begin, and my night watch is over. 'Allah ho Akbar! Allah ho Akbar!' The east grows gray, and presently saffron; the dawn wind comes up as though the *Muezzin* had summoned it; and, as one man, the City of Dreadful Night rises from its bed and turns its face towards the dawning day. With return of life comes return of sound. First a low whisper, then a deep bass hum; for it must be remembered that the entire city is on the house-tops. My eyelids weighed down with the arrears of long deferred sleep, I escape from the Minar through the courtyard and out into the square beyond, where the sleepers have risen, stowed away the bedsteads, and are discussing the morning hookah. The minute's freshness of the air has gone, and it is as hot as at first.

'Will the Sahib, out of his kindness, make room?' What is it? Something borne on men's shoulders comes by in the half-light, and I stand back. A woman's corpse going down to the burning-ghat, and a bystander says, 'She died at midnight from the heat.' So the city was of Death as well as Night after all.

Georgie Porgie

Georgie Porgie, pudding and pie,
Kissed the girls and made them cry.
When the girls came out to play
Georgie Porgie ran away.

IF you will admit that a man has no right to
enter his drawing-room early in the morning, when
the housemaid is setting things right and clearing
away the dust, you will concede that civilised
people who eat out of china and own card-cases
have no right to apply their standard of right and
wrong to an unsettled land. When the place is
made fit for their reception, by those men who are
told off to the work, they can come up, bringing
in their trunks their own society and the Decalogue,
and all the other apparatus. Where the Queen's
Law does not carry, it is irrational to expect an
observance of other and weaker rules. The men
who run ahead of the cars of Decency and
Propriety, and make the jungle ways straight,
cannot be judged in the same manner as the stay-
at-home folk of the ranks of the regular *Tchin*.

Not many months ago the Queen's Law stopped
a few miles north of Thayetmyo on the Irrawaddy.

There was no very strong Public Opinion up to that limit, but it existed to keep men in order. When the Government said that the Queen's Law must carry up to Bhamo and the Chinese border the order was given, and some men whose desire was to be ever a little in advance of the rush of Respectability flocked forward with the troops. These were the men who could never pass examinations, and would have been too pronounced in their ideas for the administration of bureau-worked Provinces. The Supreme Government stepped in as soon as might be, with codes and regulations, and all but reduced New Burma to the dead Indian level ; but there was a short time during which strong men were necessary and ploughed a field for themselves.

Among the forerunners of Civilisation was Georgie Porgie, reckoned by all who knew him a strong man. He held an appointment in Lower Burma when the order came to break the Frontier, and his friends called him Georgie Porgie because of the singularly Burmese-like manner in which he sang a song whose first line is something like the words 'Georgie Porgie.' Most men who have been in Burma will know the song. It means : ' Puff, puff, puff, puff, great steamboat ! ' Georgie sang it to his banjo, and his friends shouted with delight, so that you could hear them far away in the teak-forest.

When he went to Upper Burma he had no special regard for God or Man, but he knew how to make himself respected, and to carry out the mixed Military-Civil duties that fell to most men's share in those months. He did his office work and entertained, now and again, the detachments of fever-shaken soldiers who blundered through his part of the world in search of a flying party of dacoits. Sometimes he turned out and dressed down dacoits on his own account ; for the country was still smouldering and would blaze when least expected. He enjoyed these charivaris, but the dacoits were not so amused. All the officials who came in contact with him departed with the idea that Georgie Porgie was a valuable person, well able to take care of himself, and, on that belief, he was left to his own devices.

At the end of a few months he wearied of his solitude, and cast about for company and refinement. The Queen's Law had hardly begun to be felt in the country, and Public Opinion, which is more powerful than the Queen's Law, had yet to come. Also, there was a custom in the country which allowed a white man to take to himself a wife of the Daughters of Heth upon due payment. The marriage was not quite so binding as is the *nikkah* ceremony among Mahomedans, but the wife was very pleasant.

When all our troops are back from Burma there will be a proverb in their mouths, ' As thrifty as a Burmese wife,' and pretty English ladies will wonder what in the world it means.

The headman of the village next to Georgie Porgie's post had a fair daughter who had seen Georgie Porgie and loved him from afar. When news went abroad that the Englishman with the heavy hand who lived in the stockade was looking for a housekeeper, the headman came in and explained that, for five hundred rupees down, he would entrust his daughter to Georgie Porgie's keeping, to be maintained in all honour, respect, and comfort, with pretty dresses, according to the custom of the country. This thing was done, and Georgie Porgie never repented it.

He found his rough-and-tumble house put straight and made comfortable, his hitherto unchecked expenses cut down by one-half, and himself petted and made much of by his new acquisition, who sat at the head of his table and sang songs to him and ordered his Madrassee servants about, and was in every way as sweet and merry and honest and winning a little woman as the most exacting of bachelors could have desired. No race, men say who know, produces such good wives and heads of households as the Burmese. When the next detachment tramped by on the war-path the Subaltern in command found at Georgie Porgie's table a hostess to be deferential to, a woman to be treated in every way as one occupying an assured position. When he gathered his men together next dawn and replunged into the jungle he thought regretfully of the nice little dinner and the pretty face, and envied Georgie Porgie from the bottom of his heart. Yet *he* was engaged to a girl at Home, and that is how some men are constructed.

The Burmese girl's name was not a pretty one; but as she was promptly christened Georgina by Georgie Porgie, the blemish did not matter. Georgie Porgie thought well of the petting and the general comfort, and vowed that he had never spent five hundred rupees to a better end.

After three months of domestic life a great idea struck him. Matrimony—English matrimony —could not be such a bad thing after all. If he were so thoroughly comfortable at the Back of Beyond with this Burmese girl who smoked cheroots, how much more comfortable would he be with a sweet English maiden who would not smoke cheroots, and would play upon a piano instead of a banjo? Also he had a desire to return to his kind, to hear a Band once more, and to feel how it felt to wear a dress-suit again. Decidedly, Matrimony would be a very good thing. He thought the matter out at length of evenings, while Georgina sang to him, or asked him why he was so silent, and whether she had done anything to offend him. As he thought, he smoked, and as he smoked he looked at Georgina, and in his fancy turned her into a fair, thrifty, amusing, merry, little English girl, with hair coming low down on her forehead, and perhaps a cigarette between her lips. Certainly not a big, thick, Burma cheroot, of the brand that Georgina smoked. He would wed a girl with Georgina's eyes and most of her ways. But not all. She could be improved upon. Then he blew thick smoke-wreaths through his nostrils and stretched himself. He would taste marriage. Georgina had helped him to save money, and there were six months' leave due to him.

'See here, little woman,' he said, 'we must put by more money for these next three months. I want it.' That was a direct slur on Georgina's housekeeping ; for she prided herself on her thrift ; but since her God wanted money she would do her best.

'You want money?' she said with a little laugh. 'I *have* money. Look!' She ran to her own room and fetched out a small bag of rupees. 'Of all that you give me, I keep back some See! One hundred and seven rupees. Can you want more money than that? Take it. It is my pleasure if you use it.' She spread out the money on the table and pushed it towards him with her quick, little, pale yellow fingers.

Georgie Porgie never referred to economy in the household again.

Three months later, after the dispatch and receipt of several mysterious letters which Georgina could not understand, and hated for that reason, Georgie Porgie said that he was going away, and she must return to her father's house and stay there.

Georgina wept. She would go with her God from the world's end to the world's end. Why should she leave him? She loved him.

'I am only going to Rangoon,' said Georgie Porgie. 'I shall be back in a month, but it is safer to stay with your father. I will leave you two hundred rupees.'

'If you go for a month, what need of two hundred? Fifty are more than enough. There is some evil here. Do not go, or at least let me go with you.'

Georgie Porgie does not like to remember that scene even at this date. In the end he got rid of Georgina by a compromise of seventy-five rupees. She would not take more. Then he went by steamer and rail to Rangoon.

The mysterious letters had granted him six months' leave. The actual flight and an idea that he might have been treacherous hurt severely at the time, but as soon as the big steamer was well out into the blue, things were easier, and Georgina's face, and the queer little stockaded house, and the memory of the rushes of shouting dacoits by night, the cry and struggle of the first man that he had ever killed with his own hand, and a hundred other more intimate things, faded and faded out of Georgie Porgie's heart, and the vision of approaching England took its place. The steamer was full of men on leave, all rampantly jovial souls who had shaken off the dust and sweat of Upper Burma and were as merry as schoolboys. They helped Georgie Porgie to forget.

Then came England with its luxuries and decencies and comforts, and Georgie Porgie walked in a pleasant dream upon pavements of which he had nearly forgotten the ring, wondering why men in their senses ever left Town. He accepted his keen delight in his furlough as the reward of his services. Providence further arranged for him another and greater delight—all the pleasures of a quiet English wooing, quite different from the brazen businesses of the East, when half the community stand back and bet on the result, and the other half wonder what Mrs. So-and-So will say to it.

It was a pleasant girl and a perfect summer,

and a big country-house near Petworth where there are acres and acres of purple heather and high-grassed water-meadows to wander through. Georgie Porgie felt that he had at last found something worth the living for, and naturally assumed that the next thing to do was to ask the girl to share his life in India. She, in her ignorance, was willing to go. On this occasion there was no bartering with a village headman. There was a fine middle-class wedding in the country, with a stout Papa and a weeping Mamma, and a bestman in purple and fine linen, and six snub-nosed girls from the Sunday School to throw roses on the path between the tombstones up to the Church door. The local paper described the affair at great length, even down to giving the hymns in full. But that was because the Direction were starving for want of material.

Then came a honeymoon at Arundel, and the Mamma wept copiously before she allowed her one daughter to sail away to India under the care of Georgie Porgie the Bridegroom. Beyond any question, Georgie Porgie was immensely fond of his wife, and she was devoted to him as the best and greatest man in the world. When he reported himself at Bombay he felt justified in demanding a good station for his wife's sake ; and, because he had made a little mark in Burma and was beginning to be appreciated, they allowed him nearly all that he asked for, and posted him to a station which we will call Sutrain. It stood upon several hills, and was styled officially a 'Sanitarium,' for the good reason that the drainage was utterly neglected. Here Georgie Porgie settled down, and found married life come very naturally to him. He did not rave, as do many bridegrooms, over the strangeness and delight of seeing his own true love sitting down to breakfast with him every morning 'as though it were the most natural thing in the world.' 'He had been there before,' as the Americans say, and, checking the merits of his own present Grace by those of Georgina, he was more and more inclined to think that he had done well.

But there was no peace or comfort across the Bay of Bengal, under the teak-trees where Georgina lived with her father, waiting for Georgie Porgie to return. The headman was old, and remembered the war of '51. He had been to Rangoon, and knew something of the ways of the *Kullahs*. Sitting in front of his door in the evenings, he taught Georgina a dry philosophy which did not console her in the least.

The trouble was that she loved Georgie Porgie just as much as the French girl in the English History books loved the priest whose head was broken by the King's bullies. One day she disappeared from the village, with all the rupees that Georgie Porgie had given her, and a very small smattering of English—also gained from Georgie Porgie.

The headman was angry at first, but lit a fresh cheroot and said something uncomplimentary about the sex in general. Georgina had started on a search for Georgie Porgie, who might be in Rangoon, or across the Black Water, or dead, for aught that she knew. Chance favoured her. An old Sikh policeman told her that Georgie Porgie had crossed the Black Water. She took a steerage-passage from Rangoon and went to Calcutta, keeping the secret of her search to herself.

In India every trace of her was lost for six weeks, and no one knows what trouble of heart she must have undergone.

She reappeared, four hundred miles north of Calcutta, steadily heading northwards, very worn and haggard, but very fixed in her determination to find Georgie Porgie. She could not understand the language of the people ; but India is infinitely charitable, and the women-folk along the Grand Trunk gave her food. Something made her believe that Georgie Porgie was to be found at the end of that pitiless road. She may have seen a sepoy who knew him in Burma, but of this no one can be certain. At last, she found a regiment on the line of march, and met there one of the many subalterns whom Georgie Porgie had invited to dinner in the far off, old days of the dacoit-hunting. There was a certain amount of amusement among the tents when Georgina threw herself at the man's feet and began to cry. There was no amusement when her story was told ; but a collection was made, and that was more to the point. One of the subalterns knew of Georgie Porgie's where-abouts, but not of his marriage. So he told Georgina and she went her way joyfully to the north, in a railway carriage where there was rest for tired feet and shade for a dusty little head. The marches from the train through the hills into

Sutrain were trying, but Georgina had money, and families journeying in bullock-carts gave her help. It was an almost miraculous journey, and Georgina felt sure that the good spirits of Burma were looking after her. The hill-road to Sutrain is a chilly stretch, and Georgina caught a bad cold. Still there was Georgie Porgie at the end of all the trouble to take her up in his arms and pet her, as he used to do in the old days when the stockade was shut for the night and he had approved of the evening meal. Georgina went forward as fast as she could ; and her good spirits did her one last favour.

An Englishman stopped her, in the twilight, just at the turn of the road into Sutrain, saying, ' Good Heavens ! What are you doing here ? '

He was Gillis, the man who had been Georgie Porgie's assistant in Upper Burma, and who occupied the next post to Georgie Porgie's in the jungle. Georgie Porgie had applied to have him to work with at Sutrain because he liked him.

' I have come,' said Georgina simply. ' It was such a long way, and I have been months in coming. Where is his house ? '

Gillis gasped. He had seen enough of Georgina in the old times to know that explanations would be useless. You cannot explain things to the Oriental. You must show.

' I'll take you there,' said Gillis, and he led Georgina off the road, up the cliff, by a little pathway, to the back of a house set on a platform cut into the hillside.

The lamps were just lit, but the curtains were

not drawn. 'Now look,' said Gillis, stopping in front of the drawing-room window. Georgina looked and saw Georgie Porgie and the Bride.

She put her hand up to her hair, which had come out of its top-knot and was straggling about her face. She tried to set her ragged dress in order, but the dress was past pulling straight, and she coughed a queer little cough, for she really had taken a very bad cold. Gillis looked, too, but while Georgina only looked at the Bride once, turning her eyes always on Georgie Porgie, Gillis looked at the Bride all the time.

'What are you going to do?' said Gillis, who held Georgina by the wrist, in case of any unexpected rush into the lamplight. 'Will you go in and tell that English woman that you lived with her husband?'

'No,' said Georgina faintly. 'Let me go. I am going away. I swear that I am going away.' She twisted herself free and ran off into the dark.

'Poor little beast!' said Gillis, dropping on to the main road. 'I'd ha' given her something to get back to Burma with. What a narrow shave though! And that angel would never have forgiven it.'

This seems to prove that the devotion of Gillis was not entirely due to his affection for Georgie Porgie.

The Bride and the Bridegroom came out into the verandah after dinner, in order that the smoke of Georgie Porgie's cheroots might not hang in the new drawing-room curtains.

'What is that noise down there?' said the Bride. Both listened

'Oh,' said Georgie Porgie, 'I suppose some brute of a hillman has been beating his wife.'

'Beating—his—wife! How ghastly!' said the Bride. 'Fancy *your* beating *me!*' She slipped an arm round her husband's waist, and, leaning her head against his shoulder, looked out across the cloud-filled valley in deep content and security.

But it was Georgina crying, all by herself, down the hillside, among the stones of the watercourse where the washermen wash the clothes.

Naboth

THIS was how it happened; and the truth is also an allegory of Empire.

'I met him at the corner of my garden, an empty basket on his head, and an unclean cloth round his loins. That was all the property to which Naboth had the shadow of a claim when I first saw him. He opened our acquaintance by begging. He was very thin and showed nearly as many ribs as his basket; and he told me a long story about fever and a lawsuit, and an iron cauldron that had been seized by the court in execution of a decree. I put my hand into my pocket to help Naboth, as kings of the East have helped alien adventurers to the loss of their kingdoms. A rupee had hidden in my waistcoat lining. I never knew it was there, and gave the trove to Naboth as a direct gift from Heaven. He replied that I was the only legitimate Protector of the Poor he had ever known.

Next morning he reappeared, a little fatter in the round, and curled himself into knots in the front verandah. He said I was his father and his mother, and the direct descendant of all the gods in his Pantheon, besides controlling the destinies of the universe. He himself was but a sweetmeat-seller, and much less important than the dirt under my feet. I had heard this sort of thing before, so I asked him what he wanted. My rupee, quoth Naboth, had raised him to the everlasting heavens, and he wished to prefer a request. He wished to establish a sweetmeat-pitch near the house of his benefactor, to gaze on my revered countenance as I went to and fro illumining the world. I was graciously pleased to give permission, and he went away with his head between his knees.

Now at the far end of my garden the ground slopes toward the public road, and the slope is crowned with a thick shrubbery. There is a short carriage-road from the house to the Mall, which passes close to the shrubbery Next afternoon I saw that Naboth had seated himself at the bottom of the slope, down in the dust of the public road, and in the full glare of the sun, with a starved basket of greasy sweets in front of him. He had gone into trade once more on the strength of my munificent donation, and the ground was as Paradise by my honoured favour. Remember, there was only Naboth, his basket, the sunshine, and the gray dust when the sap of my Empire first began.

Next day he had moved himself up the slope nearer to my shrubbery, and waved a palm-leaf fan to keep the flies off the sweets. So I judged that he must have done a fair trade.

Four days later I noticed that he had backed himself and his basket under the shadow of the shrubbery, and had tied an Isabella-coloured rag between two branches in order to make more shade. There were plenty of sweets in his basket. I thought that trade must certainly be looking up.

Seven weeks later the Government took up a plot of ground for a Chief Court close to the end of my compound, and employed nearly four hundred coolies on the foundations. Naboth bought a blue and white striped blanket, a brass lamp-stand, and a small boy, to cope with the rush of trade, which was tremendous.

Five days later he bought a huge, fat, red-backed account-book, and a glass ink-stand. Thus I saw that the coolies had been getting into his debt, and that commerce was increasing on legiti-mate lines of credit. Also I saw that the one basket had grown into three, and that Naboth had backed and hacked into the shrubbery, and made himself a nice little clearing for the proper display of the basket, the blanket, the books, and the boy.

One week and five days later he had built a mud fire-place in the clearing, and the fat account-book was overflowing. He said that God created few Englishmen of my kind, and that I was the incarnation of all human virtues. He offered me some of his sweets as tribute, and by accepting these I acknowledged him as my feudatory under the skirt of my protection.

Three weeks later I noticed that the boy was in the habit of cooking Naboth's mid-day meal for him, and Naboth was beginning to grow a

stomach. He had hacked away more of my
shrubbery, and owned another and a fatter account-
book.

Eleven weeks later Naboth had eaten his way
nearly through that shrubbery, and there was a
reed hut with a bedstead outside it, standing in
the little glade that he had eroded. Two dogs
and a baby slept on the bedstead. So I fancied
Naboth had taken a wife. He said that he had,
by my favour, done this thing, and that I was
several times finer than Krishna.

Six weeks and two days later a mud wall had
grown up at the back of the hut. There were
fowls in front and it smelt a little. The Municipal
Secretary said that a cess-pool was forming in the
public road from the drainage of my compound,
and that I must take steps to clear it away. I
spoke to Naboth. He said I was Lord Paramount
of his earthly concerns, and the garden was all
my own property, and sent me some more sweets
in a second-hand duster.

Two months later a coolie bricklayer was killed
in a scuffle that took place opposite Naboth's
Vineyard. The Inspector of Police said it was a
serious case ; went into my servants' quarters ;
insulted my butler's wife, and wanted to arrest my
butler. The curious thing about the murder was
that most of the coolies were drunk at the time.
Naboth pointed out that my name was a strong
shield between him and his enemies, and he expected that another baby would be born to him
shortly.

Four months later the hut was *all* mud walls,

very solidly built, and Naboth had used most of my shrubbery for his five goats. A silver watch and an aluminium chain shone upon his very round stomach. My servants were alarmingly drunk several times, and used to waste the day with Naboth when they got the chance. I spoke to Naboth. He said, by my favour and the glory of my countenance, he would make all his women-folk ladies, and that if any one hinted that he was running an illicit still under the shadow of the tamarisks, why, I, his Suzerain, was to prosecute.

A week later he hired a man to make several dozen square yards of trellis-work to put round the back of his hut, that his women-folk might be screened from the public gaze. The man went away in the evening, and left his day's work to pave the short cut from the public road to my house. I was driving home in the dusk, and turned the corner by Naboth's Vineyard quickly. The next thing I knew was that the horses of the phaeton were stamping and plunging in the strongest sort of bamboo net-work. Both beasts came down. One rose with nothing more than chipped knees. The other was so badly kicked that I was forced to shoot him.

Naboth is gone now, and his hut is ploughed into its native mud with sweetmeats instead of salt for a sign that the place is accursed. I have built a summer-house to overlook the end of the garden, and it is as a fort on my frontier whence I guard my Empire.

I know exactly how Ahab felt. He has been shamefully misrepresented in the Scriptures.

The Dream of Duncan Parrenness

Like Mr. Bunyan of old, I, Duncan Parrenness, Writer to the Most Honourable the East India Company, in this God-forgotten city of Calcutta, have dreamed a dream, and never since that Kitty my mare fell lame have I been so troubled. Therefore, lest I should forget my dream, I have made shift to set it down here. Though Heaven knows how unhandy the pen is to me who was always readier with sword than ink-horn when I left London two long years since

When the Governor-General's great dance (that he gives yearly at the latter end of November) was finisht, I had gone to mine own room which looks over that sullen, un-English stream, the Hoogly, scarce so sober as I might have been. Now, roaring drunk in the West is but fuddled in the East, and I was drunk Nor'-Nor' Easterly as Mr. Shakespeare might have said. Yet, in spite of my liquor, the cool night winds (though I have heard that they breed chills and fluxes innumerable) sobered me somewhat; and I remembered that I had been but a little wrung and wasted by all the sicknesses of the past four months, whereas those young bloods that came eastward with me in the same ship had been all, a month back, planted to Eternity in the foul soil north of Writers' Buildings. So then, I thanked God mistily (though, to my shame, I never kneeled down to do so) for licence to live, at least till March should be upon us again. Indeed, we that were alive (and our number was less by far than those who had gone to their last account in the hot weather late past) had made very merry that evening, by the ramparts of the Fort, over this kindness of Providence; though our jests were neither witty nor such as I should have liked my Mother to hear.

When I had lain down (or rather thrown me on my bed) and the fumes of my drink had a little cleared away, I found that I could get no sleep for thinking of a thousand things that were better left alone. First, and it was a long time since I had thought of her, the sweet face of Kitty Somerset drifted, as it might have been drawn in a picture, across the foot of my bed, so plainly, that I almost thought she had been present in the body. Then I remembered how she drove me to this accursed country to get rich, that I might the more quickly marry her, our parents on both sides giving their consent; and then how she thought better (or worse maybe) of her troth, and wed Tòm Sanderson but a short three months after I had sailed. From Kitty I fell a-musing on Mrs. Vansuythen, a tall pale woman with violet eyes that had come to Calcutta from the Dutch Factory at Chinsura, and had set all our young men, and not a few of the factors, by the ears. Some of our ladies, it is true, said that she had never a husband or marriage-lines at all ; but women, and specially those who have led only indifferent good lives themselves, are cruel hard one on another. Besides, Mrs. Vansuythen was far prettier than them all. She had been most gracious to me at the Governor-General's rout, and indeed I was looked upon by all as her *preux chevalier*—which is French for a much worse word. Now, whether I cared so much as the scratch of a pin for this same Mrs. Vansuythen (albeit I had vowed eternal love three days after we met) I knew not then nor did till later on ; but mine own pride, and a skill in the small sword that no man in Calcutta could equal, kept me in her affections. So that I believed I worshipt her.

When I had dismist her violet eyes from my thoughts, my reason reproacht me for ever having followed her at all ; and I saw how the one year that I had lived in this land had so burnt and seared my mind with the flames of a thousand bad passions and desires, that I had aged ten months for each one in the Devil's school. Whereat I thought of my Mother for a while, and was very penitent : making in my sinful tipsy mood a thousand vows of reformation—all since broken, I fear me, again and again. To-morrow, says I to myself, I will live cleanly for ever. And I smiled dizzily (the liquor being still strong in me) to think of the dangers I had escaped ; and built all manner of fine Castles in Spain, whereof a shadowy Kitty Somerset that had the violet eyes and the sweet slow speech of Mrs. Vansuythen, was always Queen.

Lastly, a very fine and magnificent courage (that doubtless had its birth in Mr. Hastings' Madeira) grew upon me, till it seemed that I could become Governor-General, Nawab, Prince, ay, even the Great Mogul himself, by the mere wishing of it. Wherefore, taking my first steps, random and unstable enough, towards my new kingdom, I kickt my servants sleeping without till they howled and ran from me, and called Heaven and Earth to witness that I, Duncan Parrenness, was a Writer in the service of the Company and afraid of no man. Then, seeing that neither the Moon nor the Great Bear were minded to accept my challenge, I lay down again and must have fallen asleep.

I was waked presently by my last words repeated two or three times, and I saw that there had come into the room a drunken man, as I thought, from Mr. Hastings' rout. He sate down at the foot of my bed for all the world as it belonged to him, and I took note, as well as I could, that his face was somewhat like mine own grown older, save when it changed to the face of the Governor-General or my father, dead these six months. But this seemed to me only natural, and the due result of too much wine; and I was so angered at his entry all unannounced, that I told him, not over civilly, to go. To all my words he made no answer whatever, only saying slowly, as though it were some sweet morsel: 'Writer in the Company's service and afraid of no man.' Then he stops short, and turning round sharp upon me, says that

one of my kidney need fear neither man nor devil;
that I was a brave young man, and like enough,
should I live so long, to be Governor-General.
But for all these things (and I supposed that he
meant thereby the changes and chances of our
shifty life in these parts) I must pay my price.
By this time I had sobered somewhat, and being
well waked out of my first sleep, was disposed to
look upon the matter as a tipsy man's jest. So,
says I merrily : ' And what price shall I pay for
this palace of mine, which is but twelve feet square,
and my five poor pagodas a month ? The devil
take you and your jesting : I have paid my price
twice over in sickness.' At that moment my man
turns full toward me : so that by the moonlight I
could see every line and wrinkle of his face. Then
my drunken mirth died out of me, as I have seen
the waters of our great rivers die away in one night;
and I, Duncan Parrenness, who was afraid of no
man, was taken with a more deadly terror than I
hold it has ever been the lot of mortal man to know.
For I saw that his face was my very own, but
marked and lined and scarred with the furrows of
disease and much evil living—as I once, when I
was (Lord help me) very drunk indeed, have seen
mine own face, all white and drawn and grown old,
in a mirror. I take it that any man would have
been even more greatly feared than I ; for I am
in no way wanting in courage.

After I had lain still for a little, sweating in my
agony, and waiting until I should awake from this
terrible dream (for dream I knew it to be), he says
again that I must pay my price ; and a little after,

as though it were to be given in pagodas and sicca rupees : 'What price will you pay?' Says I, very softly : 'For God's sake let me be, whoever you are, and I will mend my ways from to-night.' Says he, laughing a little at my words, but otherwise making no motion of having heard them : 'Nay, I would only rid so brave a young ruffler as yourself of much that will be a great hindrance to you on your way through life in the Indies ; for believe me,' and here he looks full on me once more, 'there is no return.' At all this rigmarole, which I could not then understand, I was a good deal put aback and waited for what should come next. Says he very calmly : 'Give me your trust in man.' At that I saw how heavy would be my price, for I never doubted but that he could take from me all that he asked, and my head was, through terror and wakefulness, altogether cleared of the wine I had drunk. So I takes him up very short, crying that I was not so wholly bad as he would make believe, and that I trusted my fellows to the full as much as they were worthy of it. 'It was none of my fault,' says I, 'if one-half of them were liars and the other half deserved to be burnt in the hand, and I would once more ask him to have done with his questions.' Then I stopped, a little afraid, it is true, to have let my tongue so run away with me, but he took no notice of this, and only laid his hand lightly on my left breast and I felt very cold there for a while. Then he says, laughing more : 'Give me your faith in women.' At that I started in my bed as though I had been stung, for I thought of my sweet mother in

England, and for a while fancied that my faith in God's best creatures could neither be shaken nor stolen from me. But later, Myself's hard eyes being upon me, I fell to thinking, for the second time that night, of Kitty (she that jilted me and married Tom Sanderson) and of Mistress Vansuythen, whom only my devilish pride made me follow, and how she was even worse than Kitty, and I worst of them all—seeing that with my life's work to be done, I must needs go dancing down the Devil's swept and garnished causeway, because, forsooth, there was a light woman's smile at the end of it. And I thought that all women in the world were either like Kitty or Mistress Vansuythen (as indeed they have ever since been to me), and this put me to such an extremity of rage and sorrow, that I was beyond word glad when Myself's hand fell again on my left breast, and I was no more troubled by these follies.

After this he was silent for a little, and I made sure that he must go or I awake ere long ; but presently he speaks again (and very softly) that I was a fool to care for such follies as those he had taken from me, and that ere he went he would only ask me for a few other trifles such as no man, or for matter of that boy either, would keep about him in this country. And so it happened that he took from out of my very heart as it were, looking all the time into my face with my own eyes, as much as remained to me of my boy's soul and conscience. This was to me a far more terrible loss than the two that I had suffered before. For though, Lord help me, I had travelled far enough from all paths of decent or godly living, yet there was in me, though I myself write it, a certain goodness of heart which, when I was sober (or sick) made me very sorry of all that I had done before the fit came on me. And this I lost wholly : having in place thereof another deadly coldness at the heart. I am not, as I have before said, ready with my pen, so I fear that what I have just written may not be readily understood. Yet there be certain times in a young man's life, when, through great sorrow or sin, all the boy in him is burnt and seared away so that he passes at one step to the more sorrowful state of manhood : as our staring Indian day changes into night with never so much as the gray of twilight to temper the two extremes. This shall perhaps make my state more clear, if it be remembered that my torment was ten times as great as comes in the natural course of nature to any man. At that time I dared not think of the change that had come over me, and all in one night : though I have often thought of it since. ' I have paid the price,' says I, my teeth chattering, for I was deadly cold, ' and what is my return ? ' At this time it was nearly dawn, and Myself had begun to grow pale and thin against the white light in the east, as my mother used to tell me is the custom of ghosts and devils and the like. He made as if he would go, but my words stopt him and he laughed —as I remember that I laughed when I ran Angus Macalister through the sword-arm last August, because he said that Mrs. Vansuythen was no better than she should be. ' What return ? '—says he, catching up my last words—' Why, strength to live as long as God or the Devil pleases, and so long as you live, my young master, my gift.' With that he puts something into my hand, though it was still too dark to see what it was, and when next I lookt up he was gone.

When the light came I made shift to behold his gift, and saw that it was a little piece of dry bread.

L'ENVOI

My new-cut ashlar takes the light
   Where crimson-blank the windows flare;
By my own work, before the night,
   Great Overseer, I make my prayer.

If there be good in that I wrought,
   Thy hand compelled it, Master, Thine;
Where I have failed to meet Thy thought
   I know, through Thee, the blame is mine.

One instant's toil to Thee denied
   Stands all Eternity's offence,
Of that I did with Thee to guide
   To Thee, through Thee, be excellence.

Who, lest all thought of Eden fade,
   Bring'st Eden to the craftsman's brain,
Godlike to muse o'er his own trade
   And Manlike stand with God again.

The depth and dream of my desire,
   The bitter paths wherein I stray,
Thou knowest Who hast made the Fire,
   Thou knowest Who hast made the Clay.

One stone the more swings to her place
   In that dread Temple of Thy Worth—
It is enough that through Thy grace
   I saw naught common on Thy earth.

Take not that vision from my ken;
   Oh, whatsoe'er may spoil or speed,
Help me to need no aid from men
   That I may help such men as need!